Ace Books by Ru Emerson

THE PRINCESS OF FLAMES
SPELL BOUND

The *Tales of Nedao* Trilogy

TO THE HAUNTED MOUNTAINS
IN THE CAVES OF EXILE
ON THE SEAS OF DESTINY

The *Night-Threads* Trilogy

THE CALLING OF THE THREE
THE TWO IN HIDING
ONE LAND, ONE DUKE

RU EMERSON
NIGHT-THREADS

BOOK TWO:
THE
TWO IN HIDING

ACE BOOKS, NEW YORK

This book is an Ace original edition,
and has never been previously published.

THE TWO IN HIDING

An Ace Book / published by arrangement
with the author

PRINTING HISTORY
Ace edition / May 1991

ISBN: 0-441-58086-6

Ace Books are published by The Berkley Publishing Group,
200 Madison Avenue, New York, New York 10016.
The name ''ACE'' and the ''A'' logo
are trademarks belonging to Charter Communications, Inc.

PRINTED IN THE UNITED STATES OF AMERICA

10 9 8 7 6 5 4 3 2

For Doug

And for my darling mother and father,
who bear no resemblance whatever to
any parent in this trilogy

I would like to express sincere thanks to the Dallas, Oregon, Public Library staff for all their research help over the past several years, and particularly on this series of books. You guys are absolutely great!

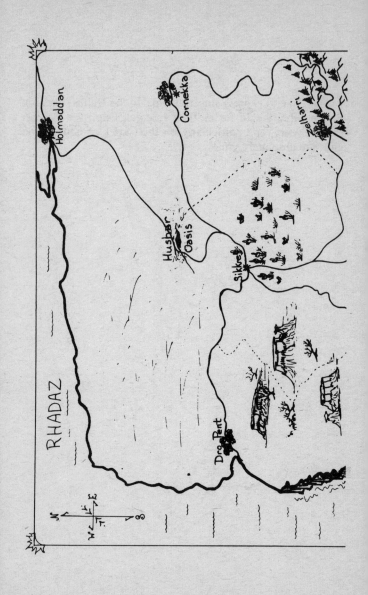

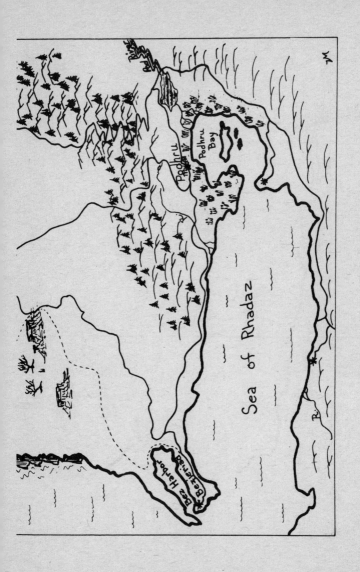

i

THE kingdom of Rhadaz stretches from the Bay of Holmad-dan in the north to the Sea of Rhadaz and along its southern shores; from the Podherian Mountains that block eastward travel in all save the warmest months of summer to the great western ocean. So great is the land between these boundaries that a man ahorse might not cross it, north to south, in fewer than six days. So vast and varied the terrain of Rhadaz that a previous Emperor found it feasible to divide his kingdom into smaller entities and give their ruling into the hands of his nearest friends, thus founding the Nine Households. The Dukes were thereafter responsible directly to the Emperor for maintaining the laws of the Empire and for forwarding taxes and trained armsmen to the capital. And despite the warnings of his nearest advisors, the Emperor was proven to have been right in his choice of friends, rather than relations, as his Dukes: the founders of the Nine Households were extremely loyal to their Emperor, as were their first descendants.

Only once in two hundred years did the Emperor call for the fighting men which were his due: The current Shesseran, known as the Golden, did so when Lasanachi raiders sent their sleek raiding ships against the coastal city of Dro Pent. Shesseran XIV otherwise made few demands on his people or his Dukes, so long as an outward appearance of peace reigned, and so long as taxes were paid. In his youth, he was largely interested in the game preserves of his own Duchy of Andar Perigha and the artists, actors and musicians in the capital port city of Podhru. The improvement of oversea trade attributed to Shesseran was brought about largely to facilitate cultural exchange and arranged by brilliant—and anonymous—men in his advisory cabinet.

Late in life, weak from many illnesses and fearing death, Shesseran lost what little interest he had had in Rhadaz and turned to religion, devoting his time and thought to lengthy festivals and ceremonies designed to appease the various gods and saints.

I

Shesseran XIV knew of activities within Rhadazi boundaries his grandfather might have taken exception to: the Thukar of the vast desert market Sikkre, who bought and sold goods, information, even people, to the highest bidder; the secret forays by Lasanachi into Holmaddan and Bezjeriad to purchase or sell illicit goods and to buy slaves for their ships; the slow but noticeable increase for the first time in five hundred years of the deadly magic Hell-Light and its once-outlawed wielding Triads; the rather suspicious, fatal accident to Duke Amarni of forested Zelharri and the subsequent marriage of Amarni's brother Jadek to a nine-day widow; the fact that though Jadek's nephew Aletto had come of age three years prior Jadek still held Zelharri as his own.

But Shesseran did nothing. The Thukar, after all, kept peace in Sikkre and sent the largest twice-yearly tax to Podhru—that he kept a variety of sorcerers (some not precisely legal) was unimportant, so long as he kept them private; the Lasanachi likewise kept low profiles and contributed a certain amount of money to the coffers; those Rhadazi they bought were ordinarily poor folk and so of little importance. The Bez merchants did not deal in lethal narcotics. And Jadek's proffered reasons for marrying his brother's widow and holding his nephew's seat were persuasive: Lizelle had the responsibility of raising two small children at the time of Amarni's death. She needed a man to see to the responsibilities of the Zelharri people, the markets and the roads, to deal with military training and collection of taxes. Later, after Aletto's near-fatal bout of marsh-sickness left him badly weakened and permanently crippled in one leg, it seemed only right that Jadek continue to hold the post. And after all, the heir showed little interest in anything but a wine bottle.

And then rumor spread from Duke's Fort that Aletto and his sister had fled Zelharri. Soon after, gossip circulated through the Sikkreni marketplace that the heir had been seen in Sikkre, searching for men once loyal to his father to aid him in a bloodless coup, and such gossip was spiced with curious and tantalizing rumor: It was said that Zelharri sin-Duchess Lialla, a barely competent novice Wielder of Night-Thread Magic despite years of hard study, had a novice of her own—a beautiful young outland woman brought into Rhadaz from another world. This woman was accompanied by an older woman and a boy, also outlanders and kindred; the older woman, some whispered, was a shapeshifter, though it was considered rare and wondrous that an outlander should be able to practice such a skill, with no Rhadazi blood and no training. The Thukar's heir Dahven was said to have helped his friend Aletto and the nera-Duke's companions evade both his father and Jadek, and it had cost him dearly, or so men said. A Sikkreni thief whose father had once served Duke Amarni now traveled with Aletto, his sister and the outlanders, and he carried information that directly implicated Jadek in his own brother's death.

By the Emperor's lights, however, there was peace throughout Rhadaz, and he turned his attention and that of his court and his port city of Podhru to the Blossom-Month Festival: Fifth Month, Sixth Day of the year 789. Emperor Shesseran the Golden, gaunt with fasting and meditation, was at peace with himself and his soul.

* * *

IN Zelharri, within the walls of Duke's Fort, the aged Wielder Merrida sat in her circular chamber surrounded by silver protective Thread and contemplated what moves she might safely make to aid her novice Lialla and those with her. *Not much*, she thought gloomily. Jadek had moved his Hell-Light Triad to Duke's Fort and any active use of Thread might well reveal her part in Aletto's escape. She did not particularly care for her own aged hide, but Jadek's Triad could use her to locate Lialla.

She drew Thread nearer, as if to warm herself, and contemplated the three Americani she had pulled from their world into her own. The young virgin Chris and his mother—both useless, probably, unless Aletto found an outlet for his foolish, romantic notions in Robyn. Though admittedly Chris's purity had permitted Thread to choose Jennifer, and to take her. With her music and her level-headed strength, Jennifer could become a better Wielder than Lialla, given the opportunity. One could only hope Lialla was sensible about that, that Lialla would realize Jennifer was useful to Aletto's cause, that she would not actively thwart her new novice. Merrida wondered briefly where they were now; she knew they had escaped Sikkre and were moving toward Bezjeriad, paralleling the south road and sensibly staying off of it. But she didn't truly want to know; such knowledge could be dangerous to her and to them.

* * *

IN a hidden chamber behind the Duke's hall, Jadek observed three gray men—so still, all of them, they might have been statues. He fought impatience, knowing it interfered with his Triad's work. All the same, that a full Triad could not discover where one crippled, sottish young man and his arrogant, whining sister were! These rumors of outlanders—but, then, they were no longer rumors, were they? For his friend Dahmec of Sikkre sent

3

word: He had seen two obviously outland women with Lialla, when he'd had them taken, but they had vanished from the high tower prison room, leaving behind three crippled guardsmen and a dead sorcerer—a man said to have once been outlander himself. They had also left Sikkre buzzing with wild rumors.

Dahmec lost them, Jadek thought furiously as he watched long and extremely white fingers touch and slowly move in a pattern that set yellowish light to glow dully between six palms. But it didn't matter; what was lost could be again found. And though rumor had it Aletto was on his way to Dro Pent now—rumor substantiated by the Thukar's son, who'd been seen with a Dro Pent-bound Red Hawk caravan that same night—Jadek thought it highly unlikely. Podhru, most likely, or Bez—and he himself opted for Bez, where Aletto might have hopes of adding to his paltry following.

Aletto had to be stopped, quickly; before he could reach the Emperor's ear with his tale of a birthright withheld. Before he could increase his following to the point where Shesseran must listen to him, and perhaps order Jadek to return to his old estates. *It is my Duchy; I worked hard to keep it in good shape after Amarni died. I will not hand it over to a sodden, ill-prepared boy!* Had Lizelle given him children—but she had not, and he wondered how much of that was the doing of her personal woman, that old hag Merrida. Lizelle had once Wielded herself, of course—before they wed—but she'd put it aside at his orders, or so he had believed. If she had found the nerve to actively thwart him—!

But the Triad was finally moving more quickly; he must make his own contribution to their spell. He drew the knife from his belt, pricked his thumb, and let three drops of blood fall on their joined hands.

* * *

ON the road to Dro Pent, a line of thirty enclosed wagons moved slowly down the last stages of a scrub-forested pass and onto a windy, sandswept road. The banners of the Red Hawk trading clan were prominently displayed, a safety measure since travelers along this road were often set upon by bandits, but no one was fool enough to threaten the major clans.

Gray-green brush dotted the landscape as far as any eye could see; a line of brightness away to the west might have been the sea. Wind bent dry clumps of grass and brought the scent of hot sage. The Holmad River, a broadly shallow flow in the drylands, veered south from the road and now paralleled it. A bright line of trees and willow followed its banks, readily marking its path.

4

Some leagues behind the Red Hawk wagons—still on the downslope of the western side of the pass—came a lone wagon, an open cart flanked by two mounted men. They made no effort to catch the caravan. But no desert raiders would threaten three Lasanachi seamen.

In the rear of the cart a bound man sat very still, staring blankly at his bare feet and the heavy shackle around one ankle, at the thick chain that ran to a staple fixed just above the cart's axle. He flexed his shoulders once, but before he could ease the growing discomfort in his back and arms, or find a better place to rest wrists chafed by the thick rope that held them behind his back where the knots dug into his spine, one of the horsemen reined back and slapped him.

Dahven somehow kept the cry behind his teeth; he felt enough shame at having been sold by his father so his twin younger brothers could become heirs. He would not show further weakness before these men—until he must. *They say no man survives the oars in a Lasanachi ship for two years; my father made a contract for three.*

Perhaps he would waken momentarily: in his own bed, badly hung over. *If I do, I shall never set foot in a pub again, or drink sweet red.* He stretched, but more cautiously this time; the raiders paid him no heed. It helped very little, though, and his fingers had long since gone numb.

His father had sold him; Deehar and Dayher had watched it being done. *May they rot before I do.* It seemed unlikely; the Lasanachi had an endless supply of men and saw no reason to treat them well. He let his eyes close momentarily, let himself see Jennifer as he had seen her last: that wonderful, thick spill of black hair; large, intelligent blue eyes; long fingers curled around the neck of an a'lud while she sang songs from her world to him. The misery he'd felt at leaving her, the matching misery in her face—*No.* He dared not think of Jennifer; he could only hope she would never know what had become of him.

* * *

On the windswept, barren mesa, not very far away, Jennifer slept with fingers wrapped around the silver protective charm that had been Dahven's parting gift. Lialla moaned; Jadek haunted her dream and again tried to force her betrothal to his horrid cousin Carolan, as he had that last dreadful afternoon. Aletto, who was sleeping with an exhausted Robyn, came partway awake and sat up but Lialla was once more quiet.

Chris perched on a flat rock, saddle pad under him to protect sore muscle and bone, and tried to stay awake until it was time

5

to waken the next watcher, but Edrith came out to spell him long before the hour. *Odd, how fast we made friends*, Chris thought. *Or maybe not.* They were nearly the same age and had a surprising number of things in common, given their different backgrounds—Chris an Angeleno high school senior interested in rock music and high-tech sound equipment, role-playing games, maps, history; Edrith the Sikkreni market thief who of course knew nothing of such things but who also liked hearing tales about the past and looking at maps. His mother had bad taste in men, too, but unlike Robyn, Edrith's mother never bothered to keep them from harassing her son.

The south road was long; the ordinary trip could be hard and exhausting, particularly in summer. But they could not use the road: Aletto was too identifiable with his game leg and the scars on his face; the Thukar might have given descriptions of Lialla, Jennifer and Robyn to his men and set them searching the roads; or Jadek's own men might still be looking. Between Sikkre and Bezjeriad the land had broken and folded; high desert and mesas were split by canyons and draws; dry washes cut into open flats. Water was not as scarce as in Dro Pent but could be difficult to locate; food might become a problem if anything slowed them.

And Bezjeriad was only the second leg of a much longer journey. It looked daunting even to Chris and Edrith. Fortunately, neither one could foresee how difficult the journey would become.

I

JENNIFER woke when rising sun hit squarely in her eyes. She stretched cautiously, groaned as a variety of muscles protested, rolled onto her other side and pulled the thick, gaudy woven blanket over the top of her head. The wind that had come up with the sun was icy.

Dahven's gift slid across her throat, warm from contact with her skin; she smiled and closed her eyes resolutely. It could not be later than five-thirty, real time. Real, of course, being home—Los Angeles. Santa Monica, actually. She ordinarily didn't have to fight early sun like this; her apartment faced west, toward an ocean she couldn't actually see from her second-floor windows. It had; it wasn't hers any more. That was gone. *Gone.* It washed over her—overwhelming, unbearable loss: career, apartment, car—everything.

She bit her lip and fought tears. Merrida had manipulated Night-Thread to find an armed guard within Rhadazi borders for Aletto and Lialla, or so she'd told them. But the magic had found them instead: dragged them from their world to this one on the way home from a Saturday picnic at the Devil's Punchbowl. Chris had lost out on his D&D night; Robyn—Robyn probably on a Saturday night drunk. Jennifer didn't want to think what she'd lost. A bright if predictable future in a Century City law firm, her apartment, her cello, the brand new red Honda. Concerts, movies, classical music on the radio, makeup, a perm when her hair started growing out—the things she'd taken for granted, the way people did, until she didn't have any of them.

Damn Merrida. Manipulative, arrogant old woman. Jennifer wasn't certain she believed what Merrida'd said about the magic choosing, about her own music and Chris's virginity combining to catch hold of them. Even though she no longer doubted the magic itself. *Magic. Who would have thought?* Merrida's talent had filled her, going with her as far as the cave where Lialla and her badly wounded brother were hiding; she'd used Merrida's magic to heal a ghastly cut in Aletto's arm.

Oddly, Merrida had been right about music, though she hadn't explained that any more than she'd explained anything else. Jennifer could *hear* Thread. And she was developing a formidable talent in the few short days since she'd walked into that cave.

Which made life with the prickly Lialla that much more difficult. *It's not my fault,* Jennifer thought sourly as she tugged the blanket tight against the back of her head to shut out drafts before she tucked chilled hands between her knees. Jennifer knew little about Lialla's own training, but the sin-Duchess apparently didn't hear the music Thread made, and thanks to her own temperament and Merrida's teaching, she was so hidebound she couldn't accept any alternate approach to the magic. *When I told her I could see the stuff in daylight, I thought she'd have me burned at the stake.* Jennifer rolled her eyes under closed lids. *I can see it, and hear it, she's just going to have to come to grips with that. And it isn't my fault the woman was bad-mouthed by her uncle.* Beaten, too, judging by her reaction in that tower. Jennifer still felt guilty remembering the look in Lialla's eyes, the way the woman had flinched away from her. *As though I'd have actually hit her. I've never hit anyone, ever.*

Well, it was a pity: Like her brother, Lialla could be a nice person to be around; at least when she wasn't overreacting to things. She came unglued too easily, and at the damnedest times. At least Aletto was fairly predictable. He was touchy about his limp, about the scars left on his face by marsh-sickness, about the hitched shoulder; he didn't like being reminded that Jadek had kept him from learning a nobleman's weapons, didn't like being dependent on magic or women—on anyone but himself, though he was painfully aware he didn't know how to take care of himself. He was rather touchingly protective of Robyn—at least, Birdy put up with his heavy-handed chivalrous behavior; it would have driven Jennifer mad. Chris—who'd babied his poor weak mother since he'd been able to walk—was visibly irked by Aletto's obvious ''case'' on his mom, but for once he was keeping the whole thing to himself instead of pouring it all on his aunt. Jennifer wondered whether he was spilling his guts to Edrith, if he was simply giving up on the situation. Then, too, perhaps he was being realistic about it all: Robyn was ten years older than Aletto, after all; she was outlander and common both. Jennifer couldn't see any chance of a permanent relationship, whatever Aletto said.

Poor Birdy. Robyn's taste in men had always been rotten. Sweet, dependable Chris seemed to spend half his life helping his mother put her life back together after the Arnies and Terrys and Johns left.

Jennifer sighed deeply, rolled onto her back and glanced around. Robyn was still asleep, and so was Aletto: His cheek rested on her long, blonde hair and another strand of it blew across his pale face, hiding the pockmarks. Chris was a wad of blanket at the base of a scrawny bush, only recognizable by the large high-topped sneaker sticking out of one end. Edrith was wandering around the mesa, gathering bits of dry wood for a breakfast fire. Lialla was somewhere out of sight; her blankets were folded and stacked.

Jennifer snugged the blanket around her shoulders once more, then pulled her knees up to her chest one at a time to stretch out her back. The ground had been very hard, and she would have been stiff from a flat-ground ride covering that many miles. But the way they'd come to reach the top of the mesa had been— God, it had been grim. She couldn't remember specifics; she seemed to recall climbing past the same trees and riding through the same cleft between crumbling, dry banks of a slender stream ten or twenty times. As though they'd ridden in circles for hours. Her first glimpse of the way they'd come, when they first arrived on the mesa, showed an appalling drop. She hadn't seen anything that might have been Sikkre out there, either.

Horses. *I hate riding,* she thought with an inner groan. She should stretch everything out, keep stretching so she didn't freeze up. After all, they'd probably be riding again this evening—and every evening from now on, at least until they reached Bezjeriad. They didn't have enough food and water to fool around getting to that prosperous merchant center, and she personally didn't want to spend any more nights like this last one than she could help. Stretch and massage, she thought, but fell asleep again instead.

* * *

SHE was wakened hours later by a familiar odor: *Pancakes?* The blanket was still over her head but it had rucked up above her feet; fortunately, since a cool ground breeze blew along her legs, keeping the actual temperature under her thick cover near bearable. Hair was plastered to her forehead and flat under her ear where she'd slept on it; the morning air felt downright cold when she threw the cover aside and breeze struck wet skin. She found her chambray shirt and blotted sweat with the tails before it occurred to her she wouldn't be able to wash the shirt any time soon. "God," she mumbled. "Or my hair. Disgusting." The leather bag that held her drinking water lay next to the saddle pad, close to the leather shoulder bag she'd brought with her before Merrida sent the Honda back to that two-lane blacktop road. "God," she said again as she fumbled through it for the precious aspirin bottle. "Next time I lay a couple of these out before I go to sleep, right?" Her head was pounding madly from sleeping on hard ground; the down-side hip was, too, but that was probably as much the discomfort of riding a broad-backed horse, of the curious saddle—though even a western saddle would have left her limping after that last night's ride. She rubbed her eyes, yawned and stretched, groaned as more muscles protested. Everything ached.

But the smell was definitely pancakes, and there was Robyn, squinting against the sun, cussing in English when the wind blew ash and smoke all over her, fighting with the strange pans. Edrith and Chris were eating rolled-up cakes with their fingers.

Robyn must have been watching for movement; she stood partway and shaded her eyes. "Finally awake, are you? You'd better hurry up or these two varmints will finish everything."

"Pancakes," Jennifer inhaled deeply as she walked tiptoe on

9

bare feet across sandy ground. "Birdy, I knew you were good, but how did you manage *that*?"

Robyn snorted good-naturedly. "You always use a mix or something? They're just flour and milk and eggs. The flour's a little coarse and the flavor isn't quite the same, but we won't be able to keep that skin of milk fresh and I wouldn't want to fool with the eggs beyond tomorrow." She scraped at the pan with a wide wooden spatula, slid a round, thick cake onto one of their tin plates and held it out to her younger sister. "Lialla had hers plain; the boys found a pot of some kind of mixed fruit butter Aletto bought in one of the packs. It's not too bad." She emptied batter into the pan and nodded at the grubby pan she'd used for mixing. "You two earn your keep; go find a way to clean this up for me without using half the water, all right?" She glared at Chris, transferred the look to his companion. "This is mine. You want to live long enough to have seconds when we get to this Bez place, go clean the pan and keep your grubby paws away from the contents of this pan."

"Yes'm," Chris said; Edrith laughed and grabbed up the mixing pan.

Jennifer scooped thick, dark sweet stuff out of the brown glazed pot with two fingers and dumped it in the middle of the cake, sucked her fingers clean and rolled the pancake around it. "Lord, Birdy, this is just great. I don't think I'd have dragged myself out of that godawful bed for anything else."

"Not bad," Robyn allowed. "Lialla wants to talk about which way and how far, once you've eaten. I think we'd better have a good understanding about the food—like, how much we have and how far it's going to go." She flipped the pancake, set the pan down at the edge of the fire. "I want you to step on her, if you have to, Jen." She glanced up. "You know?" Jennifer, mouth full of pancake, nodded. "Good. I don't think she likes me much."

"She doesn't like me much right now, either," Jennifer mumbled around her food. "She has enough sense to pay attention when she has to, though."

"I'm glad *you're* sure about that," Robyn said dryly. She gingerly picked up the edge of the pancake between two fingers and peered at the underside, swore as it burned her and slid it out onto Chris's empty plate. "You want this?"

Jennifer shook her head. "You said it was yours, remember?"

"Just to make sure you got enough. But I'll eat it if you don't."

"Do it. They're huge, Birdy, I couldn't possibly eat two."

"Don't you go shorting yourself food—"

"Don't you," Jennifer said. "That's more your style than mine, Robyn—I seem to remember a few years ago when you lost the food stamps; Chris ate, and you didn't."

Robyn waved sticky, fruit-buttered fingers. "Come on, it wasn't that bad! He was growing and I was fat. So it was a good opportunity to go on a diet."

"If I'd known—"

"Well, I didn't tell you," Robyn said rather shortly. She licked her thumb, smiled apologetically. "Sorry. I don't do charity from family, remember?" Her face fell and she bent over the plate, very carefully rolling pancake around the fruit butter. "Well—I didn't. Guess that's behind us now, isn't it?"

"Oh, Robyn—"

"Shhh. I'm not going to unglue on you or bleed all over you, Jen. I told you, first night that old witch Merrida grabbed us, all I ever needed was you and Chris. I've got that. I'm luckier than both of you that way. My poor kid." She bit into the pancake, plate held high under her chin to catch spills. "He had his senior year, all the good stuff that means—I was looking forward to it as much as he was, maybe more 'cause I never had that. I—God, I think I was living just off the Strip with half a dozen people in a two-room apartment when I was seventeen. Even then I didn't care much about possessions, but Chris—he was saving for a car, he had that fancy disk player. I know he misses the music, the concerts, TV—all that." She chuckled. "I guess you were still asleep this morning; I could see him out there with Edrith, trying to show him some of that new dance stuff, rap or whatever it is. I don't even try to keep up with it."

"Missed that." Jennifer grinned and wiped crumbs and spilled fruit butter from the plate with the last bite of pancake. "Sorry I did, too. That was terrific, Birdy. What are you doing with plates?"

"A dribble of water on a bit of cloth for the sticky stuff; that's it until we find running water. Chris says the map shows some; Edrith said he doesn't think it's too late in the season. I guess it's like where we were. They go dry once it gets hot."

"Makes sense."

"Gimme," Robyn said, and took the plate from her hands. "The boys are on K.P. until further notice. Anyone eats like those two do better have to pay for it somehow."

"Sounds fair to me." Jennifer stood, bent over to stretch out the small of her back. "God, I ache!"

"Could have been worse. We might have been on foot."

"I could handle *that*." She straightened up, dug both hands

11

into her hipbones and bent back, to one side and then the other. "I'm not sure that helped a lot; we'll pretend it did. I'd better go find Lialla." She sighed. "You've seen her today. How is she?"

Robyn shrugged and stacked plates in the pan she'd used for pancakes, set the pile aside and began hand-shoveling sand and dirt over the fire. "You know Lialla. She's not actively pissed off at anybody yet, so I guess you can call that a good mood." She sat back, pushed hair off her forehead with her wrist and looked at her hands glumly. "I feel like what's her name, Lady Macbeth." The English name jarred, as English words did in the middle of Rhadazi, frequent reminder that they were speaking a language somehow grafted onto and into them—Merrida's one truly useful gift. "Grubby hands forever, *you* know."

"I know. My hair—"

"Don't," Robyn implored. "I do not want to even *think* about my hair. And this black thing shows dirt so bad, I think I'm gonna go back to my jeans. At least I can dust my paws on those without the prints being visible all the way across the plateau."

"It's fine with me," Jennifer said. "Unless we're going to be meeting people, I don't see why we have to try to dress like locals. And I think jeans might be better for riding." She touched the inside of one thigh and winced. "I think all that material that makes up the crotch of these so-called Wielder novice blacks was rubbing my legs all night. I'll bet anything you like I've got blisters."

Robyn shook a finger at her. "You check on that. We set up the latrine just off the edge, down past that dead bush; see it?" She used the finger to indicate direction; Jennifer turned to see where she was pointing and nodded. "Check right away, because if you blistered we'll have to do something about it before you get back on that horse. People get gangrene in this kind of climate—"

"Bite your lips," Jennifer interrupted hastily. "I'll go, you save the horror stories for Chris."

Robyn nodded. "All right, deal. I think Lialla said she brought a first-aid kit from the fort—what passes for that kind of thing here. Probably herbal stuff, but that can be just as effective. If you're rubbing, get out of those goofy britches and back into your jeans, girl."

"Yes'm," Jennifer said, consciously aping Chris. Robyn grinned up at her.

"Smart kid; I see where my brat gets it now. It's all those months I let him stay with you. Thought you'd be a good influence; I should've known better."

12

"Yah. Think of all the bad influence he had on me. I actually started *liking* M.C. Hammer."

"Never heard of it," Robyn said firmly. "Is that post-Baez?"

"Possibly." Jennifer laughed, gave her shoulders one last stretch and went back to get her shoes. The ground was rough, there were splintery things everywhere—and it was getting too warm to walk on anyway.

The black pants were built like middle eastern trousers—pictures she'd seen of such trousers, anyway: There was a palm's worth of air space between body and the diamond of fabric that was the crotch. The pants themselves were extremely baggy and fabric gathered into the waist, into the crotch. It wrapped around her thighs and knees when she walked; apparently one did not stride in them, the way she normally walked. The material was a loose weave—useful for a hot climate where one wanted the breeze to pass through. But it was hard on her skin, and at the moment even her shins were sensitive to the feel of it rubbing against flesh—against stubble, she thought vexedly. "I can't shave them any more," she told herself. A small animal took off from under the dry bush at the sound of her voice; she jumped nervously. *Snake country looks just like this.* "I'll bet Birdy isn't worried about tarantula legs, I'll bet she hasn't shaved hers since 1967. If she can do it—" *I can, too, but I'll just hate it.*

Her inner thighs were rubbed red in two long, matching streaks and the skin hurt to touch, even lightly. Another night of riding would bring out the blisters she'd half expected to find. "I'd rather wear real clothes anyway. Besides, who's going to see us out here?" If Jadek could somehow tune in on them, he'd certainly know Lialla or Aletto. Three outlanders disguising themselves as natives wouldn't fool him for a moment, and Chris said the few villages off the Bez road were very well marked on the maps.

Presumably, since Edrith said people raised goats, they'd be able to *smell* villages long before they ever saw them. Jennifer grinned, retied the waist of her novice blacks and went to find the pack holding her clothes and the rest of her belongings.

* * *

IT took her a while to find Lialla; Wielder blacks seemed to blend right into the dust-colored landscape until one was right on top of her. It helped, of course, that the sin-Duchess was sitting cross-legged in the shade of a ratty little tree, only an occasional gust exposing her to an increasingly hot sun, and she was not moving at all, except for the very tips of her index fingers and thumbs. Jennifer moved into what little spare shade

13

there was and watched, fascinated: Lialla was working a complex string figure with bright red twine.

"It's a dexterity exercise," she said in preamble, and without taking her eyes from what she was doing. One index finger slid over two loops, under a crossing and pulled up another loop; the shape of the figure suspended between her hands changed completely. "It's how Merrida teaches a novice to handle Thread." She glanced up, fixed Jennifer with a brief, expressionless look, went back to her cat's cradle. "She never said anything to me about music."

"Maybe she didn't know."

"Perhaps. Sit down, why don't you?" Jennifer brushed rock and bits of dry, stickery brush aside, sat, and scratched at the side of her palm to get splinters out. "I don't know that she's tone-deaf; I've never seen her take any pleasure from music, though. I don't particularly, but music to me always meant sitting next to my uncle Jadek while it was played."

"Under the circumstances, I wouldn't have liked it either," Jennifer said.

"No." Lialla said the word with finality, closing the subject. She made two more changes to her figure, then released it and began folding up the long loop of red twine. "We need to talk—you and I, before we all do." She stuffed the twine deep in a pocket somewhere under the side-slit overshirt. "About this getting my brother from here to Bezjeriad. Quite frankly, I don't believe he's capable of making it, if the rest of the journey is going to be like last night's."

"If it is, *I* won't make it," Jennifer said. "I nearly wore holes through my legs last night."

"Is that why you're back to wearing outland britches?" Lialla considered this, finally shrugged. "Well—why not? If the Thukar or anyone else should find us out here, there won't be any doubt who we are, however you're clad. But—about Aletto. You know he's had marsh fever; I told you boys die of it. He came out of it fairly well, though he and Merrida still don't talk to each other because he thinks she could have done more—and so does she."

"I understand that."

"I just wanted to be certain. He limps; you've seen it get worse when he's tired."

Jennifer nodded. "But he rode all the way from that cave to the oasis, and without any bad effect that I saw—"

"That was an easy ride, Jen. It was road, and even when we went to trail it was flat. This isn't going to be like that."

Jennifer held up a hand for silence. "Wait. You aren't thinking of going out to the road, are you?"

"Not to use it all the time!" Lialla replied sharply. "But if we're traveling at night anyway—ordinarily people don't; we wouldn't be passing anyone, we could move out into the countryside an hour before dawn, find some place to hide before it gets light. I think it makes better sense."

"They might be expecting just that kind of reasoning from us."

"They? Who, the Thukar, the Emperor—Jadek? His Hell-Light shaping Triad?"

"Any and all of the above! The Emperor shouldn't have any reason to bother with him, if I understand local politics, but the Thukar got his pride slapped and I don't think he'd take that very well. And he's pretty devious; that might be just the way he'd think."

"Or maybe Dahven—" Lialla stopped abruptly and flushed a deep and unlovely mottled red. "I'm sorry," she mumbled. "I didn't mean he'd tell his father—"

"Never mind. At least out here, we have a better chance of seeing horsemen coming and avoiding them or just plain hiding. Your uncle—I don't know. Does Hell-Light work so he could find us, or his Triad could?" For answer Lialla shrugged. Her color was still high and she wouldn't meet Jennifer's eyes. For her own part, Jennifer was angry enough she could feel the skin over her cheekbones coloring. She touched the silver charm, at least partly for reassurance. "I don't think I can back you on this one, Lialla, but if you want to run it by the others and they agree with you, then fine. Birdy wants to run down some ground rules on the food anyway; she's worried about it going far enough to get us down to the south coast."

"We can supplement; there are the villages and places along the road. Either way." Lialla closed her eyes briefly, drew a deep breath and expelled it in a rush. "Let's go do it. We're going to ride all night and it's going to get pretty hot in another hour. I'd like to find a shady hole and crawl into it before then."

"I'd like that myself." Jennifer stood and held out a hand to help her companion up. "Let's get it over with."

They let Robyn talk first. "Food isn't a problem as long as we get somewhere to replenish stuff. Otherwise we probably have enough for six or seven days but most of it you won't like much: it'll be bland at best." She sighed. "I can do a lot but not miracles, just keep that in mind. I'm worried about one other thing, though. If something happened, and we got separated, or some of us got lost—I want to divide up the food and water, spread it out over the two pack horses and with each of us. I mean, that trail to the oasis, when we—when we lost a horse? If that happened, and all the food was on it—''

"Point taken," Aletto said. He caught her hand in both of his and pressed it, smiled when she looked up at him. "And a good one, too. Unless anyone objects?" No one did.

"You don't need us for anything, do you?" Chris asked. "Because we can start getting all the bags into one place—like maybe over there? That way Mom can get everything figured out and we can reload so we're ready to go tonight." He and Edrith took off so quickly, Jennifer wondered if they'd had a premonition of what was next.

Because Aletto objected strenuously and angrily to his sister's plan. Lialla went on the defensive at once, and her voice up in pitch. "Look, Aletto, I was just trying to—''

"Trying to baby me? Trying to remind me I'm not as good on a horse as you are?"

"It's not like—!" Lialla began, but Aletto overrode her, his own voice rising until Jennifer thought it would crack.

"I swear, Li, sometimes you're as bad as—!"

"Don't you *dare* say what I think you're going to say!" Lialla shouted. "I am not as bad as Jadek! I'm not! He never meant it when he said he was just trying to protect you, and you know it! But I'm not trying to protect you, I'm trying to keep all of us alive! Do you really have the nerve—*or* the right—to object to that?"

Aletto was halfway to his feet when Robyn's hand caught his and tugged him back down. "Um, look," she said diffidently. "I think I've heard this argument before, or another version of it. I *really* do *not* want to hear any of it again, if you don't mind." She looked away from Aletto long enough to give Jennifer a very intense look. "And maybe before I agreed with you, Lialla—about the guys going into the market at night, all that. This time, I think I'm on Aletto's side."

Lialla drew a deep breath; Jennifer, interpreting her sister's stare as a plea for backup, held up a hand to catch the sin-Duchess's attention and shook her head. "Wait. Let her finish, then yell at both of us, because I think I agree even if our reasons don't turn out to be the same ones."

Robyn cast her a grateful smile. Her fingers tightened around Aletto's. "If I've heard right, you had this disease when you were a kid, right? It left you terribly weak, your leg is partly numb and partly touchy, you limp all the time but particularly

16

when you're tired. Have you ever tried working it?'' Aletto shook his head. ''There are diseases where we came from that paralyze people, mess up the muscles and bones. Accidents do that, too. Usually, the first thing that gets done once the fever lets up, or the disease hits a plateau or the accident's in the past, people learn to work their legs or arms—whatever doesn't work. It isn't easy or simple, and it can be pretty damned painful, I know people who've gone through it. But sometimes you can't tell after a while that there was any problem.'' She looked at Aletto again. ''There isn't any guarantee it'll help you, but I say you have a right to find out. There are two people here who can work magic; Jennifer can heal probably enough to help if you hurt too much to bear. I can't do that, but I give a good massage; your leg stiffens up, I can rub the cramp out.'' She drew a deep breath, glanced at him rather nervously. ''You're the only one who can say if you want to try, if you think it might be worth it to you. You're the one who'll hurt, if it hurts.''

Aletto sat very still and silent for some moments; when Lialla stirred and would have spoken, he simply looked at her and she shrugged. ''No one ever offered me that before. I—look, Li, I know it wasn't because you think I'm no good, or because you're trying to baby me. Really I do, it's just—well, never mind.'' He closed his eyes briefly. ''Li, you know it hasn't been easy. I— all right, it probably wasn't easy for anyone else, but for me, it was the end of everything. I've tried everything else: I cried like a little boy with cut knees when it happened. I hoped for the longest time I would just die, rather than live like that. Jadek— he was always so *nice*, so sympathetic, and I could see it in his eyes. In any man's eyes in Duke's Fort. Amarni's son, his only heir, is a worthless cripple, he can barely walk, can't run, ride, can't fight—can't do any of the things Amarni did with his men, except drink.'' He seemed to suddenly realize he wasn't simply talking to himself or to his sister; his pale face flushed.

After a moment, he went on. ''I didn't die. So then I thought maybe I'd drink myself to death—it looks that way now that I'm away from Duke's Fort and that life, away from Jadek. He—I think he must have done that deliberately, too, whether he planned the attack of marsh fever or if he only took advantage of it.'' Robyn squeezed his hand and he cast her a smile. ''You must think I'm mad. To believe the man who is my uncle, who married my mother, who helped her raise us both, would delib- erately try to convince me I had no worth, and to do it like that—so subtly, I never saw it all the years I lived in Duke's Fort with him.''

17

Robyn shook her head. "I don't think that. There are men who do such things." Lialla shifted her weight abruptly, shook her head in turn as Aletto glanced at her inquiringly. "It wasn't you, it was him. Or, mostly him. Men like Jadek need victims. You were too young and innocent to understand what kind of man he is. I—" She drew a sharp breath and let it out in a gust. "I know, from experience." And, in a deliberate and abrupt change of subject, "It's behind you; try and understand it if you want to, let it go otherwise; you'll chew yourself to bits for no good reason. There's enough to concern you here and now, all right?"

Aletto looked visibly relieved. "Sensible lady. A bargain between us, then: I'll try your way, you help me. I've never attempted to work through this. I don't know that I have the inner strength to stick it through." He sighed. "Let alone the physical."

"Maybe you won't," Robyn said. "I won't lie to you, I don't think it'll be easy. I've pushed soft muscles of my own too many times, I know how that hurts. Muscles that might be atrophied—I just don't know. But we don't know you can't. I think you owe yourself the chance. You try, I'll help all I can; I'll bully you when you want to quit, I'll stick with you when we're riding and help you forget what you're doing. I'll rub you down when we stop."

Lialla opened her mouth, shut it again without saying anything. Aletto wasn't paying any attention to her anyway. "Do *you* think I can, Robyn?" She nodded; he gripped her hand hard and let it go. "Then—then I'll do it." He shifted so he could look at Lialla. "Li, I appreciate your idea. I know you were only thinking about saving me a lot of misery, about keeping the rest of us safe. But we'll go the way we originally intended."

Lialla managed a small smile, enough to satisfy him. Only Jennifer saw her cast up her eyes as soon as he turned his attention back to Robyn.

2

LIALLA pulled the red string from her pocket, worked up a complex figure and wandered off a few minutes later—long enough, Jennifer thought, so Aletto and Robyn wouldn't think she was upset. It was a nice performance, but the two weren't watching her. Robyn was showing the nera-Duke a set of very basic, very simple stretching warm-up exercises and Aletto was rather cautiously mimicking her actions.

Jennifer got to her feet and looked around. Now that her eyes were properly open and the sun was out of them, she could see better—not that there was much to see. The tabletop mesa dropped off steeply on this north edge, ran up to a rocky lip to the west and appeared to stretch out southward almost forever. Between her and the horizon it was all the kind of high desert terrain she would have expected in the open country north and east of Los Angeles. Desert, but the sand was at least half gray dust and dirt, the rest rock. In this mix of brush, thin grass and trees somehow survived between rainy seasons. She wondered how far they were from such a rainy season and hoped it wasn't due soon—dry heat was preferable in Jennifer's book to thunderstorms and gully-washers. Or serious winter rains; if this was anything like the Palmdale region, those winter rains could get damned cold and miserable; snow wasn't impossible.

Wonder how Chris's games and books would account for that kind of situation, she thought in mild amusement. Realistically, none of them were set for bad weather.

Then, too, Lialla or Aletto would know the seasons, however naive they were otherwise. *God, I hope they would,* she thought fervently. But Dahven—Dahven would surely have sent them with good boots, warm clothing. Some kind of tent. *Am I going to feel myself blush every time I think the man's name?* It was as irritating as it was unexpected. Who would ever have thought that self-sufficient Jennifer Cray, associate corporate law attorney, woman nearing thirty—who'd have foreseen her going silly over a Duke's son the way Chris's girlfriends did over rock stars?

But how fortunate, since she'd been struck by lightning—it certainly *felt* that way—that it had struck twice. Poor Dahven. If it was unnerving to her, how much stranger and more embarrassing for a man who'd by his own admission been sowing wild oats all across Sikkre for years?

Leave it, she ordered herself. *Even Robyn's going to notice you standing here mooning eventually. Do you really want that? Besides, you said you wouldn't think about him constantly this way; it's not exactly a useful activity.*

Think about Night-Thread Magic, she told herself. Better yet, get a feel for the land around here, see where you'll be going tonight. While you can, if you can. Which meant finding a way to look down from the south end of the plateau where they currently sat.

According to Chris and his maps—if she remembered what he'd said the night before—this should be the largest mesa in the vicinity, possibly the largest in the entire high-desert region. If the map gauge was accurate—if Chris had translated Rhadazi distances to something he could understand—it was about a U.S. mile side to side, and near the northern end of the region. Westward, one came to a low coastal range eventually, through that to the sea; east, one lost altitude rapidly down to the Sikkre–Bez road, went on down to patches of low desert interspersed with small rivers and farming or herding land. Beyond that, eventually forest and the north-south range of mountains that separated Rhadaz from whatever neighbors it had beyond; no one had mentioned them and Jennifer had little interest in such things at the moment. Chris was more taken with history than geography, apart from maps.

Doubtless she'd find out, eventually. If no one killed them, she'd have the rest of her life to find out. *What a lovely thought. Go take a hike, why don't you? Quit thinking, damnit!*

She stretched and stifled a yawn. It was too hot to nap and she wasn't particularly tired anyway. A mile wasn't much—make that two, out and back—and now that she was on her feet she could feel a puff of breeze that was at least cool against sweaty skin.

Aletto leaned forward, arms wrapped around bent knees; head turned to see how Robyn was doing the stretch so he could copy her. Jennifer smiled, shook her head and left them. Neither noticed her go.

Lialla was nowhere in sight—sensibly in the shade, no doubt. Sulking, probably; she did a lot of that when someone crossed her, or when things didn't go the way she wanted them to. Jennifer dismissed Lialla; it simply was not her fault that she could work Thread in ways Lialla couldn't—notwithstanding the Zelharri woman's years of practice. Barring a miracle, Jennifer didn't expect the situation to improve; Lialla was her own age, at least as stubborn, and despite her dreadful uncle, used to getting what she wanted, or at least trying for it. This wasn't a good situation for two strong—*all right, hard-nosed*—women, particularly since they seemed to be on opposite sides of nearly every decision that had to be made.

The sun was a white disk in a deeply blue and cloudless sky, the wind too seldom now for comfort. "At least it's a dry heat," Jennifer told herself. Something under a dry bush skittered away at the sound of her voice.

It took her a while to reach the south end of the mesa top, even longer to find a vantage. There were a few faint game trails leading down the draws to lower, level ground. Most of them looked impassable even on foot. "If Chris thinks I'm riding down one of those—" She shook her head firmly and turned away. If this was the way they were going tonight, it would be a damned slow trip down, with Jennifer on foot all the way.

She found a tiny pool, traced a thin trickle of water back into rock and located the spring that fed it. The water was icy, too cold to have taste. She drank, caught more in her hands and pressed them against her forehead. Chilled skin protested; her temples ached fiercely for one brief moment. She took another double handful and drank, more slowly this time. The cold-on-nerve-endings headache faded and for the first time all day she felt awake and fully alert.

"I hope that came from underground and it was clean," she said, then shrugged. After drinking water in Sikkre, she was probably living on borrowed time anyway.

There were prints everywhere: a few like deer that she recognized, others that could have been anything from raccoon to bear. "Don't think bear," she ordered herself. *Don't say bear around Birdy, either,* she added silently. She and Robyn had spent their early years in Wyoming; they'd camped and hiked in wilderness areas, had never seen bears except in campgrounds, around the garbage cans. Robyn still had a horror of bears and irrationally preferred campgrounds—where she felt safe—to trails.

"Probably not bears. This doesn't look like bear country." It was a lousy argument, the kind her first pre-law classes would never have let her get away with. It was good enough to get her mind off unidentifiable prints, and back to her immediate goal:

a look across open country. She finally found a rock outcropping near the ravine with the spring, climbed it gingerly with full awareness that similar country in *her* world would hold spiders, scorpions, snakes—"All the good stuff," she mumbled. "Maybe it doesn't look like snake country either. Maybe Saint Patrick came here when he left Ireland."

The sun was at midday when she reached the top of the eroded stack and located a flat place to sit. The breeze which had died away to nothing while she climbed had only been blocked by the ledge; it came straight at her here, blowing the hair off her forehead. It felt wonderful.

At first, she couldn't make out anything around her; the land was unfamiliar, there was nothing to pin down or name. Finally, away to the east, she saw a pale, slender line that might be a road—that must be a road, very possibly the main one. It ran north and south, vanishing behind the edge of the mesa, and a long distance to the south she lost it among hills. Everything out there was dry-looking: grays, gray-greens, tans, dust and browns. Mesas, ravines. It made her tired and thirsty, just looking. "At least we have horses," she told herself. "I hope my backside gets used to the darned things before we go much farther, though."

Farther to the south, blurry even for her good eyes, she thought there might be a line of yellow-green: willows or something similar, marking water. Beyond that, hills, then mountains. The land rose more abruptly to the west, blocking any possible view of the sea, but she thought they would be too far away to see even a reflection of light on water. If Chris had worked out his distances, if that particular map was at least in proportion, if not as accurate as the maps she was used to.

At the moment, Jennifer had only a vague idea of where Bezjeriad was—somewhere *out there*, to the south—and an even muzzier notion of how far distant it was. They'd need more maps, or they'd need to each study the ones Chris had. If they were separated, if Chris somehow lost the map or it got damaged—"Brrr! Think of something pleasant, why don't you?" She glanced automatically at her watch, swore rather despairingly. It was working again; it had only stopped those first hours after Merrida tore them from their own world. But it read 8:45 p.m.

Birdy probably had the right idea about time; she'd taken off her watch years ago, when she'd left their aunt and uncle's home in the San Fernando Valley for the Sunset Strip and a variety of hippie crash pads. She hadn't worn one since. Jennifer swore

22

again. "Well, I'm not Robyn, and I'm not going to try and manage without my watch—not as long as it's running." She glanced at the sky, at the lack of shadow around her, reset it to 12:00 p.m. "Near enough. If Chris is right, this has to be a twenty-four-hour world, too. Hell, it's *ours* with a twist in the history somewhere, if he's right." She looked at the solid, sensible rectangular face, sighed and shook her head. The battery on this particular digital was supposedly good for five years. Jennifer didn't want to think about five more years in Rhadaz. Didn't want to consider what five years might bring her. "Five years: shit. I was going to make partner at Heydrich & Harrison in under five, that's the last thing Jimmy and I talked about."

Well, she wasn't about to be a sixteen-year-old Aletto and just give up! She set her lips in a hard line, pressed buttons and silenced the various alarm beepers. That might add a little time to the battery; maybe she'd figure out a way to run it on Thread. "Million-dollar-making idea," she said aloud, and suddenly grinned. "Need at least one a week, never know what's going to sell, make you rich, let you retire early." The grin faded and she sighed. "Travel, have adventures, see the world—yeah, right. As far as I'm concerned, today is Thursday the seventh. I'm *not* going to try and remember how to shift the date over."

She stood, pulled the legs of her jeans down where they belonged and gazed back northward across the mesa. From here, there was only slightly rolling, dusty ground, wind that swirled dirt around the base of dry brush. A few trees and very little shade. She couldn't see far, not as far as she'd seen from the campsite. Hell, she couldn't even *see* the campsite; it made her nervous. "As if I were the only one left." Not a good thing to think. She climbed down the rocks considerably faster than she'd gone up them. Heat kept her from hurrying back across open ground, but she moved as quickly as she could.

* * *

CHRIS, Edrith and Robyn sat by the dirt-covered ashes that had been the morning fire; they were surrounded by bags, open cloths, ties, ropes and bundles of food, cook pans, water bags. Robyn was sorting, the boys repackaging, all three of them arguing cheerfully—Edrith had lost no time copying Chris's flippant way of talking to his mother, and Robyn gave him as good back as she gave Chris. Jennifer watched and listened for several minutes, finally mentioned her worry about maps. "Take them both, please," Robyn pleaded. "I mean, look at this, they're causing more work than they're doing."

"You just don't trust us around the food, ma," Chris replied.

"I can't think why not," Robyn said dryly. "I'd as soon trust—"

"Yourself around a carton of filter cigarettes?"

Robyn narrowed her eyes. "*That* was really cold, kid. Scram, do it now."

"Just trying to cheer you up, ma. Look how much longer you're going to live—"

"Sure, it already seems like six years since I got up this morning. Isn't there a nice cliff around here you can fall off?"

Chris grinned. "I'll see what I can do for you, after I take care of the map problem. Would you like me vanished, messily dead or just a little battered?"

Robyn held up a fist—a soft little hand, short-fingered, thumb tucked inside. "Battered *I* can manage. Scram."

"Yes'm, ma'am," Chris replied. Robyn was scowling ferociously but there was a grin tugging at the corner of her mouth; the game they'd played for years demanded he leave before she started laughing and spoiled the whole thing. "One copy of each of my two maps and an extra in case, all right, Aunt Jen?"

Jennifer nodded. "Your lawyer bag was on the horse last night?"

"It's a purse."

"Sure. Your mode of transport was a BMW, too. I went to school with girls who carried purses. That black thing isn't one."

"Haven't you had enough fun pulling people's chains?" Jennifer asked. "The bag is over there with my blankets. Keep it in the shade if you can; I have makeup in there that'll melt and make a hell of a mess. And take it easy with the paper, that's all we have."

"Tell *me*," Chris said feelingly. "Talk about unrenewable resources—at least out here in the middle of nowhere. But you've got six legal pads in the bottom of that thing, minimum, right?"

She laughed. "Probably only five. I was taking a day off, remember?"

"Want me to use both sides, one map per side? No." He answered his own question before she could. "I know, what if something happens to split us up, and something happens to the piece of paper?"

"Smart kid," Jennifer said. "Get going, all right?"

Robyn settled cross-legged in the midst of baggage and watched them. "I thought one was bad; it's almost like Chris cloned with the two of them around. That poor kid," she added softly.

"Who, Chris?" Jennifer shoved a bag of meal aside and eased down onto the blanket. Robyn shook her head.

"Edrith, of course. Imagine a mother who didn't want a kid

24

like him.'' She sighed. ''Guess this must be a version of our world; the people haven't changed, whatever else did. She sounds like me, but with even less heart. At least I love my kid.'' She sighed again and held out a hand. ''Hand me that dark blue sack, will you?'' She looked inside it, pulled the string ties and knotted it. ''That goes in the pile behind you.''

''Got it. Where's your aerobics partner?''

''Where's—? Oh. Aletto?'' Robyn grinned. ''I sent him for a short walk; he should be back any time. Aerobics.'' Like Jen, she used the English word. ''Boy, that sounds strange; no wonder they get so cranky when we toss in outland language. I feel like I haven't spoken good old American in months—'' Her face fell abruptly; she swallowed, fixed her eyes on her hands and began deliberately separating a bag of hard biscuits into six piles.

She started as Jennifer touched her arm. ''Birdy, don't think about it, all right?''

Robyn looked up at her. ''What—don't think that I was talking good old American only two days ago? With a man I—with a man I killed?'' She shifted into American, words spilling rapidly. ''What, don't think about turning into a bird the size of my old apartment—for which, by the way, Aletto would never, ever forgive me; do you know how he feels about shapeshifters, that kind of magic?—and broke some guy's neck.'' She laughed mirthlessly. ''Some guy! Vinnie Harris, for God's sake. The Thukar's favorite wizard, El Serpente from the Whiskey and I not only run into him, I—''

''Birdy—''

''Don't call me that!'' Robyn clapped a hand over her mouth; the words seemed to echo between them. After a moment, she shook her head, and Jennifer went on, also in English. Better— *safer* if Aletto should come back unnoticed.

''Robyn, whatever he called himself, he was a first-rate creep, a genuine power tripper—isn't that what you used to call people like him? He had all three of us helpless, he threatened you, me, Chris—Robyn, *I* would have killed him for what he said he'd do to Chris!''

''Look, I know what he was,'' Robyn said. Her hands became still. ''I still can't believe the shitty luck, for me to get dragged out of L.A. into *this* kind of place and then to run right into Mr. 'Look at me, I'm the next Jim Morrison,' *with* local magic under his belt! God. My lousy luck.'' Jennifer touched her arm again, this time in wordless sympathy. Robyn merely nodded and after a few moments began counting biscuits into piles again. ''I still say what I said two nights ago. He deserved what he got.

He forced it. I'll still probably have nightmares about Chris forever. I just—'' She shrugged. "I don't know."

"I know."

Robyn glanced up again. Her lashes were damp. "Yeah, right. Good old Birdy the pacifist." She looked around rather cautiously. Aletto wasn't anywhere in sight yet, Chris and Edrith had taken one of the blankets and moved into shade some distance away and were both bent over Chris's maps. "You know, I used to get so pissed at people who called themselves pacifists—the ones who harassed the cops during the Johnson visit to Century City and got pounded, the guys who said they were nonviolent and then in the very next breath told you how to cream somebody who was hassling you, or the guys like Roger—remember Roger?"

"Sweet peace and flowers Roger who broke your arm and put you in County General?" Jennifer asked dryly.

"Roger who was so damned piously pacifist except against his girlfriend, right. But I was never *like* that," she went on angrily. "Even when guys hassled me, I put them down with lip, I never hit anybody, I never even threatened to. I avoided situations where I'd get pissed enough to want to pound anyone, when I demonstrated for farm workers and they hauled a bunch of us off, some of the guys got physical but I never did, I just went limp. Even when the cops got smart and groped, trying to get some of the chicks to go at them. If it was something I felt *really* angry about, I didn't go, that's all. Maybe that's not a true pacifist, if you still get mad even if you don't act it out, I don't know. I wasn't ever into philosophy, not like that." She sighed. "I'm glad I'm not; I could tie myself in knots, trying to work out the whole thing. I could hate old Vinnie forever, for what he made me do; that's poisoning your system but I can't help it."

"Robyn, you said it yourself, it's only a couple days, it just seems longer because so much has gone on between. Give yourself some time."

"Time. Yeah, right. Jen, you know what scares me most? I know that wasn't the end of it."

Jennifer shook her head. "No. I wish just once I could tell you a candy-coated lie and make you feel better."

"Me, too. Never has worked that way for us, though, has it?"

"Never has. And I have a bad feeling you're right. I can't see how that was a one-time shift." She watched Robyn package biscuits and move on to the next bag, then sighed in turn. "I wasn't going to say anything about this, but if I'm handing you the truth I can't hold any of it back, can I? Merrida warned me, that first night—when you and Chris were packing up the picnic, she told me to watch out for you. She said your temper—''

Robyn laughed derisively. "Me? Temper? What temper?"

"That's what I said," Jennifer replied. "But the Cray family temper is a pretty nasty one, if you recall Mom and Dad's fights. Or Grandpa blowing up when he was working on his truck. I used to take off whenever he popped the hood, remember? We all have the Cray family temper, I know I do. I don't let it out much; it cost me a couple friends in law school. You just buried it deeper than the rest of us. Merrida said it could have dire consequences. I didn't think any more about her warning than you would have, I'm afraid. I'm sorry."

Robyn laughed again, quietly this time. "What for?" she asked finally. "You think it would have helped if you'd told me? That I'd have believed you—or her? Or that anything would have changed in that tower room?" She sobered. "God. If Aletto finds out—"

"Give him a little more credit than that, Birdy. He has a deep distrust for magic—particularly Night-Thread Magic, because Merrida soured him on it, but any magic to some degree or other. He makes faces and snotty little remarks whenever Lialla or I Wield, or even just talk about it. But I notice he puts up with it when it's useful. And I notice he didn't refuse that market-bought charm magic of Dahven's, did he? I'd wager if he ever finds out you shapeshifted to escape the Thukar's palace, it'll be all right, because you did it. And he knows you, he's fond of you."

Robyn shook her head; her mouth was set in a stubborn line. "He *is* fond of me; I like him a lot. But I won't test how much he cares, if you don't mind. Not unless I have to."

"That's up to you. I can say I'd tell him if it was me, but maybe not. Only you and I and Lialla know about it, though; she and I certainly won't say anything to him."

"I know that. Thanks."

"I—here he comes. I'll leave you."

"You don't have to."

"No. I want to see how Chris is doing anyway. If you want to try and talk this thing through, I'm here. Don't forget."

Robyn nodded and smiled up at her as she stood. "I won't. Thanks, Jen."

Aletto was limping but not badly and he looked fairly pleased with himself. Jennifer gave him a thumbs-up sign on her way

27

by, which seemed to confuse him, but he made a thumbs-up in reply.

* * *

EDRITH was watching in fascination as Chris lettered in a map; half a dozen lay between them. Two of the finished maps bore English words; the others were detailed with landmarks but no writing. "Remind me to strangle that old bat Merrida," Chris swore between clenched teeth as Jennifer's high-top sneakers came into his line of sight. He didn't look up. "She gave us spoken language but not written. How's a guy supposed to fill in maps when he doesn't know how to write in Rhadazi?" He glanced at his companion. "And this fella's no help at all, he can't read it either."

"They don't collect all the poor market children into groups and teach them letters," Edrith said.

"They should."

"Why? I know what the thing I'm stealing looks like, I don't have to know my letters to find what I want. I think *your* world must rely too much on such things."

Chris shook his head. "If you can't see the point, I probably can't convince you, so let's drop it. All the same, there must be some written history in this world!" Silence. "Isn't there?" he asked in a small voice.

"Oh, books again? There are plenty of them, if you're wealthy enough to afford them, to have a decent house to keep them in, time to read them."

"You're giving me a headache, you two. Chris, why don't you ask Lialla or Aletto to show you the basics?"

"Show me—?"

"How to read and write, isn't that what you're griping about? I have to admit, I hadn't particularly thought about it until just now; maybe you and I should form a class of our own."

"Yah. I'm sure either one of them would *love* to teach *me* how to read and write Rhadazi. Lialla thinks I don't show them proper respect for rank and all that crap. And Aletto—oh, hell, he's nice enough when he wants to be." He scowled at his partly finished map. "I guess now that he's coming onto Mom, he'll be a lot nicer to me. They usually are. At first, anyway."

"I don't think Aletto has much in common with Arnie and his ilk, do you? Honestly?"

Chris looked up at her. Finally, slowly, he shook his head. "Honestly—no, I guess not. Hell, don't mind me, I get this way every time."

"I know that. You need a girlfriend—or six. Birdy's growing

28

up; one of these days she'll leave home on you, and then where will you be?'' As she'd intended, he laughed.

"Yeah. Girls are so plentiful around here."

"The local ones sleep with their goats," Edrith offered, straight-faced. As Chris turned to look at him, horrified, he grinned.

"It can't smell much worse than a musk-based perfume," Jennifer said blandly. "In fact, it's probably the same base. I'll get Lialla to show me how to read, and then I'll teach you, sound fair?" Chris snorted with suppressed laughter.

"Oh, sure! You two fight worse than—well, pretty bad, anyway. I'm with Mom; you two conduct these high-volume seminars far away from me."

"Your mother's right," Jennifer said. "There's a ledge around here with your name on it, kid."

Chris ignored this, finished his map and added it to the growing pile in front of Edrith. "Listen. Not to change the subject or anything, but I had an idea this morning. I wanted to run it by everyone except then I could see Her Prissiness was about to get everyone's back up—"

"Chris—"

"Oh, all *right*. Anyway, no way I was going to open *my* mouth after all that crap went down. So Edrith and I talked it out, and we thought, maybe run it by you. We need some kind of protection. I mean, no; this isn't coming out right. Wait, listen." He sat up, shaking out his pen hand. "Let me see if I can't lay it all out logically before you pick me apart, Lialla-style, okay? Aletto got knives and things in the market, I have a bow and arrows the old bat got for me. You and Lialla got magic, however useful that might be in a fight."

"It's not too bad," Jennifer said soberly. It hadn't been too bad once Lialla showed her how to make rope, how to use such a simple, practical thing to trip up and immobilize even a large, armed man.

"Fine, then. But whatever you can do might not protect us all, and what if we get separated or Jadek or someone finds us and sends out a whole mess of swordsmen? Maybe we'll just be dead no matter what, in that case. But as far as I'm concerned, not without a fight on *my* part!

"Thing is," he went on somberly, "much as I hate to admit it, the old—Merrida was right about one thing: This is real. I haven't used a bow in a million years, and only in camp, shooting dull arrows at straw bales. I never shot a sharp arrow at a real person, except in games. I only ever used a sword in games—

in my imagination, or in a computer simulation. Oh, once at school, remember that play I was in two years ago? That was a fake sword and a choreographed fight, and I lost it. I don't know anything about fencing except that you don't pick it up overnight, and that fencing isn't real swordfighting, and that the guys we'd be fighting have been at it for years, they've been trained for it, they're paid to do it right. People like me don't just pick up a low-tech weapon like that and get good with it, not in the real world.''

Jennifer applauded silently as he paused and looked at her. ''I agree. I hate to admit it, Chris, but I never would have thought you'd catch on to that so quickly.''

''Yeah, I'm real bright, aren't I? Add to that,'' Chris went on, ''that Mom raised me to think like she does. I—maybe, if I really had to, I could shoot someone in a 'him or me' situation, or to protect someone like you or Mom. I could probably kill someone if I had to, from a distance or in the middle of a fight to stay alive. I—I hope I could look back on it that cold-bloodedly and say I had to, and live with it.'' He picked up the pen and picked up the yellow pad. ''I'm afraid the time's going to come when I'll find out if that's true.''

''I hope not,'' Jennifer said. ''But nothing's certain, is it?''

Chris shook his head. Blond, spiky hair trembled and spilled across his forehead; he grumbled and shoved it upright. ''You wouldn't happen to have any hair spray or mousse or *any*thing in that bag, would you? This stuff is driving me buggy!''

''Whatever's in there, have at it.''

''Thanks. I'll finish these first. Anyway, this is getting way off track, what I was thinking: Lialla has magic; so do you. Edrith claims to be pretty good with a knife but he also says he doesn't like blood and *he's* never killed anyone.''

''The Thukar had really ugly laws to take care of people who kill. Besides, I've always found running a better answer than fighting,'' Edrith said. ''If someone *does* find us—someone like the Thukar or Jadek—I'm afraid running won't be the answer any more.''

''And a knife doesn't give you as long a reach as a man with a sword has,'' Chris said. ''But we've already decided swords are out. The ones we have with us aren't great, and none of us know how to use them.''

Edrith nodded. ''They *look* good in a belt, probably good enough to keep anyone with my kind of morals from trying to take the horses or anything else we have.''

''That's all they have to do,'' Chris said. ''Because we don't

30

have years to learn how to swordfight right, and do it reflexively and with the notion that you can kill if you have to.''

"This has to be leading somewhere," Jennifer said.

"Yeah." Chris shoved hair aside once more. "Bojutsu. Staff fighting." Jennifer shook her head; neither the word nor the phrase conveyed anything to her. "Remember when my friend Carlos was getting into karate and all that, and he and I were hot on the ninja games and the movies—?''

"Oh, God," Jennifer breathed reverently. "Ask me if I remember that *bad*, horribly dubbed ninja movie you had on my VCR the one night I came in late!''

"Rather not." Chris grinned. "Anyway, Carlos had taken a couple of years of karate and he went off and studied some of the more esoteric stuff—and because I couldn't afford the classes he worked out with me, so he reinforced what he learned and I learned almost as much as he did. Remember?''

"I remember you crawling out at the break of dawn this past summer to do Tae Kwon Do," Jennifer said. "Which was at least *quiet*. And I remember some awfully strange conversations about centering and meditation and the like.''

"Right. I wish I remembered more of that; it's important to any Oriental fighting style you pick up. But anyway, staff fighting," Chris said. "Bojutsu has some really good points, as far as we're concerned: It's different, Edrith says he's never seen or heard of anyone in Rhadaz using it. It's hard to come up against a totally unfamiliar style of fighting.''

"Let me get this straight. A wooden stick against a sword?" Jennifer's eyebrows rose. Chris nodded.

"Hardwood staff, anywhere from three to six feet. And the ninja who historically fought with bo used them against swords. The basics are pretty simple and fairly easy to pass on, I haven't done it in a while but it wasn't that long ago—jeez, it sure seems forever! Anyway, I remember enough to improvise on. It's something even Aletto should be able to do, or Mom, if we can convince her to give it a try, it doesn't take as much strength as a sword would. And a six-foot hardwood staff gives you a lot longer arm than a man with a sword has.''

Jennifer considered all this, finally nodded. "All right, that's so far logical. What's the problem?''

Chris sighed. "You sat through that three-way catfight this morning and still ask me that? Mom's going to bitch about the K-word—you know, kill? She knows I don't want to just go out and slaughter people and she still gets weird when I bring up something that could protect us against other peoples' violence.

31

Hell, you know how Mom is. Aletto's going to bitch about how he can't do it and it's not going to work. Lialla's going to bitch because that's all she's good for—''

''I'm going to bitch if you don't stop whining,'' Jennifer warned, only half humorously. ''Don't write everyone off without giving them a chance, Chris. You do that too much.''

''Yeah,'' he mumbled. ''Sorry.''

''You're not, really, but I accept the apology.'' He glanced up, gave her a rueful grin and went back to his map. ''Work out what you want to do and how you want to present it, then do it. Don't apologize for your idea, don't figure out the opposition arguments in advance, just lay it out and see what happens.'' He nodded. ''Personally, I'm willing to at least see how you do it. If it looks good, I'll try it, fair enough?'' He nodded again. ''Good. Finish the maps. My hair stuff is in a clear zip-lock in the very bottom of my shoulder bag.'' She stood and eased the shirt away from damp skin. ''If we're going to ride all night, I think I ought to find a patch of shade and at least rest. It's hard enough staying on that damned horse when I'm awake.''

''Yeah,'' Chris said. He grinned impudently. ''You think last night was bad, the first part tonight's gonna be *down*.''

''I saw it. You're just trying to make me feel good,'' Jennifer retorted, and walked away. Behind her she could hear Chris mumbling something, Edrith laughing in reply. ''Be nice or the hair stuff stays in *my* possession,'' she called over her shoulder. Chris slapped an exaggerated hand over his mouth, but she could hear him snickering through his fingers.

3

〵

T HE journey down off the mesa was every bit as horrible as Jennifer had feared it would be, but after the first hundred yards or so she decided she would be safer on the horse. By the time they reached lower ground, her legs ached from holding onto the horse's barrel, her back ached from leaning back at an exaggerated angle on the riding pad—she knew, rationally, it wasn't necessary to lean that far back but couldn't convince her trembling knees—her hands hurt from clutching so hard at the reins, the horse's mane, the front edge of the saddle; and she had to climb off again and walk as soon as they reached more level ground. Both feet had been trying to cramp most of the way down.

They had followed a broad ravine that dropped off the southeast side of the tabletop, abandoned that for a westerly branch partway down. There was a moon, but it was still low in the sky, and shadow was thick in the deep dry cleft. Once on flat, open ground, it looked at first as though they could see a considerable distance, but that proved to be illusion: Shadow was thick under brush and rock, piled boulders, in gulleys and dry washes. The blue-white moonlight that paled open ground did odd things to proportion and distances, so that a seemingly insurmountable stone cliff shrank to a wall of rock that went no higher than a rider's knee and perhaps a hundred feet in length. Jennifer finally gave up trying to see where they were going or how far they'd come, and simply rode.

After a while, she edged up close to Lialla. The sin-Duchess glanced at her and offered what might have been a tentative smile; the motion of her mouth indicated as much but her eyes were unreadable. "Tell you things?" she asked.

Jennifer laughed quietly. "Am I as easy to figure out as that?"

"It's what you always say," Lialla replied.

"I guess it is. But why not? I want to know things, I hate being ignorant. Never mind that my ignorance *here* could get us killed. Besides," Jennifer shifted cautiously as they started down a shallow slope, "it might take my mind off a few bruises in unnameable places. Particularly if we have as many hours to go tonight as I'm afraid we do."

"You aren't a rider?"

"Believe it or not, there *are* things I don't do, yes. I don't hunt or fish, even though I was a child where that's done; I have never used any kind of weapon—well, unless you could count the little judo I used on that guard. And as to horses—God. I used to ride a cousin's horses when I was *very* young, years ago. Not very often, either. I was small enough and his horses were tall enough that they scared me." Jennifer considered this and sighed. "I have a bad feeling they would still scare me."

Lialla laughed briefly. "I'm sorry, I didn't mean to insult you," she said.

"I don't think you could on the subject of horses."

"Well, I can't call myself a rider, really," Lialla said. "My uncle Jadek would have kept me from horses entirely, like everything else that gave me any independence, if he could have found a decent reason. He did prohibit me all but the most placid, and I never had a riding master, but I rode whenever I could. As much as I could, and I watched others who *were* learning, And copied everything I could.'' She sighed. ''I do like horses, though I haven't the nerve to attempt any but gentle ones. And of course, riding gave me time away from the family apartments, so even an ancient horse or a timid one was better than none, an hour or two better than no time. I don't think I've spent as many hours horsed all my life in Zelharri as I have these past days, and this last night! I'll ache tomorrow.''

Jennifer groaned. ''I ache already. Tomorrow night is going to be purest hell.''

''It may not, if it's only ache and not skin rubs. But I wish I'd had opportunity to search out a decent herb-merchant in Sikkre; there are a few salves that even ease rubs that have blistered.''

''You can't use Thread?'' Jennifer asked, and immediately bit her tongue.

Lialla snorted. ''You ask the strangest things! *I* don't know, I can't heal, remember?'' But she sounded less irritated than usual. Jennifer paid attention to the horse for the next several moments, and when Lialla spoke again, her voice had lost its edge. ''*You* tell *me* things for a little, why don't you?''

''Things. All right.'' Jennifer shrugged, winced as Chris urged his horse into a trot and the rest followed. ''Such as what?''

''Like—oh, what it's like where you come from. You have strange possessions, you talk oddly—your sister tells me she doesn't care to put herself forward, but even so she's more outspoken than most Zelharri women. And you—'' Lialla sighed. ''Tell me things about yourself. Or about your music—if Merrida says the magic chose you because of that, why? How does it work? Why do you manipulate Thread the way you do?''

Jennifer considered this. ''All right. Where we come from— it's a city, larger and more complex than Sikkre. The streets are all smooth-covered. There are many times more people.''

''I find it hard to picture anything bigger than Sikkre,'' Lialla said. ''Though Podhru is considerably larger, they say.''

It took time. Lialla interrupted frequently, demanding better descriptions of things that had no name in Rhadazi: cars, planes (she had less trouble imagining air travel than automobiles, for some reason). The ideas of air conditioning and refrigeration appealed to her; movies and television made no sense even after a long and earnest discussion into which Chris entered, and they

34

finally had to abandon it. Chris tried to explain computers and got even more tied up in nontranslatable words than before.

"Never mind," Lialla said finally, and very firmly. "I think I should like to see some of these things, somehow; I doubt I would want any more than that."

"Nice place to visit, wouldn't want to live there," Chris and Jennifer chanted together, in English, and both laughed. Chris shook his head and urged his horse forward; he was still laughing. "Sorry," Jennifer managed after a moment. "Old joke." They rode on in silence for some distance. "Anyway, music."

"Music," Lialla agreed with relief. "I heard you in the wagon, two nights ago. You and Dahven. The songs were—they sounded similar to me."

"If Chris is right, they should be. About this being a variant of our own world, about being the same part of the same continent. If he's right, things changed between my world and yours no more than six hundred years ago. In six hundred years, a lot of our music has evolved and probably you wouldn't recognize it as music at all. I'm sure there's sound here that would strike me the same way. But the basic stuff, the folk music—where I come from, much of it hasn't changed in hundreds of years. He—Dahven—told me it's static here, too. It's been handed down, unchanged, father to son to son's daughter, for as long as anyone remembers."

Lialla rubbed her forehead. "So you think there might be a time, far enough back in our history and yours, where they touch? That if you looked far enough, you might find songs that were the same."

"I have to admit I never thought of that," Jennifer said. "It's possible; it might be a better way to track that than Chris's approach, but I'm not as concerned about that as he is. And whether Merrida can send us home again or not, I don't know that it's important to place ourselves." She shrugged. "I can't think in that many directions at once, anyway. I think I'm better off concentrating on Thread and on here and now."

She stood in the stirrups as the horses started down a steep but fortunately short gorge wall. At its base, they turned left to ride down a broad wash. Jennifer cast a troubled eye upward, finally shrugged. It didn't look or feel like rain; there wasn't a cloud anywhere. She was talking quietly enough that she'd hear water rushing toward or behind them before it struck. But all those years in the L.A. region had left her extremely sensitive to the dangers of dry washes. When she began speaking again, Lialla had to ride closer and lean toward her to hear her.

"As to the magic choosing me because I'm a musician—I don't know. What I observed of Merrida that night and what you've told me since—I don't know if that's entirely the truth." She glanced warily at her companion. "I hope that doesn't offend you."

Lialla shrugged gloomily. "Merrida has always had a way of telling me things that leaves more unanswered than if I'd never asked. Like my uncle—like Jadek—" She fetched a deep breath, "I don't believe I noticed things like that, until I was away from them. Even a little time. I'd somehow never questioned that Merrida knew everything—even though she clearly did not. Now—"

"I understand. Sometimes there's no reason to question. Or there is, but you don't dare for your peace of mind. Music, though: At first, I thought she must mean the kind of education a classical musician goes through, the way you learn to think about music, about notes written on paper. It might be a little of that, but it's more the music Thread makes. I—Merrida never taught you anything about Thread and music?" She saw the sin-Duchess's hair fly, blue in the moonlight, as she shook her head. "Nothing—" Jennifer hesitated momentarily. "Nothing about the *sound* Thread makes?"

"It doesn't," Lialla began automatically. She stopped herself. "I'm sorry, I promised myself I would not argue with you this once. Even when you tell me something like that, something that goes against everything *I* learned. What *sound*?"

"You've never listened to Thread? You—wait. When you manipulate Thread, you do it quickly, don't you? In, do what you have to, out?"

"It's how I learned," Lialla replied, only mildly defensive. "Merrida always warned me to plan for emergencies beforehand—like making the rope in the stable the night Carolan caught us. I know that spell inside and out, I can probably make rope in my sleep. I don't have to search for the particular Thread it takes. Merrida taught me to use color, thickness, the way it vibrates, the—I don't know." She shoved a hand through her hair. "That was why she made me work from childhood with the string figures, so I'd learn the necessary speed and dexterity. Because one doesn't always have the comfort of plenty of time to plan and work a spell. Thread and sounds—I—well." Lialla thought about this in silence for some time. Jennifer felt the subtle shift of the fabric around them, Lialla touching Thread, manipulating certain of it—actually, Jennifer thought in wonder, testing a new idea, instead of screaming it down. "How truly odd!"

Jennifer slewed sideways to watch her. "You *never* heard it before?"

"I *heard* it—the way you hear things. You know: like now, there's wind, the sound the horses make on the sand, that kind of thing. I wasn't paying attention to that either, until just now. Were you?"

"No," she admitted. "But Thread doesn't just make a background noise like wind in the brush. At least, that's not what I hear."

"Maybe not. I'm not a musician, like you are; maybe that's the difference."

"You don't play any instrument? You don't sing? Dance?"

"Everyone sings, don't they?" Lialla asked. "And of course I dance—when I have the opportunity."

"You *do* hear music as music, then."

"Oh—I see." Lialla nodded. "Merrida told me once she didn't like the harvest banquets because there was so much of that—everyone sings the harvest cycle, there's other songs, new ones the players make up, and then the dances. She says the noise makes her head ache, and when it's necessary that everyone sing, Merrida bellows along on one note. It's awful to be anywhere near her." Lialla considered this, then actually laughed aloud. "And of course, no one wants to simply walk away from her, and chance offending her. She's kept it fairly quiet she's a Yellow-Sash Wielder, because of Jadek, but even the newest of the servants know she does magic of some sort, and it makes them cautious."

"She's tone-deaf," Jennifer said. "It's a problem some people have where I come from, too. But if *you* can hear music, if you can sing it—then you should be able to hear Thread. Just the ones I know how to use, since I can find them by sound, it's easier and faster than touch. Like touch, each one is different."

Silence. She wondered if she'd offended the woman once more, pointing out another way to utilize magic Lialla had known all her life—and been barely able to wield. This time, she wasn't touching Thread; the air all around them was quite still. Jennifer tried the shift Lialla had taught her that first night on the road from Zelharri, the one that let her move in the "real" world and still see the underlying Thread that bound it all together. The Night-Thread that let a Wielder work magic.

From horseback doubled vision was disorienting in the extreme; Jennifer jolted forward, both hands grabbing for mane, and held on until she could shift back into straight reality. *Don't do that!* she ordered herself.

"I don't know," Lialla said finally. "I'm being honest with you, Jen; it's not easy, either. Thinking that maybe Merrida knew about the sound, she'd *have* to, wouldn't she? Not because she heard it but because *her* instructor did. Thinking that, knowing she knew the way that would let me try for a White or Silver Sash and she didn't tell me. That she's responsible for me being such a bad Wielder, that maybe it *isn't* my fault for being impatient, or for wanting it so badly—"

She drew a deep, shuddering breath; Jennifer leaned over to touch the back of her hand and shook her head hard once she had Lialla's attention. "Don't think about that, Lialla. If I were you, I know I would be simply furious, even considering she might have held me back. You can't afford that distraction just now, you need all your wit and your skill right here, with us. It might not be true anyway. Save that thought for when you see her next, and ask her."

"Hah," Lialla growled. "She'll tell me she did it for my own good, or that it wasn't her fault, that Thread doesn't work that way. You don't know her."

"I know her well enough." Jennifer smiled grimly, remembering the autocratic old sorceress. "She might tell you any of that, or all of it. But between us, I'd wager we will be able to get answers for you, Lialla." She heard the other woman laugh.

"Somehow, I don't doubt that, Jen. It's curious," she went on after another little silence. "How many days is it since Aletto persuaded me to leave Duke's Fort, and I made him agree to come with me—it can't be only six? Seven?"

"Time gallops when you're having fun," Jennifer said dryly.

"You people have strange humor. Seven days ago, I was told I had to marry Jadek's cousin Carolan, and I'd have done anything to avoid that." Jennifer felt her shudder.

"Why Carolan?" she asked, her voice low and carefully neutral. Lialla had not volunteered any of this before; clearly, though, she needed to get some of it out of her system. In the dark like this, no one close to them, her face largely hidden as Jennifer's was, it would surely be easier for her to talk about it. "Why Carolan?" she asked once again.

"He was Jadek's nearest relation—save Aletto and me, of course, and Carolan was from his mother's side. Older than Jadek—he was horrid, soft as too-old fruit, unclean. If I'd married him, our—our son would have been next in line after Aletto. And if something had happened to Aletto—Jadek's own son by our mother would have been after Aletto, of course, but mother never gave him children.

38

"I wanted to refuse him but—" She drew a deep, shuddering breath. "Jadek wouldn't let me. Later, Aletto and I decided to leave but somehow Carolan found out. That was—was how Aletto was hurt; when you found us and healed his arm, Carolan did that. And then—Aletto stabbed Carolan. I—when his escort tried to finish matters, I made rope—like we did in the tower in Sikkre—and when Carolan's man fell, he fell on his knife."

"Good Lord," Jennifer breathed. "How awful for you, Lialla!" No wonder the woman had been such a jittery wreck when she, Chris and Robyn found them. And then, her brother as badly wounded as he'd been, Lialla unable to do anything but stop the bleeding . . .

"It was the worst thing so far. I tell myself things can't get any more dreadful than that; it helps." Lialla shrugged. "I told myself that before Sikkre, too. It still does help, a little."

"Keep in mind both times you came out in pretty good condition, so it can't all be luck. But let's hope we put the excitement behind us when we left Sikkre," Jennifer said.

They rode in silence for some time after that; Lialla immersed herself in Thread, humming very faintly under her breath, trying to match Thread-sound with her own voice, shifting up and down the scale. Jennifer found this vaguely unsettling until she discovered playing Beethoven in her head effectively screened what the other woman was doing. It muffled the shift of Thread, too. She was deep in the third movement of the Seventh Symphony when Chris and Aletto called a halt.

Chris came back to talk to them. "There's open ground for miles ahead, and the moon's pretty bright for something that thin. Besides, my backside went numb an hour ago. I think it's time."

"Good planning," Jennifer said. She waited until Chris went in search of Robyn before trying to ease herself quietly out of the saddle—no easy task since she was stiff and sore and her legs trembled so much they didn't want to hold her. Hands which were stiff and cramped from clinging to heavy reins and harsh mane wouldn't grip the saddle hard enough to hold her up, either. Somehow, she managed one step, a second—it came a little easier after that, but it didn't ache any less. *At least I didn't make a fool of myself in front of Chris,* she thought. Not that Chris was an equestrian either; but he was eleven years younger than she, more athletic—teenage-boy resilient—and he now and again thought it funny to bug her about it.

It was only mildly amusing at the best of times, and tonight certainly was not one of those. *And I'm too damned stiff to kick his backside, the way I normally would.*

The drinking water was very warm—almost hot—even though they'd kept the bottles in shade most of the day and the air temperature was nearly too cool now for bare arms. Jennifer firmly told herself to ignore the taste and managed to swallow some of it. The half of an oat cake Lialla gave her got rid of the leather and stale water taste but left her thirsty once more. The apples Robyn handed around were mealy, the little juice left in them cloyingly sweet. Another swallow of water to wash *that* down, a very tiny nibble of oat cake that might be enough to kill the taste but not dry her mouth, this time. . . . She sighed. Better.

Chris rattled paper. "According to this map, there's a spring—not where we'll be stopping tonight, but tomorrow night," he said. He'd watched her take that last drink, and he knew how she felt about cold and clean-tasting water.

Jennifer sighed. "I'll live that long. What's at the end of the flatlands ahead?" And how far is it—but she wasn't sure she wanted to know *that*.

"According to the map, it runs on a long way without any change, just grass, the kind of sand that's about half dirt—you know, like the Punchbowl, gets you really grubby when the wind blows? Anyway, a few bushes, not much else. It heads back into some gulleys—actually, if I read this thing the right way, the gulleys come off a couple really broad mesas, but we won't be close enough to the mesas to matter. So after that, sometime before dawn, there's a long rock overhang, a ledge that we'll have to get around and up before dark tomorrow. A few miles after that is water, but there's no way we can make *that* tonight." Chris held up the map once more; yellow legal-pad paper crackled in the stiff breeze that now blew steadily from the west. "I added real miles to yours and mine and Mom's, Aunt Jen—as close as I could figure them. I'm not certain what a Rhadazi league is, but it doesn't seem to be even close to three U.S. miles like a league should; it's worse than furlongs or kilometers or any of that."

"Do we really want to know any of this?" Robyn groaned. It was the first thing she'd said in hours.

"Probably not," Chris replied cheerfully. "If you do, the important stuff is right there, and forget all the mathematics that went into it, okay?"

"Swell, kid." Robyn sagged and let her head fall forward into her hands. "*God*, I could use a drink," she mumbled. But when Aletto leaned across to ask her what she'd said, she shook her head and glanced up at him. "Said, how are you holding up, after all that workout earlier today?"

"I think I'm still alive," he said. He sounded faintly surprised. "I—it's strange, just *feeling* things; they don't hurt or ache, nothing like that. Yet, anyway. I just *feel* them."

"That's good, then," Robyn patted his arm. "Tell me if something does start to hurt, will you?" She stretched cautiously. "In fact, why don't you help me up and walk me around a little? I think *I* need it."

They walked off together, along the floor of the dry wash. Edrith leaned back against his rolled cloak and closed his eyes; Jennifer worked off one sneaker to check sore toes. Chris stood and silently applauded. "Nice job, Ma," he added under his breath, in English. Jennifer cast him a glance but he'd already turned and was busily tucking the yellow-pad map into one of the bags hanging from his saddle.

* * *

THEY had been riding for about another hour, according to Jennifer's watch, when Chris drew his horse to a halt and held up a cautious hand. They came up even with him. "I saw a light," he whispered. "Or I thought I did—out that way."

"Light—oh, God," Robyn groaned and clapped a hand over her mouth. Ghost riders, ghost camels and a horse vanishing horribly—she wasn't the only one who immediately thought of that. Aletto caught hold of her other hand where it gripped the saddlebow.

"Not that kind, I don't think," Chris added hastily. "Sorry, Mom. Like a lantern, or something, maybe a fire. But I looked again, and there's nothing."

"Do those things travel?" Jennifer asked Lialla. "That Spectral Host?"

"If you can trust the stories armsmen tell, they're all over Rhadaz, or something like them," Lialla whispered. She brought her horse around and stared out into the darkness. "Is there a village out that direction?"

"Nothing on the map, this is past where most of the western mesas are. Maybe a little ways up the slope of one of the last ones," Chris replied. "Or maybe a hill somewhere. I can't really tell distances, not as dark as it is now."

"Jen—" Lialla turned; Jennifer could see the whites of her eyes in the starlight but little else of her face.

"I know." She knew, all right: A Spectral Host couldn't be sensed by ordinary means—at least, none she'd found that first night, none Lialla had heard of. People, however, could. "You

41

watch around us, I'll try first.'' Thread felt cold and tense, like an overtight cello string. Or maybe that was her inner sense or her hands trembling. She took momentary comfort from the fact that a comparatively long time had passed since Chris claimed to have seen that light and the present moment; back on the desert between the Zelharri border and that oasis, they'd been attacked twice by now. Besides—''I found them—I mean, there are people out that way.'' She pointed, west and a little south. ''Not very near, I don't think. I can't tell much else, they aren't close enough.''

''Which is just fine,'' Chris said grimly. His words jangled Thread all around her; she covered her ears and shook her head.

''Don't,'' she implored. ''Lialla, you'd better double check me. It could be a village, or a summer camp for herders if they do that here. I don't know.'' She disengaged with relief.

Lialla was quiet for some moments, finally shook her own head briefly, moaned and clutched at her temples. ''That was awful! Something's strange out here. I can't tell what they might be either.'' She turned to Chris. ''But I don't think there is a village or a camp around here; there isn't water marked on your maps, is there?''

''None marked.''

''This isn't the right time of year for high camps in this kind of climate anyway,'' Lialla went on.

''So what do we do now?'' Aletto asked. He still had hold of Robyn's hand; Robyn looked only slightly relieved to hear their distant company was human. ''If one of us goes to look—''

Edrith sighed faintly. ''A professional thief, maybe? I suppose I could, if no one minds waiting a while.''

''Are you mad?'' Lialla hissed in her brother's direction. ''If it's Jadek or the Thukar—!''

''Then we'd know for sure who is out there,'' Aletto began. Lialla shook her head and he stopped.

''No! If it's Jadek, he might have sent ordinary men via the road, but what if he didn't? What if he used his Light-Shaping Triad to send men, or one of his petty magicians, or even part of the Triad? Or what if the Thukar did? He lost face badly, you know, plus whatever reward Jadek offered for us. They could take us—''

''If that's how it is,'' Aletto said flatly, ''then they already know we're here, right now.''

There was a chill little silence. ''Ah.'' Edrith cleared his throat and everyone jumped. ''I take back what was never a serious offer at any time. Perhaps, sensibly, we'd be on our way. And

42

after all, it might only be a sleeping village, or a hunting party of ordinary mortals. Rhadaz is a vast land, if you remember, and even one of the great Triads from the Hell-Light wars couldn't possibly scan all of it.''

''No,'' Lialla admitted as she turned her horse and started forward. ''If it was the Thukar, though, he might know which way we went because—'' She gasped as strong fingers dug into her forearm, near the elbow.

''Don't say that,'' Jennifer said in a low, flat voice that stayed between the two of them. ''Don't even think it.''

Lialla jerked her arm free, numbing her companion's hand. Bared teeth gleamed in the starlight. ''Why? Because you find him attractive? Women do, you know. You wouldn't be the first to go soft over the Thukar's heir, nor the first to discover he's not entirely civilized. Or that he thinks of himself before any other.'' She dug her knees into the horse and rode ahead.

Jennifer managed to keep her horse from following, reins digging into stunned flesh and numbing it further. ''What brought that about?'' she whispered. Dark, long ears twitched back toward her, shifted forward once more. She'd thought they had finally buried the hatchet, she and Lialla, and now this—''He—Dahven would not reveal us to his father,'' she told herself. *Not of his own free will,* came an unwilling response. Her fingers sought the silver spiral charm he'd placed about her neck two nights before, but for the first time the feel of smooth, cool metal gave her no pleasure.

* * *

THEY rode as quickly as possible, each with a nervous eye to the west. The darkness was near complete, though, now the moon was down. Finally, Chris declared a brief halt. ''We need someone out front with good eyes, to watch for holes and sudden drops,'' he said. ''We can make out gullies and hills but not the subtle stuff.''

''Sensible,'' Jennifer said and slid from the back of her horse. ''I'll go first; you know my night vision's good. You stay right behind. You can read my signals.''

''Make them really broad,'' Chris urged. He swore under his breath as he shifted in the saddle. ''You got an ulterior motive for doing this, Aunt Jen?''

''Who, me?'' she replied dryly. ''And how's *your* backside, kid?''

''Can I trade this hoofed thing for a Chevy?''

''Make it a good chopper and a pilot instead. You're the kind of kid who'd have a junker break down after five miles.''

"Chevy," Chris insisted. "With a killer sound system." He groaned as he sat back up, but this time, Jennifer thought as she started out on foot, leading her own mount, it was less muscle pain, more the remembered misery of a lost CD player and the kind of music that went with it.

Her feet had quit cramping once they came down out of the hills, and walking quickly loosened her leg muscles. She put Chris's troubles—Robyn's, her own—aside so she could concentrate on their physical surroundings. She shut herself firmly away from Thread, too. Lialla would know to handle that; at least, she'd better.

* * *

AFTER a while, Chris took over for her, then Robyn took Chris's place, and Edrith took hers. The night stayed black, the shifting of stars overhead the only outward sign that time had passed, or that they had moved; it seemed as though they'd been walking and riding in place, with the black line of high country to their west blotting out the lines of individual hills and mesas, with no sign of light—or any other indication of human habitation. There was no change to the east, either, where there was little for miles between them and the road. A cool breeze brushed across them now and again, or a night bird or insects set up a racket—Jennifer was uncertain what she heard, and none of their Rhadazi companions knew, either.

Eventually, the high western line cutting across the sky came down low enough that they could be certain they had passed the last of the mesas. Not long after, Edrith raised a warning hand and Chris turned in the saddle to warn the rest of them: a narrow ditch of a wash, crossing just in front of them. Beyond it, more. They scrambled through half a dozen narrow gullies, down a slope. A few bushes screened a broad, gravelly span, and chill air alerted them to water. The horses pulled them on.

There wasn't much, a trickle scarcely capable of wetting the tops of the pebbles it flowed between. Chris and Edrith knelt to drag rock aside and with Aletto's help got the horses an unexpected drink each. Jennifer went a small distance upstream and pulled gravel down to form a dam. She drank from cupped hands, too thirsty to care about unfiltered, untreated water at this point, then splashed two doubled handfuls over her face before climbing back to her feet and leaving the little pool to the others.

She blinked, startled, as she turned and came face to face with Lialla, but when she would have turned back, the sin-Duchess touched her shoulder. "Jen, I'm sorry. I was scared half stupid but that wasn't any reason to say what I did."

"It's all right," Jennifer said.

"It's not."

"All right, it's not. But I hadn't thought, when we were out there looking for Chris's light, what you might be going through. I understand." She touched the hand still resting on her shoulder. "Don't worry about it, Li. You're the one who said it first; you and I will be getting under each other's skins a lot on this trip."

"I didn't mean it like that," Lialla mumbled, but she sounded fairly relieved.

4

It took what seemed hours more to Jennifer, once they'd found the ledge, to locate actual shelter under it. Chris's precious map seemed to need a little fine tuning, but she was too tired and cross to say so, and Chris wouldn't have appreciated the comment anyway. He was at least as tired as she—he'd walked the last miles when Jennifer was too tired to do anything but hang onto the horse and hope she didn't fall off and die before they reached someplace she could fall down and sleep. And at the moment, he seemed to be extremely depressed; hours of low-voiced talk with Edrith or with Aletto apparently got him no more ahead on his theory of an alternate world, let alone on where and when they might be in relationship to their own Los Angeles.

Finally, he had given up; he and Edrith had gone off on a discussion of mothers. Jennifer hadn't intended to eavesdrop, but she'd been too worn out to fight with a horse which wanted to hold its present position in the pack. Neither Chris nor Edrith seemed to notice she was right behind them—or maybe they didn't really care. Chris knew his aunt knew how he felt about his mother, anyway. "She's great. I worry about her a lot, you know? But she's got heart."

"I can see all that," Edrith replied, rather glumly. "Your mother really cares about you, too: She talks like she doesn't, but it wouldn't fool anyone. *Mine*—" He fetched a deep sigh.

45

"I can't remember when mine didn't have men around, lots of them. Lots of different ones—any kind as long as he had some money. For wine, or food—for something new for her to wear. *You* know." He sighed again. "Most of them drank more than she did; none of them liked it that she had a boy around, so after a while I just left. It was better than getting hit all the time."

"Yeah," Chris said feelingly. "Mom never seemed to care much for herself, but some guy started getting down on me, she really took 'em apart. No one lays a hand on the kid, that was her first rule. Any guy that forgot it, too bad, out the door." It was Chris's turn to sigh. "Too bad she didn't keep that rule for herself. She was all the time lying to me about how she got a black eye, or how her nose got bent up. Can you believe she went into the hospital," he used the English word out of necessity, "for a broken arm, she's laying there doped to the teeth for pain, and she tried to tell me she fell on the front steps?"

"I don't know about *hospital*," Edrith said. "I do know about black eyes. It *is* a shame." He shook his head. "I can't change her, I tried. It's her life; she doesn't approve of mine, either." There was a long, easy silence between the two, which Edrith finally broke. "I can see light, out to the east. We should be able to make out the ground soon."

"That's good. Maybe I can see where we actually are—"

"Shhh. Don't let anyone hear you say that!" Edrith hissed.

"It's all right," Jennifer mumbled from right behind him. "I had a hunch we were lost at least an hour ago."

"We *aren't* lost," Chris replied patiently. He glanced over his shoulder, but besides Jennifer, no one was near enough to hear him. Most of the sound behind her words had gone into her horse's mane. "You're sagging, lady," he added critically. "Aren't you supposed to be in good shape from all those Yup things you do—tennis and stuff?"

"Ooooh, smart kid," Jennifer said. "Tennis isn't Yup, you."

"Yah. Tennis whites and a two-hundred-dollar racquet coming out of a BMW, tell *me* it isn't Yup. You're flabby."

"Right. Tell me something new. Law requires you to sit on your backside and read thick books; I ran out of time for staying in shape, remember?"

"I remember you making noises about it, sure. Anyway, we aren't—what you said," he added in a suddenly cheerful voice. Jennifer sensed rather than saw Aletto and Robyn come up behind her. "Very nearly there; we'll just need daylight, like I said earlier, to find the holes in the rock. You won't want to stay

46

out in the open around here when the sun comes up, I'll bet you.''

"No, you won't," Jennifer groaned. Chris laughed and shook his head.

"*Mom's* in better shape than you are," he informed her.

"Yeah, I got more padding where it counts, kid," Robyn said. "We going somewhere, or did you get us lost?"

"Why," Chris demanded of Edrith in an aggrieved voice, "does everyone seem to think I'm a brainless nerd with a map?"

"If I knew what that meant," Edrith began seriously. Chris waved a hand in negation and started off. "I trust you," Edrith added.

"Isn't that a contradiction, you being a thief and all?" Chris asked over his shoulder.

"I *trust* you," Edrith repeated. There was a subtle twist to his words that Jennifer didn't follow. Chris apparently did; his shoulders tightened, visibly even in the dark. He let Edrith catch up to him and held out a hand, which the other took.

"Yeah. Right. Didn't even make sense, did it? But I guess it's been so long, I forgot."

"Forget again. It was rude of me to bring it up. Very against code," Edrith replied.

* * *

THREAD was fading; so were the stars. Eastward, a very pale line of yellow outlined otherwise featureless low hills. Lialla caught up with Jennifer. "I tried—what you said before. I can't touch it, I can't work with it. I can see Thread. I couldn't do that before." She paused. "I'm sorry."

"Sorry?" With an effort, Jennifer roused herself. She'd half fallen into a doze where she sat. But Lialla being Lialla, she might well take sleepy monosyllabic responses as an insult—or more likely, a freeze in reply to Lialla's earlier cutting remarks about Dahven. "Why sorry?"

"For at the inn, telling you it was impossible," Lialla said simply. "I—look. I think I keep saying this; I just want you to know it's not *you*. I—the way I learned—"

"Don't," Jennifer said. "I'm not Robyn; I don't particularly like to argue but I don't mind it. It's one of the things I was paid to do, back home, remember? You're at least willing to go back later and examine the facts, as you know them—that's better than most people. And to admit when it looks as if you were wrong, that's better yet. Frankly, I'd rather a good, hard, full-out fight than have you disagree with what I say and just keep it to yourself." She glanced around, lowered her voice. "Robyn's always done that. I love her dearly but if I could change anything about her, I would give her backbone and the will to stand up for what she thinks.''

''I—thanks,'' Lialla said, and reined back. That was the last conversation Jennifer remembered. Some time later, under a brilliant blue sky and with the least edge of sun touching at the eastern mountains, she half-fell from her horse into Chris's arms, barely managed to catch herself before she overbalanced both of them, and staggered back into a crumbly rock ledge. Dirt sifted down from somewhere above her, slid under her shirt collar and down her back; a blade of rock bored into her spine. Moments later, Edrith had her by the arm, his other arm around her shoulders, and he led her along crumbling stone, through shifting and treacherous dirt overlaying uneven, loose rock. She wondered muzzily how anyone his size—he was not really any taller than she, and certainly no heavier—could put so much strength into holding her up. She certainly wasn't contributing very much to the effort.

Daylight vanished and for a moment, she went blind. Edrith eased her down, moving in a half-turn so she faced the entrance of the shallow cave and her shoulders were against rock. ''Wait here, we'll bring your things,'' he told her, and vanished back the way they had just come.

Jennifer groaned, tried to stand. ''I can't let them shove me in here like an old lady while they do all the work,'' she mumbled. But her legs had quit communicating with her brain; they simply wouldn't respond at all. She yelped when she tried pressing her hands against stone, to help pull herself upright. They were unbearably sore, palms red and mottled. Her fingers didn't want to uncurl; they wouldn't flatten unless she pressed them against her legs, and that hurt. The muscle running along the back of her forearm and into her elbow hadn't burned that way since the aftermath of her first head-on racquetball game. ''God, I'm dying,'' she moaned, and sank back against the wall.

Robyn looked almost as bad as she felt, and she had no wisecracks at all for Chris, who carried her in. Aletto had somehow managed to stay on his feet, but his limp was a side-to-side lurch, and he leaned heavily on the wall. A walking stick Jennifer didn't remember seeing before was clutched in his other hand, held out to the side as a counterbalance. He had a pack over one shoulder, a blanket slung over that. He and Chris between them got Robyn down on the blanket, and Aletto dropped down next to her. It could only have been a matter of a split moment's difference which of them slept first. Jennifer was vaguely aware of Edrith and Lialla, of the water bottle Edrith pressed into her hands and up to her mouth. Of her own mouth shaping the words, "Somebody ought to keep a watch," before her eyes closed and she sank back. One of them had shoved something under her head—her leather jacket, by the familiar smell of it. It was the last thing she remembered for quite a while.

* * *

CHRIS was nearly as tired as everyone else and weak with relief at having finally found the ledge. The distances on that damned map needed overhauling, badly; it had shaken him more than he wanted to think about. Somehow, though, everyone was under shelter; he and Edrith fought sleep long enough to bring the horses along to where they were, to run a rope line between a pair of boulders. He could only hope the sun would travel the way he thought it would, that the map didn't lie about the ledge. Those poor horses would be cooked without shade, and unless the ledge provided it, there wouldn't be any around here.

They dragged saddles and bags free and simply dumped them in a disorganized heap in front of the rope line.

Edrith had poured water down everyone else. Now he drank a little himself, crawled into the shallow cave and dropped bonelessly onto the sandy floor. "By my mother's old gods, that feels just wonderful," he mumbled, rolled onto his back and fell asleep. Chris tossed a cover over him, knelt rather cautiously to slide the flat edge of one of the cloth food packs under his face so he wouldn't choke on the thick dust; Edrith didn't even notice Chris's touch.

Chris pushed back to his feet—it took both hands pressed against his thighs to give him the leverage—and staggered back outside for a blanket for himself. "You guys got enough water back at that wash, didn't you?" he murmured to the horses. He'd have to hope that was so; he didn't have enough coordination left to deal with horses and water, finding and opening the staler bottles and digging out the low-sided leather buckets that had been stuffed in one of those bags—somewhere. "Sorry, guys," he mumbled. "We'll get you grass later tonight, I promise, okay?" He was talking English, he realized; talking rather stupidly to horses who probably wouldn't understand the same babble in Rhadazi. *Oh, well, they'll pick up on the tone of voice.* He clutched at the blanket that had padded his saddle most of the night, managed to turn around without falling over, and made it back into the cave. "Jeez, maybe Mom's in better shape than *I* am. Hell, what a thought!" Everything ached, right now, and he was exhausted—astonishingly so for a guy who'd pulled plenty of all-nighters, studying, partying, running games at a downtown L.A. convention last year.

Aletto and Robyn were sound asleep, both gently snoring; for once, Chris thought, his mom's bubbling little snorts wouldn't bother him at all. Lialla was a wad of black fabric just beyond her brother, the hood of her blacks between her face and the ground. His aunt sprawled against the wall, her face so pale she looked dead. Chris shook that thought aside hastily. *Pale, like she used number 200 sunblock,* he improvised. Not great, certainly better. "I should maybe do a watch," he told himself. Obviously no one else was up to it at the moment. Unfortunately, he wasn't either. "Luck," he murmured to the roof of the shallow cave, lay back and fell asleep.

* * *

THE luck apparently held. Jennifer woke to see horses staring in at them. The air was hot and dry; the wind blew in gusts, ruffling the gear piled in front of Chris's tie line. Shade covered everything within fifteen feet of the ledge they sheltered under. "North facing," she mumbled. Chris had told her that; her one coherent thought when she'd first seen this almost hole in the wall was that they'd fry in here when the sun got them.

Her second had been about watches. That woke her, got her partway on her feet before muscles howled in outrage. "God," she moaned. "Aspirin." The bag was outside, with everything else. There was a water bottle next to her jacket, though. She managed to get to her knees—they were sore but not bruised, they only hurt if she tried to straighten them—got one curled-up hand against the wall for support, and edged around Robyn, who was curled into Aletto's arms, past Edrith, who lay flat on his back like a starfish, arms and legs wildly sprawled. Past Chris, who slept, as he always did, on his stomach, arms tucked under him, legs together, face barely turned out enough to let him breathe. Lialla was a curled-up mass of black draperies, only one fist and the tip of her nose visible.

It was even cooler outside the shallow cave: Wind came across the entry in a continuous flow and there wasn't any trapped body heat out here. Jennifer rubbed the nose of the horse nearest her with a knuckle, knelt to fumble through the piled things for her bag. It was almost on the very bottom, of course, and the enormous aspirin bottle as difficult to find as it ever was. For one heart-stopping moment, she thought it might have somehow fallen out, but it had merely buried itself under the toiletries bag. The child-proof cap was almost a Jennifer-proof cap at the moment, with her hands as dreadfully stiff and sore as they were and her nails trimmed short, but it finally came off. She eyed it appraisingly, finally shook out three and swallowed them down with a large gulp of now extremely warm and leathery water. The resulting shudder set her head to pounding. She looked at the bottle once more, shook out a few more of the tablets to take back with her.

The leathery taste coated her mouth. *Some people carry breath mints,* she thought grumpily. *Or gum.* Another thought brought her up short. She had toothpaste; that would kill the taste. . . . "I am *not* going back out there," she told herself in a near-soundless whisper as she felt her way over her companions and back onto her makeshift pillow. The jacket was hard and ungiving, and had probably contributed to that headache. She closed her eyes and settled back into it gratefully. It was hard, yes; it was also familiar and comforting. It smelled like home. The aspirin would fix the headache, eventually. She remembered the day she'd bought the jacket, the bonus the partners had passed out to everyone who'd helped with a massive research issue that won a large jury trial. The jacket had taken about half of her share, but it was something to remember her first bonus as an attorney. Later, she had thought at the time, there would be other big cases won, so many she would never remember them all—or the things that she bought with the extra money. This: She rubbed the collar with one knuckle, smiled faintly, and fell asleep again.

* * *

SHE woke quite some time later—by her watch, at least four hours. The headache was indeed gone; her hands still ached abominably and she was not certain she was ready to test her legs once more.

Nearby, someone groaned. She rolled over to look: Aletto lay flat on his stomach, face twisted in concentration or pain, Robyn straddling his back. Her hands were working his shoulder and upper arm muscles. As he groaned again, she lifted her hands, looked at him worriedly. "Don't stop," he mumbled. "It feels good, honestly." Robyn looked as though she didn't believe a word of it, but obediently went back to rubbing. She nodded a greeting as Jennifer edged up onto one elbow. Aletto opened one eye at the nearby sound and motion, let it close again when Robyn's hands kneaded his right triceps.

"I wish I had a heating pad," Robyn said vexedly, and in English. "Or some rub. I mean, *I* feel like an old woman someone beat with a baseball bat, but he's *really* in bad shape."

"I know. You've given me an idea, though," Jennifer said. She sat up cautiously and by dint of slow, careful movement managed to get herself cross-legged on the packed sand floor. "I don't know if this will work, it's daytime, it's something really off the wall—hang on."

"Sure," Robyn said curiously. Her hands kept working. Jennifer let her eyes close and concentrated on Thread. After some time, she sighed and shook her head.

"I think it's there; I'm awfully tired and it's hard to concentrate, and Thread isn't as easy to work during the day. I think there might be a way to do what you want. I'll try again later, maybe after I wake all the way up. Meantime—Aletto, how is your stomach?" He rolled his head cautiously, opened one eye again. "Does it hurt after you drink wine?" He shook his head. "Hurt when you get upset?" He shook it once more, groaned and let it back where it had been. "Good. Birdy, when you're done there, give him this."

"Aspirin—you think only one?"

"I bet he's never had one in all his life before. One should be plenty. You want—?"

"I don't take pills," Robyn began severely. She stopped short and blushed. "That was dumb. I don't take over-the-counter," she amended neatly. "And I guess I don't take prescription or street types any more either, do I?" She considered this, and her shoulders sagged. "God. It's hot enough out there, I wouldn't drink wine if you had it for me. A beer sure would be nice, though." Her fingers moved down Aletto's back, dug gently in above his kidneys. "Yeah, lady, leave me one. I might not take it, but if I do that'll be plenty."

* * *

CHRIS and Edrith worked out the watch for the rest of the day, setting up a system that allowed everyone to get as much sleep— or at least rest—at a time as possible. The day wore on slowly, rather boringly. Even Chris moved slowly and carefully after so many hours of riding; the water was stale and no one really felt like eating. The afternoon was oppressively hot; clouds came up black in the west and wind blew over them late in the day, but any rain fell well to the north of them. The air did not actually cool until after sunset.

Apparently no one followed them, however; none of the watch saw any sign of pursuit, at least, and by midafternoon, Jennifer was able to conduct a search that verified the physical lack of company. "No one within miles," she announced.

"The mesa," Robyn said. "Last night, that light Chris saw?"

"I can't be certain I was touching on distance like that, Birdy. I didn't find anyone out in that direction, however. They might have just been locals, sleeping out for some reason. Whoever they are, they haven't come anywhere close to us." Robyn seemed assured by that; Lialla didn't particularly look it, but she kept quiet. Jennifer found something else, too: the healing Thread she'd used that first night on Aletto, to mend the knife cut in his arm. *Bach,* she thought dreamily. Whatever that particular Thread had reminded her of before, something baroque, it was definitely Bachlike now. Bach-ish.

Something to ease muscle ache. Mmmm—heat did that. Deep heat, vibration. Some of each. She had felt warmth when she healed Aletto, her fingers had become almost hot, working with that sticky cobweblike stuff. What if someone laid *that* on an aching muscle? Well, she didn't have far to go to find a guinea pig, did she?

Her right hand warmed rapidly as she overlaid it with Thread. She kneaded the fingers with her left hand for some moments, quit when the warmth became an almost unpleasant, itchy heat. It faded back to soothing. Faded again, was gone. The fingers weren't anything she cared to own, even yet, but she could flex them, could flatten them out against her jeans without wanting to cry. She made a fist around one of the countless rocks at her feet; her fingers held on, and for the first time all day, something didn't hurt. Jennifer smiled faintly, detached herself from a faded, blurry, daytime vision of Thread, and opened her eyes. "Birdy? How's your legs?" For answer her sister shook her head and closed her eyes. "How'd you like to try a little something for them?"

* * *

IT wasn't anywhere near perfect, even after considerable practice throughout the late afternoon. But she certainly wasn't lacking in stiff and aching subjects to practice on. It did help. And Lialla, who had been inclined to throw one of her usual "It won't work" fits, kept quiet when she saw Aletto actually walking a little, for the first time all day.

"I can't heal," she said stubbornly as Jennifer applied heat to her left knee. She sat in silence for some time, finally flexed her leg cautiously. "I know I can't. I *still* can't work with Thread in the daylight. But after dark—show me how this is done."

"Maybe it's different," Jennifer suggested. Lialla shrugged.

"Maybe. I'll try." She pulled herself up by the rock ledge, flexed her leg again. "It did help," she added rather grudgingly.

"However you thought of that, it's something worth knowing. It would be worth the try."

* * *

ABOUT an hour before sunset, the wind kicked up, blowing gusts of dirt, dry seed pods, small sticks and sand high into the air. The small cave was uninhabitable; people grabbed things and vacated hastily. Outside, Chris squinted at the westering sun, at the sky, mumbled something under his breath as he looked at his watch. "There isn't any point in staying here any longer, is there?" he asked generally.

"None," Jennifer said. "Personally, I think it's going to take us forever to get all this stuff back on those animals."

Chris smirked at her. "Softy," he said, and ducked as his aunt took a swipe at him. "You swing just fine, I notice."

"I kept my arm below my shoulders," Jennifer retorted. "You try raising yours lately?"

"Hey, you know?" Chris dropped into English. "I'm not a chair jockey. I *do* stuff, all right?"

"I mean, you know?" Jennifer said dryly. "D&D takes a lot of muscle, right?"

Her nephew laughed. "Truce," he managed finally. "Anybody object?" he added in Rhadazi. "Sooner we leave here, sooner we locate that water."

* * *

LIALLA was concerned about traveling in full daylight, but she merely said as much before easing down to help Robyn sort out the stack of bags. Her worries were unfounded, Jennifer's all too well grounded: It took Edrith and Chris working together to get saddles up and onto the horses. Aletto did the first sets of straps, but couldn't manage any more; he still needed his stick to stand, and he apparently hurt sufficiently that for once he didn't object when Lialla told him to go sit while she finished for him.

Jennifer dug into her shirt pocket for the plastic sandwich bag. "Aletto. Did the pill help earlier?" He nodded, winced and began rubbing the back of his neck. Jennifer untied the bag, pulled out an aspirin and gave it to him. "Let me know if you want another later; no one should have to put up with that kind of ache."

Aletto moaned. "To think I used to envy men who rode! I didn't know when I had it good!"

Lialla turned away from the bag she was tying in place to frown at him. "I hope you're jesting."

"Only in part. Get me through this and I swear I'll never ride again!"

54

"It gets better after a while," Robyn assured him. He cast her a sidelong and very doubtful look. "Like anything. The muscles adjust. I'd wager you every one of those men you envied started out just as stiff the first few days they rode hard. This hasn't exactly been an amble through the market, you know."

Aletto was still looking at her dubiously. Lialla rather surprisingly came to her support. "She's right, Aletto. It's hard country for anything, it's a damned hard ride and I don't know about your horse but the one I'm riding has a trot to loosen teeth." She turned back to finish her task, took another bag from Robyn and worked it onto the other side of the animal's neck. "Don't be so hard on yourself, brother. You're doing much better than I would ever have thought when we started this."

"I am?" Aletto looked surprised by this, then slightly offended. He opened his mouth to say something, closed it, thought, finally smiled. "I suppose that's good, isn't it?"

"Believe it is," Lialla replied seriously. "Can someone hold this damned bag in place," she added in a sharper voice, "while I tie it? My wretched arms just won't *do* it!"

* * *

THE sun was down, the sky still blue when they moved out. The sharp gusts had become a continuous hard-blowing wind—a surprisingly chill one, given the heat of the day. Jennifer found it refreshing; it blew away the last of a loggy, hot-nap-in-the-afternoon headache and left her feeling awake for the first time since some time the morning before. She still ached; they all did. Fortunately, once they skirted the long edge of the rock wall they'd stayed under, the land was absolutely flat, nearly featureless. Even after the horses scented water—not long after full dark—and eased into a trot and then a canter, it wasn't unbearable.

The river was a narrow stream in a very broad, shallow bed filled with rock, boulders, uprooted trees and brush. Water gleamed silvery in the light of new-risen moon. Neither Jennifer nor Lialla could sense anyone nearer than the eastern Bez road. "The village we want is out that way, it may be outlying houses," Lialla said. Chris and Edrith still walked stiffly but they had enough energy after watering and unpacking the horses to conduct an on-foot search to both sides of them—slightly offending Lialla but reassuring Aletto, who visibly could not quite believe in Thread.

They had picked a spot not marked by recent campfires or other signs of men—a stand of ash and willow blocked the west wind, tall brush would shadow them when the sun rose. The stream ran in front of them, a few paces into the open and down the waist-high bank.

Aletto ran the horse lines while Chris and Edrith went off to look for any signs of people, game trails, another way out of their camp should they need it. "Playing Indian," Robyn mumbled to herself. She had dragged through her purse, emptying everything, searching for one last, perhaps lost, cigarette. There hadn't been one, only an empty pack. Jennifer gave her a wide berth, and went down to the water to take off her high-tops and soak her feet. Robyn silently handed her an oat cake on her way back from the stream, set out two for Chris and Edrith—they hadn't returned but could be heard crackling through the brush nearby, and talking in low voices that still carried. Robyn glanced in their direction and muttered something before dropping back onto her blanket.

5

JENNIFER was wakened by the smell of biscuits, and for one startled half-asleep moment, she thought herself six years old and camping with her parents in Wyoming. But the baking-bread smell wasn't quite right, the air much too warm. The voices—though one of them was raised in exasperation—not right, either.

The language wasn't English; that brought her fully awake. The stream seemed even smaller in the early sunlight, the woods much more open.

Robyn saw the movement as her sister sat up, and waved a hand in her direction. She was tending a small fire. Her makeshift Dutch oven—a Sikkreni footed copper pot with a thick lid—was half-buried in coals. She sent the lid flying with a thick, short branch, peered into the pan. Hair fell over her face; she swore and held it back with a forearm. "I'm going to burn myself up yet, damnit. Jen, you'd better come get one of these while they're hot, I can't guarantee they'll taste like anything once they've been off the fire a while, and I—damn, I think I burned the bottoms after all." She wrapped a length of cloth around her hand, cut into the contents with one of the hunting

56

knives Aletto had bought. "You'd better eat a couple before those boys get back. You know what they're like."

"Yeah." Jennifer ran fingers through sleep-flattened, snarled curls, stretched and patted around her blanket for the two bags that contained her precious coffee-making supplies. The flat red sack holding the copper bean-roasting pan was buried under everything else, after the nature of such things: whatever might be wanted on any kind of trip was bound to be on the bottom, if not missing entirely. For one horrid moment, she feared the two bags of raw coffee beans might fall into that latter category, but she finally located them on the other side of her blankets. *I'd better tie them together; raw beans aren't much good without the equipment, and that is worthless without beans—at least until we reach Bez.* And she wasn't much good without the final product. "Without coffee, I'll be lucky to reach our next stop, the way I feel this morning," she mumbled, and made one more attempt at fluffing squashed hair into some kind of decent shape.

What would she do once that permanent grew out? *Guess I'll go straight once more, won't I?* Maybe there was some way around that, like the coffee. At least, if she had to do without one or the other, it wasn't coffee she'd have to forego. Jennifer spared one brief sympathetic thought for Robyn, even more firmly hooked on cigarettes than her sister was on caffeine.

Only a brief one. Coffee and cigarettes weren't in the same league. And she and Chris had been trying for years to get Robyn to quit. Unsuccessfully. Robyn might be irritable just now, but Jennifer noticed already she wasn't coughing as much. And *this* time, she wouldn't be tempted into backsliding after a few weeks.

Jennifer drew a fistful of beans from the bag and let them slide into the roasting pan. The pan went into the fire where Robyn's biscuit cooker had been. Jennifer sat down to juggle one of the hot biscuits and watch her beans. "Where *is* Chris? And is there anything to go on these?"

"I hope you don't mean butter," Robyn said.

"Nope. I know how fast butter goes rancid and I know we didn't get any in Sikkre anyhow. Wasn't there honey or something?" Robyn handed her the small clay jar of fruit butter that had gone into pancakes two mornings earlier. "Great." She broke the biscuit in half, dumped in jam and rubbed the halves together to spread it. "Smells wonderful, Birdy."

"Yeah," Robyn said. "Always could cook."

"I love stuff like this for breakfast. Why didn't I ever hire you to cook for me?"

Robyn laughed. " 'Cause we'd kill each other after three days, and 'cause I don't do windows, remember?"

"Right, forgot." Jennifer finished her biscuit, took a second and shook the coffee beans to turn them. "All the same, we haven't murdered each other yet, have we?"

"This is different," Robyn said. "Maybe it's more like camping; we always could do that together. Even if we didn't very often. Or maybe it's because we don't have a choice." She half-stood, turned to gaze out across the streambed. "What *is* that kid of mine doing?"

"I don't know, is this a trick question?" *Hot beans into small grinder, small grinder—right, it turns the opposite direction of what you'd expect.* She found Robyn's bucket of cooking water just outside the fire pit, dipped her small brewing pot into it and set the pot where the roasting pan had been. "Where is he?"

"Across the water, with Edrith. They're cutting sticks, I think."

Sticks, Jennifer thought in mild confusion. It took a moment to remember his suggestion about self-defense. "Oh. Sticks."

Robyn turned to look at her sister. "He's being pretty damned smug and godawful secretive about it. This something you know about, maybe?"

Jennifer shrugged. She seemed to remember late the previous evening, a half-formed thought of breaking the idea to Robyn beforehand, but in daylight, and with her sister gazing down at her thoughtfully, the notion died an immediate death. Robyn wasn't going to like it, whoever said what; let Chris take the flak. "Not enough to get it all straight. I'll let him tell you. Where's Aletto?"

As a change of subject, it was a good direction. Robyn brightened noticeably. She dug out another biscuit, scraped the bottom with the knife blade. Black flakes rained on ash and rock; at Jennifer's growled suggestion, Robyn moved her messy task away from the pot of nearly boiling coffee water. "Out walking. He's stiffer than I am this morning, but he's willing to keep going." Robyn sighed, scowled at the still very dark-bottomed biscuit, tore off a corner and ate it. "He's got courage, that boy."

"He's got good people helping him keep pushing," Jennifer corrected her.

"Yeah. Well." Robyn brushed sooty crumbs from her jeans, wiped the knife across her knee, sighed heavily and wiped the new line of crumbs away.

"I'm serious. Don't sell what you've done short, Birdy, it's apparently just what he's needed." *Water just short of boiling, grounds on top.* She pushed buttons to set the timer on her watch so the dubious-looking mess could cook, finally dumped half a measure of cold water over the top and poured coffee quickly into her cup. They said the grounds didn't rise again; she didn't care to test that on her first cup of truly from-scratch coffee. She wasn't about to wait, anyway. "Oh, God, that's wonderful," she sighed happily. It wasn't really: it tasted burnt, it was overly strong, very acidic—almost another beverage entirely from her usual purified water, gourmet beans, drip-maker liquid. There was no sugar, of course. Fortunately, she could drink it black, even if she didn't like it best that way.

She offered Robyn a cup; Robyn shook her head. "You may not be able to find more."

"That's all right—"

"No. It wouldn't be all right, if it were me. Besides, I never was that crazy about coffee, I can't believe this is a good time to get hooked." She considered this statement gloomily. "Hooked on something else," she amended.

"Yeah. Sorry, Birdy."

"Me, too. I'd kill for even a menthol filter right now, you know? Here comes Chris and his shadow; help me hide a couple of these biscuits for Aletto, will you?"

"How about Lialla?"

"Went downstream to bathe, took my share of those oat cake jobbies, didn't want anything else." Robyn made a sour face. "She's welcome to them; they remind me of very plain granola bars, health-nut stuff for the brown rice and herb tea set."

Jennifer laughed. "You drink herb teas, Robyn."

"Yeah. I'm not a fanatic, though. You know, I think I left that commune where Chris was born as much because of the rice as because they all dried out? Think about it: overnight, from ordinary food, wine, acid, pot—to brown rice and none of the other stuff. Didn't Dante have something like that in his version of Hell?"

* * *

CHRIS dropped down onto his blanket with three six-foot lengths of straight tree, still covered with small branches and leaves. Edrith had one more, already peeled down.

"Ash," Chris announced. "This is terrific." He looked over at Edrith. "I still can't believe no one's come up with saws here yet. I described one and *he* never heard of such a thing." He laid the ash pieces across his lap and shook out his hands. "I had to carve them down with a knife, can you believe it?"

"Eat, before these get cold," Robyn said. Chris stuffed a biscuit in his mouth, dropped the others in his lap with the ash.

"Right," he mumbled around an oversized mouthful. "Good stuff, Ma."

"Swallow first, then tell me what you're chewing down trees with a knife for?"

Edrith tucked a bite in his cheek. "Staves," he explained, waving his. "For fighting." Robyn's eyebrows went up, and Chris sighed. He waved an imperious, silencing hand.

"Let me," he said as soon as he could manage to swallow. "And maybe after the others get back here. Then I'll tell you all about it and I won't have to twice." He bit another biscuit in two and began lopping branches from one of his lengths of ash. Robyn rolled her eyes heavenward, turned away and gathered up the Dutch oven.

"Anything you say," she replied sharply. "Let me know when you feel like filling me in, all right?" She strode off to the stream, scaling down the bank more rapidly than was sensible. Chris came halfway to his feet, sat back down as his mother made it to the water without falling.

"What's eating *her*?" he demanded of Jennifer in English. "I mean—oh. Right. No morning smoke, right?"

"No morning smoke and one cryptic kid. Don't push her, all right, Chris?" Jennifer finished her coffee and rinsed the small pot. "Remember what I said: I'll go along with you, but it'll be easier for all of us if you don't get any backs up. Got it?"

"Yeah, right."

"Yeah, right," Jennifer mimicked, and Chris looked up at her from under a falling thatch of blond hair. After a moment, his mouth quirked in a rather shamefaced grin. "I know you want to try this, I understand your reasoning. Give her a chance— give Aletto and Lialla a chance, for that matter. They just might see it too, all right?"

"It's just that I got it all worked out—"

"Fine. Keep in mind your mother has had a lot of years to work out her feelings about nonviolence. I know you understand how she feels about fighting," Jennifer went on, overriding Chris, who had opened his mouth, clearly to protest that he knew as much. He sighed. She waited until he nodded. "I'm not trying to put down your ideas simply because they aren't mine, Chris. Or because you aren't twenty-eight years old, didn't go to college, don't have a law degree—did I cover it all?"

Chris grinned, shook his head and laughed aloud. "Jeez, Aunt

Jen. Make a guy feel like an ass while you're at it, why don't you? I mean, you know?''

"Jeez, I mean, I don't know, you know?" she replied dryly. "I'm just telling you. Try not to step on any feet, you'll get a lot farther with this. Let me know when you want a guinea pig, I'll give it a try. I took one quarter of judo when I was in college and one of those defensive training for working women seminars last year. So I have a little feel for how to move and how to fall—a very little," Jennifer amended honestly.

"I hope I remember more than that, when it comes to the point," her nephew said rather gloomily. "Thanks, Aunt Jen. I'll try and go easy on Mom, all right?"

"Do that," Jennifer said as Chris went back to peeling and de-branching. He passed a clean, thick branch to Edrith, who began running it through a primitive smoothing device: a headcloth filled with sand from the stream. "Keep in mind I'm the one she'll dump on." She got up to take her coffee-making supplies back to her blankets and went rummaging for her shoulder bag and the toiletries it contained. There had to be somewhere downstream the way Lialla had gone where the water was deep enough to let her bathe, perhaps wash the sand and dirt from her matted hair. At the moment, deep enough would be anything that covered her instep. Warm enough—well, if she could keep her feet in a pool that deep and still feel them, it would do.

* * *

To his credit, when Chris had everyone in camp, he made a decent job of presenting his idea. "What it comes down to, none of us are fighters. Unless it's very different here, no one learns to use a sword overnight, and we don't have good ones anyway, or enough of them. The same goes for our other weapons. As far as I know, we have a bow, several knives, a couple of swords—the best we could buy, which doesn't make them very good.

"Now, again, unless it's different here—" Chris sighed. "If no one minds, I'm not going to keep going through that, all right? Enough things track between our world and this one that I'm going to assume my logic tracks, too. If I'm seriously off, one of you Rhadazi natives tell me.

"Learning to use a sword is hard work. It takes time, lots of practice, and instructors to show you the right way to do it. We don't have the time, the teachers, and even if any of us somehow learned to use one of those swords—to fight with, to defend us—they'd be up against men who've been using swords for years. Men who are good at it, who are *paid* to learn how and to be good at it. I know damned well I'm not even going to *try* to use one of those swords for anything besides what we got them for: show.'' Aletto shifted his weight and frowned. "That's what it comes down to, isn't it, Aletto? So that men who might pick on an unarmed company would leave us alone, seeing us armed and assuming we wore swords because we could use them?''

"Well—it's not how I'd have said it.''

"Me, either,'' Chris admitted. "Not then. I don't want to now, either, but I don't think we have much choice if we're going to reach this Bezjeriad.'' He shook his head sharply. "No, wait— I'm just saying, in case we get set upon. And we have to presume there's one party looking for us, probably two. We don't know either that Jadek will find us, that the Thukar will—or that they want to. After all, it could be everyone has misread both of them.''

"It could be ships fly,'' Lialla replied sarcastically.

Chris spread his hands wide and shrugged. "Where I come from, some do. But I am not arguing with you, if only because I think it would be really dumb to underestimate those two. I'd rather be stupid the other way, jumping at my own shadow, than not see someone else's before he gets me.

"So we assume they're after us. Or waiting somewhere. Sorry, Mom.''

Robyn had gone rather white but her voice was steady. "Why? I don't like your picture but that doesn't mean it's pure fantasy.''

"Thanks. Assume, too, that we ought to be able to protect ourselves. I know we have two magic wielders but there are six of us all together. They might not be enough, or we might be separated.''

"*One* of the Wielders might not be able to do anything,'' Lialla said flatly. Jennifer shook her head.

"I don't think he meant that, Lialla.''

"Maybe not. I did, though.''

"Either or both of us might not,'' Jennifer said. "I've had good luck so far; it might run out. Or I—*we*—might find something strong enough to stop us both. Go on, Chris.''

"We need a kind of fighting that isn't like any of theirs—the trained men. Something fairly simple, because we don't have a lot of time and we might need it soon. That's what this is for.'' He held up a polished ash staff. "A while ago, a friend of mine was taking—Jeez, *why* don't any of these things translate?— taking a kind of hand-to-hand fighting. I couldn't afford the lessons, so he taught me. That way, he got practice outside his class and I had the chance to learn Bojutsu.''

Robyn sighed heavily. "Oh, Christopher! Damnit!"

Chris turned on her. "Damnit what, Mom?"

"This is *real*, Chris! You can't play out scenes from your stupid ninja movies—!"

"You think that's what I'm doing?"

"What, you going to make long steel forks and those stick and chain things, like those cartoon frogs on TV have?"

Chris snorted, anger momentarily forgotten. "Turtles, Mom, honestly!"

"You're making an ass of yourself, kid—"

"Mom, damnit, will you just shut up and *listen*, just for once?" Chris overrode her furiously. Robyn was startled into silence. "All right, I admit I like that kind of stuff for entertainment, the cartoons, the bad dialogue and goofy fight scenes, all of that! And yeah, those practice sessions with Carlos started out as a lark! But I'll tell you something, Mother, I still learned a lot, damned practical things we can use, just in case something goes wrong, and magic can't protect us. All right? Just—instead of *telling* me what I'm doing, or acting like I'm ten years old and showing off, why don't you *listen* for once and find *out* what I'm trying to do?" Dead silence. Chris breathed heavily through his nose; Robyn still stared at him. Aletto and Edrith shifted very quietly, and Lialla coughed. "Look, I'm *sorry*! I wasn't going to get pissed, and I didn't mean to come down on you. Just—just listen. Please! All right?"

"All right," Robyn agreed faintly.

"Thank you. Really." He still sounded exasperated. "What I'm talking about is fighting with a bo, a staff—a long piece of wood. The method I learned, you can use something this long"—he held up the six-foot length—"or something like Aletto's stick. Even one shorter than that. The main thing about it is, it's a form of fighting that I think any of us can learn, at least the basics." He glanced at the attentive, if rather embarrassed audience, and added, "To be honest, I barely learned anything beyond the basics, and I've probably forgotten a lot of the fancier stuff. That doesn't matter. It's partly a way of thinking, partly a sensible way to use your body. If you can absorb that, it's possible for you to beat even a man with a sword. And that is particularly true here, in this world. Because the man with the sword won't know anything about Bojutsu. It'll surprise him."

"He still has a sword," Aletto pointed out.

"Of course. But think about ordinary men who are paid to use swords. Think about what that kind of surprise will do to him, all right?" Aletto considered this, nodded thoughtfully.

"Also, it's just logic: Your reach is longer with a stick like this than with a sword. Add better leverage and you *could* beat a man with a sword." Silence. Chris looked at each of them. "Look," he said finally. "I can't say we'll need this, that any of you will want it—Edrith said he'd try it, Aunt Jen said she would. I can't say for sure I can teach any of you anything, or that even if I can, it'll really work. I'm just saying, I think we need *some*thing. This is what I know. Kind of," he amended carefully. "I'm willing to try it if you are."

He sat down abruptly and fixed his eyes on his hands, which were rubbing the smoothed long ash staff. Finally Aletto sighed; faint as the sound was, Lialla started. "I'm so tired and stiff already," the nera-Duke said, and he sounded tired. "But you are right about enough of it; I have to think your logic holds true for the rest. The swords I bargained for in Sikkre are good enough to intimidate someone who doesn't use a sword. And it's foolish for all of us to depend on our two Wielders. Father told me once, when he took me hunting, one plan of attack is never enough. There should always be two or more, or plans and backup plans." He smiled, very faintly. "Odd, how that came back to me just now; I could not have passed my sixth summer and I had forgotten it all these years since. You all know by now I have—limitations. I—I can only try."

"Good," Chris said. "Edrith?"

"You know I'm ready."

"Jen?"

"I said I would try." She laughed faintly. "As long as it's not physically beyond *me*." Chris raised his eyebrows. "*You* told me not long ago I could learn break dancing! I think I could almost walk after a mere week or two of sheer agony."

"Hey, Aunt Jen, always there to help, right?" Chris laughed.

"Break dancing?" Edrith asked. The phrase came out very oddly in Rhadazi and couldn't have meant anything like the English original.

"Never mind," Jennifer told him.

Chris grinned. "Don't trust her, buddy, I'll show you later." He looked around the circle and spread his hands. "Thanks, all of you. It may not—well, never mind, we'll worry about how useful it is after we try it out." He handed the long stick to Edrith and jumped to his feet. "We're going to go work out some basic practice moves. Are we staying here tonight?"

Lialla and Jennifer looked at each other, shrugged, and Jennifer turned to Robyn. "Birdy, are we going to cut ourselves short on food if we do?"

64

"We're all right for another three days, if you allow for nothing fresh," Robyn said. "How far is that village from here?"

"A very long night, according to the map," Chris said. "I just asked because I know how bad *I* still feel after all that riding three nights in a row. I bet the horses would like a night off, too." He stood at the edge of the stream bank. Lialla shrugged again.

"We could go mad, trying to second-guess our uncle. Or the Thukar." She spread her hands rather helplessly. "Or anyone else, come to that. So I see no reason why we shouldn't stay here another full day and night."

Robyn let Aletto pull her up. "I felt ghastly when we got here, short as that ride was last night. If I had to pay close attention to anything right now, I'd be in a lot of trouble. I'm still too tired to concentrate. I think we should stay."

"That by itself is a good reason," Aletto said. He was leaning on his stick, trying to look as though it weren't at least half his support. "What if Jadek *did* find us? We can't ride out across country like drugged or half-dead men. I say we stay."

His word carried it. Chris nodded briefly before dropping down into the streambed, Edrith close behind him.

Aletto's word: Jennifer bit back a sigh. Lialla, of course, would ordinarily support whatever her brother said, whether he knew what he was talking about or not. Robyn was showing an alarming tendency to do the same thing. *Male authority*, she thought tiredly. *Where can I buy some of it, so people will listen to me like that?* But this time Aletto's reasoning had been good. They would have been in a sticky situation the previous night if she'd had to Wield against any kind of attack. She'd been glassy-eyed, hurting, stiff to the bone and dry all the way to the soles of her feet. None of the rest of them had been any better off, and some, like Robyn, had been worse.

Aletto might not be able to use Chris's bo, but he was using his brains. The only times he'd spoken during the entire meeting, he'd been sensible, practical, honest about his limitations—very different from the touchy, sensitive, arbitrary Aletto she'd first met outside that cave on the western border of his father's lands. Interesting. Perhaps there was a Duke in him after all.

* * *

LATE in the afternoon, after the sun dropped below the trees and the evening breeze started up, Chris and Edrith got the rest of them down onto a patch of hard-packed sand next to the water. Both were red-faced, sweating, stripped to the waist. Edrith's knuckles were skinned and there was one very visible bruise across the back of Chris's right hand. Robyn frowned at that; her son followed her gaze and laughed shortly. "I won't die of it, Mom. You won't get one, either—that's from early, like his hands." He gave her a flash of teeth. "Aren't we nice? We worked out the bugs for you."

"Yeah, great kid," Robyn muttered. "I've got to figure out what to feed you; is this going to take long?"

"If I get a lot of interruptions," Chris began. Jennifer chopped a hand in front of his face.

"Go," she ordered. Chris turned back to Edrith, gave him a sharp nod. Chris stood still, the staff held lightly across his thighs. The young Sikkreni matched his position, then went into a low crouch and brought his *bo* up in a slashing overhand arc. Chris caught the staff on his own. "Watch now!" he shouted over the click of wood against wood. "It's a pattern of five moves! He'll do them, I'll defend, then I'll do them, *he* will defend. We'll do it at speed first, then break it down for you."

Lialla shook her head. "I can't—" Aletto touched her shoulder.

"Wait, look for the pattern, Li. It shouldn't be obvious at first."

Good advice, Jennifer thought dryly, to one who was supposed to have studied patterns most of her life. But she herself couldn't see what Chris was doing until they'd traded offense twice, until they'd slowed it just a little. When they slowed it down a second time, and Chris began counting the moves in a loud voice, it began to make better sense.

"Halt," he called out finally. Edrith stepped aside, back straight, staff held lightly against his thighs. "All right, that's starting position. You'll always go back to that, whenever your instructor calls 'halt' or whenever you disarm your opponent or the opponent gives up—in practice, among us, that is. The positions—you see what they are now, all of you?" Four nods answered him. "Those are the basic strikes and parry maneuvers. The most important thing before any of you start: You don't reach with your arms. We didn't. Watch again." Edrith came forward; they executed the pattern twice, very slowly. "See that? I am using my leg muscles. If you push the stick that way, you get a lot more strength than if you just use your arms. Halt." Edrith went rather self-consciously back to the basic position. Chris nodded; he looked a little self-conscious himself, but most of his attention was on what he was doing.

His mother was right, Jennifer thought. Chris would make a wonderful teacher. "We obviously won't have time to become really skilled at this. What I hope is, you'll all learn the basic maneuvers so well that if you need them, they'll be automatic. If they are, then you have an edge in speed on an opponent who has to think about what he's doing, and how to parry what you've done. If you use your legs for the strength, let the skills soak into your muscles so you don't have to think about them, then—well, that should be enough. If you—Mom, this is for you, particularly, and it's part of the philosophy, not just something I'm telling you to make you feel better about this—if you use your mind only to think about the person who's attacking you, to realize that you have every right to defend yourself against him, that you have every right to protect yourself and the rest of us from whatever pain he wants to inflict—that you are absolutely right to use your weapon to subdue him so that he cannot hurt you any more, so that you can get away from him before he hurts you again—use your mind for that. All right?'' Three nods. Robyn looked at him doubtfully. ''Mom,'' Chris said gently. ''You always said you'd fight to keep your family safe.'' His mother closed her eyes briefly. ''That's all I'm saying. If you do this, if you want to do it well and do it right, you need to *know* that it's okay. That's all. Are you all right?''

''Sure.'' Robyn opened her eyes and managed a faint smile. ''I'm fine, kid. Get on with it, all right? If you want to eat tonight, anyway.''

* * *

He had sticks for all of them, but no one got to use those at first: Chris made them stretch out horse-stiff muscles. He put Robyn and Aletto together then. ''You two need a little more loosening up, first, and there's only two of me and Edrith anyway. Arms: Do those circle things, I guess, Mother; whole arm ones. Get some blood down into your fingers. Maybe some—Aletto, how well does that shoulder work?''

Aletto's eyebrows drew together before he apparently remembered he was going to be honest about his physical shortcomings. ''It gets stiff when I'm tired; my neck muscles don't work well and my head goes over, I get headaches.''

''The arm, though? The shoulder itself?'' Aletto shook his head. ''Down your back this way?'' Chris went on, drawing a line with his index finger from the other's shoulder across the top of his shoulder blade and down into his spine just above waist level. ''Doesn't give out or hurt if you use it?''

''No. Not much, and not when it's hot and dry. Why?''

''Try this,'' Chris said. He dropped down onto his stomach, pressed up onto his arms and knees in a modified pushup, down

67

again. "It'll do good things for your upper body, if you can handle them."

Aletto looked down at him, at Robyn, over at Lialla who was some distance away, concentrating fiercely on what Edrith was telling her. He shrugged, got down with much more care and pressed himself up.

"Keep your back straight," Chris advised. "Better. How does it feel?"

Aletto, back up a second time, managed a twitch of his shoulders that might have been another shrug. "It doesn't *hurt*," he said finally.

"Do six of those," Chris said. "Wait a little and do six more. Stop if it hurts." He looked over the prone nera-Duke, nodded in his mother's direction. "Mom, if you can handle the same thing, you should; your upper arms need it."

"I said I'd try this, so I guess I'm stuck," Robyn said. "If I grow muscles, kid, you'll be real sorry!"

"Oooh, I'm worried," Chris retorted. As he passed Jennifer, he murmured, "Anybody tells that guy he's doing girl pushups, and they're dead." Jennifer laughed under her breath and followed him into the open.

6

⚅

Two full days and an extra night in one place helped considerably: Jennifer discovered the second morning she had wit and energy, even before her coffee was brewed—enough wit to remember the precious packets of sugar buried deep in her bag. A packet divided between two cups was well short of her usual dose but it still vastly improved the flavor.

She was still stiff in places—where scarcely padded bone came into contact with unyielding saddle. Her hip joints would probably protest the unnatural stretch riding put on them for days to come, though at least she could sit and stand without holding onto something for balance. Her hands now ached not only from clinging tightly to reins but from holding onto the bo Chris had made her, from one stinging crack she'd received across the back of her left hand, from the jarring her hands and arms took as two staves slammed into each other.

She'd worked with Chris first, while Edrith instructed Lialla, and Robyn and Aletto stretched out. Later, Chris had put her against Robyn. Birdy had been pretty tentative about the whole thing at first, until Jennifer's bo caught her on the crazy bone. She'd given her sister a decent workout after that, until lack of stamina caught up with her.

Perhaps because it was his first opportunity to learn any kind of weaponry—or because he wanted to show he could keep up— Aletto finished the first afternoon almost a match with Edrith. Lialla was as grimly determined as her brother to learn how to defend herself, but she had even less strength in her legs and shoulders than Aletto did. Chris left it to Jennifer to start the sin-Duchess on modified pushups and situps; Lialla still took offense at half of what any of them said, but she sometimes listened to Jen.

By the end of the second day, the workout had at least loosened up arms and shoulders: the saddling went quickly, the loading of bags easily, and not even Lialla needed assistance in mounting. They left the streamside camp just after sundown, crossed the water and rode back north a ways before turning east to parallel the line of trees that marked its path. The village they sought was somewhere on this west side of the main Bez road, on the north edge of the water. Lialla had argued earlier against following the stream closely—which had been Aletto's idea—and she brought it up again as they prepared to ride out. "We have plenty of fresh water with us now; we can't possibly lose the village as long as we keep the stream south of us. And I wouldn't feel safe riding in the trees. Anyone could be in hiding, or just be camped as we were. There isn't any advantage in calling attention to ourselves, is there?"

"I thought you could tell where people are," Aletto began stiffly.

"It's possible to find people, if we're actually looking for them, and if they don't have a way to hide from us," Jennifer said before Lialla could say anything to precipitate another fight. "But we've gone over this already, more than once: The men who want you two have access to magic, so we have to assume they *can* hide. And it isn't easy to Wield from horseback—at least, I find it damn near impossible to ride and read Thread at the same time."

Lialla eyed her sidelong. "You can't think how glad I am to hear you say that. I thought I was losing my touch entirely two nights ago. We can take in turns to walk and search, or stop now and again. That will reveal anything ordinary.''

"Good," Aletto said dubiously. He slid the walking stick into place between the chest strap and the bags tied behind his saddle, then threaded the six-foot bo in over it. Lialla scowled at his back but apparently decided to let it alone. Jennifer caught her eye and nodded once.

"I can handle it on foot. You and I can stop if need be, catch up to the others. But we'll need breaks anyway. I'm nowhere near ready for a nonstop ride."

"Even if you are, the horses aren't," Robyn said. She let Chris tie her bo to the pack horse; just as well, Jennifer thought, considering how little progress she had made with it.

Chris, surprisingly, agreed with Lialla, though for slightly different reasons. "We ride down the streambed and we'll be two days getting to that village. That's if no one's horse breaks a leg; there are rocks, downed snags, trees, logs and limbs from flash floods—hell, you've seen it, you know what it's like. All those little skinny trees are murder to get through, and that's when you can see what you're doing. If we ride at night, we should at least be out where we can see a little ahead. But yeah, it would be just our lousy luck that someone was hanging out in the brush and we fell right over them. I don't want to get caught at all, but some guy smirking at us because we got caught dumb like that—no way, all right?'' He consulted the map a last time before mounting. "There should be hills; the main road runs into them for several miles before that village, and it's built on higher ground so we should see it even before we see the road.'' He looked around. "It's a pretty good ride, though, people, so let's get going.''

* * *

IT was considerably warmer out in the open, and Jennifer felt dangerously exposed at first, being able to see so far in so many directions. But with the sun out of sight behind the western foothills, the sky got dark quickly. The moon, one night nearer full, was almost an hour later in rising so they rode at a walk until nearly midnight.

Jennifer tried the shift while riding, with the same results: She simply could not manage to keep her balance and keep control of Thread at the same time. *It's only been a couple of days*, she reminded herself. But somehow, she couldn't see herself as a rider, even after months or years. Horses weren't like dogs—or better yet, cats. She liked other people's dogs; she'd looked forward to getting an apartment or a condo where she could have a cat or two. You could talk to a dog or a cat, could feel like the animal was responding, even if not to the specific words. She had no sense of communication with any of the horses, felt no warmth toward the creature that carried her at the present moment. Her legs were beginning to ache again, her hip joints protested crampingly at being held at this unnatural angle. The hair was rough, the mane rougher; the harness and blankets smelled unpleasant. The horses themselves smelled: a compounding of sweat, dust, the base odor of their skin, their breath. Jennifer supposed if you liked that smell—She found it mildly offensive, enough so that she never quite got used to it. Like Birdy's cigarettes, or Lisa Heydrich's musky perfume that lingered in the hallway for what seemed hours after the senior partner's wife swept through the offices. "Well," she told herself. "At least there's two things I don't have to worry about smelling any more." At the moment, she would cheerfully have traded— well, not Robyn's gagging smoke, but certainly that cloying Musky Death (as Jimmy had called it) for the smell of hot horse.

Lialla rode by herself a good deal of the time, or, like her fellow Wielder, walked when the pace allowed. Jennifer could feel her handling Thread, sensed rather than heard her soft humming. Jennifer stayed a distance from her, since Lialla's activities still shifted her own balance. When that didn't work, she went back to Beethoven's Seventh Symphony, using music to separate herself from the sin-Duchess and her tinkering.

During the first of their rest stops, she walked away from the rest of them and dropped to one knee, caught hold of the mauve Thread Lialla had called red, and felt its length as far as she could, in all directions. There were people along the stream: two or three of them with a herd of small animals—probably the goats Edrith had mentioned. Farther downstream, another, similar group. Behind them, more to the south as though they were across the water and out of the trees, men and perhaps horses. Five or six of each. Unlike the herders, they were absolutely still, men and horses alike, and so almost certainly all asleep.

When she rejoined her companions, she set Lialla to searching in the same direction; Lialla found the three different groups also, but learned nothing new about them. "If we tried to join forces," Jennifer began tentatively.

Lialla began shaking her head but stopped almost at once and stood thinking for several long minutes. Finally, as Chris got to his feet and bent over to stretch out his spine, she shrugged. "We can try that, if you like." She didn't sound hopeful it would work, but at least she didn't say so. Progress of a sort, Jennifer thought. But it proved impossible to manage a joint search, or even to lend strength one to the other to extend the search area. If anything, it was more difficult to tell what was around them; simultaneous use of the same Thread obviously wasn't going to work in such a straightforward manner.

Jennifer waited until they were on the way once again, and dropped back to where Lialla brought up the rear. "Are there Wielders in Bezjeriad?"

Lialla considered this. "I would think so, but I don't know. Thread isn't proscribed and Wielders aren't exactly rare." She was silent for some moments. "Why? Do you mean—do you want to find a Wielder, a high-ranking Wielder, who might answer some of your questions?"

"Not to insult you or your own instructor, but that's exactly what I had in mind," Jennifer said.

"If I can't answer you, why should I object if you find someone who can?" Lialla sighed. "Don't answer that, please; it occurs to me I've done little but object since we met."

"That's true," Jennifer said mildly. "But under the circumstances, I can't blame you. However, we're dealing too much from ignorance; that's not the safest thing. It could get us all killed."

"I know. And some of your questions—I'm beginning to wonder about things myself. There *should* be a way to join strength; I think Merrida said something once about an exercise her instructor did with her—I can't even remember what now. If there are Wielders in Bez, I can't think how we'll find such persons."

"No phone books," Jennifer agreed. She shook her head as Lialla scowled at her. "Never mind. I hadn't thought; I'm used to a world where people are easier to locate."

"One of the Zelharri we're to meet might well know; a wealthy merchant family could conceivably use the services of a Wielder. It's not unheard of. But if we *do* find a pale-sash Wielder—an Orange, a Yellow like Merrida, anything above that level—there's no guarantee she'll want to answer questions."

"I understand that," Jennifer said. "Wait, though. She? Aren't there male Wielders?"

"Of course. I've never met any, though; all *I* know are Merrida, myself, Mother. Merrida's old instructor Erryn, she really was a distant relation to Red Hawk Clan." Lialla sighed heavily. "They say she was also very good; I know she wore the palest Red Sash there is; there is only White above that, and Silver, of course." She named both rather wistfully. "She gained that level after her second testing, Merrida told me that. Merrida herself took fifteen years to reach Dark Green. Seven tests before they gave her Yellow.''

"Stubborn determination, rather than innate talent," Jennifer said.

"She's not the only one who—"

"Don't say that. You can't know that, not when all you've ever had is the one instructor.''

"*You—*"

"I have had more luck than I deserve, combined with a good teacher,'' Jennifer overrode her. She gestured toward the rest of their party, now some distance ahead. "I think we should catch up to them, even if we're alone out here tonight, don't you?''

* * *

THE night wore on, the moon rode high and began its slow descent toward the western mountains. They made a long stop just after midnight and once Jennifer and Lialla pronounced the land around them vacant, they went back to the water so the horses could drink. Jennifer bathed her face and the back of her neck, and felt considerably better—and more awake—than she had. She still hurt when she first dismounted and it took several minutes of walking up and down to ease the cramps out of her hips and feet.

The land changed almost at once when they set out again: less sand underfoot, replaced by hard-packed, pavementlike dirt. "Dry lake," Chris mumbled. "Should be good footing for the horses," he said aloud, "and we can see a long ways but that means we're visible too. So now what?''

"Keep going," Aletto said before Lialla could say anything. "It can't be very long, can it?''

"Not if the distances on my original map are even remotely accurate," Chris replied. "The road is—I can't translate the damned distances," he mumbled vexedly. "Hell, it's not that far.''

"Keep going," Aletto said. "We're visible, so is anyone else.'' He slid the long staff back and forth to make certain it was fairly loose and urged his horse forward. Robyn kneed her mount so she stayed right beside him; the others fell in behind. Edrith moved up to take the lead and set a quicker pace. The party strung out behind him, Chris and the pack horse bringing up the rear.

According to Jennifer's watch, it took them perhaps twenty minutes to cross the flat, barren lake bed—twenty harrowing minutes that felt like hours. Her head was beginning to ache from twisting to try and see in all directions at once and her stomach hurt. But she had to rely on her eyes and ears here since she certainly couldn't dismount. At the pace Edrith was setting, she wouldn't be able to keep up if she ran. And it would be a serious mistake to try and Wield *now*; the wretched horse was jolting her half out of the saddle as it was.

She drew her first deep breath in what seemed forever when Robyn and Aletto slowed to a walk and followed Edrith onto what might have been a game trail worn down into the dirt. Brush and grass grew more thickly here. Sere grass rustled against her ankles, seeds caught in her socks and the lower edge of her jeans. The sharp smell of sage was all around them, the dry bushes waist-high, then above their heads. She only noticed they had begun to climb after several moments.

Hills. Chris called another halt so he and Aletto could study the map, so Edrith could ride along the hill and partway up it, to see if he could make out their destination. "Stay off the top," Chris told him and Edrith sighed in heavy exasperation.

"Jeez! I learned that kind of thing *years* ago, I mean, you know?" And he was gone. Jennifer bent over the saddle and clapped both hands across her mouth to keep from laughing aloud. The so-called "Valley" slang sounded even funnier laced into native Rhadazi than when Chris used it.

"Good Lord." Robyn's voice sounded pinched, as though she was trying not to laugh herself. "Chris, you're going to leave such a mark on the language—!"

"Hey, Ma, *living* language, only Latin's dead and who speaks that any more, huh?"

"Does that mean you have to kill it yourself?"

Jennifer swallowed another attack of giggles. "Like, your age group and mine never, like, did that, right?" she asked Robyn in English. "Fer shur?"

"Good Lord," Robyn said again and she chuckled. "I'm hip. All the same, the mind boggles, doesn't it?"

* * *

THE remainder of the night's ride was a slow one, along the slopes of low hills or between them, down narrow gullies with moonlight sending long shadows before them, making footing treacherous. They finally went back to the pattern of two nights before: one person afoot to lead, the rest to follow.

They found the village an hour or more later, but the few huts were empty, the fences missing, no sign of habitation, and even the smell of goat so faint that it must have been deserted a long time before. They moved on through it, past the dry well in the midst of the one narrow cart-track and didn't stop to rest or discuss their next move until they were again in the open.

"Thank you," Robyn said as Chris reined in and turned back to face the rest of them. "That gave me the creeps."

"Pretty strange, empty little houses in moonlight," Chris admitted. "You feel like—well, never mind, I know *you* don't want to hear anything spooky. There's supposed to be this village, like, a real village with people in it? I thought this was a recent map. What now?"

Silence. Robyn shifted, glanced behind them. "We have enough food to get us down to Bez without the stop, I guess. No one's going to like it and probably no one's going to feel full, but we can do it."

"That's good to know," Lialla said. "And there are a few other villages along the road, if it becomes necessary to find supplies. But this—it looks to me as though the water gave out here is all. They probably dug a new well and moved the village. They shouldn't be far." She glanced at Jennifer, turned to check the eastern horizon. It was barely visible as a more opaque black against the sky. "All the same, it's odd they would leave so many buildings behind, especially here with wood in such scarce supply." She dismounted, leaned back against the horse, closed her eyes. Thread vibrated Jennifer's teeth; one of her back fillings ached until she put a Verdi aria between her and Lialla's search. She was trying to remember Italian words learned by rote, years before, to put to the melody when Lialla stepped into the open and pointed east and a little north. "It's there—at least, a habitation that's big enough and close together enough to be a village is that way. I think it has to be the same one, don't you?"

"I think I don't care, if we can buy milk and eggs from them," Chris said. "How far?" He shook his head before Lialla could reply. "Never mind, I probably wouldn't understand even if you told me. Will it take long?" Lialla shook her head in return.

"I'd like some water," Robyn said. "If someone has a bottle handy, I think mine's under things again." Aletto fumbled his free and held it out. Jennifer took the opportunity to dismount and feel along Thread for herself in the direction Lialla had indicated. People—dozens of them, most still and so likely sleeping. Beasts that could either be horses or goats, possibly both, and people with them, a little apart from the main number. Water—the stream bent north just ahead of them and ran through the relocated village, if she wasn't mistaken. The thick blue Thread that marked the presence of water conveyed just that to her, as it had the first time she'd used it. The New Age–like

75

music was as difficult for her to pinpoint as it had been then, too: This particular Thread was easier to find by touch than sound. As to distance—Jennifer bit back a frustrated sigh. Somehow, *some*how she must learn more; it was utterly maddening not to understand certain things! Things like telling horses from goats, near from far with more precision—men from women! Ordinary village people from men who carried weapons and intended harm! And how far from where she stood to where the damned creek went through the village!

Distance, though: There might be a way to work around the damned vague water Thread; she'd use that mauve stuff to locate people and judge it. It wasn't easy to judge, to set aside irritation and frustration to try and work out what was still an awfully inexact thing.

"Chris. Well under an hour, at the rate we're riding. Could be considerably less."

"Thanks, Aunt Jen. Anyone else thirsty?" he asked. "Need anything else? I'd really like to get this over in one more ride, not break it up any more." No one else needed anything, apparently. Robyn returned Aletto's water bottle, Lialla remounted, and they started down the rough track toward the main road.

They rode in silence, single file, Chris now in the lead with Edrith right behind him. The track plunged between two hills; the faint, narrow road vanished in a rubble of dirt, dust, dry brush and loose rock. Jennifer, riding in third place, heard Chris mutter something but he was too far ahead for her to catch the words. Edrith's response made little sense at first: "I know, I thought it looked familiar, too." She could see the boy's head in outline against the stars, looked the direction he seemed to be looking and frowned. *Damned strange*, she thought. The rock formation up there—there had been one just like it before the deserted village, hadn't there?

Her nerves prickled and a chill ran across her shoulders as the line of horses came into more open terrain. Hills unfolded on both sides of them. Deserted buildings, a narrow cart track, a dry well . . . Chris reined in so hard his horse danced sideways and Edrith nearly ran him down.

"Hey!" he demanded in outraged English. "Who put the loop in the video tape?"

"It's the same place," Edrith said at the same time in dazed Rhadazi, "the same all over again! That's not right—!"

Lialla overrode them both. "Moebius spell! That's Hell-
76

Light!'' She stood in the stirrups, brought the horse around in a circle.

"It's not, it can't be!" Jennifer protested. "There's none of the light—"

"It's a Moebius spell," Lialla shouted. "If we stay, it'll trap us for good! Ride, go, fast! Get out of here!"

"Well, right! Which way?" Chris yelled, but Lialla dropped back into the saddle; her horse bolted past his and took off at a dead run down the road. The rest followed.

There was only one way to go. Even in the moonlight, they could see the hills on both sides were steep, rocky, pitted with burrows or ridged with animal tracks: dangerously unstable. Back was no answer, either, particularly since Lialla was already well ahead, a fast-moving shape heading down a frighteningly twice-over familiar cleft.

Beyond it, open hills, deserted houses, a dry well . . .

Aletto kneed his horse and forced his way ahead, caught hold of Lialla's bridle and dragged her to a halt. "Stop this!" His voice was low, urgent and got through to her. "Panic won't help, we'll only wear out the horses!" Silence. The rest of the party caught up, milled around brother and sister uncertainly. "If it's a trap, a circle of some kind, how do we break out?"

"It's a Hell-Light thing," Lialla whispered. She was shaking violently. She gasped and drew her breath in a little, thin shriek as Aletto's fingers bit into her arm. "I'm trying to tell you, I don't know! Except that we can't stay in one place like this!"

"We aren't," Aletto said. "The place is staying around us. *How do we break free?*" He shook her arm. Lialla's head snapped back, she yanked her arm free.

"You don't listen to me!" Her voice shook. "I *told* you, I don't know!"

"All right," Chris said grimly. He flung his leg across the horse's neck and jumped to the ground, dragging the bowcase down with him and setting a heel on the trailing bridle. Aletto turned away from his sister and stared where the outlander was pointing: back the way they'd come. "So you don't know. Why don't we ask them?"

"Them?" Robyn echoed faintly. She turned to look and let out a little scream. Four mounted men sat unmoving, shoulder to shoulder, blocking the track behind them. At some unseen signal, the horses started forward. Jennifer's warning shout tore their fascinated attention from the parade-ground maneuver coming up the narrow, dark road toward the empty village: More

77

men, at least four more, rode in the same tight formation from the east end of the track.

"Trap," Aletto said grimly. He slid from his horse, drawing a horrified babble of protest from Lialla, but only to drag the bo from its sheath. Remounted, he touched Robyn's arm and nodded at her. "It's all right, stay near me and I'll protect us both."

God, Jennifer thought, and could see the same despairing thought mirrored in Lialla's eyes and the set of her mouth. The sin-Duchess shook her head. "Do that," she told him. "Stay on that horse!"

"I intend to. You get us out of this!"

"We'll try. Birdy—" Jennifer shook her head and turned the horse; Robyn was clinging to her horse's mane, staring open-mouthed at the four men now riding at a matched trot. They were near enough to make out the metal badge on each man's shoulder: Thukar's men.

Lialla wheeled and rode partway uphill, dragging her mount to a halt next to a low rock wall. There was a three-sided shed on the other side of it. She dismounted and scrambled over the wall, wrapped the reins around her arm and clutched two-handed at Thread. *She has something to make rope*, Jennifer realized. Eight men to six of them, such as they were, though: She leaned low across her horse's neck, forced the nervous animal around and back past Aletto to ride up the hill south of the road. There was loose stone here, the rubble of a wall like Lialla's, several thick fallen branches from a dismantled fence. The horse scrambled for footing. Jennifer lost one stirrup and nearly fell from the saddle. She wrenched her shoulders but somehow landed feet first instead of on her head. She remained where she found herself, half-kneeling, trying to hold a four-footed, dancing menace and staring down at the converging horsemen. She jerked hard on the reins. "Stop that," she hissed. The horse, startled, stared at her and subsided. "I knew I didn't like your kind; I didn't know you'd actively try to do me in. God, what am I supposed to *do* with you now?"

She dragged the momentarily quiet beast back a few paces and tied him to the largest remaining pile of stones in the wall. He lost interest in her at once and began nosing at the ground. Jennifer glared at his ample backside and slid partway down the hill.

Rope: It might be the answer, but she was afraid to simply immerse herself in braiding it. They were outnumbered, and this time—unlike in the Thukar's tower—what Lialla was doing fragmented her thoughts. She could access Thread; she'd need better concentration than she could manage right now to Wield it. *Why?* she wondered briefly. Something to ask, later. Something Lialla wouldn't be able to answer.

Stop it! she ordered herself angrily.

The moon was westering, not yet half full; it was bright enough to let her see all too clearly. Four men came from the east, horses at a walk, no space between them, and one at least held a drawn blade. Facing them, right in the middle of the track, Chris stood, staff held loosely across his thighs. Edrith was a pace or two away, turned slightly so the two commanded a wider view. He had brought the bo up, one leg back. Defensive pose, Jennifer thought; to draw the unwary. "God, they're mad, both of them," she whispered. To actually pit a hardwood branch against mounted men with steel—

From the other direction, the four now advanced slowly. Robyn, her long, blonde hair fallen loose down her back, hunched over her horse's neck, behind Aletto. The nera-Duke had thrown aside his cloak and half-stood in the stirrups, staff resting across the saddlebow. As she watched, one of his adversaries came forward; he said something she couldn't hear. Aletto kneed his horse, coming upright at the same moment, the bo sliding gracefully between his hands. The end caught his enemy under the chin; the Thukar's man fell and did not get up. His horse shied sideways, turned and ran. Aletto shouted, a wordless cry, and came back to center, awaiting the next attack.

Jennifer glanced across; Lialla hadn't moved, and there was movement by her feet. Rope. Jennifer fought her way into contact with Thread, humming under her breath to counter the dizziness Lialla's Wielding was causing her. There wasn't anything on this side of that road she could use for rope-making, anyway; just as well, because a simple three-part braid would've been beyond her just now.

And there was something else to deal with: Beyond the sin-Duchess, farther up the hill and to the east, one of the enclosed huts began to glow, as though someone had turned on a floodlight inside. Light leaked between ill-fitting boards, around shuttered window openings and a door; light spilled from holes near the roof line, from holes in the roof itself; light crept from spaces between the outer walls and the ground. Pale, buttery yellow light . . .

Hell-Light, Jennifer realized. She didn't dare give herself time to think; she dropped down to sit on hard, prickly ground, gripped the earth hard with her feet, and concentrated her full attention on that building.

There was a man there—outside the building, she thought as her fingers wove into Thread. Outside the Light, at least; she could feel where he moved Thread, where the building did. And then—not nothing, exactly. Nothing solid, nothing with parameters. The old mystic line about the inside being larger than the outside: If there was ever a place it held true, this deserted hut pulsing with Hell-Light was it.

No one inside. She felt it slide across her arms, almost unbearably hot, felt it folding into the spaces between Thread. She withdrew hastily. There had been something—*Later,* she ordered herself. *Sort it out later.*

There were only two men still mounted and facing Aletto now; the nera-Duke had moved some distance back down the track, leaving Robyn by herself. She still sat hunched over the saddlebows, as if afraid to move. Probably she was. Aletto was between her and the two; she was as safe there as she was going to get. In the other direction, one who fought Edrith. Chris had turned to look up the northern hill; he waved his staff, pointing it somewhere behind Lialla. Edrith, to his credit, didn't allow himself to be distracted. Jennifer stared through the darkness. There were more men back there—half a dozen at least, afoot.

Useless to shout—Chris was nearer Lialla than she was, and the woman didn't appear to have heard or seen him. Jennifer forced her way back into Thread and found Lialla, found the four-part rope the woman was braiding, caught hold of it and tugged hard, three times. Lialla stopped plaiting at once. The ensuing pause seemed to stretch forever, until the rope was tugged three times and yanked from Jennifer's grasp. She came briefly out of Thread to look across the draw. Lialla was standing very still—searching, apparently, because she turned to fling several lengths of rope into the darkness. Two men, shadows against the hillside, vanished behind the stone wall. Lialla bent down to run along the downslope side of the wall; she slid into a ravine and out of sight half a breath later.

Behind her—? Jennifer couldn't sense anyone there, but that last clutch of men made it nearly impossible for her to concentrate on Thread or anything else. She didn't dare trust her grasp on magic to reveal enemy, and Lialla's rope was disorienting her badly. She could feel the skin between her shoulder blades prickling.

Get the staff from her horse, go fight. Even if she wasn't as coordinated as the boys, as strong or determined as Aletto. She could back someone.

And maybe she'd be better help if she was a little hard to pick out. Maybe—if she could blur. It was worth a try. Her horse was several paces back up the hillside, up a hard scramble over shale and dry, sharp-pointed weeds. It rolled its eyes and tried to evade her until she caught the stirrup and yanked down on it, hard. The bo had been tied into place and it seemed to take forever to undo the knots. Half her nails felt pulled from the skin before it finally came loose.

She strode down the hill, blurring as she went. It took concentration, but less than rope. Enough concentration to keep her from being frightened as four new men came running around the northeast end of the hill, near the Hell-Light filled hut. They piled down the slope with a yell, straight for Chris, who shouted something extremely obscene back at them. Robyn would be shocked.

Edrith had gone after the last of the mounted men; the two boys had become separated just enough that they weren't able to guard each other's backs any longer. Jennifer lengthened her stride until she was running, angling across the track, behind Edrith, around a loose horse and across a fallen man. The blurring felt right, and it must have been working properly. At least, the approaching men didn't see her. Edrith was too busy to notice the shadow that passed him and his horsed opponent.

Chris was sweating, breathing heavily. He spared Edrith one swift glance and his mouth drooped a little as he turned back. "Bad odds," he mumbled. "Why couldn't I have been Bruce Lee if I was going to do this?" He didn't see Jennifer until she touched his arm with the staff. He yelped; the four men slowed and eyed him warily. "Jeez! Warn a guy, why don't you?"

"What do you think I was doing, kid?"

"You're damned hard to see; what are you *doing*?"

"Trying to even things out a little, all right? Look out, here they come!"

"Oh, really?" Chris said sarcastically. "Well, leave me a couple, all right?"

"Anything you say, kid." Jennifer turned aside to let the first man pass her and take Chris's staff across the temple, stepped back and slid the smoothed wood between her hands as she straightened her knees. The tip slammed into metal; the man she'd attacked was wearing light armor, plates fixed to leather. It was still enough to knock the wind from him and when he went down she snapped a blow against his exposed throat. The man nearest him stared down at his gasping companion; Chris caught him across the back of the head.

"Chris! Here I am!" Edrith shouted; he came up on Chris's

right shoulder and brought his bo down on bare knuckles. The swordsman yelped and swore viciously but somehow kept his grip on the hilt.

Jennifer backed away and left him to Chris and Edrith. Two other men had stopped and were now backing slowly away. The end of her staff cracked into a kneecap; the man howled and dropped to the ground, clutching his leg. The second simply fell; Thread vibrated all around her and she could see Lialla, hands above her head, forming knots in the night air. Behind her, she heard metal clatter on stone; the armsman fighting her nephew had just lost his blade.

There were no enemy standing anywhere around her. Jennifer dropped the blurring with relief.

There were men everywhere, a dozen of them at least: fallen men, some wrapped in awkwardly knotted rope, one almost at her feet, still trying to remember how to breathe. Several who didn't move; just unconscious, she hoped. Edrith was standing at the ready, watching, while Chris moved from man to man. Both boys were momentarily distracted as Lialla's rope moved on to wrap around another man's arms and ankles. Chris touched his friend's arm, glanced at Jennifer, nodded toward the track. "Nice to *see* you again," he said sarcastically. "Is this stuff all right? This rope?" He glanced up the hill and into darkness. "She's making it, right?"

"Works fine," Jennifer assured him.

"Good. I want something off one of these guys; a badge or something. In case Aletto needs proof somebody wants to kill him."

"Good idea."

"I—Jeez. What's *that*?" Chris had looked up the northern hill once more and his eyes were locked on the lit hut. "That wasn't like that a minute ago, was it?"

"No. And it's Hell-Light, stay away from it—" Jennifer began. Chris chopped a hand to silence her and shook his head.

"I can tell that; you think I'd mess with a lit building around *here*? There's something out there, moving, the other side of it."

"I didn't see anyone, Chris."

"Check," he urged. "Use the magic, because I swear I just saw—" He spun around on one heel to stare down the track. "Oh, God. Jen—where's Mom?"

Jennifer turned. There were several horses at the western end of the track but only Aletto was still mounted. Three fallen men—no, four. Between her and the nera-Duke, though, nothing. No sign of Robyn.

7

I T was dark on the hillside; so dark, she couldn't see the man who had come between her and Aletto, who now had her bridle, and was leading her away from the others. Robyn clutched at her horse's mane to keep from falling, tried to fight enough air into a panic-closed throat to shout a warning, to scream for help. It was all her worst acid trips, all her nastiest nightmares rolled into one: impending doom, claustrophobia, and she couldn't breathe, couldn't move, couldn't make a sound.

There was a shack ahead of them, pale yellow light spilling from cracks and holes. Hell-Light, she realized, and for one horrid moment, she thought the man was taking her straight into the building, dragging her into that evil magic. Like Aletto's father, who'd been a man until he fell into the stuff; Aletto's father, who'd died a blackened, shriveled, giggling lump of shivering *thing*—Aletto's description of Amarni's last hours had been enough to give her the crawling horrors. She whimpered, a strangled little noise that didn't sound human. The man didn't seem to hear it; he didn't turn. *Why should he, though?* Robyn thought bitterly. There was nothing to fear from *her*. *Wet, limp, shivering thing*, she berated herself. *Spineless, chickenshit old broad,* do *something! You'd fight to save your son; aren't you worth anything, even to yourself?* Her shoulders sagged and she gave herself up for lost.

But her captor skirted the building, keeping it on their right shoulder as they crested the hill. It was even blacker down the back side, and for some reason she couldn't hear the sounds of fighting any more. As though a door had closed between her and her family. She couldn't seem to see back that way either, when she shifted in the saddle. Maybe they'd already gone through some kind of door—Robyn swallowed an evil taste and shuddered. But there was enough light ahead—reflected Hell-Light from that hut, perhaps—to show her the man's face. He glanced back at her, mouth twisted in distaste, then yanked on the reins and pressed his heels into his horse's flanks. The animal turned back east and south, angling up the spine of the hill. He hadn't intended to bypass the hut, Robyn realized. He'd come around to the main entry, an open door on the north side nearly as wide as the entire building. Large enough for two people, mounted, to pass through without any difficulty.

Oh, God. She was going to throw up; bile and the taste of the oat cake she'd eaten during their last stop blocked her throat, momentarily shutting off every other sense. Somehow, she fought herself a little more upright; somehow, pantingly, began breathing again. Sickness receded; panic replaced it. *I'm not going in there, I won't, I won't!* She'd throw herself from the horse; he hadn't tied her, he wasn't even watching. She kicked free of the stirrups, braced her hands on the saddlebow. But fear of the unseen drop made her hesitate, the least moment. Too long. The horseman was beside her, her reins now wrapped around his arm, and his free hand caught the front of her shirt, twisting it hard. Soft white cotton pressed uncomfortably against her throat. "Where did you think to go?" he hissed. "The Thukars wish to see you before they sell you to Lord Jadek."

Robyn shook her head. "I don't want to see the Thukar," she managed breathily.

"Him? Ah. You'd say *that*, of course. They said you would deny any part in Lord Dahmec's death."

"They?" Robyn whispered. Was it that ghastly light? Nothing the man said made any sense! "Death?"

"Young Dahven—he was with you. Where is he now?" The hand tightened on her shirt. "And the old Thukar's sorcerer, *you* were one of those he went last to see, one of the outland women. The Thukars will be very interested to speak with you." His horse took a step toward the glowing building, hers perforce following.

Robyn grabbed at his hand with both of hers, clawing frantically at his wrist. He swore, spat, snatched his hand free and brought it across her face with a ringing slap. She screamed in pain and outrage, flailed for balance. He grabbed her shoulder and threw her back into the saddle. He brought the hand up again; the backhand slap made her ear ring. Robyn huddled away from him.

"Don't dare try that again," he snarled, and turned away to lead her into the building.

Her face burned; her whole body did. *Is there one man anywhere who doesn't use his fist to get what he wants from me?* Suddenly she was nearly as angry as she was afraid, and an inner voice prompted urgently: *Use that. Feed it. Change, force the shift to bird—do it!*

"I can't, I can't." She shaped the words, but no sound came. The light was reaching for her. "Aletto—oh, *God*, why me?" The armsman began to turn as he heard her faint whisper, as he felt a breeze against the back of his neck where none had been. He stopped cold, staring back and then up as his cringing prisoner began the shift. Her horse shied wildly; a dark shape rose with unnatural speed into the night. Huge wings furled with a snap that cracked across the sky.

He yelled and his eyes went impossibly wide. Robyn saw white all around the pupil with suddenly enhanced vision. She threw herself straight up, hovered above him. The look on his face— he wasn't so brave now, was he? She'd show him, she thought fiercely, he'd pay for everything he'd done. Wings in, close in— for the least moment, she found it odd she could still think, that she was Robyn and the bird both. Fortunately, that didn't inhibit her movements: The Thukars' man screamed again and cowered into the saddle as the huge black shape fell straight from the sky toward him. It missed by no more than the width of a feather; he felt something brush the back of his neck and the wind of its passing blew dust up into his eyes, blew the loose helm from the back of his head. His horse pawed at the sky, shied from under him and tore back down the hill, following the beast Robyn had ridden. The armsman rolled onto his back; one eye peered over a protective forearm.

Robyn sailed low across him, watched with immense satisfaction as he wailed and began scuttling backwards on hands, feet and backside toward the Hell-Lit shed. She soared back aloft and hovered. *Show him,* she exulted. It was getting harder to sense the difference between herself and the bird. The stupid, horrified look on his face, though: She wanted to erase it, forever. To kill, rend—he'd hurt, horribly; he'd want to die long before she killed him.

No! "God, what am I doing?" Strong, black wings pulled her higher, farther from him, high enough that she could no longer make him out as clearly. She hovered up there, a still blackness against the stars, westering moon shining blue against the long feathers. "Robyn, you're Robyn." She repeated the thought, over and over, watched the shivering, whimpering man vanish into the light.

* * *

JENNIFER raced up the hillside, running toward the last place she'd seen Robyn. Footsteps behind her; she didn't dare turn to look, she was going too fast and the ground was dangerously unstable. Chris came up next to her a moment later. His face was haggard in the moonlight, knuckles white around the staff he still carried. "I can't see her!" he panted. Jennifer pointed toward the hut; she couldn't afford to waste precious air on words. A shrill cry, muffled by the hillside. "I—wait, did you hear that?" Chris put on a burst of speed and sprinted up the hill ahead of her. Jennifer forced air into burning lungs and followed.

She hit level ground finally; fought for balance on loose stone and the remnants of a twig-and-branch fence. Another cry, and a horse galloped past her. A familiar clatter of wings, and a second horse followed the first. Jennifer ran forward, arms extended to keep her balance and nearly cannoned into Chris, who had stopped cold. He'd let the staff fall unnoticed and now stood with his head tilted back, staring straight up. His face had gone deathly white; at Jennifer's touch, he yelped and leaped away from her. His eyes turned away from her at once, though, and he gazed into the night sky. "Mom?" he whispered. His eyes sagged shut; his knees gave out. Jennifer caught his shoulders as he fell and nearly went down with him. Somehow, she shielded his head from rock but scraped her knee on hard ground. She let her nephew all the way down, staggered up and around him, ran the rest of the way around the hut. She was just in time to see a dark-clad man scramble through the doorway, threw an arm across her eyes as the light flared. It faded then, became an orange several shades darker than what it had been. The man was gone.

"Robyn?" she whispered. There was no answer, though, and no sense of her sister anywhere nearby. She didn't have time to worry about anything just now but this hut, anyway. The man had been wearing the uniform of a Sikkreni guard, like those who'd stood about the Thukar's dining room—he'd had an addition to that uniform, though: a large, brightly shining silver brooch on one shoulder. It was large enough that she'd have noticed it before. Perhaps a token of rank, but it somehow seemed more likely to her that it was some kind of charm, a wizard's token perhaps. Or maybe something to permit a man to move from place to place. Hell-Light as a travel device? It could mean he'd gone back to warn the Thukar the fight was going against them; it could mean men would come to help, or to take prisoners. That one of the Thukar's remaining sorcerers might come to subdue them. Jennifer snarled a curse at her lack of knowledge, then drew a steadying breath, shifted her perspective and caught at Thread two-handed before she could let herself realize what she intended to do.

Before Lialla could come and try to stop her.

Hell-Light was somehow easier to look at from inside the shifting lines of Night-Thread. Unlike the magic *she* knew, it was utterly silent, and seemed to dampen the sound of Thread nearest the shed, that in the makeup of the building itself. Light—no pattern or feel or sound to it. Frustrated, Jennifer touched what Thread she knew, feeling her way along it in an effort to learn something—*anything!*—that might help her undo what was here, or at least somehow confine it. There was nothing—nothing around the edges, at least. Near the center, however, she could see an object—no, she thought, two. There was some kind of large, angular charm or talisman in there, something that had been brought in and set—could it possibly have been brought physically in by one of their attackers and set within that shaky and aged building to fill it with Hell-Light, to confine it there? If so, then *if* she could remove it—

"Do it," she whispered. There was a straggling line of grass or hay under her feet, as though someone had caught up a load of the stuff when the village moved and spilled shreds of it at each step. She bit her lower lip, used the near-pain to focus her attention, withdrew further into Thread and began creating a fast, simple three-part plaited rope. Such a rope wouldn't last very long, but unless she was very wrong, she wouldn't need a strong one or much length. Ten feet—it would simply have to do. She caught up both ends, folded it in half and tugged, hard. It was springy and tough both, however temporarily. "God help me if I have this wrong," she muttered and knelt at the edge of the door.

It took two throws to get the loop around the object, but it came readily when she pulled. Jennifer backed away from the hut, carefully coming to her feet, sliding the rope and the thing across the hard-packed dirt floor. It might have been pulsing slightly; she couldn't tell for concentration, for Thread vibrating all around her, for the Light itself. It had a faint glow of its own, but once she slid it past the outer walls, it went inert. She pulled it several paces away from the building, just to make certain, touched it doubtfully. She might have neutralized it; she couldn't be sure. There was no reaction to her touch, though. She drew a deep breath, dropped the rope, scooped up the rough object and threw it as far as she could, turned back to gaze into the shed.

Hell-Light. It piqued her curiosity, it left more questions unanswered and unanswerable than ever. How to undo this—well, there might be a way, but *she* couldn't find it. There were shadows where moments before there hadn't been, however; as though it were fading. Thread near the outer walls touched her ears with music once again. She ran her hands along the mauve ones briefly. The second thing she'd seen in that dilapidated building was still there—a spherical object but composed of Light or something like it and not touchable by any means she could contrive. She stored the sense of it to ponder later, stepped back and disengaged from the maze of Thread. Hell-Light flared, pulsed, and vanished like a blown-out candle. There was nothing there now save an aged building that creaked ominously in the faint breeze.

She couldn't tell what had caused it to go out; whether it had been her effort or an outside agent. She sighed deeply and turned away. *Chris*, she thought worriedly. *How much had he seen just now? And—where was Robyn?*

* * *

ROBYN banked as the Thukars' man vanished. She soared in one wide circle over the deserted, moonlit village. Aletto where she'd left him, now hunched over his saddlebow, fallen men sprawled around him. Lialla nowhere in sight but Robyn heard her not far away on the same side of the road as she was, shouting her brother's name. Edrith down the track the other way, but no sign of Chris there.

Or Jen. Robyn used the long wings to pull herself higher into the night sky, flew north and east, away from them all. Dread was a choking, stomach-knotting sensation. She had a terrible hunch she knew where Jen was, and Chris. There'd been a startled shout that wasn't hers or that armsman's, just as she'd shifted and left the ground. A familiar boy's voice, yelling wordlessly. If it had been Chris, near enough to have seen—what would she do if he had?

She was sickened, all at once; ill with fright, with reaction. At what she'd become, what she'd nearly done. *Change back, do it now. If you can. While you can.* It seemed a long, long way back to that deserted village, a long way down to the ground. She sailed across the Hell-Lit hut, down the backside of the hill into welcome, enveloping shadow. The heightened vision and enhanced hearing faded; human arms flailed for balance and hands scraped across rock. There was something long dead down here. *Disgusting. Disgusting like me.* Robyn went down onto one knee and was sick.

She thought later she might have momentarily lost consciousness; she was suddenly aware once again of the smell, of Jen's anxious voice well above her. She pushed herself upright, bent hastily back over and was sick again. *Oh, God.* She fumbled an aged tissue from her jeans pocket; it smelled like dust but it was better than nothing to mop off her mouth and blow her nose. She used a corner to wipe her tongue and teeth. It helped some; she didn't think she'd throw up again, at least. "Got to get out of here," she whispered. Something rustled in the dry grass behind her—something small, running away, she tried to assure herself. Her face was hot and sweaty, her palms clammy and she was shivering violently. The hillside rose steeply above her. "I hate places like this," she groaned. Her legs wouldn't hold her upright; that was all right, she couldn't have walked up a slope like that one anyway.

She crawled most of the way up, hands clutching at holds, sneakered toes digging holes in the soft dirt, sliding down into rock and brush. It felt like forever but when she came across the crest, well down from a now dark and quite ordinary little shed, Aletto was just climbing down from his horse, and Lialla only barely off the slope, crying his name and running straight for him.

* * *

THERE were people up here. Robyn blinked sweat out of her eyes, freed a hand to rub the sleeve over her face. Jennifer knelt, back to her, arm wrapped around Chris who seemed unable to sit without her support. He was swearing in a monotone, using every English word he knew. "Goddamn it, Aunt Jen, don't try and tell me what I didn't see, sonofa—"

"Chris, don't swear." The automatic reprimand came from both women at once. Jennifer jumped and swung around, banging an already sore knee. She hissed with pain and clamped her hands around it. Chris fell forward onto his hands and knees.

"Mom?" he whispered uncertainly. "Mother?"

"Hey, kid," Robyn said unsteadily. She gripped her sister's shoulder, let herself down next to him. "Everything's all right, kid. I'm here."

Chris shook his head violently. His cheeks were wet and his mouth trembled. "Don't say that! I—God, Mom, I saw—" His voice cracked; Robyn shoved her own misery aside and wrapped her arms around him, hugging him the way she'd done when he was a small boy, waking from horrid dreams. Chris clung to her and buried his face in her shoulder. Robyn freed a hand to stroke the back of his head, to pat his arm.

"Everything's all right, kid. Shhh, don't."

"It isn't okay. God, I wish we'd never come here." He sniffed loudly, swallowed, and Robyn loosened her grip. He sat up, sniffed again and ran a hand under his nose. He wouldn't meet her eyes. "I'm—Jeez, I'm sorry."

"I understand. Don't sweat it, kid." Robyn took hold of his chin and brought his face around. He met her eyes unwillingly; his were blurred and wet. "Trust me, Chris. Never lied to you yet, have I?" He shook his head. "Get me down off this hill then, all right?"

"Sure, Mom." His voice still wasn't working right, but he wasn't as wobbly as he'd been. He got to his feet and pulled her up, wrapped a supporting arm around her shoulders and looked around for an easier route off the hill than the way he and Jennifer had come up. Jennifer was already partway down, dropping down the hill toward the wall where Lialla'd been. There were three horses there: the one Lialla had tied down and two others—Robyn's and that guardsman's apparently, either glad for the company or that there was something edible. "I can get the horses," Chris called after her. "You'll make them nervous, scare them off."

"Get Robyn down," Jennifer called back. "And go help Edrith; some of those men might wake up."

It lent speed to his feet. *I fainted*, Chris thought. It both astonished and disgusted him, passing out like a Victorian maiden with too-tight corsets or something. Then again, to look across that hillside and see his mother sprout feathers and—He swallowed, tightened his grip on his mother's very human shoulder, concentrated on the trail, the footing, on Edrith not far below them now, surrounded by still, fallen men, and a pile of rope. Shifting, moving rope. Chris bit his lip, dug the nails of his free hand into his palm, and looked back down at his feet. *His* feet, nice, ordinarily human feet—moving one step at a time down a very ordinary pathway. He suddenly couldn't bear the thought of magic, not any of it. It made him dizzy, slightly ill.

"Jen's getting your horse, Mom; you can hang onto it while I help Edrith, all right?"

"I'll help," Robyn said firmly. "I want to stay busy for the next little while, if you don't mind."

Chris nodded. "Yeah. I can understand that." He could; he didn't want to think about anything just now, either.

* * *

THE armsman's horse *was* nervous; Jennifer thought it probably was a lot more spirited than anything they had. But when she

90

untied Lialla's mount and led it and Robyn's down the hill, the abandoned animal followed.

The horse Aletto had ridden and the pack animal were tied to some of the large brush near the track; Jennifer tied the two she led, glanced up the south face of the hill to make certain hers was where she'd left it. She squared her shoulders and came up behind Aletto, who was arguing loudly with a near-hysterical Lialla. *Why doesn't this surprise me*? she thought.

"We have a problem?" she asked crisply. But when Aletto turned, she could see the problem: a long cut above his eyebrow that was bleeding freely.

Lialla looked at her and sighed with relief. "He won't let me do anything with it. Since you're here, though—"

"I'm here. This time. Next time I might not be," Jennifer said evenly. "Aletto—"

"Don't touch it," he growled and edged back.

Lialla reached for him, overbalanced and had to take a couple quick steps forward as Aletto evaded her. "You're bleeding, damnit!"

"Oh, really?"

"Stop this!" Jennifer shouted. Lialla froze, hand raised, and Aletto twisted around to stare at her, open-mouthed. "One of those men got away up there," she hissed in a low enough voice that she hoped none of the prisoners would hear what she said, "and he just might come back, with reinforcements, if I didn't somehow slow them down! I am heartily *bored* with your stupid sibling fights! Aletto, damnit, at least—here, take this." She jammed a crumpled and not very clean tissue from her jeans pocket into his hand. "And at least press it against that! Or do you like spilling blood?" Aletto was still staring at her in stunned silence; he took the tissue, eyed it warily, finally held it against his face. Jennifer rearranged the paper and flattened his hand across his forehead. "That's better. Look, I understand you're not mad about magic, you've made that all too damned clear! But if we get taken because you held us back, or slowed us up, I swear I'll kick your backside from one side of this country to the other! Personally!" She stepped back, folded her arms and waited.

Aletto glared at her but after a moment his gaze slipped and he sat, rather hard, in the dirt. "What do you want from me?"

"Let one of us heal that," Jennifer said flatly.

"If you have to," he said grudgingly. "It's not that deep; it'll stop bleeding soon enough. After all, it's just my face. Li can't heal, anyway; why should I let her experiment on me?"

91

Lialla glared down at him. "I *can* stop bleeding. You may not remember but I surely do."

Jennifer glanced over her shoulder, to where Chris and Edrith were moving among fallen armsmen. Robyn wasn't with them but she wasn't far away—she'd gone up the south slope to get Jennifer's horse. Apparently, she'd been near enough to hear the last of this latest argument. She put the reins into Jennifer's hands and knelt beside Aletto.

"I care about your face," she said simply.

"Where were you?"

Robyn gave him an unreadable look. "Some things you don't ask. Never mind that," she added. "We haven't time, I don't want to stay here any longer than we have to. You don't really want to ride with a cut like that, do you? I wouldn't." Aletto gave her a sour look, glanced at his sister and at Jennifer, finally shook his head. "Good. It's bled a lot but it doesn't seem to have affected your brains, then. Aletto—you know, I'd wager Lialla could take care of that if—"

"Robyn, don't you start on me, too," Aletto growled. He subsided as Robyn touched his cheek.

"I was going to say, she could take care of things like that, if people had any confidence in her. Don't you realize when you keep telling her she can't do things, it makes it harder for her to even want to try?" Silence. She nodded emphatically and glanced up at Lialla, who stood with arms folded across her chest, her mouth set. "I know how that is, I've lived with it most of my life. I think you have, too. Look, I know a lot of this is reaction, I'm scared and sick and worried about someone else coming. I don't think it's anything to be ashamed of, if that's what's making you cross." She touched his face again and got back to her feet. "The boys need a few more minutes. Why don't you let Lialla use them to see what she can do? In case sometime it happens again, and Jen isn't there to fix things?"

Aletto sighed. "I—oh, all right."

Lialla looked momentarily rebellious at his grudging capitulation. But Jennifer was already behind her, hands on her shoulders. Lialla sighed in turn, knelt before her brother. "All right, Lialla," Jennifer said quietly. "Whenever you're ready. The Thread you want sounds like this," she leaned close to the sin-Duchess's ear and hummed, so quietly even Aletto couldn't make it out. "It's that sound, it's sticky like cobwebs—you have that?"

"I—I can't—no," Lialla said suddenly. "Wait." She let her eyes close, one hand on her brother's forearm. Aletto winced as

92

her fingers dug in. "Give it to me again, *gods*, I can't get hold of it—!"

"Not that," Jennifer said as Thread jangled unmusically and set her teeth on edge. "Almost—that, there!"

"It won't stay in my grasp—"

"*Hold* it!" Jennifer hissed against her ear. "Hard! It's—that's it. Lay it in place, hurry, it'll stick to your hand if you don't."

Lialla leaned forward and slid her hand up Aletto's arm, the free hand clutching at Thread. Her brother eyed snatching fingers nervously. He didn't want to let go of the tissue and he yelped when it tried to stick to coagulating blood. Lialla slapped his wrist, very lightly, and began pushing sticky, webby stuff into place. Aletto hissed, tugged against her restraining hand. "Easy," Jennifer said aloud. Lialla lightened her touch; Aletto held briefly still. "It doesn't take pressure, Lialla. It's—that's right." She couldn't touch the Thread the other woman was handling but she could see what it was doing, how it was working. "That's right, good. Now—one last layer, can you ease off still more?" Lialla was trembling under her hands.

"That's it?" she whispered.

"That's it," Jennifer said. "Aletto, how does it feel?"

He reached for his forehead rather cautiously, ran a tentative index finger across it. "Hurts a little, still. Itches." He touched the hand Lialla had used to hold him still, and that she now was apparently using to hold herself upright. "You really did that, didn't you, Li?"

She laughed breathlessly. "If I had to do it twice, I think I'd die. I can't remember the last time I was this tired." She expelled breath in a loud huff. "I don't know how useful it'll be, not if it's that tiring."

"First try," Robyn said. "Some things are a lot harder the first time." Lialla met her eyes briefly, and with sudden comprehension. She nodded then. "We—can we go now?" Robyn added in a small voice. Chris came up behind her and gave her a quick hug.

"All ready, Mom. I'd like to get away from here myself, before something else goes wrong." Edrith came up a moment later leading the pack horse and their two mounts. "We tied them, but look, I don't want to just leave these guys here like that. They could die."

"Serve them right," Aletto said grimly.

"No. They're hired men, what if it's not their fault they're working for the bad guys? But—hell." Chris scratched his head

93

and began playing with the spiked ends. "We can't turn them loose, either."

"I wouldn't worry about them," Jennifer told him. "The guys who sent them know where they are. Someone is bound to come looking for them."

"Take the horses as far as the road," Edrith suggested, "and leave them. And if we take their boots, so they can't follow us on foot, either—"

Chris considered this, nodded. "Not bad. We can leave the boots a ways on, maybe."

"Do it," Jennifer said. "But let's hurry, shall we?"

Chris headed for the nearest bound and still unconscious men. "No argument here. I'll get it done faster with help, though."

* * *

THE track went between low hills as soon as it left the abandoned village, but this time there was nothing familiar about the terrain. After several minutes went by, Chris let out a loud, relieved sigh and dropped back to ride beside Aletto. "I am *really* impressed," he said. "The way you worked that bo, and on horseback, too! You sure you never did any of this before?"

Aletto visibly expanded under the praise. He shrugged. "Well—I knew I wouldn't be as strong at it as you or Edrith, and I don't have other experience with weapons—but you know that. So I thought about it yesterday, when it was too warm to sleep. What I would do if different things happened—if one man attacked, or if several did, or if I was already on the horse. Exactly what I would do, each move. I—it seems to have helped," he added.

"That's how good self-defense fighters work it out," Chris said. "Figure what might happen, and then work out how to deal with it. I have to admit, when I came up with the idea I wasn't sure it would be workable. But you'll do."

"Thanks," Aletto said. "I did learn one thing, though: a good sharp sword has one advantage over one of these staffs. Mine is a hunk shorter." He touched his forehead. "Went right through the wood and into my head."

"The wood must've slowed it enough," Chris said. "Or you wouldn't be here to tell me about it. We'll cut you another bo, as soon as we find the right kind of wood."

Aletto shook his head. "I don't know. Maybe I should keep this one—as a reminder not to get cocky."

"Keep it," Chris said and grinned. "But not to fight with, we'll cut you a new one."

* * *

94

JENNIFER and the pack horse brought up the rear. At the moment, she was afoot, leading both animals so she could make certain there was no one and nothing moving behind them. That lack of sound that marked Hell-Light within the deserted hut would warn her, she thought, if another charm had been set.

She needed the time alone to think, too: not about Hell-Light, though. She would have to wait until they stopped for the day to think through what she'd seen, what it might mean.

Sensibly, she needed to wait to think about what the Sikkreni armsman just told her, but she couldn't let that go; it played in her mind over and over. She could see Lialla standing before the men at the east end of the track, telling them the rope would dissolve around sunrise, that they'd find their footgear a distance up the trail, the horses farther on but short of the main road—unless someone came for them first, of course.

"Someone will come, if we don't contact them before dawn," one of the men had told them—an older, thickset, bearded man. "But they'll send someone to find you well before then."

Lialla had shaken her head in puzzlement at that; Jennifer had laughed. "If you mean through that building atop the hill, you're wrong. There *was* a device to hold Light but it's gone; I did away with it."

"It won't stop them, just slow them a little." He had peered at her uncertainly then, finally nodded. "You're the women who lunched with the old Thukar, and *you* are the one—I would watch my back, if I were you. The Thukars have a number of questions to put to you, personally, about their brother, the traitor Dahven."

"Traitor—" Her lip still hurt where she'd bitten it, to keep the words in.

"Traitor. He murdered his father to gain the ruling, and when he was found out, he fled Sikkre—market rumor and evidence alike say with you, the outlander woman advocate. The brothers Deehar and Dayher now rule in his place and they have vowed to find the traitor and bring him to justice."

"You're lying!" Jennifer had hissed. But that would convince no one of anything, save the intensity of her feelings. She somehow had regained control of herself. "You must be mistaken. I met this Dahven, of course. But only over the course of a meal taken with the rest of the Thukar's family. He seemed an amusing young man and no woman would be indifferent to his face, of course." She had smiled then, and no one—particularly this armsman—could know what that cost her. "A pity if he's done something rash. I find it difficult to believe; from what I saw of him he didn't seem the type to commit murder. Of course that is no evidence, is it? But I would find it difficult to obtain evidence, even from him, since I have not seen him since Sikkre.''

She'd seen doubt on the man's face before she turned away, as though indifferent to the whole matter. Let him feed *that* into market and court rumor!

But Dahven—*oh, God*, Jennifer thought, and clutched at the horse for support. Her knees wanted to give out; she wanted to cry, or throw up. He hadn't killed his father—he didn't want Sikkre, certainly not yet! She'd *never* believe he'd murdered anyone! He'd make an excellent scapegoat for those horrid twins, though. Particularly if he simply vanished.

''What have they done with him?'' she whispered.

8

T HEY reached the main road just before dawn. The village was visible from where they sat at the edge of the packed-dirt surface; it stretched across two hillsides and there was a small, shabby roadhouse a distance away where the stream flowed under a wide, high bridge.

''I don't like it out here,'' Robyn said in a very low voice to Chris.

Chris touched her arm, as if to reassure himself she was still there. ''I know. Feels like someone's just around the corner, ready to pounce. Or in one of those houses—ow!'' He ducked, too late; Robyn's well-practiced swing caught him upside the head.

''I don't need examples of *why* I don't like it, all right? God, my arms ache.''

Chris opened his mouth, shut it without saying anything. He wasn't certain what would be a safe thing to say, anyway: He still felt sick over having seen that shift, woman to bird, the horror of realization that it was his *mother* doing the shift, not a market woman trying to keep herself alive by entertaining male chauvinists. Robyn had always been open to magic but this—this wasn't dabbling with Tarot cards, I Ching coins,

Ouija boards and the rest of that crap Chris couldn't possibly believe was real, that he doubted otherwise common-sense Robyn honestly believed. He'd felt weird all along about this Thread stuff of Lialla's—possibly because of Merrida; anything *she* did couldn't be completely good, could it? That his aunt Jennifer worked the same stuff made him faintly uncomfortable, when he thought about it, but compared to what Robyn had done, it was as ordinary as walking to the Circle K for Cokes and a pack of gum!

Besides, what *could* he say? Robyn had looked awfully sick when she found him; her hair had smelled like sick. *Yeah, I'd have lost it too, if it was me,* Chris thought. *Just from being up in the air like that with just my arms to keep me there.* Of course, if Robyn knew how Aletto felt about shapeshifters, she *really* had cause.

Later, he told himself. But for his own peace of mind, maybe once the initial shock wore off, he'd have to find a way to bring it up, to talk to her about it.

He pulled himself out of gloomy thoughts. Lialla and Aletto were arguing—when weren't they?—about this village. Aletto wanted them to all ride in, which struck Chris as typically not-very-bright Aletto planning maneuvers. If they ever got him back to Zelharri and he deposed Jadek, he'd damned well better get that Gyrdan or someone like him to take care of any military planning that needed doing. Lialla wanted to leave everyone else down by the stream and go herself—as if no one was looking for a black-clad novice Wielder, Chris thought, and opened his mouth to tell her so. Edrith fortunately spoke up first.

"Every one of you is instantly recognizable—three outlanders, two Zelharri nobles with notable features, one clad as a novice Thread Wielder. Even the least intelligent peasant would either recognize you, or would remember you later should someone ask after we've moved on. I'll go. No one will expect someone like me; even those men who attacked us didn't seem to take any note of me. I'm not particularly outstanding anyway," he added. "I've worked hard most of my life not to be; a thief who sticks out in a crowd isn't going to be much of a thief."

Silence. Lialla digested this, finally nodded. "I—you're right. Even if those men were here before they set upon us and this village knows about our company, there's a good chance you won't be thought of as part of our party. Unless one of them is there *now*," she added and looked over at him, brows knit.

"I've also cultivated swift feet," Edrith said gravely. "Let me go now, get whatever we need, get us on our way before anyone has that chance to get free and come looking.''

''That's good sense,'' Jennifer said before anyone else could voice an argument. ''We need—Birdy, you know better than anyone else what we can use. Lialla, I suppose you know what we're likely to get instead. Why don't you two work it out?'' She looked east, across the small village. The sky was definitely getting lighter, chickens and geese were making a racket in pens, and as they watched a few lights were lit in glassless windows. A trousered figure walked slowly from one building to another, back again a few moments later.

Robyn had a mental list all ready. ''Milk, some kind of jam, eggs, salt. I'll cook chicken for us if you like and if you can get a *very* fresh one, but not any other kind of animal.''

''Chicken,'' Lialla agreed. ''Eggs, salt might be too expensive, I'm not certain about jam. We might be able to get a little butter. Milk—a little, perhaps.''

''It'll be goat,'' Jennifer warned.

Robyn nodded. ''I don't mind, even if I know you won't drink it. There isn't that much difference. Butter if you can get it, enough for today but no more than that, it'll gc bad. If you can get yogurt that's all right, too.'' She laughed briefly as Jennifer made a face. ''It'll last longer than milk, Jen.''

''Around me, it'll last forever,'' Jennifer said firmly. ''Because I won't eat it. Particularly *goat* yogurt.''

Edrith was finally dispatched with a few copper coins to see what he could bargain from householders. ''I'd stay clear of that road house,'' Chris said. ''Just in case.'' Edrith looked at him rather huffily and Chris threw out his arms. ''Yeah, well, all right, I was just saying!''

''Jeez,'' Edrith said in disgust; he sounded just like Chris. ''I'll meet you in the trees, other side of the bridge. Why don't you go now, before someone sees you? I lie better when the circumstances support what I'm saying. I can't be traveling alone if you're all out in plain sight, can I?''

''Irrefutable logic,'' Jennifer said dryly, and turned her horse down the road. It seemed very strange, riding such a broad, clear way after so many days of cross-country. She had to fight not to keep looking over her shoulder, though, and she breathed an audible sigh of relief as they made it to the bridge apparently unnoticed. Chris rode past her and led the way down a hard, dry bank, over a rough stone ledge and the shallow, pebbly stream, up the far side and into a broad, sparsely shaded grove of cottonwood.

"We can wait here," he said quietly. "Until Edrith comes. I think after that we'd better move farther from that road; we're awfully close to the inn or whatever." No one seemed to want to disagree with him, for once. "Particularly if we're going to have a cooking fire and all that."

The sun lit the tops of the tallest trees but nothing else yet when Edrith found them. He had bargained hard and had a handful of coins to return to Lialla. "If I hadn't argued price, they'd have wondered," he said, in apparent expectation of censure. Lialla merely nodded and returned the coins to the little cloth bag tucked under her black sash. He pulled a pack from the front of his saddle and held it up. "Everything but the yogurt, including a chicken the housewoman cleaned and dressed just before dawn."

Robyn glanced up at the sky, at the line of sunlight creeping down the trees. "Good job, kid. Let's get out of here, can we? I'm about dead after last night. I'd like a good long nap before I start cooking."

"I'd like someplace safe for that nap," Lialla mumbled. Her brother snorted.

"Find a place like that in all of Rhadaz, why don't you?"

* * *

IN the end they traveled nearly a mile up the stream, heading west and a little north, crossed the water and settled into a grove of cottonwood and willow a few dozen paces back from the stream. Robyn sent Chris and Edrith for the driest firewood they could find and Aletto to find her large covered cookpot, the sharpest knife. By the time Lialla had a fire built and the boys a stack of wood next to Jennifer's stone firepit, Robyn had the chicken cut into pieces and in the pot, covered with water and herbs. She now poured a handful of the dried soup vegetables from one of the stoppered clay jars and pushed the small pieces around with a finger. She picked out several, bit them cautiously, finally nodded and threw two fistfuls in with the chicken before setting the pot between rocks and brightly burning large sticks. "I'd kill for fried chicken," she said gloomily. "But any will do, I guess."

Aletto settled in close to her. "Fried chicken?"

Chris was stacking wood away from the rocks but still within Robyn's reach. He whistled. "Wow. You *are* alien, aren't you?" His mother glared up at him. "Well, jeez, Ma. It just brings it home with a vengeance, okay?"

"I thought I raised a kid with manners," Robyn said reprovingly. But as Chris opened his mouth to protest, she laughed and

99

waved him away. "Never mind, kid. Haven't you got something worthwhile to do?"

"Sure. Wait for that to cook."

"Remember the line about watched pots?" Robyn asked. Chris laughed again and leaped to his feet. Robyn sighed. "That's right, make me feel aged and feeble, I'd need a crane to get up at this moment." *Or wings,* she thought, and could feel the blood draining from her face. To keep Aletto from noticing, she bent forward to check the pot, pulled it a few inches back from the fire. He hadn't noticed; at least, he hadn't expressed concern the way he normally did when she freaked. Chris had. When she glanced up, he was looking at her with a face that was at least as pale as hers felt.

But he managed a grin and stepped back. "I gotta cut this guy a new bo; maybe I can do you a pair of crutches. All right, Ma?"

"Go play in the traffic, rotten kid."

* * *

THEY ate an hour later. "Stewed chicken for breakfast. I can't believe we're doing this," Chris grumbled, but he ate twice as much as anyone else. "No point in saving any of it, is there?"

"Sure," Jennifer said. "If you want to poison anyone."

"Pass," Chris said. He mopped up the last of a thin broth with Robyn's biscuits. "Am I on K.P. again?"

"Think of it as paying for that hollow leg, kid," Robyn told him.

"Fill it with water and bring it back," Lialla said as he stood and caught up the empty cookpot. "We need to talk before anyone sleeps, and I'm about tired to death right now." She waited until he came back, watched her brother throw dirt on the last few burning sticks, then turned to Jennifer, who sat cross-legged across the firepit from her. "Last night," she said.

Jennifer nodded. "Whose men were they? The uniforms I saw were Sikkreni."

"Mostly, they were the Thukar's men," Edrith said. "There were four in Zelharri uniform, though, those who came from the direction of the road."

Lialla considered this in pale-faced silence. "We already knew that Dahmec was cooperating with Jadek, at least for now."

"There was Hell-Light," Chris put in. Both Jennifer and Robyn looked ill at ease, and Chris didn't feel very happy about that part of things himself. He went on, trying to sound normal and not very sure he was succeeding. "That old barn on top of the hill. It *was* Hell-Light, wasn't it?" Jennifer looked at Lialla, who nodded. "Did those guys come that way? And was that stuff there all along and we just didn't see it? Because, frankly, that scares me. I mean, that it could just be anywhere, and no one notices it until too late—"

"No," Lialla said flatly and with such conviction Chris knew he couldn't believe her.

"Well, but no one noticed that—! I thought it was like that mess in Zelharri, remember that, Jen? Mom? The first night, by the road? The old bat said that was Hell-Light, and it wasn't going anywhere."

"It's not all set, or attached to one place," Lialla said. "I—look. I know less about Hell-Light than I do about Thread, but I do know what everyone knows, from the civil war: If you're a Triad or if you shape Light through a Triad, you can open or close set pools like that, and you can use certain spells to form Light. But that takes a lot of strength to just reach out and set Light, and it takes an enclosed place with walls—"

"Like a goat barn," Chris finished for her. "So if you can close a set pool, how come that one's still sitting next to your back road out of—Sehfi, isn't it? Your city?—where anyone can trip over it?"

Lialla sighed in exasperation but rather mildly for her; perhaps she was as tired as she claimed to be. "No one will trip over *that*," she said. "Everyone in Zelharri knows it's there. In Podhru, they know where such things are; there are maps and books telling where the still-open pools are, where the faded ones are that might be hard to see but are still active. But to close one—you would need a Triad for that, and they were illegal until a year or so ago."

"So no one would admit to being in one, or having one, is that it?" Chris asked. Lialla let her eyes close and nodded limply. "And since Light's the bad stuff, and since Triads are barely legal, no one would trust a Triad to close something like that, that right?" She nodded again. "Makes sense, I guess. This Hell-Light from last night, though. How did it get where it was? I mean, if any of those guys we fought were sorcerers, they can't have been any good because why would they fight us like that, physically, if they could just zap us somehow?"

"Zap—?" Lialla began. She waved a hand. "Never mind. Go on."

"Logically, none of them could use real magic," Chris said. "So how'd that hut light up like that?"

Lialla shrugged. "They came by road, I'd almost swear to it.

The horses had been ridden; that was real sweat on them, not fear-sweat from a shifting spell.''

"That's possible, though?" Chris asked.

"Don't know," Lialla said. "I don't *think* you can do it with Thread; Merrida never said so I have no way of knowing about it. Light—I *think* it's possible. Again, it would take a full Triad, and some kind of spell device both." She sighed. "I think it would. Gods, why are you asking me?"

"Because you might not know much, but we know diddly-squat," Chris said flatly. The American slang sounded strange even to him. "Nothing, in other words."

"I was closer to that hut than any of you," Jennifer said. "Maybe if I tell you what I saw, it would help." She described the device on the armsman's shoulder, the thing she pulled from the hut and threw down the hill. Lialla stared at her, unblinking, until she'd finished. Jennifer sat back and waited for the usual explosion, but Lialla merely shook her head and her eyes never left the other woman's face.

"Gods of the Warm Silences, but you have courage," she said finally. "After what I told you happened to our father and you *still* dared—!"

Jennifer shrugged. "Someone had to. I thought at least some of those men that came that way, that more would follow. It seemed to me that someone had better try something. Your father went into Light bodily; I was very careful not to touch it."

Robyn stirred uncomfortably. "The man—the one who grabbed me?" Her voice barely reached them, and Edrith had to lean forward to hear her. "He said we were going back to the Thukars that way."

"Some kind of transfer portal," Chris said. The three Rhadazi looked at him confusedly. "Instant travel," he said.

"How did you get caught?" Aletto pressed Robyn's near hand.

She'd expected that, Jennifer thought. Robyn was a rotten liar unless she put a lot of thought into her story, and this one held water well enough to convince anyone who didn't know Robyn. She didn't look at any of them as she spoke. "Um. You kept moving forward, Aletto, and I was—I just couldn't get my nerves under control, the damned horse was as scared as I was and you were suddenly that far away and the guy came up behind me, had the reins out of my fingers and over the horse's head before I could do anything." Aletto looked at her with a stricken expression. Robyn couldn't have seen that but she felt the renewed pressure on her fingers; she glanced up, touched his cheek with her free hand. "It wasn't your fault; you had your hands full, after all. At least they didn't get you, and I did—I got away before anything happened.'' She drew a deep breath, expelled it with a loud sigh, and told them about the hut, the sudden light, the man's words. "I—I was so scared I could have died of it. I *couldn't* go in there, so I managed to throw myself out of the saddle. I rolled all the way down the back of that hill, and it took forever to get back up it.'' She sighed again, more quietly this time. "I hate steep places, too. If I hadn't been so scared of those guys, I'd have yelled for help or tried to go around, but I was even more afraid of getting lost or one of *them* finding me again.'' She spread her hands. "That's all I know. But that man definitely said he was going to take me into that hut and back to Sikkre.''

"To the Thukars,'' Aletto said. He was frowning. "There's only one.''

Silence. Then: "There *was*,'' Jennifer said past a tight, dry throat. "The man I spoke with, just as we left? There've been—changes since we got out of Sikkre.'' Somehow, she got it all out, a dry recitation of stated facts as she'd been given them. "He may have lied but if so, he was very good.''

Aletto stirred. "I—no. Dahven wouldn't have killed his father. Not for Sikkre.'' He shook his head angrily. "I won't believe that. But if Dayher and Deehar rule in the old man's place—'' He let his head down into his hands. "I can't see they're any worse than their father was, from our point. They're apparently cooperating with our uncle, but so was Dahmec.''

"It doesn't matter,'' Lialla said flatly. "We have enough to worry about without fretting about Sikkreni politics. This Light, though: If they sent armed men on horses, and one carried that charm you found, Jen; if that was set in the enclosed place to permit them to at least bring two mounted people back to Sikkre—gods, that's no good thing for us!'' She drove both hands through her hair. "And as little as we know—!''

"We know enough to start with,'' Jennifer broke in. She leaned over to touch the other woman's arm and nodded as Lialla looked up at her, she hoped reassuringly. "We at least know such a set spell can be broken fairly easily; the Light faded at once when I threw that object down the hill.''

"You might not get so close or have so long at it, next time,'' Lialla grumbled.

"No. I might get faster, too.'' Jennifer muffled a yawn against her sleeve. "Look, I don't think there's much else we need to chew on right now. And I could use a couple hours of sleep before it gets too hot. Are we drawing sticks for first watch, or do we have a volunteer?''

* * *

SHE slept heavily, woke at Edrith's touch for an hour and a half of guarding, by her wrist watch, passed the duty on to Robyn and moved into shade where her sister had been. But sleep evaded her now, and she found it impossible to get comfortable on the hard-packed sand. There were ants crossing the corner of her blanket, running across her fingers now and again. She sighed, got up, shook out the blanket rather ferociously, moved it a little farther into brush and lay down once more.

Dahven's charm was warm against her throat, but it brought her no comfort. Finally, she rolled onto her back, stared up at white branches and pale yellow-green leaves overhead, at the dark blue sky between them. *Think about Hell-Light,* she ordered herself. It took an effort, shifting from dread and worry to the rather unnerving puzzle that was magic in this world.

Hell-Light: According to Merrida, it was strictly evil stuff. It had been the cause of a long and desperate war several hundred years ago. It killed people. It had killed Aletto's father, rather horribly. Lialla said much the same thing; the people in the market who sold charms had intimated the same kind of thing—Night-Thread was good, Hell-Light bad. And the Thukar and the Thukar's outlander magician had certainly reinforced that, though poor old hippy rock'n'roller Vinnie Harris—El Serpente himself—hadn't been a Shaper. Now, of course, he wasn't anything at all, thanks to pushing Robyn the way he had. Well, Jennifer thought tiredly, he'd been trying to get her mad; apparently he hadn't been able to read Birdy the way old Merrida had. Surely he hadn't realized her temper would force her first shift. He'd have protected his neck, literally, if he'd known that.

Enough, she told herself. *You're mentally blathering.* A lawyer was supposed to be capable of sticking to a point; she didn't seem to be able to handle it just now. "Try, damnit," she told herself in a low, hard voice.

So: Light bad, Thread good, the two obviously not related, according to the locals. So why was it that she herself had felt *nothing* in the presence of Light, after that initial fear—a fear based in what others had told her, not what she actually felt? It might not be truly neutral but the magic itself didn't feel any more evil than Thread felt good. It was—just magic. If it had been initially used for bad ends, if Triads continued to use it the same way, generation mindlessly copying the previous generation of Shapers, that might account for its reputation. If no one

104

knew how it was used, only what it had once done—This time, however, she certainly couldn't ask Lialla. The woman could barely accept the concept that *Thread* could be felt in the day; she wasn't ready to believe it could be *used* during daylight hours. She'd probably see Jennifer burned at the stake—or however they dealt with heretics—for even *thinking* such thoughts. All the same, Jennifer thought defiantly. All the same, she'd felt Thread all around that hut, and she'd handled Thread inside it; she'd had hold of both ends of that rope, then hold of the thing, the spell, that had been inside the hut. At no time had she felt the way something bad should leave her feeling.

And the thing that had still been there, when the Light faded—it was damned odd, exceedingly strange. A ball, from which Hell-Light itself seemed to pulse. It was silent, of course, like the rest of the Light. But it wasn't solid, or so she thought when she'd examined it as closely as she'd dared: It was made up of threads of some kind, an extremely fine, exceedingly tightly compressed wad, as though someone had taken a huge ball of twine, one the size of a six-foot weather balloon, and compressed it to the size of a golf ball.

Were the two magics related? Jennifer let her eyes close and sighed wearily. "Who the hell could I ever ask about that?" she wondered aloud. She rolled onto one side, tried to settle down for at least a decent rest if not actual sleep. Her shoulder was going to sleep, her hands ached, and her eyes burned. She rubbed them cautiously, rolled over onto her stomach and brought up her right leg. Mozart, perhaps. The cello sonata that had won her the statewide competition her junior year of high school. . . . She slept before she had a chance to run all the way through the first movement.

* * *

THEY—Chris, Edrith and Aletto—were still talking about the previous night's excitement when she woke late in the afternoon. Mostly, it was the fighting itself: Aletto was still fairly thrilled by winning against extremely stacked odds and perversely proud of what was left of the cut on his forehead. Lialla's healing had left a scar, faint but considerably more noticeable than the one on his upper arm from Carolan's dagger. Aletto wouldn't let either Wielder near it, although Jennifer suspected it was still giving him a headache, and he seemed to have a hard time not scratching it.

Chris was verbally patting the nera-Duke on the head, praising his efforts and his fledgling skills; Aletto couldn't have helped but warm to him. Her nephew was also rather cleverly keeping the conversation directed away from his mother and that hilltop hut, Jennifer noticed. For the most part, anyway. She rummaged in her packs, found one of the lavender-scented soap bags and a drying cloth, went downstream in search of someplace to wash herself and possibly her hair, which felt thick with dirt and sand; besides, after that nap, every time something tickled her scalp, she thought, *Bugs.* It was making her skin crawl and she was starting to itch all over.

She came back still damp under jeans and the tee-shirt she'd worn under her long-sleeved chambray to the Punchbowl forever ago, hair wet and twisted up in the cloth. Robyn and Lialla were sitting with Chris and Aletto now, discussing Sikkre, the old Thukar, Dahven. Edrith was standing, glaring disgustedly down at them, and as she came into sight, he turned and strode away. Jennifer felt anger filling her, maybe the same anger the young thief felt: Dahven wasn't here to defend himself, none of them had any idea what was truth, what lies—Dahven might not be anywhere in Rhadaz or in this world at all, to defend himself. She couldn't bear it. As Chris glanced up and saw her, waved a hand to draw her into the conversation, she turned and went to her blankets, dug out her handbag and fished through it for a tie and pins to get the wet hair off her neck. Suddenly, she couldn't stand any of them, couldn't stand to stay here another moment. Out. A little solitude, a little time all to herself . . . She glanced at her watch, up at the sky. The hour was late, the sun westering, a breeze picking up. It was warm but not insufferably hot. She'd run in hotter weather than this, back in L.A.

She shoved the bag back under the top blanket, sat back on her heels to free damp hair from the thin towel and wind it into a knot. She'd have to get it wet again before they rode out, but right now that wasn't important; just getting it off her neck and out of her face was. She became suddenly aware of someone behind her. Chris squatted beside her. "You all right?"

"Sure," she replied shortly. "Go on back to what you're doing over there."

"I—right. Look, I'm sorry, I know you like the guy—"

"Let's not talk about it right now, all right?" Jennifer said crisply. "Maybe later. Right now I'm going for a run."

"Run? In this heat?"

"It's not so hot. I need it, Chris."

"Yeah. Endorphin freak," he replied and grinned.

"I don't run often enough any more to get a runner's high. Or long or fast enough." She sat back and began snugging up the laces on her high-tops.

"You can't run in those, you'll break something."

"They're good shoes—"

"The jeans, lady. Hey, though, I keep forgetting. Your bag from the car, you know?"

Jennifer let the loose ties fall forgotten. "Chris. Are you possibly trying to tell me something worthwhile?"

"Your Nike bag, the one I got out of the trunk to put stuff in? I left the tennis balls and all that in the car, but your other stuff—"

"Get it," Jennifer ordered. She had both high-tops unlaced and off her feet by the time he came back. It took her several minutes to unearth her things from under his spare clothes and other Sikkreni market goods, but there they were: one expensive pair of cross-trainer shoes, a wrinkled pair of white tennis shorts, a sleeveless mesh pullover shirt. "Stay here and turn your back, kid." She moved back into the bushes and changed. Odd, how unclad she felt after so few days in Rhadaz; she'd never thought twice about wearing even shorter shorts anywhere in L.A.

The three Rhadazi stared in wide-eyed surprise. Jennifer walked past them, tapped the face of her watch and nodded at Robyn. "I *need* this, you tell them, Birdy. I'll be back in an hour, maybe a little less." Before anyone could say anything, she broke into a slow, rather shuffling trot and headed through the trees toward the open. Behind her, as she broke free of trees and brush, she could hear Aletto's rather plaintive, "Run? Like *that*?"

"How better?" Jennifer mumbled to herself, and lengthened her stride as she turned west and a little south, keeping the wind on her right cheek. Suddenly, she felt her spirits lift. She pressed buttons to start the stopwatch, surveyed the land ahead of her with a practiced eye, and swung into pace. God knew she'd ache for this tomorrow. "Hell, I'll ache anyway, damned horse." But for nearly an hour, she'd have an absolutely empty mind. And for now—*damn*, it felt good, bare arms and legs under a hot sun, open ground ahead of her, and no one and nothing to get in her way.

9

W HEN Jennifer returned to the streamside camp—sweaty, a little wobbly in the knees and very pleasantly tired—they were talking about it again: about Sikkre, the old Thukar, Dahven. She could tell by the look on Chris's face when he saw her, the sudden lack of conversation around the cold firepit, the distinctly uncomfortable expression on Robyn's face. It irritated her immensely and for a moment she wanted to jump all over them. But the run had done her some good that way, at least letting her realize the anger before she unleashed it, letting her put it aside. Of course they were talking about it; why wouldn't they? And knowing—at least in part—how she felt about Dahven, of course they'd react just the way they were reacting when she got within hearing. So she merely waved a hand at them from a distance and shook her head when Chris got up and started to say something. He was red right into his hairline. *Spare him having to lie politely*, she thought.

"Hold on, kid, unless it's vital, I'll be back in a few minutes. I reek and I want to rinse my hair." Lialla's astonished, but unintelligible, comment followed her down to the water, and Jennifer grinned. *She* couldn't understand someone like Lialla, outwardly an extremely neat young woman, feeling no urge to bathe after riding a horse all night and sweating through long naps all day—and in the same awful black cottony clothes. It was a wonder Lialla didn't reek. *My nose must be broken*, Jennifer thought and shivered as she peeled out of shorts and stepped into the ankle-deep, chilly water. *She doesn't even smell like that four-footed, foul-tempered brute she rides.* "Yeek!" she yelped, as she knelt to splash water across her legs and check the soles of her feet. They'd felt unbearably hot—at least, until a moment ago—but there were no red places, no blisters. At the moment, they didn't *feel* at all.

She gritted her teeth, squirmed out of the limp, clingy white shirt, finished washing down, scrunched her hair damp and curly again with stream water. It dribbled down between her shoulder blades when she stood up, and she yelped again. "Damn." She'd have to put the sweaty clothes back on; she'd left her other clothes on her blankets and that miserable, thin excuse for a towel was over there, too.

"Bless Chris for whatever possessed him," she muttered as she squeezed water through the thick white socks. Whether he'd intentionally left her gym clothes in the bag or just forgotten to pull them out when he stuffed the contents of the picnic basket in it—it didn't matter. She doubted she'd have many opportunities to wear the shorts or the shirt, except someplace like this where she could only scandalize a couple of Rhadazi. The look on Lialla's face!

But a second pair of socks—a nice, thick pair—what an unexpected present.

* * *

THEY had changed the subject by the time she got back. Someone had built another fire and Robyn was scrambling up the last of the eggs in the last of the butter. While she cut reconstituted dry peppers into them, Lialla watched, wrinkling her nose doubtfully. Edrith and Chris had retreated to Chris's blankets to go over the map once more—far enough away that their conversation wouldn't distract everyone else, but near enough to let them keep an eye on the food.

Jennifer went into the brush to change into jeans, went back down to the stream to wash her running things. She draped hand-wrung shorts, shirt and socks over a bush where she wouldn't be likely to forget them and set the cross-trainers on her blankets to air. She cast a glance at the sky rather doubtfully. It was still warm, but not particularly hot here; the sun had gone off them and the wind was light. Chances were, her things weren't going to dry in time, and they'd have to go across the back of her saddle, still damp. She certainly couldn't afford to let them mildew, though: There wasn't likely to be any laundry additive for that around here. She dragged her blanket nearer the firepit and dropped onto it cross-legged. Her hips protested, and she shifted at once. "God, I'm wiped out," she said.

"I'm not surprised." Robyn used a pair of wooden paddles to separate eggs into quarters, dumped each of the four wedges onto plates with a biscuit each, broke the remaining eggs into her small saucepot and stirred them vigorously. "These done ones are ours; what's left goes to the bottomless pits over there. The bread's probably hard; they're from this morning."

"Amazing," Jennifer said. "How'd you hide biscuits?"

Robyn grinned, sniffed the heavy clay jug of milk and poured some in with the eggs. "Wasn't easy. Chris usually manages to count them when I start." She unfolded the much-reused piece of wax paper salvaged from their Punchbowl picnic, scooped out very soft butter with an index finger and plopped it onto the pan where it sizzled madly. Jennifer finished her plateful in record time, leaned over to take hold of the pan and held out her other hand for the saucepan of raw egg.

"Give that here, and you eat, Birdy. Nothing worse than cold eggs, and even I can scramble them once you've done the hard work."

"Don't burn anything," Robyn warned, but she settled back and picked up her plate.

"I don't plan on it," Jennifer replied. She picked up one of the wooden paddles and began stirring. It was pleasantly quiet around the fire for some minutes. Aletto finished eating and went over to help with the maps, Lialla gathered up plates, knives and the eggy little saucepan to wash.

"You don't have to do that," Robyn began rather indistinctly.

Lialla shook her head. "Call it an apology, for having thought what you were doing wouldn't be edible. It looked terrible when you started cooking it, and it smelled strange but I liked it." She nodded in the direction of the navigators. "Besides, you may have insurrection on your hands if they have to wash every night."

Jennifer looked up from the pan of nearly cooked eggs as the sin-Duchess vanished in the trees. Robyn was staring that way, too, mouth open. "That's a *noblewoman* doing our dishes," she said. "It makes me feel funny, you know?"

Jennifer shrugged. "Maybe they do, here. No one's said, have they?"

"No—guess not. But *that* noblewoman doing dishes boggles *my* mind, Jen." She rubbed the last bite of biscuit across her plate and popped it in her mouth. "How was it—your run?"

"Great. Think I did about four miles."

"God," Robyn breathed and closed her eyes.

Jennifer laughed. "Want to come, next time?"

"Trying to kill me off young?" her sister demanded.

"You keep telling me you're old; I couldn't kill you off young. Besides, think how much faster you'll clean all the crap out of your lungs."

"Yeah." Robyn set her plate aside and sighed gloomily. "Could have used *that* last night."

Jennifer leaned across the dying fire to touch the back of her hand. "Want to talk about it?" Robyn shook her head, hard.

110

Her eyes went sideways, toward Chris. "If you're sure. But if you do, later, let me know. All right?"

"Sure." Robyn pushed to her feet. "Better get some water to put this out, clean my own plate. I'd feel better about having Princess Di wash up after me than *her*."

"Don't say *her* like that, it's common," Jennifer said. Robyn looked down at her and laughed.

"Grandma's old etiquette book, God, I'd forgotten about it. But it's only common if she's around to hear me." She turned and raised her voice a little. "Hey, you two, you can smell eggs and you aren't over here? You sick or something?" She picked the flat leather horse bucket from its hanging place on a shoulder-high branch and went on down to the stream, plate in her other hand. Barefoot, Jennifer noticed with amusement. Barefoot across all those rocks and everything else. You'd need feet with soles of iron. Of course, Birdy'd walked from one end of the Sunset Strip to the other for years, barefoot. Once a hippy—and then Chris and Edrith descended on her and the pan she was holding.

* * *

The land south of the stream was largely open, all very low brush, scrubby gray-green ground cover, tumbleweed, a few tight rosebud patches of cactus. There were hills to the west—rounded, green-looking things cut by numerous washes. The desert looked green like that, too, at a distance: It wasn't, Jennifer knew. Those hillsides would be covered at the same widespread distance by the same kinds of plants, the dirt between them hard-packed grayish stuff, pebbly, sandy, or cracking mud flat where water had run across it at some time this past season.

Running along the edge of dry high desert country this afternoon had been exhilarating but riding across it, even the thought of such a ride, made her tired all over. "Give it a break, Cray," she told herself in a low, English undertone. "You're just plain tired all over. Four miles after the months you've taken off, sitting on your butt writing briefs—" She sighed, blinked as Chris led them into the open, into fading evening light and what was left of a brilliantly blood-red sunset. "Then again, I didn't do bad for a flabby broad." She made herself sit a little straighter when Robyn dropped back to ride beside her.

She indicated the sunset with a wave of her hand. "Pretty neat, huh? As my kid would say, awesome."

"Which kid?" Jennifer asked dryly. "You ask me, Edrith has you on inverse condemnation—"

"Watch that dirty lawyer talk around my shell-like ears, kiddo."

"You have two of them," Jennifer said. "Two kids." Robyn cast up her eyes and shook her head. "And one sounds about as bad as the other, these past couple of days."

"Jeez," Robyn said sarcastically. "Rully?" She rolled the "r" the way Chris did when he made fun of some of the Valley Girl types he went to school with. Both women laughed. "You gonna fall asleep back here?"

"Do I look that tired?"

"Not yet. A little saggy around the shoulders. Just because I don't run doesn't mean I don't know how it hits people. If I see an empty horse back here, I'll yell for the rescue squad, okay?"

"Swell." Jennifer managed to stay pretty much upright when Robyn urged her horse back up where Aletto was, waved cheerfully when Chris turned to look at her a few minutes later. As darkness fell, she found it considerably easier to wrap the reins around one hand and rest both palms on the high saddlebow. If she kept her hands spread wide apart and her elbows locked, or if she crossed her arms and leaned on her forearms, she could actually doze a little while the horse followed the rest of the horses.

They took a rest around midnight, when the moon came up; later they stopped for a few minutes so Chris and Edrith could check the map against the one visible landmark: a tall, pointed hill between them and the road. When they went on, Chris took them away from the base of the hill, almost due west, and they kept on that way for an hour or so, finally turning south again.

Jennifer was bent over the saddlebow once more, but this time to rub out cramped and stiffened calf muscles, a tight Achilles tendon. "At least I'm awake enough to stay *on* this wretched beast," she mumbled through clenched teeth. The horse's head came partway around and what looked like a displeased eye met hers from way too close for her tastes. "What are *you* staring at?" she asked it. "One of us is supposed to be watching where we're going, you know!" Just ahead of her, Chris chuckled.

"Way to go, Aunt Jen. When does it start answering you back?"

"It's doing *that* with attitude," Jennifer groaned. She sat back up and dug her knuckles into a painfully tight hip.

"At that camp when I was a little kid, they told us the horse picks up how you feel about it, you know—"

"*I* know that," Jennifer snapped.

"Hey. Just telling you. We're almost where we're going, there

112

might be water.'' He turned around in his saddle to look at her. ''You can tell about where water is, can't you?''

''Not while I'm on the horse. It's like drinking a wine cooler and turning cartwheels, makes you dizzy.''

''It would make me puke. The horses'll tell us anyway; they can scent it long before we can.''

* * *

THEY were riding just too fast for Jennifer to think about leading her horse and walking, and she spent the next hour or so being very sorry for that fact: She was starting to ache in earnest now. The horse Chris rode brought his head up and whickered softly, picked up his pace. Jennifer's followed. ''See?'' Chris said. ''Told you.''

''Yeah,'' she said in a low voice that wouldn't carry beyond him to the others. ''Why do I detect relief in your voice?''

''Watch that,'' he said even more softly. ''The guy with the map always knows where he is, remember?''

The water turned out to be what was left of a pool, sheltered on the east by several dead trees and an enormous, daunting screen of cactus twice as high as any of them. Edrith jumped down to shove horses back so Chris could dig out wet sand. Eventually, they had a little water bubbling up. Enough to keep Chris's hole partway filled, and to let the horses each drink. ''I don't think I want any of this,'' Aletto said doubtfully. It was the first thing he'd said in hours; Jennifer couldn't remember his having said anything through dinner, either. Aching himself, maybe; he was carrying his shoulder high, and his head at an angle. ''There's a lot of dirt down in there.''

''We have plenty of water,'' Lialla said. ''Particularly if we don't have to share with the horses. Where's the next?''

Chris shrugged. The moon was westering, and now bright enough to show them up well—bright enough to play cards by, as Jennifer's grandfather would have said. ''There aren't a lot of things marked from here down. I'm pretty sure that hill we went by is Hat Mound; there isn't much else it *can* be. Which puts us not quite halfway to where we're going.''

''Not quite halfway.'' Lialla sighed, but when Aletto scowled in her direction she shook her head. ''Nothing. We're making pretty fair time, actually, considering the land we're riding across.''

''There's a regular water stop on the west side of Hat Mound,'' Chris said. ''But Edrith and Aletto and I—we thought it would be dumb of us to go there, so close to the road and after last night. This wasn't a sure thing, but like you said, we were pretty

113

full up, so it wouldn't have been a disaster if the hole had been completely dry. Tomorrow—we can move around this one-sided barrier to stay out of the sun, I guess; there isn't a lot of shelter but at least there's a little. The next water, I'm afraid we're either going to have to head across to the road, or up into the western hills.'' He gestured, realized his hand was swinging toward the cactus wall and yanked it back. ''Watch that thing; if none of you have picked up spines before, they hurt like nothing else in this world, and some of them are ugly to get out. Anyway, you can tell by the cactus, and what we rode through the past hour or so. We're heading downhill and away from even the sagebrush stuff. According to the map there's a lot of sand due south of here and not much else, for at least two days. Maybe more. I'm gonna strangle the guy who made this map,'' Chris added dispassionately. ''Because I swear he had less sense of distance than—well, he didn't have any.''

''The sand is the Great Sink,'' Aletto said. ''It's in books, even in Zelharri; there were nomads and camels there, years ago. They say it's deserted now except for animals that can take the dry and the heat. Snakes, maybe. You don't cross it on horses.'' He sounded stiff, unfriendly—the way he had that first morning. *Hurting again or just in a bad mood*, Jennifer thought. She didn't feel like asking him just at the moment; *she* hurt, she was deathly tired suddenly, and she wasn't in much of a good mood herself. At least he wasn't spilling his mood all over them.

''No,'' Lialla agreed. If she caught the tightness in his voice, she was ignoring it too. ''So—hills or back to the road. The road is probably being watched, the hills would add days to our ride, and Jadek or the Sikkreni might assume we'd go that way, as against the easier way.''

''We can second-guess ourselves blind,'' Jennifer said. Her voice was rather muffled and a little strained; she was folded nearly in half, stretching out her back and kneading tight muscles in her thighs. ''Let's not bother. Sensible people would presume they're watching both ways, and probably the other side of the road, too—whatever it might be like. We use all our resources to watch for them, to fight them, if we have to.'' She came cautiously upright and extended her arms, twisting at the waist and wincing at the outside of each turn. ''We haven't done too badly so far, you know. That's no cause to get complacent, of course. But we don't need to shake in our boots, either.''

Lialla looked like she wanted to dispute some or all of this, but Aletto handed her the blanket and personal bags from her horse. ''She's right, you know.'' For a moment, he sounded almost friendly. "We did prove we can fight back, last night. We can do it again."

"You're right, of course," Lialla said. "And we can think about it tonight, talk about it tomorrow, can't we?" She smiled at her brother. But after he turned to lead the horse over to Edrith's tie line, she scowled at his back. He was limping badly again. When he came back, he had the bo in his left hand and he was leaning into it as he walked.

* * *

THE rest of the night was too short, the daylight hours hot, windy and horribly uncomfortable. Jennifer woke to find her lower body in full sun. Her jeans and the legs under them felt like they were about to burst into flame, and she rolled onto her side, yanking them up to her chest. But it wasn't much cooler in the shade; the constant wind was a blast furnace. She dug through her bag, found one of the black scarves and bundled the longest of her hair into a knot at the base of her neck, then wrapped the whole sweaty, sandy mess in the scarf. She could feel the skin of her hands and face being drained of moisture; lotion didn't help much, just gave the dirt something to cling to.

Despite their extreme caution, both Edrith and Lialla picked up cactus thorns. Robyn proved to be the best at getting them out with the least pain.

No one wanted anything to eat, not even Chris. Robyn finally broke out an oat cake and made a face at it but gamely bit off a corner and chewed. "You," she said. She had to raise her voice against the whine of wind through holes between cactus bulbs and the rattle of dry branches. She held up the oat cake. "All of you, pull one out and eat the damned thing, and wash it down with a good drink of water. You can't ride all night on an empty belly, and you'll be *real* sorry if you dehydrate. You trust me on this one, and you do it. I don't want to hear any argument, got it?"

"She's right," Jennifer said, before anyone could object to either the idea or Robyn's tone of voice. Though no one looked particularly capable of objection at the moment, not even Lialla. Jennifer unwrapped one of the crumbly rounds and broke off a piece. "Chris, you know what a nasty headache you get when you don't eat, and I'm not wasting any of my precious aspirins on stupidity."

"Nice to know you love me," he grumbled, but he sat up and pulled the bag he'd been using as a pillow from under his head before leaning over to tap Edrith on the shoulder. "Hey. Better dig out one of those horse-feed things, those oat cakes, before these guys come down on *you*. They're getting *adult* on us, you know? I mean, rully,'' he added to Jennifer, huffily, in English.

"Rully," Edrith echoed with equal indignation, as he worked at the knot holding his personal bag closed. Jennifer rather hastily dropped part of the oat cake on her blanket, between her knees, so she had to bend down to look for it. The constant whine of wind fortunately covered her giggles.

* * *

ALETTO spoke very little during the day; he slept or at least rested. He ate when bullied into it. But when Robyn rather timidly offered to rub him down, he sighed loudly and shook his head. "Why bother?" Before she could reply, he fought his way to his feet and went over to the horses. The limp was at least as pronounced as it had been the night before.

"What did I say?" Robyn asked of no one in particular. Chris shook his head.

"Don't sweat it, Ma. Did you see him against those guys? I mean, it really was a great idea he had, using the horse to reinforce the moves. I'm gonna do that myself, if I ever have to. But he was partway out of the saddle for a long time, I mean, like, *crouching* over that horse. It makes *my* thigh muscles scream just thinking about it, and I'm in halfway decent shape; imagine what *he* feels like. And I'll bet you his hands are at least as sore as mine, just from absorbing the counterblows they were dealing; those guys weren't exactly pulling their punches like we did for each other." Chris glanced over to the horse line, lowered his voice as Aletto started back, bo clutched in his left hand to ease the swing of his walk. "Bet you anything he hurts something awful and he thinks he's the only one because he's so damned egocentric."

"Don't swear, kid," Robyn said, and Chris, as predictably, replied, "Damn isn't swearing, Ma. Listen, trust us on this one, will you?" Aletto came back into earshot moments later and Chris flexed his hands and groaned. "God. They don't want to go flat, you notice that, Edrith?"

"My hands are just fine, it's my forearms," Edrith replied gloomily. "I probably use my fingers a lot more than you do."

"Yeah," Chris retorted. "That's living the clean life, I don't use my hands the way *you* use yours!" The conversation between them moved on to other things, came back to aching muscle later. Aletto lay down on his blanket, in shade, eyes closed and apparently paid no attention to them. But some of the tension seemed to leave him, and late in the afternoon when Robyn sat down next to him once again, he didn't object when she began massaging his bad leg.

* * *

THE horses were saddled, loaded and ready to go when the sun dropped behind the mountains. They turned their backs on it, on the now even more strongly gusting wind, and began riding south and east, on a course that would bring them to the Bez Road somewhere around midnight. After that, they would be able to decide whether to stick with the road itself, or to parallel it from one side or the other. Lialla had suggested as much, late in the afternoon, and no one had argued with her. None of them liked the look of the gray-brown foothills to the west, particularly with water so chancy and with the Sink stretching southward between the road and the hills.

Jennifer found herself increasingly nervous as the night wore on, but even when she walked and tested Thread, she could find no physical cause. She dismissed any notion of sixth sense or other foreshadowing as nonsense, and finally put it down to their near-disastrous experience the last time they'd gone for the road—it sounded better, at least, than Chris's smart-mouthed suggestion of "girl-nerves"—a suggestion deliberately calculated, if she knew Chris, to play on her feminist-sensitive outrage and to make her stop worrying. It worked, to an extent. Besides, she told herself, Jadek couldn't possibly have men stationed all the way down this road; even the Thukars couldn't have that many to spare. It might not be paranoia if they really were after you, but that didn't mean they always were, after all.

She finally remounted and edged forward to join Lialla, who now led. "About Hell-Light," she began. "What do you know—fact, rumor, anything at all?"

Lialla sighed faintly, shook her head. "Less than about Thread. Some rumor, more folk tale, though, and it's little or none of it capable of being proved. You want that?"

"Anything," Jennifer assured her.

"Mmmm. Well. I already told you, it's old but not as old as Thread. Thread was—I don't know, found? Already there, and people who were adept found it, and discovered how to work it. Hell-Light was one of the created magics, and—" She paused, as if to choose her words. Shook her head, hard. "I'm trying to be fair."

"I appreciate that."

Lialla eyed her sidelong, apparently searching for sign of sarcasm and finding none. "Good. Hell-Light is evil, it kills."

"You're certain of that?"

"Of that last? It killed my father, horribly. I'll never forget the last time they let me see him, how he looked. That wasn't the last anyone saw of him, though. It kills," Lialla repeated flatly. "But, I—in fairness, I'm trying, I swear it. I am simply not certain of anything, any more. The only uses I know for Hell-Light, the only uses anyone ever made of it, *are* evil. Those in Zelharri histories, the ones my tutor made me study, name it as evil. But—I don't know!" She sighed loudly and was silent for a while. "If that man of the Thukars told you what you told me—then it can't *all* simply kill the person who goes into it; that much is very obvious. There has to be a way to use it as transport, or to use it with magic that utilizes charms or spells that can create transport. I've heard of it via tales, but no one *ever* suggested to me it was possible in the real world, to go from place to place like that." Lialla sighed. "It would be nice, wouldn't it? Getting out of this desert without riding out of it? I never thought I'd be tired of riding and horses, and"—she lowered her voice cautiously—"I am becoming bored with trying to keep Aletto happy. We should have gone the road, it would have been easier and faster. Instead—" She shrugged.

"Maybe there are penalties to pay for that kind of travel," Jennifer said finally. "The kind of penalty that—maybe that's why Merrida never told you about it, if it exists. I have to admit, it didn't look safe to *me*, and the man using it looked like it was only as the least of two dangers. Robyn—" It was her turn to sigh and fall silent.

"I know," Lialla said. "It's a wonder we kept that from Aletto at all, but I find myself a little angry we need to."

"Perhaps we don't, and only Robyn doesn't know it," Jennifer said somberly. "I have an uncomfortable sense we'll learn all too soon."

"I have a fear you're right," Lialla returned glumly. "About the travel. Remember it. If we can find a Wielder in Bez, like you suggested, perhaps we can learn more. Merrida *might* have known. There might even be Thread that controls it, but she never told me. She's like that, you know."

"I got that feeling from our one meeting."

"It's part of the sorcery for her, you know," Lialla said, a little defensively. "The mystery. The less noninitiates know, the more important she looks." She shook her head. "That's so stupid, it can't make sense."

"It doesn't," Jennifer assured her. "But that doesn't mean it doesn't happen; people in our world do the same thing, whatever their profession is. Hell-Light, though—is there anything—anything at all else—you know about it?''

''Nothing,'' Lialla said after a moment's thought. ''It's evil—I still believe that; what I saw last night was as foul as anything I've ever encountered in Zelharri. But I felt no desire to explore that hut myself, before or after the Light went out of it.''

''No.'' Jennifer nodded agreement, and decided to keep her odd discovery to herself. Anything to maintain this rare cooperation between them, and Lialla's even more rare openmindedness. Besides, she wanted a better opportunity to study what she'd seen and felt before she passed anything on.

Lialla went on, following her own train of thought. ''Wielders have to *use* Thread, to handle it—you know that, you have to touch it to work it. They say a Light Shaper, particularly a Triad, can function at a certain distance, though it weakens the use.''

''So you can have a single person to Shape—''

''Or a Triad. They say a Triad functions like—the way one very strong person might, not as three individuals. I don't know that, either, though rumor makes the individuals of a Triad extremely strange—not individual beings at all, any more. Hell-Light, they say, is visual magic, not primarily tactile. But the spells are best worked if they can touch and see what they're Shaping, it's said; they're still strong if the Triad can see but it's not in reach. If it's out of sight, that depends: Supposedly you could Shape Light from here to where the road is and still have a tight spell, but at any great distance, you need spell devices of some kind. If you're right about that man, if Robyn heard him right, then the Thukars' men had some kind of device with them, and once they found us, one of them took the device and went into one of the deserted buildings with it. I know other kinds of magic use devices that way, at least, to set spells over distance. The Thukar's magician Snake—he was apprenticed to one of old Dahmec's best wizards—I would wager *he* could have created the Moebius spell: It's a nasty one.''

''I'm convinced. Just as well we don't have to worry about him any more,'' Jennifer said.

''So it is. Anyway, I warned you, I really don't know anything about Light, except it killed Father. And—honestly, it may not be evil of itself, but I've never heard of *any* use for it that isn't evil. Anything anyone ever did with it is evil; I think someone would have said if there was another way to Shape it, wouldn't they?''

''I don't know,'' Jennifer said honestly. ''If we can find out, so much the better, don't you think? But thank you. What you've told me tells me more than I knew before.'' She dropped back to think over what Lialla had told her. It was almost less than nothing; it tantalized. *Damn*, she thought, and could only hope that teasing desire to know was her own curiosity kicking in and not Hell-Light drawing her from that one too-close contact. Unfortunately, like everything else, she didn't *know*.

* * *

IT was late night once more when they were attacked. There were only five men, this time, but three of them had been in that deserted village two nights before and they were all ready for a fight, prepared for a company of six who would fight against them. Unfortunately for them, at least Aletto and Edrith were spoiling for a fight, too. And Jennifer had been able to give them advance warning: She'd felt the jangle of Thread while they were riding, and had insisted Chris—who was now in the lead—slow down so she could slide off her horse and properly search.

This time, fortunately, there was no strange and unnerving Moebius spell to loop them over and over through the same terrain, but as flat and featureless as the land around them was, it would have been hard to tell anyway. As the five rode for them, Chris yelled a terse order: He and Edrith moved with swift precision to put Robyn between them, with Aletto on her right. Jennifer and Lialla wheeled to take on the man who split off and tried to come up behind them; Jennifer's staff distracted him long enough for the smoothed end of Lialla's to catch him square on the temple and send him flying. One of the others was already down, Aletto engaged a second and the two women came back to attack one of the two who were backing Edrith away from Robyn. Robyn had her staff in one hand but anyone could see at once she was afraid to use it.

It was over quickly; four men down. The fifth turned and spurred his horse toward the road, and Chris went after him. Robyn's shout reached him; he waved a hand that was probably meant for reassurance but didn't try to turn to yell back at her. At a dead-out run, it would probably have been a mistake. Jennifer sought Thread, backed out of it immediately and threw herself into the saddle. ''Wait,'' she ordered. ''Something odd out there; it might be more men, a trap.''

She could see Chris a little ways ahead of her, pale arms standing out from the dark of his clothing and horse. Beyond him, another shadow that was the fifth enemy horseman. As far as she could tell from the deceptively bright moonlight, Chris was gaining on him. She gritted her teeth, leaned forward and kicked her horse in the belly. The ground flew beneath its feet

120

and she tried not to think about falling off. She drew a deep breath. "Chris, come back—!" The wind of her passage blew the words away. *Louder*, she thought, and dragged in another deep breath. And stared before her. Her horse slowed, turned sideways and danced off nervously.

Moonlight shone coldly down on a barren, flat landscape. There was Chris, still ahead of her. He'd reined in and was staring about in surprise; she thought he swore aloud. Apparently he too saw no sign of the man he had been chasing.

There was nothing between them but a discordant clangor of Thread that nearly unseated her, but her horse balked, and when she dismounted and started forward on foot, dragging at the unwilling beast, she discovered why: There was a wall there, invisible but otherwise very real. Somehow it had let Chris through, but it stopped her cold.

10

J ENNIFER took a step back, rubbing her left shoulder and swearing under her breath. It surely felt real, whatever it was. Chris—she could still see him, now riding slowly in a circle, peering all around him. There wasn't anything out there big enough to hide a lizard, let alone a grown man on a horse. There *was* a line of scrub brush marking the far side of a shallow ravine, but it was simply too far away for the man to have reached; he'd only appeared to be a few paces ahead of Chris when he vanished. Jennifer swore again and put out a tentative hand. Maybe if she got back on this rotten animal and found a way *around* the barrier. . . .

Her hand touched something thick, smooth, pulsing; when she tried to snatch it back the thing opened, costing her her balance. She stumbled forward; the horse pulled free and wheeled away, galloping back the way they'd come. *Typical*, she thought sourly, and paid no further attention to it, other than to call it an extremely obscene name.

It couldn't have heard her, even if it hadn't been a hundred yards away already, she didn't think. At least, *she* couldn't hear anything from the outside world: the insects, the occasional nightbird, the gusts of wind that had rattled dry weed and grass or whined through their clothes and the horses' tack. She sensed rather than felt that opening seal itself behind her, and she took an involuntary step forward. It reminded her of tide-pool creatures, the sea anemones she'd touched as a child: thick, smooth, clinging—a little sticky on the inside, holding onto its prey.

That wasn't a good thing to think, in *her* position. "Knock it off, Cray," she told herself firmly.

The outside world was fading as the thing that held her began to opaque from a spot overhead. She sought Thread and found to her surprise it still responded; for a moment, it even held back the fog that was beginning to enclose her. *Don't think enclose*, she told herself even more firmly. A good dose of claustrophobia was the last thing she needed just now.

There was no sign of anyone else near to hand, no one else within this—place. She could still, just, make out her party, enough to see that Lialla had her lousy horse by the reins. Well, that was a piece of luck. What few things she had were on its back and she'd really *resent* losing her cross-trainers. Resent it enough to do something drastic about it. *I wonder how the rulers of Sikkre and Zelharri would like to die for a spare pair of socks,* she thought grimly. Robyn was staring after her, radiating worry. But she was—all of them were—getting harder to see, as though moonlight shone on dirty glass. She spun around to look out in the other direction. Chris seemed to have given up on the immediate area and now rode toward the line of brush, the only shelter where anyone might be hiding. Jennifer had only the briefest impression of the men who came out of shadow: clad in dark, flowing garb that covered even their lower faces, dark camels. Chris was surrounded. She caught a last glimpse of his blond head and the flailing bo before the trap that held her hazed over.

"Goddamn it!" She strode forward, slammed into the opposite wall almost at once. How long, she wondered as she turned back to survey the inside of the trap, before Lialla realized where she was? And would she be able to do anything about it?

Can I? The silence was unnerving. She could see Thread, but only with effort; there was little color to it and less sound. Impossible to tell which to touch—even if she knew which of it might free her from this thing. *If this is what Lialla sees, no wonder she can't work it very well.* She gave it up, folded her arms across her chest and brought her chin up. The Cray temper was trying to take the upper hand; she'd better not let it. "All right. I know you're there, say whatever you have to say."

Silence. Had she misjudged? Whoever had rigged the trap had to be studying her; those nasty twins would certainly do so, and from what she'd heard of Jadek, so would he. Then again, this thing might be designed to transport her or simply frighten— even kill. *God. Maybe I did misjudge.* But a yellow light was forming in the center of her spherical prison. She had the impression of presence; then she could see eyes, nothing more. Dark, chill eyes. "Is that the best you can do?" she demanded crisply. "If it's intended to scare me silly, I've seen worse in movies."

A dry, humorless laugh answered her; a little more definition, then—the sense of a head with a thick fall of dark hair, heavy brows. Shoulders clad in something silky. "My poor old friend Dahmec told me you were fearless. One of the last things he told me, before his son removed him from his seat—*and* his life." He paused, perhaps to gauge her reaction. She gave him none. "Well. I am glad to see you are a sensible woman, and it is a pleasure to deal with an intelligent and beauteous one." He paused again, this time awaiting a response.

Jennifer shook her head. She wouldn't have been fooled by his heavy-handed style anyway, and she was too angry to accept it now. "If that was a compliment, you can save it. I ordinarily consider the source when I hear such things, and in your case I fear it's empty flattery. If you have a point for all this, I should like to hear it, please."

"Yes. Well. You've heard one side only of a certain story; I should like to tell you the other. An advocate should have both sides of a story before weighing them, shouldn't she?" Again silence; Jadek apparently waiting once again for her to protest angrily. Once more she waited him out. "My niece is unstable and hysterical, my nephew physically unsound and emotionally dependent on drink."

"So I've heard," Jennifer said calmly. "They seem to do fairly well away from your influences."

"I knew you'd heard only one side," Jadek replied. "I helped their mother raise them, you know. I feel responsible knowing I somehow failed them both—"

He stopped abruptly. Jennifer was laughing. "Look," she said finally, and the laughter was still in her voice. "Please, spare me the rhetoric, will you? Do you think you're the only child abuser to be found out? If you want to talk, let's find another subject, shall we? Because if you hope to win me over to your side on *this* particular issue, it won't happen. Where I come from, there are too many people like you, and they all defend themselves just the way you're trying to defend yourself. Let it drop. I'm not interested in hearing it again, just because the rank is different and so is the language.''

''All right,'' he said crisply. ''A bargain, then.''

''Now we come to it. What do you plan to offer me, and for what?''

''Your lives—''

''Something better than that. This is a hard world, Jadek. Anything might take our lives in the next few hours, not necessarily caused by you, or preventable by you.''

''Your lives in your own world, then.''

''Taking into account the difference in how time passes, here and there?'' Jennifer shook her head. ''There is no way for you to prove either thing is possible, is there? Particularly not with you wherever you are, and us here. Personally, I don't care to trust your word that you can.''

''Let that go for now, then. But don't forget that I offered such a thing, woman. The offer was genuine, and will remain so. Whatever you have seen of this world, or heard of me, men don't readily take lives here, the Emperor frowns on his Dukes setting themselves up as petty despots, and personally I dislike killing.'' *At least directly,* Jennifer thought sourly. ''That doesn't mean there aren't ways around the central government in Podhru, or that I won't kill all three of you, if I must. However. It was the old woman who brought you, wasn't it?'' Jennifer shrugged. ''I've known all along she was a Wielder, of course; she left it alone for long enough that I ignored her. Perhaps she and I should talk—but that has nothing to do with you, has it?''

''I thought you wanted to talk to me. There's no old woman in my pocket.''

He laughed. ''Oh, very good. I like that. But I was saying: A Triad has certain powers not held by other users of magic, certainly not by Wielders of Night-Thread—if you came by those Wielder blacks you wore to Dahmec's table honestly, you'll be aware Thread has limits, or you'll surely become aware. If you're foolish enough to remain here, and lucky enough to survive to Wield it. All the same, it is possible to Shape a portal and to shift you into the proper time. Don't take my word for it, however—''

''I certainly don't intend to.''

''Do not interrupt me!''

Jennifer laughed again. ''Why? Because you're noble and I'm not, or because you'll strike *me*?'' She sensed rather than heard his exasperated sigh. "Go on. I'll hear you out, if it means so much to you."

"Find those in Bez who know Light—there are a few sole Shapers attached to various households—and ask. The offer will remain open, if you wish it. In exchange, you will leave my misguided young kin." Silence.

"Speaking of your young kin, they'll be wondering out there where I am," Jennifer said finally. "Doesn't that worry—I'm sorry—*concern* you?"

Jadek's laugh rang in the hollow sphere. "Why? Will Lialla use her pitiful magic and spring you free?"

"She's not so pitiful as all that, away from your kind attentions."

"Time is moving differently in here; that's the need for the shading. They'll barely notice you've been gone. I see you aren't mad to return to your own world."

"Say, I'm not leaping to an uncertain chance offered by a man who isn't known for completing contracts of honor. Such as giving up Zelharri on his nephew's twenty-fifth birthday?"

"That is nothing to do with you—!"

"Oh, no? It's only the—never mind. I'm certainly not prepared to argue that just now, with you or anyone else. Say, if you choose, that I'm waiting to hear the alternatives you have to offer."

"Very well." Jadek had faded to eyes once more. *Taking its toll on him*, Jennifer thought, and filed the thought for later. "Consider this as an alternative, then: The life of the golden-haired young man, in exchange for which you, the shapeshifter and the boy will leave the nera-Duke and the sin-Duchess. I will arrange a place and time with you for an exchange."

"I see. You have the boy, have you? So many people claim to have had him, and to date no one has. I'm not certain I believe you do, either."

"The man he went after was my man; he wore a transference stone and when the boy caught him just now, he pinned the brooch to the boy's saddle. You won't see him again unless I choose that you do."

"I see." Jennifer considered for one brief, frightening moment that he might actually be telling the truth this time. She finally rejected that; Jadek seemed unaware she'd been able to see out of the trap for some moments before it opaqued. He certainly didn't mention dark men on dark camels. "Let me see him or hear him."

"No. If I feel later you've earned that right—"

"No," Jennifer cut him off sharply. "Either I know here and now that you have him alive and well—unhurt in *any* fashion—or there's no bargain."

"There is a bargain on my terms or none!" Jadek shouted furiously. Jennifer bit back the least of smiles. The man didn't have Chris. She could worry later—if there *was* a later for her—about what had happened out there by that dry wash.

She wasn't particularly worried about herself, either, though. Perhaps because there was nothing about this trap that suggested it could be used the way the shed two nights ago had been used. Mostly because she couldn't see why Jadek would continue to try and bribe an uppity outlander woman if he could strike her down and be rid of her for good.

After all, despite what he had said earlier, who would complain—to the Emperor or anyone else—about a missing outlander or two? And to what point? And having spoken to him now, she didn't doubt for one minute he'd kill. That combination of practical and egocentric would make it easy for him to both commit murder and justify it to himself.

"Come," Jadek said persuasively. "It's foolish to set yourself on the wrong side of an issue, particularly in a land like ours. As you say, it's a hard one, and punishment for those who lose is not pretty, or pleasant. Aletto is simply unfit to rule. There is no cure for marsh-sickness or for the injury it gave him. It affects the brain as well, you know."

"I didn't know. Go on."

"He's not as enfeebled as some but he's not in full possession of his wits. Test him, if you don't trust me. You'll see he's incapable of the kind of thought and planning a Duke needs. As for Lialla—she is weak and hysterical; she imagines things and thinks everyone against her. I'm certain you'll have discovered that long since, though. She certainly has no control over her temper or her hysteria. Poor little girl has been that way for years, you know. Would you believe it, she tried repeatedly to spread the rumor that certain of my men were touching her, that my secretaries trapped her in empty rooms. That one of the cooks fondled her." He paused briefly. "You need not believe that, of course; I merely repeat some of the more astonishing tales she told at various times."

"I know nothing about any of that," Jennifer said calmly. "I don't form opinions on a complete lack of data, or only one side of the data. Go on."

"As you please. The Emperor has been satisfied with the job I've done, caring for my poor brother's lands. I fail to see why

126

he would choose to take them from my stewardship and pass them to a boy unready and unfit to take the same care of them.''

"Perhaps because they are his by birthright?" Jennifer asked. "And if he's unfit—wasn't it your task to ready him to rule?"

"I did my best with the boy," Jadek snarled. "As for the girl, if she'd wed the man I chose for her—" He paused, and when he went on he'd shed the anger. "Yes. Well. Poor cousin Carolan, he was devoted to her. He's dead, you know. They might not have told you they killed two men, one noble, when they left Duke's Fort. However things fall in your world, it is against the laws anywhere in Rhadaz to murder, and there are harsh penalties for murdering the gentry. You may tell Lialla and Aletto there has been an inquiry from Podhru about the death of my cousin Carolan. I of course have said nothing about their part in it—either to the Emperor's men or to their mother, by the way—and whatever is so far suspected, there have been no warrants of arrest issued.''

"How very kind of you to still look out for them," Jennifer said dryly.

"Arrogant woman. Be still! I see that it's foolish to talk with you at all. Your emotions put you on their side, whatever your intelligence tries to tell you. Tell my brash young kin," Jadek went on smoothly, "since you seem as immune to sensible behavior as they, that there will be another heir in Duke's Fort. The Duchess Lizelle's unfortunate barrenness has been cured, and she now carries my child. Tell them that, from me. Once she bears me a son—but even Aletto can work out the logic of that, don't you think?" He laughed, one brief chuckle, and all sense of him vanished from the sphere. Half a breath later, the sphere itself dissolved. Where it had been were the withered remains of a man, nothing about him recognizable save the clothing and the silver brooch. Jadek had used his man to set the trap and had ruthlessly drained everything from him to keep it active.

Jennifer sat down, hard, and let her head fall forward. She wasn't going to be sick, she wasn't going to pass out. She hoped.

It was a near thing. She finally shifted, turned herself around so she didn't have to look at the mummylike *thing* sprawled on the ground. That helped; now she was simply dizzy, something that might have been an effect of dealing coolly with a slick customer like Jadek. *I thought Dahmec was bad; at least he wasn't out to actively raise hell.* Now that it was over, she wondered if she'd handled him right; if she'd given anything away. She didn't think she had, but for a moment, she had to close her eyes and grip the ground, until she could breathe normally. When she opened her eyes once again, there was only a clear *one* of everything, not doubles, and things stayed where they belonged.

That, of course, might not be nerves—*Chicken-shittedness*, Jennifer amended to herself, and Robyn's pet phrase brought up a faint grin. "Maybe it's not futzed nerves," she said aloud. Her voice was steady, at least. It might have been reaction to Jadek's magic, to that sphere or perhaps the time shift. Jadek apparently hadn't lied about the time shift: When she looked up, Lialla was winding the extra length of her horse's reins around her hand and keeping watch, turning her own horse so she could see all around them. Aletto was just standing up from binding the fallen man. Robyn was still peering uncertainly eastward.

Robyn saw her first and spurred toward her. Jennifer scrambled hastily to her feet to avoid being run down as her sister practically fell from the saddle and snatched at her shoulders, hard. "God! For a minute I couldn't see you, like there was a fog or something! Was I seeing things? Are you all right? What were you doing on the ground? And *where's Chris*?"

"I'm fine, let's talk about it later, all right? As for Chris—" She turned and pointed toward the black line of shadow that marked the brush. It didn't look as far as it had before—spell or moonlight. "Ow, Birdy, loosen up, will you?"

"Oh. Sorry. He's over there? But I can't see him—!"

Aletto caught up with them a moment later. Edrith was right behind him, swaying and clutching at the saddlebow. His face was unnaturally white, his eyes half-closed. Lialla brought Jennifer her horse, held it so she could mount.

Aletto glanced over his shoulder. "What about the man we took?" he asked.

"Leave him, we'll come back," Lialla said. "Where did you go, Jen, and where's Chris? And—gods, what's *that*?" She pointed a shaking hand at the dead man.

Jennifer shook her head, mounted and turned her horse's nose east. "Worry about him later, all right? He's not going anywhere. Chris, on the other hand—" She pointed toward the brush. "I saw him over there, and he wasn't alone." She held out a warning arm as Robyn would have passed her. "Birdy, you stay right with one of us; you looked like a damned victim out there! No wonder they keep trying to grab you!"

"Well, sorry!" Robyn huffed and dragged her horse back. Aletto touched her shoulder and set a pace to match hers.

Jennifer winced as her backside touched the saddle; apparently she'd sat harder than she thought. She pointed again. "That streambed. He lost the man who's back there, somehow. Apparently he thought the guy made shelter.''

"Then where is he?" Robyn asked faintly. She stood in the stirrups. "I don't see him!"

Jennifer dismounted short of where she thought she'd last seen her nephew and held up a warning hand. "Stay put. There are prints here, where the dirt's soft. I'd like to get a look at them before you ride all over them."

"Excellent idea," Lialla said. She dismounted, took hold of the horses—hers, Jennifer's and Edrith's—and led them a few paces away. "Edrith, you said once you knew prints. Do you think you could—are you all right?" she added rather sharply as she looked up at him.

"My head hurts—never mind that, I'm fine. Where's Chris?" He threw a leg forward and slid to the ground, wincing as his feet hit.

"We're trying to discover," Lialla said. "Didn't you see him go?"

"I—yeah. Sure. Something got between us, though, lost sight of him."

"He was over here," Jennifer said grimly as Robyn and Aletto dismounted. "Back a little, Birdy, all right? He's not here. Somebody grabbed him, several somebodies."

"Oh, Jesus," Robyn breathed. She stood very still, didn't even seem to notice when Aletto came up to stand behind her and take hold of her shoulders. "Where is he, Jennifer? I—that fog thing, is that it?"

"No. Save that for later; it's nothing to do with Chris. That was Jadek, but Jadek didn't take Chris." Edrith edged forward, used Lialla's arm to let himself down to his knees. He peered uncertainly at the disturbed ground. Jennifer described what she'd seen—or thought she'd seen. Lialla considered this in silence for some moments as Edrith tried to move himself so he wasn't casting a shadow across the prints he was trying to study.

"Cholan nomads," Lialla said finally. She sounded doubtful. "At least, there *used* to be Cholan nomads in the southwest deserts. They lived around the Sink and where it now is, before things dried out."

"Edrith?" Robyn asked fearfully. He shook his head, clapped a hand to it and held it still.

"I can't see very much here, the moon isn't as good a light as it might be. Camel prints—there were camels here. I could tell more if I could *see*."

129

"I can't make a blue light," Lialla said. "It needs a container and time—it would be almost daylight by the time I fixed it."

"Wait," Jennifer told him. She ran back to her horse, found the leather bag and fished through it. The spare keychain was still hooked to the shoulder strap, the tiny flashlight still hooked to it. She flashed it once experimentally; it wouldn't last long, the things didn't, but it was still fairly bright. She rezipped the bag and took the little flash back with her. "Here. Push that. Use it as sparingly as you can."

Edrith did, and for one brief moment he managed a pleased grin. It faded quickly; he really did look awful in the brighter light. "Hey. Chris told me about your lights. Neat-o." He let go of his head, leaned forward onto that hand and played the flash over the ground for several long moments. Robyn's light, panting breathing was the only sound until Edrith sat back and groaned. "There were six of them at least. All camels. How did you say they looked?" Jennifer told him. "Sounds like nomads to me. Sometimes you see them in Sikkre, always a tight little pack of them, on foot—it's said they're afraid the city folk will steal their mounts, so they leave them outside the walls with an enormous guard. You never see one alone, or even just two or three together. They're considered cowards; they probably think it's caution." He frowned. "Why would they come after us? I mean, I can see them taking *one* of us, if there were a lot of them, but why come after us in the first place?"

"Ransom?" Lialla suggested.

"Oh, God, Chris," Robyn whispered. Aletto leaned forward and murmured something to her. She shook her head frantically.

"Anything is possible," Jennifer said. "I wonder why they'd think we looked like we could *pay* a ransom."

"We'll get him back," Edrith said. He pushed up onto his knees and groaned. Jennifer held out a hand and pulled him upright. He handed her the flashlight and gave her a faint, rueful grin. "I got a little too smart with my staff; one of the guys who ran clipped me with the hilt of his sword. Right there." He pointed, carefully keeping the hand away from the left side of the forehead, just above the hairline. "Makes me feel sick whenever I move too fast and, man, it hurts!"

"Dizzy?" Jennifer asked him. When he nodded cautiously, she said, "That's the mix of your language and *our* slang, probably. Seriously, you probably have a concussion. Hold still." She shone the flashlight in his eyes briefly. "Your pupils are the same size, so it's not bad, just painful. I know, I did that once. Can you live with it for a little while?"

"Get Chris first, if you can," Edrith said flatly. "I can live with it."

* * *

ROBYN had pulled out of Aletto's grasp and was forcing her way through the bushes, calling her son's name in a low, desperate voice. Lialla skirted the brush where the prints were, moved away from them all and closed her eyes. Jennifer felt the preliminary jangle of Thread against her back teeth and began humming. She walked back past the horses, began looking along the dry wash, using the flashlight to check for footprints—human *or* camel. There was nothing back this way. When she found a way through the brush onto the east side of the wash, she discovered another tight clutch of prints: mostly camel, one set of very square-toed boots. Apparently the nomads had waited here.

How had they known to do that? If they'd been camped here and taken what looked like a lucky chance for money, she could understand that, but there was no sign of any camp, just men waiting in a desert landscape otherwise devoid of humans. It bore thinking about.

In the meantime, though, she sighed, turned off the little flashlight and went back to hook it to the handle of her shoulder bag once more. Chris was absolutely not here. She didn't look forward to breaking that news to Robyn.

* * *

ROBYN had already come to that conclusion herself. She sat where Edrith had, staring down at the patch of hoofprints, silently crying. Aletto knelt just behind her, one hand on her heaving shoulders, visibly uncertain what he should say or do. "Robyn," he said finally. "There wasn't anything you could have done."

"There was." Robyn's voice was muffled by her hands. She ran one of them under her nose and sniffed loudly. "I could have—I could have stopped him from going after that guy."

"How? He was gone before anyone could have said anything. You don't think he'd have stopped if you'd yelled for him, do you?"

"He—I don't know," Robyn mumbled.

"There wasn't anything you could have done. And if you'd been with him, they'd have taken you both."

"No." Robyn shook her head fiercely and slewed around to face him. "I could have stopped him—I could have stopped them, if I'd just done it and not worried about—"

"How?" Aletto was beginning to sound exasperated. "You

haven't much strength in your arms, you don't use the staff, you couldn't bear to help me tie up an unconscious man—!''

"I could have!" Robyn shouted. "And I didn't because I was afraid what *you'd* think when I—" She spun to her feet and shifted, alarmingly, from human to bird, back again almost at once. Aletto fell back from her, lost his footing, dropped heavily to his knees. His face was white, his eyes wide. His mouth twisted. Robyn, human again, stared down at him and her face was as pale as his. "You see? The look on your face! I knew you'd be that disgusted, and I *liked* you and I didn't want you to hate me! And I let them take my kid instead—oh, *God*!" She turned, eluded her sister's outflung arm and ran back the way they'd come.

Aletto pushed himself slowly back to his feet. "I didn't know," he said dazedly. "Was that what—is that how she escaped the Thukar's man? How she got free in Sikkre?"

"I'm sorry," Jennifer said. "We tried to keep it from you. No," she added hastily as he took a tentative step in Robyn's direction. "Let me—"

"No." Aletto took hold of her wrist and set her hand aside. Robyn sat in the open, near where they'd fought, back to them, head down. "I—this time, I can't let you. If we're to understand each other, she and I, we have to talk. Shapeshifter," he said blankly. "I—gods. Poor Robyn." He started back after her, walking with a noticeable limp but with determination. As he closed the distance between them, his pace slowed.

Lialla came up beside Jennifer. "I don't know if he can convince her," she said. "He's had a thing about shapeshifters since he was a boy; I don't know if it was an experience in Sikkre the time he and Dahven snuck out, if it was before that, Duke's Fort—he's been like that about them as long as I can remember."

"I think he's willing to try," Jennifer said.

"Oh, of course. Because it's Robyn. I hope she can meet him partway, though. Traveling with a mess like *that* in our midst won't be pleasant at all." She continued gazing after her brother, who now knelt beside Robyn. Robyn turned a little, keeping her back to him. "Gods. You realize," she went on crisply, "that someone—Jadek or the twins, I can't think of them as Sikkre's rulers—might have paid Cholan nomads to track us and capture or kill anyone who got separated from the rest?"

"Possible," Jennifer said. "We'd better not do that any more, then, had we? Will we get a visit or a note asking for money, if it's simple ransom?"

Lialla shook her head. "They don't speak Rhadazi, or in the stories I've heard, none of them do. They have no written language, either. Does Chris—he writes, he wrote on the maps."

"Chris writes," Jennifer said. "It's common, where we're from."

"Oh." Lialla turned her attention to the open ground where Jadek's sphere had been, to the flat, once-human shape. "That man. The one Chris was after?" Jennifer nodded. "What did that to him? And what was wrong out here?"

Jennifer told her about the sphere. Lialla stared down at the dead man. "I don't know about *any* of this. Time-shifts. We *have* to find some answers."

"Bezjeriad," Jennifer said. "We will."

"It *was* Jadek, wasn't it?" Lialla sounded almost too calm. Jennifer nodded. "What did he say?"

"That you and your brother aren't good for much, that the Emperor won't listen to you. That there's been an inquiry from—Podhru, is it?—to Duke's Fort, over the deaths the night you left. He *says* he hasn't told them you were responsible."

"No," Lialla said faintly. "He wouldn't. He'd hint, and wring his hands, and worry about his missing, foolish young stepchildren, and let them draw their own conclusions." She sighed heavily. "We won't dare go to the Emperor now, you know. Or anyone in the central government. They'd simply hold us at best, or—well, I won't think about the worst."

"Don't."

"This man, though—" Lialla stared down at the remains dispassionately. "They could blame *this* on us, too, you know. It—somehow, we might be able to prove Aletto was justified in killing Carolan, we might be able to get someone to listen to our side of the story. This—it could—Jadek could use it to bolster his position that Aletto's not safe outside his rooms. If it's tied to us."

"We can do something about that," Jennifer said. "I saw your brother tying one of those assassins; is he still there?"

Lialla peered across the open, finally nodded and pointed. "There."

"Let's get him over here, then." Jennifer dusted her hands together. "Let's show him what he's siding with, and the kind of value Jadek puts on men."

11

ROBYN was still sitting on a patch of bare ground, knees drawn up, head buried in her arms. Aletto knelt just behind her, talking in a low, urgent voice. Jennifer couldn't tell what he was saying or if Robyn was listening. She didn't seem to be crying as hard, though. As the women walked by, Aletto turned and looked up at them. "What are you doing now?" He sounded exasperated; taking out some of the frustration he felt toward Birdy on his sister, Jennifer thought. Or toward the situation in general and his inability to cure it.

Lialla nodded in the direction of the bound, and now awake, man in their uncle's colors. "Want to help us talk to him?"

"Why?" Aletto demanded sourly. "You think that will help anyone?" But he patted Robyn's shoulder awkwardly and got to his feet. She touched his hand, sniffed loudly. They couldn't see her face; Aletto's was still very troubled indeed. He looked over at Jadek's man. "Give me a moment, will you? Before I do something—wait." They waited. Aletto ran a hand through his hair, briefly buried his face in it. When he looked up again, he was nearly expressionless. He squared his shoulders. "All right."

Jennifer already stood looking down at the captured man. When the nera-Duke came up behind her, she dropped down cross-legged in front of him. The armsman looked at her, set his lips in a tight line over clenched teeth and shifted his gaze to a point past her shoulder, a man clearly expecting the worst. "No one's going to hurt you," Jennifer said in some irritation. "We'd like to talk to you, and we'd like you to listen to what we have to say. As someone told me a little while ago, you've only heard one side of a story. And we'd like to show you something."

The man had been cautiously testing the ropes that held his arms behind him. He shook his head, hard. Jennifer waited. He looked at her again, curiously and a little longer this time before turning his gaze back toward the horizon. "They said there was an advocate woman, an outlander who talked the Thukar to a standstill. Was that you?"

Jennifer shrugged, offered him a faint, friendly smile that he probably didn't see. It was making her mad, his cringing attitude, damnit! She tried to force herself to be fair: Any man who served either of the Dukes she'd met probably had every right to expect torture to extract information; she really couldn't blame this poor boy. He wasn't much older than Edrith, probably not half as bright, either. All the same, she wanted to shake him until his teeth rattled. *Right*, she told herself ruefully. *Smack him one so he pays attention when you promise you won't hurt him.*

"I talked to the Thukar. I wasn't aware I'd talked him to a standstill, however. He was shouting, turning purple, not even trying to make sense after a certain point, if that's what you mean. I didn't convince him of anything. He isn't the kind of man who'll listen to a sensible argument, though. I'm hoping you have more intelligence than that." She folded her arms and waited. He set his lips in an even tighter line and wouldn't look at her. She sighed. "All right. Then if you don't have brains maybe you have a survival instinct. There are four of us to your one, armed with staffs—I think you know by now how effective they are, don't you? We all have knives, and the Duke carries a nasty sword. And, of course, two of us Wield Thread." He eyed her dubiously, looked beyond her to where Lialla stood; for a moment, Jennifer thought he might laugh aloud. "The sin-Duchess is no master of the craft but she's more skilled than her uncle knows. I don't do too badly myself." The understatement seemed to convince him more than any bragging might have; the laugh went right out of him. "We don't want any difficulties with you. Personally I would rather not hurt you. We intend to talk, though, and by that I mean dialogue, with you at least paying attention if you won't contribute. Do you understand that?" Silence. Just as she was about to give up on him, though, he shrugged, twisted his mouth. Finally nodded rather sullenly. She decided to ignore the attitude, simply accept the agreement. "Thank you. Personally, I'd think you could pay better attention to us if you weren't twisted up in rope. Don't you?" Silence. He stopped fidgeting, frowned at her—confused by her approach, no doubt. He nodded once more, a little more quickly this time. Lialla stepped behind him to loosen physical knots in real rope, to dissolve those created of Thread. She stood looking down at him rather thoughtfully as he eased his arms around, rotated his shoulders cautiously.

"I know you," she said suddenly. "You're Garret, the son of Sehfi's best baker, aren't you?"

"I'm Garret," he replied warily.

"You used to saddle my horse when you first came to Duke's Fort. And you were on the curtain wall most of this past winter, I used to see you from my windows—getting wet, most often. You must be due to leave or sign for another spell of duty under my uncle, aren't you?" He nodded again, wary still but visibly surprised and perhaps pleased that she should have remembered him. "I'm glad to see you at this moment, Garret. Because you're Zelharri born, you know things no outsider would."

"I do?"

"Of course." Lialla nodded. "You know my brother is three years past age to rule." Aletto shifted impatiently and Lialla sent him a warning look. Jennifer could see the nera-Duke's feet shifting in the dirt, could hear the sand crunching under his boots, and hoped Lialla could keep him quiet long enough to try and win this rather simple young man over.

"Everyone knows that." Garret turned his attention to his wrists, rubbing first one and then the other with great care. He wouldn't met her eyes any longer. "But there are—there are reasons—" He glanced at Jennifer. "*You'll* let me speak frankly?"

"I'd appreciate it if you did," Jennifer said. "If I'm an advocate, I need all sides of a story, don't I? But we didn't ask you to simply agree with whatever we say because we hold you prisoner. I said dialogue, and I meant it."

He squirmed, gave Aletto a rather helpless look. "The young—Duke Amarni's son is—sir, I'm sorry, Lord Jadek's named you incapable because of the fever and the drink."

Jennifer would have answered him but Aletto's voice stopped her. "Don't be sorry," he said mildly. He walked slowly across open ground, the limp scarcely noticeable, the bo in his hand but swinging free. For a wonder, he was keeping his voice under control, too: It was low, deep—no wonder Chris had been impressed when Aletto talked to Gyrdan that night in Sikkre. "It's all right, Garret. I've heard what my uncle says. And, of course, it's true, to a point. I had marsh fever and I drank, particularly when the weather was damp and my movements restricted. Since I left Duke's Fort—well, that doesn't matter, anyone can say anything. I could tell you I no longer drink, that I've grown physically stronger since I've begun to do things for myself—it's still only words, isn't it?"

The armsman forgot about his wrists. He sat very still, watching Aletto closely. "You fought well enough tonight for any man, let alone one who had marsh fever, or one who stayed in his rooms drinking for days on end. There's no look of drink about you." He stroked his upper lip thoughtfully, finally said, "Perhaps it isn't only words."

"Perhaps," Aletto said. "However that falls out, my uncle was wrong to simply withhold my rights from me, as though I were still a child or mentally feeble. I am neither."

"If Jadek fears our vengeance—" Lialla began. Aletto dropped a hand to her shoulder, silencing her, and minutely shook his head.

"There is no need to even speak of vengeance. Not against Jadek, any who serve him—not against anyone. The past is gone; why dwell upon things that can't be changed? All Zelharri knows that Jadek acted as he did out of care for a nephew and his late brother's son." Jennifer glanced up at him; she couldn't tell if he was serious or not. From the astonished look on her face, Lialla couldn't tell, either. "I surely have no reason to want revenge against my uncle. He's kept my birthright intact, my house in good order. Again, anyone can say what he chooses, true or not. But the Emperor would not countenance me to wreak havok upon my uncle.

"All I want is what is mine. Or what should be mine. I know my uncle thinks me unfit because I was, for so long. But things have changed. I am older. I have had long enough to think about things, to come to terms with them. I think it very likely Jadek, with his many concerns in Zelharri, has simply not noticed that I have matured—and changed. He and I need to talk."

"We'd return you to Duke's Fort," Garret began dubiously, but he stopped at once and shook his head. Aletto was already shaking his. "You wouldn't accept such an offer, would you?"

"No. I do not entirely trust my uncle, or I would not have left Duke's Fort in the first place. And now, because of the death of Carolan—it was self-defense, I bear a scar to prove that—I fear Jadek's anger for his cousin's death, and because the sin-Duchess and I fled Duke's Fort when we discovered we could not talk to him, about her future or mine." Aletto shrugged. "Surely you can see I have no reason to believe from our past relationship that I could return to discuss the future of the Dukedom with him as civilized men might.

"And so, I would ask you to take him a message. I ask that he meet with me—in Bez or Podhru, in the presence of neutral witnesses—to discuss the future of Zelharri and my father's Ducal chair."

Silence while the man considered this. "Um. What if he won't?"

"Then I will bring the discussion to Duke's Fort, with enough of my father's old followers to ensure my freedom to leave again, if I desire. Understand," Aletto added quickly, "that I will never *fight* for Zelharri. Even if I were fool enough to believe my birthright worth killing any of my own people, the Emperor would never stand for that! Besides, my mother is still in Duke's Fort.

"So tell Jadek for me: a meeting. I will have that much. At his choice of place—or mine if he ignores this message."

Silence. Jadek's man chewed on his lower lip, finally looked up. The moon was bright enough that Jennifer could see his face was red to his hairline; his eyes were wide and there was no sign of the sullen look left in them. "If any man had said you'd change so much, sir, I'd never have believed it."

"I didn't change," Aletto replied gravely. "Men don't, that often. The circumstances themselves have changed."

"Perhaps." Garret didn't look convinced of that. "I'll see my superior has your message when we reach Duke's Fort, to pass up through channels. At least—" He looked around, twisting up onto one knee to check urgently behind him. "There *were* five of us." He sounded nervous again.

"Three ran," Lialla said. "But the fifth—you'd better see for yourself." She beckoned and he came after her, wary once more. Jennifer saw Aletto sag at the knees momentarily. He shook himself, glanced at Robyn, hesitated but finally followed his sister. "It's no pretty sight, I'd better warn you."

The fifth man seemed to have desiccated even further in the past several minutes; his features were barely visible and anyone who had once known him could only have recognized him by the hair and his clothing. Garret gazed down at him, shuddered and turned away to stare out across the desert. "What did this?" he whispered finally.

"A spell to enable Jadek to speak with me, in this place," Jennifer said. "Apparently through that silver brooch on his shoulder."

He digested this in silence. They waited him out. Finally he shook his head. "Poor Usrien. I asked him about the brooch, earlier. They don't permit us to wear personal decoration on duty, after all, but the officer who gave us orders and sent us out didn't comment on it at all. And Usrien wouldn't say anything about it. I thought perhaps a—well, a patron; there are women who'd buy a man such a costly gift." He turned back and brooded on the dead man. "It—it might not be the way you say it was. Lord Jadek keeps magicians, of course, but there's never been any kind of evil spell in Duke's Fort, no hint of anything since the old Duke's death. *You* might have done this."

"It's possible," Jennifer said neutrally. She was prepared to wait for him to reason it through, if he could, but Lialla stepped forward and caught hold of his shoulder.

"It's not possible! If I could work a spell that powerful, why would I have left any of you alive? We wouldn't have needed to fight you with rope woven of Night-Thread and long staves, would we? If I could do *that*, why would we have had to leave Duke's Fort at all?" She drew in a deep breath, expelled it loudly and went on in an only slightly less outraged voice. "I Wield Night-Thread. I may not be the greatest Wielder in Rhadaz but like any Wielder, I took vows when I was apprenticed: Those vows say I'll never do deliberate harm to any beast, to any innocent human. I've never broken those vows and I'll swear that to you by any oath you care to accept."

Garret still stared down at his dead comrade. He was visibly trying not to shiver. "Faced with this, there's no oath I'd accept from anyone. But—" His voice faded, his eyes were hooded. He gnawed on one knuckle for several moments. "There's some sense in what you say. But what if you couldn't work strong enough magic in Duke's Fort to set your brother in the chair? Perhaps that—" He pointed a finger in the dead man's direction, snatched it back as though he feared some residue of the spell would ensnare him. "Perhaps that kind of thing only works in open air. Everyone knows there are different times and places for different kinds of magic."

"*I* swear to you that not one of us wants any man's death," Aletto said flatly, before Lialla could form an angry reply. "Certainly—" he swallowed. "Certainly no death like that. I want only what is mine; I told you that, and I mean it. Anyone can say anything, of course."

"Anything," the man echoed unhappily. He was looking around; looking for an escape, Jennifer thought tiredly, and wondered how they were going to resolve this. There were other things that needed doing, and she was exhausted.

"I told you I'd have you take a message to my uncle, if you will. As a sign of our good faith, we'll set you free, now. We'll give you back your weapons." Lialla stared at him, open-mouthed. Aletto made a sharp silencing gesture in her direction. "In turn, as a sign of *your* good faith, you'll ride back up the main road to Sikkre and on to Duke's Fort, and deliver my message." There was an uncomfortable little silence. Garret glanced at the dead man, let his eyes close and turned away. "I would suggest one last thing to you," Aletto said. "If I were a man nearing the end of his service term under my uncle, I would consider another method to earn a living than arms service to Jadek. Whoever was responsible for this man's death—we won't resolve that here and now, so it doesn't matter. But he's dead, most unpleasantly so."

"I take your meaning," Garret said grimly. "Dead is dead, whoever strikes the blow. And for a man like Usrien or myself, riding in search of trouble and stuck between two forces, death is likely to come quickly."

"Exactly so. Call it three forces, though: The Sikkreni aren't precisely neutral at this point, are they?"

Garret managed a very weak smile; it faded almost at once. "When were they ever? Those men I rode with say if anything the new Thukars are more than the equal of the old. Well. I'll see your message delivered, but the rest of it needs thought, and this is no place for it."

"A final question," Jennifer put in crisply. "There was a sixth member of our party, the blond outlander boy. He's missing."

"We didn't do that—"

"I saw him taken," Jennifer overrode him. "Not by men like you or the Sikkreni. These were different. What do you know of men swathed in dark robes, men and camels?" The armsman shook his head. "They didn't come with you?" Another shake. "Or as any part of your ambush here tonight?"

"Men and camels?" He shook his head again and Jennifer thought his bewilderment genuine. "You mean, nomads? I haven't seen any nomads in all our days of travel from Sikkre, and I swear no one like that came with us!" His voice rose; he apparently saw his chance of freedom fading, and he spoke quickly now. "There were five of us: Usrien and I, plus three men from Sikkre ordered out by the new Thukars, to find the old Thukar's heir. He's gone missing, you know—"

"We know," Jennifer snapped. She shook her head as he paused, wide-eyed and shaking. "Never mind about Dahmec's heir. We were talking about men and camels—nomads. What about them?"

"I don't know, I'm telling you! There were only two of us from Duke's Fort, myself and—and that man. Usrien. There'd have been more, but one has a broken arm from two nights ago and my immediate superior is still seeing two of everything.

We've been together since Sikkre, though. I don't know anything about nomads, and I'd be willing to swear no one who rode with me does, either. Or about your missing boy. Unless one of the men with me—''

"No," Jennifer said flatly. "I saw him taken. Men and camels. Enough of them that he couldn't fight free."

Garret considered this, finally turned to offer Aletto a very tentative smile. "That stick. I never saw such a thing before, sir. Is it an outland thing? It's impressive."

"It'll be more impressive as time goes on," Aletto said. "You're certain you know nothing about our missing companion?"

"I knew only about an armed attack by five of us—we saw you from a long distance, sir, the moonlight made it easy to locate you once we'd figured which way you had to have gone last night. It made things easy for us, choosing a place to set ourselves. There was nothing in *any* plan I was told about that involved nomads, or a killing spell." He gestured, hand taking in what lay at his feet. "I know you've no reason to believe me, sir, but I swear it's true."

"We *don't* have any reason to believe you," Lialla told him evenly, before Aletto could say anything. "Just as you've no reason to believe us."

"Except trust," Aletto said.

She turned away from him, rolled her eyes and walked a few paces away, motioned to Jennifer to join her. "What are we going to do?" she hissed urgently. "If we let him go and he leads more men to us! Or what if he knows where Chris is?"

"We're second-guessing once again," Jennifer said quietly. "But I tend to agree with your brother's assessment. I think this Garret is a farm boy turned soldier on his first big mission, learning it's not all fanfare and glory, and it's got him scared and confused. Particularly with Aletto doing such a fine job of nobleman in exile; frankly, I didn't know he had that in him."

"Oh, he's *got* it," Lialla replied gloomily. "Just because he doesn't act that way very often—There really is a lot of our father in him. It doesn't show often, particularly like tonight, when he's hot, tired and already in a temper over something. Never mind Aletto. What do we do with Garret?"

"I don't believe he could possibly be lying; no one could be that good an actor. Did you see the look on his face when you brought him over here? He didn't know about Jadek's spell, and I'll swear he didn't know anything about the guys that took Chris."

Lialla sighed. "I—all right. But what's to guarantee he won't just turn around and come back—?"

"He could do that. The other three could come back, with or without him, couldn't they? Those Sikkreni know where we are, after all. And Jadek has done a fine job so far of finding us."

"Not tonight, if that boy's right. That was luck and those men, using a map and second-guessing us," Lialla reminded her. "Jadek just gave out a tracing brooch of some kind—you won't find anything like that in open market, by the way—and used it once we were split up."

"I can't imagine ever wanting to find one," Jennifer said. "But the rest of it—that's all assuming we can trust this Garret. He could be lying about the brooch, you know."

Lialla glared at her. "You're the one who spoke with Jadek, aren't you? I thought you had it worked out! And you said we *could* trust Garret!"

Jennifer sighed tiredly. "I did, didn't I? Actually, what I think I said was that we don't really have any other choice. If I'm not making a lot of sense just now, it's because I'm about to fall asleep on my feet. There's been a lot going on the past hour or so and I think your uncle's fog ball took a lot out of me all by itself. But *I* don't see where we have a lot of choice. We can take him with us—and I can't see the point in that—or kill him, or leave him tied and hope his friends come back, or tie him with a three-strand Thread rope and leave here quickly, except I know damned well Robyn won't go unless we can physically track Chris and the guys who took him, or—"

"Never *mind*," Lialla groaned.

"All right. Forget all that. My opinion is that Aletto's gone a long way toward winning the boy over; he's at least got him thinking. Perhaps he's done a better job of reading Garret than we have; maybe he's just not as tired and he can *think* better than I can. I think we shouldn't tamper with what he's accomplished—anything we do hasn't got any more of a guarantee, and this way at least, your brother comes out of it feeling like he's done a good job. Like he's the Duke he's supposed to be. Let's just stay out of it, shall we?" Lialla nodded. Jennifer rubbed hair back from her face and let her eyes close briefly. "I admit I'd feel better if I had any idea what to do about Chris. Robyn is going to want some answers, and I don't know what to tell her."

"One thing at a time. Let's send this man of my uncle's on his way before the others come back to rescue him and we have

142

another battle on our hands.'' Lialla flexed her hands. ''One a night is more than enough.''

* * *

THE Zelharri armsman rode out shortly after, angling to the northeast to intersect with the road. He led his comrade's horse with the man himself rolled in his sleeping blanket and tied sideways across the saddle—for proof, Garret said. And for a decent burial. He hadn't really looked like he wanted to take the mummified body; he'd kept looking behind him, as though fearing the man might somehow come to life and attack him.

There had been a brief, rather fierce argument about the brooch: Garret had wanted it at first but he abruptly decided he didn't, in case it should come to life in his hands. But he wouldn't simply leave it with Lialla and Jennifer. Finally Aletto scooped it up with a blistering oath and threw it as far as he could. It traveled in a high arc, shone chill in the moonlight, vanished with a crash of dry sticks and leaves into the brush. It wasn't a good answer, but then, Jennifer thought, there probably weren't any good answers. Neither she nor Lialla had any idea whether it still worked, or how to dismantle any spell still left on it. At least it was where none of Jadek's men could pick it up and use it to communicate with Jadek—or be used by him. Jennifer doubted Jadek could use it without a human source of strength to power it. Garret, at least, seemed to find Aletto's gesture an acceptable answer.

But Jennifer privately promised herself that given the opportunity, she'd track down the nasty thing and bury it as deeply as she could.

* * *

ALETTO went back to Robyn as soon as the armsman rode away. She still hadn't moved, except that now she rested her chin on her knees and was staring blindly back the way they'd come. He eased himself down next to her and touched her arm to get her attention. Robyn merely nodded. Aletto said something in a voice too low to carry beyond the two of them. Robyn nodded again and he fell silent.

I hope he can handle all that, Jennifer thought. It was a real problem: Robyn in one of her sulky, stubborn moods—however much she had the right to be that way; Aletto for once trying to deal with a situation on an adult level. *What a mess.* She dismissed Robyn, Aletto, even Chris from her thoughts then. Edrith had looked simply awful the last time she'd seen him, and she rather worriedly realized that had been some time ago.

She found him finally, at the edge of the wash. He'd pulled

143

one of the packs from his horse and half lay, half sat against it, eyes closed. He was extremely, unnaturally quiet and pale—even for Edrith by moonlight. His breath came and went in a soft little pant, as though anything deeper hurt. He started when Jennifer knelt to touch his arm, groaned and raised a hand to the side of his head but didn't quite touch it. "I don't know what I can do about you," she began apologetically. "I know how to heal, but this isn't the same as a cut."

"It's all right, I can manage," Edrith said faintly.

"No, you can't. Not like that."

"Well, but, if we don't ride on tonight—"

Jennifer glanced over her shoulder. Robyn was far enough away still that she'd never hear her, not if she kept her voice low. "We can't. Chris is still missing, and that man of Jadek's claimed not to know anything about him. But we certainly won't go anywhere until we decide what to do."

"Good." Edrith's shoulders sagged.

Lialla crouched down beside him. "I can fix this," she said briskly but when Edrith opened an eye and looked relieved, Jennifer could see the confidence draining out of her. "If—that is, well, I've *done* it, I did it once, when Merrida showed me how, for Aletto, bruises but it's the same thing, really, at least, I think—"

"You can fix it," Jennifer said firmly as Lialla stuttered to a nervous silence. In a moment, the woman would tie herself in such a verbal knot—"Do it, then show me what you did."

"Merrida did it—here. Put your hand on my arm and concentrate on what I do," Lialla said. She still sounded dubious, but willing to try. "It's—they're yellow, can you see them?"

"Yeah," Jennifer replied shortly. She was already dizzy from Jadek's spell, deathly tired from the heat, the long ride, the fight, worry about Chris that was threatening to overwhelm her, all at once. This—accessing a vague Thread so like half a dozen others near it, sharing physical contact and the mental touch with Lialla—made her faintly nauseous. No wonder Lialla had sounded so uncertain. Jennifer was beginning to feel that way herself, and she could see—and feel—Edrith's pain, which added to everything else was about the last straw. Being on one knee already helped. She dug her free fingers in the dirt to keep from toppling over. *Contact with the real world*, she thought dizzily. *If only a pawful of sand.* She'd have to sort the proper yellow Thread free later, by herself, if she could find it again. She couldn't properly feel it or *listen* to it, not now. Not with her

144

ears ringing and Lialla's touch vibrating right down to the soles of her high-tops. She could *see* the stuff Lialla was using, though.

It took a long time. Lialla felt around the edges of Edrith's injury, deftly touching one thing or another; she probably felt the boy's pain also, which couldn't help her use something she'd tried only once before. Probably with old Merrida glaring at her and grumbling about her lack of skill. . . . Lialla swore under her breath and tugged on something. The world tilted alarmingly; Lialla fell into Jennifer, nearly taking them both over, but the knot simply came undone, all at once—as though it were only a slip knot after all, for all the complex look of it. Lialla shook herself free of Thread. When Jennifer looked out on the normal world once more, Edrith was gingerly rubbing his forehead. He managed a weak smile. "It feels strange still and things look odd, but my head doesn't hurt any more. Thank you." The smile faded. "Little brown sand gods. What are we going to do about Chris?"

* * *

But discussion got them nowhere: The footprints of the men and camels that had surrounded the boy vanished almost at once—as though someone had wiped the ground behind them. But a little beyond the dry wash, there was a dry lake bed that would have taken no prints anyway. "We can circle it tomorrow, at first light," Edrith said. "To see if there's any sign of them emerging." Of course, the nomads could have gone anywhere, any distance, after they left the lake bed. Edrith left that unspoken; the thought was visible on everyone's face.

"I don't care about the rest of you," Robyn said flatly. "I'm not going anywhere without my kid." Her voice was thick with tears. "End of discussion." She bit her lip and said nothing after that, merely shook her head at any suggestion that would have taken her away from this place.

"It doesn't matter," Jennifer said finally. "Jadek's men can find us, here or anywhere else. I could wish for running water and decent shade, but—" She held up a hand. "I know, Birdy, don't say it. You know I'd never desert Chris. Once we have daylight—"

"I thought you could tell where people are," Aletto said. It wasn't really a challenge; somewhere in the past day or so, he'd lost some of his truculence at mention of magic.

"I tried," Lialla said. She'd also lost some of her defensiveness, or maybe she was simply too tired to rise to his bait. "There are people out there—oh, leagues away. But the road is out there, about that far." She waved an arm eastward. "Anything out there could be them; it's more likely anyone on or by the road has business on it. And I can't tell a horse from a camel, any more than I can tell a Bez merchant from a Cholan nomad. Jen?''

"If we knew how it's done—but I'm not even doing that well, at anything, just now. I tried to search right after that spherical magic phone booth released me—sorry, Jadek's spell," Jennifer said. "You and those *words*," Lialla mumbled. Jennifer eyed her side-long briefly, went on when the other woman shrugged and stayed quiet. "It could have been the spell, my reaction to it, or maybe some spell the camel-men had with them. I couldn't find a sign of anyone nearby. I could barely find the right Thread to conduct a search, and I'll take it on trust right now that the road's out there. I can't tell." She drew a deep breath, let it out in a loud gust. "But I don't understand. Why would these Cholan nomads take Chris, if not for ransom? Jadek told me *he* had Chris, but that was simply for leverage, so I'd agree to do what he wanted. He was obviously lying because he had no reason to tell me he'd used the brooch as a transfer spell if he hadn't. I saw men, camels, they were near enough that I couldn't have missed them, but since they left prints, I obviously didn't just imagine them.''

"*He* could have done that," Aletto said doubtfully. "Made you think you saw Cholan nomads; somehow made a sign of them?" Jennifer shook her head.

"Even if he could, why? If he had Chris, why bother to do all that? No. He was only using Chris as a lever; the Thukar and his wizard Snake did the same thing, remember, Lialla? Robyn?" The two women nodded. "It was about as believable, too. So. Jadek doesn't have him. These nomads, though: Is ransom the only reason they'd have to jump a party like ours? It just seems so stupid, setting themselves up for trouble. Or are they not held to Rhadazi law?" She paused. Aletto shrugged. "Well, then, could they be working for the Thukar—sorry, Thukars—do you think? The two Zelharri men who attacked us wouldn't have necessarily known about a deal like that; maybe the Sikkreni wouldn't have either. Dahmec would have thought that way; leverage. Maybe''—she swallowed hard—''maybe the twins think we really do know where Dahven is; maybe the story we got is all true, they think we'll tell them what we know in exchange for Chris—for whoever those men were able to get hold of.'' Silence. "Well?"

Lialla shrugged again; Robyn shielded her eyes with both hands and let her head drop. "That's all possible," Edrith said finally. "I don't know how likely it is. About Dahven—gods, I

146

hate to think. Deehar and Dayher are at least as bad as Dahmec was, everyone knows that. The Cholan—hard to say how *their* minds work. Traditionally, they've always gone their own way, and since they live so far from the market, no one's ever bothered to hold them to City law. They're Sikkreni; at least, the Sink and the lands all around it are within Sikkreni borders. They don't pay taxes and no Thukar has ever drawn armsmen from their clans, to my knowledge. They don't trust anyone, and since Dahmec took the Duke's chair, there have been fewer of them in the market every year. They're fond of coin, not just the things it buys, though such of them as I've seen have had a good eye for pretty weapons, bright cloth. The bead and the copper and brass jewelry merchants do good business with them." He offered them a faint, rather abashed smile. "I'm trying to 'logic it out,' as Chris says. I'm not as good at that kind of thing as he is. But logically, we'll see one of them, or some other communication from them, asking for money in exchange for Chris. It's the only thing that makes any sense."

Robyn sniffed and rubbed her nose with the back of her hand. "God," she whispered. "This is—I can't handle this. If it was me, yeah. Not my kid." Aletto touched her shoulder.

"Don't underrate the kid, Birdy," Jennifer said mildly. "It's not like they took some ordinary kid; Chris probably had five escape plans in the first half-hour."

"Yeah." Robyn said gloomily. "If he's conscious. Or—or—"

"Don't," Aletto urged, and this time took her hand between both of his. "Don't think that way; it's not fair to him, and you'll make yourself ill with worry." He frowned. "On the chance he escapes, he'll come here. So do we dare go anywhere?"

"Probably not," Jennifer said, and sighed. "I know, Birdy, you won't. I suspect you're right; Chris might well get away from them, and he'd come back looking for us. There's a good chance he's still mounted on his own horse; he may even have full control of it. But listen, since we're *not* going anywhere, why don't we try and set up some shade for in the morning? Because there isn't going to *be* any around here to speak of; those bushes won't hide us for long at all. And I'd like a chance to try another search before I fall asleep. I don't know about you, people, but that's not going to be long off."

"We stay here," Robyn said. It wasn't a question. Jennifer nodded.

"We stay here," she replied. Some of the tension went out of her sister's shoulders and she got stiffly to her feet.

12

LIALLA and Edrith rigged two of the blankets and a welter of ropes to form an overhead shade; Robyn broke out a container of dried fruit to supplement the oat cakes before going with Aletto to unsaddle and wipe down the horses. Jennifer walked out into the desert and sat cross-legged on the sand, eyes closed. The stillness and dark were unnerving, after the past few hours; she could almost *smell* Jadek's last trap, and after the suddenness of that one it was hard to believe another wasn't waiting just behind her shoulder to pounce as soon as she wasn't looking. After a few minutes she sighed, rubbed her eyes and stared unseeing at a broken stem of dry and dying brush. All right. At least the magic was working again. There were people—*men*, she thought—out where the road must be. A small number of them traveling at what must be a slow walk from the south. More unmoving, probably camped and sleeping. Water—there, in the direction the Zelharri soldier and his grisly burden had gone. Not terribly far away, certainly not far enough for her peace of mind since she was sleeping here shortly. There were men and horses there, too, where the water was. She hoped it was the man Garret and those he'd gone to meet; hoped they hadn't completely misread Jadek's man. Maybe he would actually think about what Aletto had said, maybe even accept most of what they'd told him. Not that Jadek would take his nephew's offer, no. Not the Jadek she'd argued with. At least Garret knew the offer had been made; at least one man had heard a reasonable voice suggesting compromise. *God. What the hell have I got myself into? I'm a lawyer, a twentieth-century American corporate litigator! I'm not a Rhadazi advocate, a witch, a fighter, a—God. I wasn't. I don't want to be now!* She rubbed suddenly wet palms down her jeans, then swore and brushed at her thighs. The damned pants had to stay reasonably clean; grubby handprints and ground in sand weren't going to help them any. She'd already rubbed dirt into them, falling in that deserted village and scraping her knee. At least she hadn't torn the fabric, and

148

the little blood she'd shed had washed out. But once these were gone, she could hardly go back to that beachfront shop for more.

She blinked, brushed at her legs once more and got to her feet. She wasn't doing Chris one damned bit of good out here, so tired she couldn't concentrate enough to listen to Thread. All she could hear was that scared little inner voice that said, "You're all gonna die out here, Cray, and the damned jeans won't matter then, will they?" She shook the legs down where they belonged, shoved the pockets back down where *they* were supposed to be instead of bunched up against her hipbones, and wandered back to where the others were setting up a rough camp.

There was sand in her high-tops, despite the snug way she'd relaced them two nights before. She eased herself back under the rope-and-blanket shelter, sat on her blanket and undid them, poured sand into twin cone-shaped piles and pulled her socks off to shake them. It was too warm to pull the blanket around her but a little cool for bare feet; she sighed, pulled the socks back on and the shoes, loosely, over them. Better.

Everyone else was already settled in. Lialla lay on top of the blanket next to hers, curled into a little black wad the way she ordinarily slept, nothing visible but one small fist. Beyond her, Edrith was stretched out flat on his back and beyond him, Aletto sat, gazing out across the desert, head slowly turning from side to side as he watched for visible enemy. *Fat lot of good,* Jennifer thought sourly, but kept the thought to herself—as she had earlier, when they'd drawn lots for first watch.

Robyn slept on Jennifer's other side. Aletto had done what he could to heal the breach—he'd done much more than Jennifer would ever have expected—but the silences between the two were long and uncomfortable ones. *At least he's tried.* Jennifer stifled a yawn against the back of her hand. It wasn't all stubbornness on Robyn's part, of course: Birdy was so worried about Chris her own problems had faded into a stomach-knotting background. And if Lialla had found a moment to warn Aletto about the things Jadek had said . . .

Jennifer lay back, stretched out her legs one at a time before she rolled onto one side. She groaned faintly as all-too-hard ground pressed against her hip, and her leg started to go numb. Air mattresses. Why couldn't they have air mattresses here? Or water beds? She sat up, scraped her knuckles against the blanket to hollow sand from under her hipbones and then, to distract herself, considered Thread. She understood at least a little about five kinds of it now: the one that marked the presence of others, the blue that was water. Mauve for healing—for heat to be used against stiffness—and the ones that wove into rope. Now this yellow: Lialla had used it against concussion and bruises. Jennifer found it by touch, held it tentatively while she identified the music of it—something that reminded her of Handel's Water Music, rather nice, she thought. Concussion and other bruises— that made it an extremely practical piece of stuff. How else, she wondered, might one use it? And what else was out there, how could that be used? What more could she *do* with this stuff?

* * *

EDRITH woke her near dawn for a short watch, and she used the time to search once more. There seemed to be no one nearer than before. The people by the water were where they'd been, and at present no one was moving up or down the road. Just before the sun rose, she woke Robyn, took a small swallow of water, and settled down on her blanket for whatever sleep she could get before the day turned too hot.

She came awake from an unpleasant, swathing dream; someone was shouting and the ground under her ear was shaking. It took several moments for her to realize where she was, to understand that the pounding wasn't part of her dream of appraising eyes, a compressing sphere with her inside it, suffocation. It was a horse, coming fast, and Edrith was shouting to waken them. Jennifer rubbed her eyes and tried to see against a level, harsh sun. Chris? Robyn was up and running barefoot across the open, and Edrith, with another warning shout, was right after her. The horse checked. It *was* Chris's horse, still saddled and bridled, packs making it a familiarly lumpy shape. But no sign of its rider from where she crouched. Edrith stopped short, dragging Robyn back against him. Chris's horse danced nervously away from them. Robyn somehow eluded her companion's long-fingered grip and snatched hold of the bridle; the animal jerked her half off her feet. Aletto scrambled out from under the blankets shirtless, hung himself up in ropes and swore as he tried to get free without pulling the whole thing down. Lialla staggered to her feet, looking as blankly exhausted as Jennifer felt. Edrith caught the other side of the bridle before the horse could rear once more, and between them, he and Robyn got it calmed enough to lead over.

She'd known the saddle was empty; she'd seen no sign of a rider upright, fallen forward, thrown sideways across the saddle. It was still a heart-dropping disappointment to see no sign of her nephew. Robyn tied the reins around the end of the horse line and came over to drop heavily to the ground. Edrith hurriedly pulled bags and saddle free, tossed a blanket over it and followed.

Robyn waved a small square of something yellow, but she was panting hard enough that it was some moments before she could talk. Jennifer peered at the yellow thing, rubbed her eyes and looked again. It suddenly made sense: a folded piece of legal pad, Chris's inked map on the back of it. "It was stuck to the saddle," Robyn gasped. "The stuff's all over my hand, watch it."

"I see it," Jennifer said. She took the note by one corner, avoiding the line of black saplike stuff on one side, unfolded it. "God, he's written a book; how'd he ever get away with that?"

"Read it," Robyn said. She still sounded breathless, and she let her eyes close, sagged against Aletto when he sat down behind her and wrapped an arm around her shoulder. "I don't think I could."

Jennifer glanced through it quickly. "All right. He says he's okay, Birdy—"

"Jesus, Jen! *Read* it to me!"

She cleared her throat. " 'Mom and everybody, Only one of these guys speaks Rhadazi and he's got an accent like rocks and broken glass. If I can track what he's trying to say, though, it's the usual thing: You give them money or I'm dead meat—' Sorry, Birdy," Jennifer added apologetically.

"I'll kill the damned kid myself," Robyn gritted between clenched teeth. She caught her breath on a sob. "Go on."

"Sure you will. Me too, we can take turns. 'They seem to think you guys are rich. I gather somebody in Sikkre owes us for telling these bozos that and where to find us. File that, okay? Anyway, I convinced them to let me write this. They don't write at all apparently, and I swear they argued for *hours* about who was gonna come talk to you, except they're all spooked by their own shadows and no one wanted to. So I don't know how they plan to exchange me for bread, but hey, that's their problem.

" 'I got *no* idea where I am. I was knocked out at first and when I woke up I was bagged right down to my knees, and on a camel. Camels smell worse up close, especially when you can't see anything, file that, too. Obviously I can see now, but everything looks flat and brushy like it has for days, which isn't too useful. I'll pull a back-door fade if I can at least figure where the road is, so you don't have to decide if I'm really worth any money.

" 'Oops, they say I'd better finish, guess they don't believe you need a whole page of English to say pay the geeks on camels a hundred silver ceris or the kid bites the big one, and they'll be in touch to let you know when and where. Don't panic, Ma, it's cool—' '' Jennifer gazed down at her nephew's crabbed and unusually tiny handwriting for several more moments. "That's all," she said finally. There was a little heart at the very bottom with a "C" in it; she handed it to Robyn, who glanced at it, let her eyes close and swallowed hard.

"A hundred ceris!" Lialla breathed. "That's a—that's a Duke's ransom! We haven't a fourth that among us, even with the gems—"

"It's all right," Jennifer assured her, and hoped she sounded authoritative. "They have to send someone to arrange the when and where, don't they? We can talk them down then. Chris might get away in the meantime. He's resourceful enough. Or we can find a way to follow whoever they send, or track him via Thread—" She spread her hands wide. "There are plenty of possibilities; we'll sort something out. And meantime—Birdy. Birdy?" she repeated gently. Robyn started, stared at her blankly for some moments. "The horse, Birdy."

"The horse?"

"I don't know horses like you do. Did Chris's horse come very far? Can you tell that?"

Robyn frowned, gazed down at her hands for some moments, finally shrugged and got up. She went over to the horse, ran a hand along its withers, the other down its neck, finally patted it and came back. "I don't think it came far; the skin is warm but not sweaty. If they'd turned it loose miles away, it wouldn't have come back to us, I don't think. It had to be near enough to scent the other horses." She shook her head but she suddenly looked more hopeful. "The note says he was out a while. Do you— d'you think they rode him in a circle? That he's nearby?"

"Don't know, Birdy. I tried an hour or so ago; I wasn't aware of anything moving anywhere around us. All the same, why would they take him far?"

"Cowardice," Lialla said dryly.

"Over practicality?" Jennifer asked, and Lialla shrugged. "They have to be close enough to make the exchange, don't they? Unless—do you think the offer is genuine?"

"I—I don't know. I don't know why they'd make it otherwise. I thought all along, though, that they'd never take him for Jadek or the Sikkreni; it doesn't fit anything I've ever heard about Cholan nomads. I told you, though: They had a repute once for kidnapping people. If they were told about wealthy travelers, it's possible they'd try for what they might see as easy money. If so,

I'd think they'd track us from a safe distance. Once they saw an opportunity to separate one of us from the others—''

"Chris is right," Edrith said grimly. "Someone in Sikkre is going to owe us one for this. The nomads don't ordinarily ambush travelers any more. They avoid people. Particularly since Dahmec became Thukar. He wouldn't stand for that kind of thing; it would interfere with his profit. This—"

"Let's get the kid back first," Robyn said faintly. "Then—if I ever find out who did this to us, I'll kill him myself." Jennifer raised her eyebrows. Robyn, she thought, meant exactly what she said. Unexpected—a little worrying, even.

Talk to her later. "Whoever it is, I'll hold him for you," was all she said.

Robyn glanced down at Aletto's arm crossing her chest, looked at Lialla and then at Edrith. "Listen, you people don't have to sit out here in the middle of nowhere with us, waiting like this—"

"We're not breaking up," Lialla said fiercely.

Edrith's "We do!" came at the same moment. Aletto merely tightened the arm briefly. Robyn sighed faintly.

"I'm sorry," she said, even more faintly. It sounded more like the normal Robyn than her earlier outburst had.

"Why be sorry?" Lialla demanded. Her voice was still sharp. She considered this remark, held up a hand for silence. "Never mind. I've said the same thing, and for no more cause, haven't I? It's no more your fault than his that this happened, Robyn. There isn't any point in wondering what might have happened if you'd shifted—or if Chris had stayed with the rest of us. Is there?" She fumbled the water bottle from under the edge of her blanket and drank. "We'll have to send one or two of us with the horses for water sometime, of course. Fortunately it isn't far, although I wish it weren't so near the road. Otherwise, we stay together. Anything else would be absolutely foolish."

"Rully," Edrith said. He still looked very indignant. "I mean, you know?" Robyn scowled at him.

"You don't even know what that *means*!" she snapped. Edrith grinned, spread his hands wide.

"I've heard you fighting with Chris about it. *You* say it doesn't mean anything," he retorted cheerfully. "I can figure it near enough from the way it sounds; that's good enough for me."

"God," Robyn breathed and cast her eyes heavenward.

"I like the way Chris talks; even his Rhadazi is—different. I like his odd words. Besides," Edrith added, "you make *such* faces. It's fun seeing how long it takes to cause one."

He'd done it on purpose, Jennifer thought. Sure enough,

Robyn stopped trying to fight a smile and actually laughed; the boy looked pleased with himself. Moments later, they were both somber again but the laugh had done them all good. Edrith got to his knees so he could reach Robyn's hands. "We'll get him back, you know. You ask any merchant in Sikkre: The nomads aren't bright. Chris is. And we have some unusual resources. We'll find him, and I'll wager you when we do, he'll be on his way back here."

Robyn's smile was watery now; she freed a hand to rub across her eyes. "Sure. I'm not betting with *you*, kid. You're too slippery and I'm too poor." Edrith merely smiled and left the shelter of the blankets, the end of the long bo trailing and bouncing across the ground behind him.

* * *

LIALLA and Aletto were discussing something in low, noncarrying voices; Robyn let the nera-Duke keep hold of her hand and curled up next to him, eyes closed. Jennifer decided to go back to sleep. There didn't seem to be anything else she could do at the moment. Early sun was turning the insides of her eyelids blood-red, but she pulled the black kerchief from around her hair and draped it over the upper part of her face. Ordinarily, worry, the hour, the murmur of voices would all have conspired to keep her from anything but a not very productive rest. Not this time. Reaction, she later thought. She woke hours later, hot, sweaty and disoriented, to find herself alone under the low shelter, which now consisted of only one blanket tied across bushes directly above her, the single blanket under her.

But a little farther south along the dry streambed, two of Lialla's lightweight silkcloth blankets had been knotted together over a bracing pair of bos, worked into a shelter a person could—cautiously—stand under. Lialla sat cross-legged under this, staring out westward. An occasional breath of air lifted the black cloth from her forehead; she herself did not move. There was no sign of Edrith and two horses were also gone. In the midst of the new shaded area, liberally carpeted with their blankets and the horse blankets, Aletto came slowly up on his hands in a modified pushup, went down again. Robyn lay flat on her stomach on the other side of him, head turned to watch what he did. She was speaking softly, words Jennifer couldn't hear, but Aletto shifted his hands to a broader base before he did another pushup. Two more. He dropped flat with a relieved grunt; Robyn rolled onto her knees and began kneading his shoulders.

"That's seven," she said clearly. "Your best so far."

"It's not so many." Aletto's voice was muffled by the blanket.

"I've seen Chris do—" He stopped abruptly, glanced up at her. Robyn's hands came away from his arm and went still for the least moment. She began working the muscle again.

"Oh, Chris," she replied carelessly. "He's been doing push-ups for years, he had to for school of course, but he's always been at this martial arts stuff—you know, the staff fighting and things. Just—because friends did it, or because it was something to fool around with. Men where we come from—people, really— they do all that stuff. A lot of them just want to grow big muscles."

"Oh." Aletto's voice was muffled by blanket again.

"Yeah, I agree," Robyn went on. "Crazy. I never did, you can tell; I can't even do *five* pushups without dying and I'll never even try to do them the way Chris does."

"I will," Aletto promised grimly.

"Sure. Before too many more days, I'd think. Once you're comfortable with ten of the other kind. There. How's that feel?"

"Fine." He rolled over and sat up, kneaded his left arm above the shoulder briefly and bent forward to stretch out his back.

"Careful," Robyn warned him. "You work that back slowly or you'll be *really* sorry."

"Got it." He leaned down across bent knees, straightened up and got to his feet. "I'll walk a little now. You?"

She shook her head. "Too hot for me right now."

"All right." He touched her head with his fingertips in passing and stepped into the sun. The limp was perceptible but no more than that. He moved southward along the wash and slowly walked out of sight. Slowly, but there was more strength in the way he moved, Jennifer thought.

Robyn watched him go, sighed and shifted so she could sit cross-legged. Jennifer crawled from under the blanket where she'd slept and got to her knees, stretched hard, stood up. Too quickly; the hot, clear air swam before her eyes and she folded in half, breathing deeply until she could see once more. She straightened more cautiously this time and came over into shade. It seemed cooler here, more room for the air to circulate perhaps, or just the effect of a higher ceiling. "That looked interesting. You all right, kiddo?" Robyn asked. Jennifer nodded.

"I'd be better with coffee," she mumbled.

"We didn't make a fire, but if you want one so you can have coffee—"

"Never mind. I'll conserve the beans. Not like I *have* to be awake for driving rush-hour traffic or anything."

"Yeah," Robyn said. "Edrith took two of the horses, went off toward the road. I guess there's water out there somewhere."

Jennifer rubbed her eyes, nodded, stifled a yawn against the back of her hand. "Yeah. Saw it last night."

"Saw—oh, right. *Saw.* Sounds so damned weird when you say that, girl. Since he doesn't stick out the way the rest of us do, you know? There should be a fresh bottle for you any time now."

"Good." She'd had a swallow of Lialla's water earlier; it had been absolutely dreadful and only the thought of dehydration kept her from spitting it back out. "Hot as it is, that'll be better than coffee."

"I have that tea you got in Sikkre; I think I can make sun tea in the open kettle, don't you? It would be cool for breakfast, anyway."

Jennifer laughed. "You have enough sun for it. I can spare a little sugar, if you want."

"You're probably the only one who'd want any; I don't think these guys indulge."

"Nice thought. I get to learn to drink my coffee straight."

"Oh," Robyn shoved off her right shoe with the toe of the left and began massaging her arch. "I think there's something for sweetener around here. Maybe not the kind of white death you're used to. I bet Edrith would know about it."

Lialla stood up and shook the Wielder blacks around her, walked past the horses and vanished into the brush. Robyn watched her go. "She's sure quiet this morning." She pulled off the other shoe.

"Has a lot to think about," Jennifer said. "That looks like a good idea." She eased off the sneakers she'd slept in, pulled off her socks and eyed them dubiously. They were disgustingly brown where they rubbed the tops of her shoes. "Wow. I feel about ten degrees cooler already."

"Yeah. I wanted to take those off you this morning but I was afraid I'd wake you and you'd never get back to sleep. You looked exhausted."

"I wouldn't have even noticed." Jennifer fought another yawn, jerked her head in the direction Aletto had gone. "How are you two doing this morning?"

Robyn sighed. "Well—everything considered, all right, I guess. We just aren't talking about it, I guess that's an improvement over cold shoulders, huh?"

"Guess so. Look at the bright side, Birdy: At least you don't

156

have to chew on yourself any more, worrying how to break it to him.''

"Yeah, swell. I just—*dump* it all over him, and then throw a screamy-fit in his ear. God, I can't believe I did that. I like the guy!''

"Well, don't chew on it now, for heaven's sake, it's over and done with. Has he said anything at all?''

"Just—well, not really. More or less that since it's me, it can't be that horrible maybe, but it sounds like he's trying to convince himself and not doing such a terrific job.''

"Consider the source, Robyn. That's progress against years of heavy prejudice, don't you think?''

"Sure.'' She didn't look convinced herself. "Listen, I had this idea, I don't know if it would work, what he's gonna do if I try it—guess that part doesn't matter, cause I'm going to try anyway.'' She looked suddenly shy and her cheeks were pink. "What if I—if I shifted, if I could get up there and''—she hesitated over the word—"and *flew* around, looked all around us to see if I could find him? I mean,'' she went on hastily as Jennifer looked at her in surprise, "you tried last night but it doesn't sound like you can find things—people—very far away, and I *know* I can—can fly fast and far, and I can get pretty high.'' She looked down at her hands. "If it's a dumb idea, say so, okay? I just thought—''

"It's not dumb,'' Jennifer said slowly. "I'm proud of you for even thinking of it, after everything that's happened the past few hours. I'm trying to think, though—'' She frowned.

"If Aletto—'' Robyn began tentatively. Jennifer shook her head, silencing her.

"I wouldn't let his reaction worry me, if I were you. Just—when he gets back, tell him you're going to try it. If it upsets him, tell him not to watch.''

Robyn laughed weakly, shook her own head. "Yeah, right. My all-time favorite line since I was a kid, and *you* gotta tell *me* that.''

"You're not using your brain, lady, and right now I can't blame you. My only concern is, *can* you shift during the day? Have you tried yet?''

"No. You know all the times I've tried it. At least—well, no. But it's not Thread, like what you do, after all. Is it?''

Jennifer shrugged gloomily, spread her hands wide. "I'm beginning to see how Lialla feels. Hell, *I* don't know. I don't think it is, because I don't *feel* what you do the same way. Lialla called

157

it neutral magic. I was just wondering because I've only seen you shift in the dark.''

"Only time I've *had* to, or wanted to. I guess we'll find out, though. If I can find that rotten kid of mine—" Her voice was trembling.

"I know, Birdy, don't."

"We can't stay here forever." Robyn gestured in the direction Lialla had gone. "She's worried about it; she's not saying, she's being really cool about it but I can tell she's worried about being in one place for too long and getting caught."

"She's worried about getting caught, period," Jennifer said. "She knows the same as the rest of us that it doesn't matter if we're moving or not. And she's got a lot of new things to worry about just now, remember? Being arrested for murder, for one thing. On top of being chased by a wicked uncle like Jadek— you know, I wasn't really certain I could believe half the stuff those two let slip, the things Merrida told us about Jadek. After last night, there isn't much I'd put past that guy."

Robyn sighed and let her eyes close. "God." She rolled onto her knees and pushed to her feet. "Powder room's way out there, for your information. Where she went. I think I'll go walk a little myself or I'm gonna fall asleep again, and it's way too hot for that. Maybe after Edrith gets back with the water, we can— I can try."

* * *

EDRITH returned at midday, riding slowly, water bags weighing down both horses and sloshing pleasantly. "Tomorrow I can take two of the others. There was no one there at midmorning; much better than trying to ride in unnoticed at night or late in the day. There should be enough water to keep everyone from drying out and dying tonight." He glanced at Jennifer. "But not enough for bathing."

"I'm not bathing in a collapsing leather horse bucket," Jennifer assured him. She wasn't. The remaining stale liquid in her spare bottle and the corner of her drying cloth was going to sponge away the worst of the dirt and sweat. And probably not until late in the afternoon, in case she decided to run.

* * *

ALETTO didn't look at all pleased when he came back from his walk to hear Robyn's plan, but he shook his head when she suggested he stay clear while she tried the shift. "No. If there's any help I can give you. And—" He swallowed. "If this is a part of your life, then I'll have to learn to accept it, won't I?"

"No," Robyn said.

"Well, *I* say it is," he replied stiffly.

"Look, Aletto, I *told* you! This isn't anything I asked for. If I could be rid of it—except for this, just this once, when I need it—do you think I wouldn't?" He was pale but she'd gone very white, and he held out a steadying hand. She took it and he nodded. He seemed to intend the gesture as an apology; Robyn apparently took it that way because she sounded much calmer when she went on. "It's—I don't like the way I feel when I shift, I'm afraid of high places, and flying in machines used to scare me half to death. This—I'm not afraid when I'm up there, I haven't been. But I don't feel in control of myself, either. It's—hell. I'm no good with words. Never was."

Aletto nodded faintly. "I wish I could say I understand. Honestly, I do."

"I believe you," Robyn said softly.

"Then, if I watch, maybe I can avoid thinking what I've always thought when I see a shapeshifter—"

There was a long silence between them. Jennifer was ready to break it when Robyn gripped Aletto's fingers and released them. "It's your decision," she said. "Do what you want. But if you change your mind, I won't get mad, all right?" She turned to Jennifer. "I can't stand waiting any longer. What do you think?"

"Midafternoon, only a light breeze—I'd call it good flying weather."

Robyn's eyes went wide; she relaxed suddenly and managed a weak grin. "You! I needed a smartass, I really did."

"Always happy to oblige. What do you want us to do—if anything?"

"Don't know." Robyn ran a hand across the top of her head, smoothed long blonde hair back behind her ears. She was dithering, her color high once again, embarrassed to be the center of everyone's attention. "Look, I feel like an ass, I really don't know. Just—hang on." She sat cross-legged on hard sand, in full sun, closed her eyes and rested her elbows on the sides of her knees. Her head fell forward onto her hands, loose hair spilling all around, hiding her face. Jennifer and Lialla stood side by side in front of her, watching her rather anxiously. Aletto knelt beside her, dividing his attention between Robyn, the two Wielders, and Edrith, who had stepped back a few paces and stood almost directly behind her, arms crossed and head tipped to one side. "Damn." Robyn's voice was muffled by her hands. Aletto looked up rather helplessly and Jennifer knelt, laid a hand across her sister's arm. Robyn glanced up immediately, let her head drop again. "I can't feel it."

"Feel what?"

"There's a—I don't know, I can't feel the right kind of way to do it. Oh, damn!"

"Right way? What?" Jennifer asked. "Want me to help, Birdy?"

"I don't know what you can do, though!" Robyn's forlorn little voice came up through crossed arms and the spill of long, straight hair.

"Oh, damnit, woman," Jennifer said crisply. "If it were *my* kid, I'd be royally pissed, I wouldn't be sitting there whining! I guess it's only when somebody lays a hand on you personally you come unglued, huh? Or when—Jesus!" She fell back, scrambling hastily out of the way; Lialla let out a tiny shriek and jumped aside. Aletto stayed where he was, frozen into place, eyes wide and face absolutely white. Robyn's squall of fury covered Lialla's scream entirely; she shifted with a speed that blew a whirlwind of sand into the throat of Jennifer's open shirt and momentarily blinded her. Wings cracked against still air. Jennifer swore and rubbed at her eyes. When she could see again Robyn hovered on immense wings directly overhead. She banked awkwardly, Jennifer thought, and began circling.

"She doesn't look right," Lialla murmured close to her ear.

"No," Jennifer agreed. The two women exchanged a worried look, and Aletto came to his feet.

"What—is something wrong—?"

Jennifer shook her head and tried to put the conviction she didn't feel into both her gesture and her words. "Don't think so. Not—wait, what's she doing?"

"Coming down," Edrith called out. "Fast, too." He backed away quickly. Jennifer shaded her eyes against the high afternoon sun. Wings spread wide, the bird was indeed losing altitude, and a moment later, she pulled the wings in and dropped in a series of tight circles. She was Robyn again almost before clawed feet touched earth. Aletto caught her; they went down together.

Aletto's knuckles were whiter than his face. He struggled back to his knees, bringing Robyn partway up with him. "Say you aren't hurt!"

She shook her head; she was panting heavily.

Jennifer leaned over to touch the pulse in Robyn's throat. It was pounding extremely fast. "I think she's just winded."

Robyn nodded again. "Hard to talk. Hard landing, okay?" There was silence, except for the wheezing pant, and that finally faded to something nearer normal. She finally looked up. Aletto

160

took the tissue from her pocket and used it to blot sweat from her forehead and cheeks. "Thanks. A little water, maybe?" Edrith was at her other side with an open bottle, which he held for her. "Wow," Robyn said finally. One final little gusty sigh, and she sounded almost normal once more. "*That* was a rush!"

"Tell me," Jennifer said.

"Yeah. Like dropping acid and thinking you were flying. I just *knew* it wasn't real, you know? I kept expecting to find myself halfway down to the street from my bedroom window or something, really nasty. And the height? Boy, I knew it was there this time!" She took another drink and her shoulders sagged.

"Never mind," Lialla said. "You can try it tonight, after dark. Jen's right, it was a good idea. Who'd know it wasn't going to work?"

"Yeah." Robyn forced a rather crooked smile. "Sorry we had to waste all that lovely mad, kiddo. You do that on purpose, or were you really pissed?"

"Really want to know?" Robyn shook her head. "Never mind, then. I'll think of something else for tonight. In case."

"Sure, I know you love me. Something, though: I mean, I stayed up as long as I could, there wasn't anything moving all around us, and I don't think I saw as far as the road. But that way?" She twisted around to point west. "Where you can't see it because we're too low here. There's an absolute *mother* of a thunderstorm coming our way. I think we're going to get soaked this afternoon."

* * *

THEY could see it building: a faint line of black against the distant brown and dusty green foothills, a hump of mushroom-shaped white thundercloud rising above the rest of it. Some of the storm moved past them on the north, moving rapidly inland. Jennifer watched shadow sail across the hills, felt the occasional gust of chill, damp air swirl down from that direction.

She turned her back on it, shifted her grip on the bo. Edrith had worked out a new series of moves based on something he and Chris had been doing and he was eager to try them. "We can't just sit here," he said, once Robyn was on her feet and walking around again. "That isn't smart; we have to keep doing this if it's going to be automatic, and if the muscles are going to hold up. I was about *dead*, I was so tired after last night. And some of those guys have come at us twice; we don't have complete surprise on our side any more. Anyway," he added as he brought the bo up to start his figure, "it'll make the time go faster, if we have something to do."

Jennifer had to concentrate hard on what Edrith was doing; once he'd shown them all the pattern, he worked with her first, leaving Robyn and Aletto together for the moment, and Lialla to watch. "Hands farther apart," he said. Jennifer nodded; she was already a little breathless and didn't want to have to let him hear it. She'd been kept from the fight last night—frankly, she thought, she'd rather have hit someone than traded sniping remarks with Jadek. She'd found a way to enhance what she did the time before—but that might not always be an option. It would be dumb to depend on being able to blur herself; even if she could do it with any regularity, it would be her luck to run up against someone who could see through that.

"Legs," she told herself in an undertone. *Use your legs, Cray, not your forearms, right?* There was too damned much to remember, at least until she got the feel of what was being asked of her. The only thing that kept her from despair was remembering she'd had the same problem with her self-defense classes. She'd been a total klutz there, too, until the whole pattern had come together. Once she had the pattern down, Edrith stepped back and nodded. "Great. You teach it to Lialla." He went over to work with Aletto while Robyn caught her breath and watched.

"You heard the man," Jennifer said mildly. Lialla set her jaw, brought up the bo to the first position. Wood cracked against wood. Other considerations and worries faded for the moment. Lialla was absolutely determined to make a success of this, at least as determined as her brother was. And she had none of the uncertainty about striking another woman that Jennifer had found in her contemporaries in that self-defence class. Here—she had to make her concentration total, her eyes, her reflexes, her knees and feet all ready for that one misstep on Lialla's part that would allow her to make a touch.

It came finally; both women were sweating freely and Jennifer was vaguely aware the sky was getting dark as the storm came nearer. Hair lifted from her forehead; Lialla's scarf was snapping in the sudden, rising wind, flapping around her throat. It was a distraction, a deadly one when it flailed across her eyes. Lialla found the other woman's staff suddenly inside her guard, the smoothed end touching her breastbone. She inclined her head, relaxed her grip on one end of her own staff and used the free hand to tuck the scarf ends. "I'll remember that," she said crisply, but she was grinning. "Remove my own or pin it firmly; watch the opponent's."

162

"Cheating," Jennifer said gravely, but her eyes were alight.

Lialla shook her head. "Not if it works. But that reminds me; your wrestling trick. Show me how you did that." She glanced skyward as another gust of wind tugged at her Wielder blacks. Jennifer followed her gaze: The rest of the storm was blowing right for them. "And fast," Lialla added. "Before we have to try it wet."

"Or fried," Jennifer said. "Lightning will go for either of us; we're just about the tallest things around." She cast another glance at the rapidly approaching storm. "All right. Stand still; I'll have to do it fast the first time, but I'll try not to drop you too hard."

13

L IALLA took several falls without complaint, her concentration intense and very focused. She and Jennifer were nearly enough matched in size that neither had any advantage over the other and Jennifer found it considerably harder to throw the sin-Duchess than she had the large man she'd dropped in the Thukar's tower. It forced her to pay closer attention to what she was doing, and how it worked, for the first time since she'd taken the self-defense class. *Not a bad idea,* she thought briefly. *I got sloppy with it, back home, let it slide too long.*

Lialla pulled the legs from under her on her second try. She was grinning like a kid when she held out a hand to help Jennifer up, then made Chris's time-out sign. "That's right, isn't it? A little time to talk?"

Jennifer nodded. She was a trifle breathless at the moment. "Good work. I'll have to teach you the rest of what I learned. I was thinking it probably wouldn't be useful here, but—" She shrugged, drew her first deep breath in what seemed forever and let it slowly out. She was hot and sweaty, and the sudden gust of wind felt cool against her forehead and bared arms.

"Why not useful?" Lialla wanted to know.

"It's—the things I learned were for working women, mostly used on city streets to protect them from the kinds of men who prey on women. Somehow, the way things looked here, it didn't seem that women would be on the streets by themselves, or that men would try to harm them." She shrugged. "I guess that's not bright of me; there are always people who steal or kill or—"

"It happens," Lialla said. "Even in Sehfi, which is small and part of Duke's Fort. You thought our women were—what?"

"I don't know. Guarded, sheltered. Encouraged to be helpless, dependent completely on men."

"Holmaddi women are. Caravener women certainly aren't. *I* was like that in Zelharri, not because of custom but because of Jadek. I thought I'd told you I was to have learned to use a knife and to wrestle, to ride. Rhadazi women have always had to be able to protect themselves, at least since some time after the Hell-Light wars but before the Dukedoms were created." She pushed damp tendrils of brown hair from her forehead and turned her face into the wind. "You'd really need to talk to Aletto if you want history; it's more his interest than mine, except I know some things generally. During—oh, Shesseran the Eighth's reign?—there were feuds. Several powerful and wealthy families in Andar Perigha virtually destroyed Podhru, there were assassinations in the streets, poisonings. Families had their own small armies, women—people of means went about the City surrounded by armed servants and the less well-to-do openly carried knives and swords."

"We had something similar," Jennifer said as Lialla looked at her, awaiting comment and visibly expecting disbelief. She filed the data for Chris—Medici, Borgia? It sounded like what little she knew of Renaissance Rome—which really wasn't that much. And just now, she couldn't afford the distraction; if Merrida was right, she'd have the rest of her life to explore such historical byways, if she wanted. If Aletto came into his own. *When, Cray,* she reminded herself firmly.

But Chris would be enchanted by this information. And he'd doubtless know names, he and Aletto could— Chris. God. The pang of loss and accompanying guilt caught her by surprise; she'd actually forgotten about him for an hour or more. *Don't think of him, if this is all you can feel. Wallowing in guilt won't get him back, it won't help anyone,* she ordered herself. Easier thought than accomplished. But Lialla was talking again.

"Merrida says it was then some women started wearing breeks like mine. More sensible for running, if you had to." She shook her head. "As I say, it was never an interest of mine, history. I know as much as they could bully me into learning, which isn't much. They—Jadek—wouldn't let me learn the wrestling; this is the first I've ever tried." She flexed her arms and winced. "I'm going to ache from it, too."

"New and specialized use for your muscles," Jennifer agreed. "And I hurt all over when I took the class. That's enough for one session, though. It's like what Chris said—about the bo. You only need a very few basic moves, and then you need to practice them until you can just do them without thinking. I'll work out a couple other throws for you, if you like, whatever else I can make myself remember." Lialla nodded enthusiastically, winced again as tight neck and shoulder muscles protested. "Sorry I didn't think about it before. Like I said, this seemed like something for the big city, nothing sensible for here. And I haven't done it in some time; until Sikkre, I'd forgotten all about it."

"It worked," Lialla reminded her. "Those breeks of yours. What kind of stuff are they?" She held out a tentative hand. "May I?" When Jennifer nodded, she touched the other woman's denim knee, felt the edge of the pocket. "Thick. Extremely practical, aren't they?"

"Extremely."

"A little—ah—revealing, of course," Lialla said. She withdrew her hand. Jennifer grinned.

"These are conservative, compared to a lot of them, trust me. I'll be damned sorry when they wear out, though."

"That surely won't be soon." Lialla rubbed her jaw thoughtfully. "My mother would doubtless faint if I wore such a thing."

"It used to be the same where I'm from," Jennifer assured her cheerfully. "Until mothers began wearing jeans themselves."

"Jeans," Lialla echoed. Her eyes were fixed on Jennifer's denim-clad leg. She finally shook herself and brushed her hands together briskly. "If we—you know, somehow I find it hard, here and now, to believe there will ever be anything other than this. If there is, I'll do everything I can to get replacements for those. There are excellent weavers in Zelharri, some fine seamstresses."

"It's a nice thought," Jennifer said lightly. "And I'll hold you to it, believe me."

"Do. I—wait." Lialla stood very still suddenly. Her eyes had moved to a point past Jennifer's shoulder and were now fixed there, dilated in surprise or fear. When the other woman would have turned, she held out a low, warning hand. "No, don't look yet. Wait. There's a man, a nomad. Behind you." Jennifer's back crawled and the shock must have shown on her face. "He's back beyond the brush,'' Lialla added hastily. "Not moving at all.''

"Isn't *that* reassuring," Jennifer exclaimed dryly.

"He's not—I don't *think* he's armed. Go ahead, turn around, do it slowly, though. I think he'll run if either of us startles him." Lialla's face showed nothing, certainly none of the disgust in her extremely low, noncarrying voice. "Coward," she hissed softly. "How can anyone live like that?"

Jennifer could see him now; a short, fabric-swathed figure standing motionless on the far side of the dry wash, where the brush wasn't as thick or as tall. It still covered him well above the waist. What she could see was mostly black or indigo cloth— it was hard to tell color, the sun had slipped behind rapidly advancing cloud and it was suddenly twilight. The air was noticeably cooler. Jennifer fought a shiver, certain the man facing her across twenty feet of open ground would take it for fear. *Like Charles the First,* she thought, and was immediately sorry the thought had occurred to her. One of the rare bits of history that had stuck: Charles, who'd wanted a second shirt before he was led out to the block lest his enemies mistake the shivers caused by cold air for terror of the impending ax. . . .

"What do you want?" Lialla spoke in an even, reasonable voice, as though continuing an ongoing conversation. The nomad blinked: His walnut-colored forehead and black eyes were all that were visible in the welter of wrapped cloth. "Are you one of those who took our companion?"

Silence; so long a silence Jennifer wondered if he'd heard. If he understood. If he was some half-witted wanderer out on his own, not one of the kidnappers at all. But he finally spread his arms wide, held his open hands at shoulder height long enough for them to see he held no weapons, let them fall to his sides again. "No one is to touch me, or to come near, or I go." His Rhadazi was thickly accented but he had a reasonable vocabulary. Jennifer had to concentrate to understand him. "If I go away, there will be no opportunity for you to deal with me later. One hundred ceris for the outlander boy."

Jennifer was suddenly aware of the presence of the others behind her: From the corner of her right eye, she could see Aletto, both arms wrapped around an extremely pale Robyn, as if to keep her from rushing the man. Edrith—she thought he was behind the nera-Duke, thought she had seen movement. She didn't dare turn her attention from the little man to make certain; it didn't matter anyway. The nomad cast Aletto a long look before directing his gaze to the two women once more. Jennifer

166

sent her eyes toward Lialla; Lialla was looking at her expectantly. *Advocate,* she thought tiredly. *I should never have told them.* Then again, to let anyone else negotiate for Chris . . .

She straightened, squared her shoulders. "We haven't so much coin as you ask," she said firmly.

"Then the boy dies." His eyes shifted as Robyn cried out but Aletto had a good grip on her. They came back to Jennifer again.

"No." Jennifer forced her voice to remain level, expressionless, even as she thought *Shut up, Birdy!* as savagely as she'd ever thought anything. This was any negotiation, any arbitration. Not life and death. Not important enough to any of them to provide this little man with any leverage—he'd have leverage in plenty if he knew Chris's relationship with two of them. "It would be very unwise of you to kill the boy. Dead, he is worth no coin. Besides, we find him useful. Also, if you intend to return to your own with the message to kill him, we have no reason to let *you* live, have we?" Logic like that would have cost her back home, but she was playing a different game here—and she counted heavily on the nomad's reaction to her threat. *He* didn't like the "k" word, either: He took one step back, caught hold of a bush as though to hold himself in check. "You will listen to what *we* offer, and in exchange we will let you live to take the message to your fellows."

"A hundred ceris," he insisted, but he sounded uncertain this time.

"No."

The nomad gestured toward Aletto. "This man is the young Duke of Zelharri, we have that on good authority. A nobleman. Nobles are wealthy. Do you think we do not know such things?"

"Perhaps many nobles are wealthy," Jennifer said. She folded arms casually across her chest and hoped she conveyed the indifference she intended. "But this is not a wealthy man. If he had a hundred ceris to give to any man, in exchange for a boy who is not even his near friend or a relative, why would he be in *this* place, with only a few companions and such horses as he has, with not even a proper tent to shield him from the sun?" It was damned hard to tell from shadowed eyes at such a distance but she thought he looked even more doubtful now, and she pressed the advantage. "The Dukes whose land this is will not take it well, that you waylay people, to kidnap and extort money from them. It is not good for trade between Bez and Sikkre. The Emperor will not like it." Silence again. "You will bring us the boy, and in exchange we will swear any oath you choose not to lodge complaint with the Dukes and the Emperor."

"A hundred ceris," the nomad insisted, but he was simply mouthing the words now, no conviction behind them.

"No. Bring us the boy. As an added incentive, if you do so today, at once, if he is in our hands again before nightfall, I personally will give you this." She reached slowly for the little bag that hung from the black Wielder sash she'd run through the belt loops of her jeans, withdrew one of the stones Merrida had given her. Even in the rapidly increasing gloom, it shone a clear, bright blue. Sapphire, perhaps. "Only if he is in our hands tonight. Otherwise—"

She took one step forward; the nomad took two back. "You do not touch me," he said rapidly and in a high, trembling voice.

"I do not intend to. I merely wanted to show you this stone more closely, that you may know it is real and valuable."

"Then bring it and set it upon the sand, there—"

Jennifer's laugh silenced him. "Not likely! We aren't complete fools!"

"You are fools! The offer is as I said it—"

"No. A counteroffer. Our *only* offer. We won't cause an army to hunt you down, if you cooperate and return the boy to us, unharmed. If he comes back tonight, you get this stone, as a— call it a bonus." Wind whipped hair across her eyes, stingingly; she shoved it back from her forehead and held it flat to her head. The air was very damp, downright cold compared to only moments ago. The storm must be almost on top of them. The little man must be counting on the downpour to cover his escape; she doubted he'd have come so near them otherwise.

Her hopes rose suddenly, and for the first time: There was a piece of yellow paper in the man's fingers, held up like a talisman. "If I agree? There is here a map, to take you to the outland boy; *you* will go and fetch *him*. The stone—you will give that to me now." He didn't sound very hopeful, and didn't argue when Jennifer shook her head.

"You get the stone when the boy is *brought* to us and only if that is done before sunrise tomorrow. We will exchange them, the boy for the stone. You have my word once this is done, any oath you choose, that none of you will be harmed thereafter. And also, this vow," she added grimly. The nomad took another step back and waved the scrap of yellow pad.

"Threaten me and there is no bargain!" he shouted shrilly. "If I go now, there will never be a bargain!"

"The threat will be kept only if the bargain is not. In such a case, if the boy is not delivered to us, if he is hurt, I swear to

168

you—'' She raised her right hand, blue stone clenched in the fingers. Lightning chose that moment to strike only a few hundred feet away; thunder crashed almost on top of it, stunning all her senses.

The nomad shrieked, or perhaps that was the ringing in her ears. ''A storm sorcerer!'' he wailed. Jennifer reeled, barely aware to see the flutter of yellow paper as it dropped from the man's fingers and vanished into dry brush. *Chris's map*, she thought dazedly. *Get it now!* But her feet wouldn't obey her. Lialla raced past her, running for the bushes where the man had been and no longer was. Edrith grabbed Jennifer by both arms and gave her a hard shake.

''Are you mad, standing out here?'' he bellowed. He had to, to be heard above the wind, the thunder, the sudden roar of falling rain. He kept a grip on her right elbow, turned and sprinted for the low blanket shelter, dragging her after. The tall one that had provided afternoon shade was already down, a flapping mess of cloth, ash staves, rope ends. The single low blanket they crouched under didn't seem likely to stay up much longer, the way the wind was blowing.

Jennifer crawled back as far as she could and leaned against Edrith. She was soaked to the skin from just those few moments in the open, shivering violently as the wind howled around her. Edrith pulled her close and she leaned into him gratefully.

Lialla was close behind her. She'd stopped only to wrestle the silkcloth blankets free; they trailed wetly behind her as she crawled under the madly snapping blanket. ''Here.'' She held one out. ''They're almost as good wet as dry.'' Aletto dragged a protesting Robyn in moments later. Robyn was crying, swearing, almost incoherent.

''Let me go, damnit! I can go after him, I can shift, I can find where Chris is!''

''You can't!'' Aletto had to shout for her to hear him. ''Don't you know anything about storms like this? Lightning kills!''

''She knows that,'' Jennifer said. Her teeth chattered, but she and Edrith were packed in clingy wet silkcloth that was rapidly losing the clammy, cold edge. It was blessedly windproof; enough so, she thought, that she might be starting to warm up. ''Birdy, you can't do that, not now. The little man's long gone, in the first place. In the second, you've flown in planes back home in bad weather. Remember downdrafts?'' Robyn shook her head stubbornly. ''Don't do that, damnit, your hair's getting me soaked!'' Jennifer snapped. She freed a hand to wipe the fine spray of water drops from her face and eyes. ''You know damned well you wouldn't survive, and how do you think Chris would like *that*? Matter of fact, how do you think I'd like having to tell him you wiped yourself out trying to get him back? Ultimate guilt trip? Besides—'' She stared out at the curtain of falling water, at the very thin line of blue dividing black cloud and hills. Typical desert storm, wild but brief. "Oh, Lord," she yelped, fought free of the shelter and crawled into the open before Edrith realized what she was doing. "Wait!" she shouted over her shoulder. "I just remembered—!''

Remembered too late. The nomad had indeed dropped Chris's map in his astonishment and terror. She found it a few paces from where he'd been standing, one tiny corner sticking up from the mud. Another moment and it would have been buried forever, or washed into the gully and carried away. But what she freed and gently sloshed in running water to clear it of dirt was pulpily wet. The blue lines stamped on it and the ink Chris had used ran together and what was left was utterly unreadable.

* * *

SHE crawled back into the shelter, let Edrith wrap the silkcloth around her once more and leaned gratefully against him. She'd become chilled again, just in those few moments; Edrith seemed by contrast to radiate heat. She opened her eyes, aware of Robyn's worried gaze, freed a hand to pull out the bit of yellow pad. Being crushed in her fist hadn't helped it either; probably it couldn't have hurt anything. Robyn took it wordlessly, smoothed it with extreme care and gazed down at it. Jennifer shoved dripping hair from her forehead, let her head fall against Edrith's shoulder, let her eyelids close. Thunder seemed to shake the ground; the wind shrilled through brush. She heard one of the horses and hoped vaguely that they were well tied. Someone else would have to deal with them, though. Just now, it was too much effort to open her eyes. . . .

* * *

SHE woke just short of sunset, alone under the dripping shelter blanket that had somehow remained tied off throughout the storm. The blanket under her was soggy; she could feel the water squelching through the thick fabric when she shifted her weight. The silkcloth was apparently also largely waterproof because she was wet but not as wet as lying in a puddle would ordinarily have left her. It was pleasantly warm inside the featherweight silkcloth, the breeze against her face cool. She sat up slowly, keeping the silkcloth in place. The thought of that breeze against damp shirt and jeans didn't seem at all pleasant.

A little ways away, Lialla was spreading blankets and clothing across the hedge that edged a now noticeably deeper and still-running wash. Edrith was letting the horses drink from this. Aletto was nowhere in sight but Jennifer could hear him somewhere behind her, crackling through the brush. Gathering wood, most likely. Robyn had a good-sized fire going and was stirring the largest of her kettles. Something steamed; Jennifer couldn't smell what because the wind was blowing away from her.

She hugged the silkcloth closer around her shoulders and edged her way out of shelter, awkwardly got hold of the groundcloth blanket and dragged it out with her. Lialla saw her, came across and took it. "Go on over and get warm. Dry out if you can, we all have. I'll do this."

"You're sure—"

"Go," Lialla ordered and gave her a little shove toward the fire. "You don't want to be still wet once the sun goes down, not if the wind stays strong."

"Mmmm. No." She withdrew the hand gratefully into her cover once more, squatted as near the fire as she dared and gingerly eased her arms apart. The wind was strong and erratic, blowing smoke in half a dozen different directions. Robyn had made a fan of her folded-double map and was using it to keep smoke out of her eyes. With her other hand, she was stirring a thick, dark soup. Jennifer sighed happily as heat soaked into her legs, slid back a little as the warmth on her cheeks became heat. Robyn glanced at her, went back to stirring her soup. "Damned smoke, I'm gonna go blind. You were really out, kiddo. Everything okay?"

"Yeah. I'm not wild about thunderstorms, though, and I got so cold and wet I thought I'd die."

"Yeah. Pretty nasty for a while there. You know, I'd forgotten about you and storms; I've always been the other way. You know, a good hard rain and I have to find an excuse to get right out in it. It gives me a real rush."

"I remember Aunt Betty having a fit when you went out in a downpour, way back when."

"Hah. She had fits about everything. Forget her." Robyn swore as smoke momentarily blinded her, coughed thickly. "This'll be ready pretty quick. I don't want to try flying on a full stomach, you know?"

Jennifer sat up a little straighter. "You think—?"

Robyn shrugged gloomily. "I don't know what to think. Edrith and Aletto went at that chunk of paper for—God, I don't know, a long time. They seem to think the little guy, the nomad—he apparently thought you were calling down the wrath of God on him. Impressive, but—''

"Oh, God. Birdy, I'm—''

"Don't you dare say sorry!'' Robyn hissed. She shoved hair behind her ears; it blew free almost at once. "That's the worst rotten luck ever, but it's not anything else. I'm surprised the little man stuck around as long as he did, what with the odds and everything. Anyway, the guys had a long go at the map but they just couldn't tell much. You can see the line that's maybe the Bez road. Anyway, I'm going to try another search, once it's dark. I know that little jerk is long gone, but I have to try."

"I know. I'm not going to try and stop you, Robyn. I thought it was a good idea, remember? Besides, your little jerk must have planned on the storm covering his retreat, don't you think? And he can't know about you. So they could be close by, figuring we'd never locate them by conventional means, and not knowing we have any other way of doing it.''

"They—yeah, right." She shoved damp hair out of her eyes once more with the wrist of the hand holding the paper fan. "This stuff is driving me nuts tonight. Wasn't there a hat or a visor in one of the bags? Wasn't Chris wearing one early on? Before we got to Sikkre and he went native?''

"Mmm—I don't remember." Jennifer shifted, stretched a leg out cautiously. Her high-tops were splotched with mud and sand, and soaked right through. "No, wait. My tennis hat, the yellow one. I saw it in the Nike bag when he fished out my running shorts. You want it?''

Robyn set the spoon on the piece of paper, a short distance from the fire, and stood. "I'll go. Get away from the damned smoke and besides, my knees are starting to die from squatting here.''

"Bring me my other sneakers and socks, will you? I think I put them back in that Nike bag, too." Robyn stretched cautiously and walked across the open. She was moving almost as stiffly as Aletto did after a long ride. *God,* Jennifer thought, *How's she going to get off the ground tonight if she's that done in?* Robyn passed Aletto, who was on his way in with a double armful of branches. He wasn't limping; he was walking extremely slowly, though, and his face was pinched. Lialla watched his back, worry lining her forehead. She turned away as Robyn came up and helped her dig out the gym bag. Robyn squatted down to fish through it. Her shriek brought Jennifer to her feet; Aletto dropped the load of wood and ran lurchingly back to her.

Jennifer was right behind him, the silkcloth a forgotten puddle next to the fire where it had slithered from her shoulders.

Robyn's face was red, her eyes fixed on something inside the bag. As Jennifer came up, she reached with a shaking hand and drew out a small, flat object, held it at arm's length.

It took a moment to realize what her sister had; so few days since Robyn had bought three red-and-white packs of cigarettes at that highway fruit stand on the way out to the Devil's Punchbowl, but with so much happening it might have been a lifetime since she'd seen anything like it. "Robyn!" she gasped.

"Damnit, Birdy! You gave me a goddamn *heart* attack!"

"Heart attack?" Robyn glared up at her, shaking the pack like a weapon. "I *knew* I couldn't have smoked all of those, I *knew* I was being careful, holding onto them, just doing half of one at a time. That little monster *hid* these from me! I'll—when I get hold of him, I swear I'll—!" Words failed her. Aletto stood irresolute just behind her for several moments, finally backed slowly away and went to gather up the fallen wood as though nothing had happened.

"Maybe he was saving them *for* you, or maybe he just found some you dropped," Jennifer began. Robyn glared at her and she shut her mouth.

"Sure. I don't think." She turned the open end of the pack toward her and began counting with the end of one little finger. "Seven. I'll, *oh*, when I get my hands on him—!"

"If he'd wanted to get rid of them, wouldn't he have just dumped them?" Jennifer asked mildly. "Or thrown them in the fire?"

"You'd defend him," Robyn snapped. "You nonsmokers."

"That's not fair, and you know it." Jennifer took a step back. "I've never traded stereotyping put-downs with you before, and I'm not going to start now. Have one, if that's what you want, it's your business. Settle what he was doing with them with Chris, when he gets back. You're not dying, which is incidentally what we all thought, so I'm taking my shoes and going back to the fire before I start turning blue." She bent over, found the cross-trainers and the socks stuffed in them—all still dry thanks to the heavy waterproof nylon of the bag, returned to the silkcloth and gratefully pulled it back across her shoulders.

It took a while to undo double-knotted, wet laces, longer to convince herself to ease her feet out of the high-tops and then out of the socks. Her toes were white, wrinkled and numb with the chill; the cold air was like ice cubes on the soles and arches. She tucked one under her, inside the silkcloth, held the other to the fire to dry and warm before pulling on the almost clean, wonderfully dry sock. By the time she was tying the second shoe, Robyn was back at the fire. The red-and-white cardboard pack was nowhere in sight, but she smelled faintly of cigarette smoke. Jennifer made an effort not to wrinkle her nose, shifted around so she could perhaps get her shirt and the pockets of the jeans dried out.

Robyn gingerly tested the soup, set the spoon aside once again. "It didn't even taste that good, damnit," she mumbled finally. It wasn't really an apology, Jennifer thought; but it was the best she'd get. She nodded. Robyn apparently chose to take the nod as an acceptance of apology, because she sounded less defensive and angry when she went on. "I need to make some biscuits. Would you mind watching this while I get the flour and stuff for them?"

"No problem," Jennifer assured her, and edged around to take the wooden spoon. From here, the soup smelled wonderful: peppers and some kind of herb blend thickened with rice. Too bad it wouldn't be beef-based. Even chicken would be good right now, but they didn't have any chicken, and Robyn wouldn't use the jerky for soup. She wasn't going to eat—or cook—red meat. Jennifer respected her for it, under such trying circumstances, but at the moment she found herself wishing her sister wasn't quite so—pigheaded. Yeah, right. Call it pigheaded.

They ate before it grew entirely dark, Robyn only picking at a little of the soup, half a biscuit. The biscuits were filling but bland: no butter or milk to go in them, only salt and a pinch of the soup's herb for flavor. No butter to slather on them, which to Jennifer's mind would have covered a multitude of sins. Edrith gathered the bowls together and carried them off to scour with sand. By the time he had them ready to rinse in a little of their hot washing water, Robyn was pacing around the fire, anxiously watching the western horizon. Aletto watched her, as anxiously. Lialla glanced from one to the other; Edrith ignored them all and carefully stacked bowls. Jennifer stirred, but before she could offer any help, Robyn simply shifted and rose into the night sky. Aletto bit his lip and watched her go.

* * *

SHE was gone what seemed a terribly long time. Lialla replenished the fire, went to turn blankets and to lay one under the low shelter. She came back to pronounce the upper, shade blanket dry. "I don't think it's as cool as it was earlier, just after it rained. The wind's helping, too."

No one answered. Lialla shrugged and began brewing a large

pot of tea. Aletto's eyes were fixed on the sky, now thick with stars. Edrith ate the second half of Robyn's biscuit, then went off to check the horses.

Jennifer closed her eyes, let the silkcloth fall to the ground and sought Thread. Find Robyn—she should, she realized with a sudden pang, have kept some kind of contact with Robyn all along. At least tried.

There was no movement on the ground anywhere near them, plenty of people on the road. Moving slowly, though. People in such close contact with each other, so many animals—*horses*, she assured herself—it must be a caravan. Another herder and the herder's flock beyond the road. And suddenly, very close, one rapidly moving being that set Thread to chiming like small brass Indian bells—movement that became human movement a little distance away. Robyn—surely Robyn, back in human form, shifting away from them all.

She opened her eyes and regained reality as her sister came walking into the light, slowly and unsteadily. Aletto and Edrith both jumped up and helped her over to the fire. Jennifer unhooked her own collapsing leather cup from a belt loop and filled it with hot tea. Robyn took it gratefully and sipped with caution, eyes closed. She finished it and sagged back against Aletto, shaking her head. "I—God, I must have gone most of the way to Sikkre, and I swear I could see the ocean at one point. If they're down there, they're under shelter—a cave, trees, somewhere I couldn't see." She sighed deeply. "I'll try again."

"You're too tired," Aletto began. Robyn laughed breathily.

"Oh. Not tonight. I think my arms would fall off if I tried it tonight again." She opened her eyes for one brief moment and glanced up at him. "Told you I was an old broad."

"You're not," he replied indignantly. "What you did—"

"Wasn't enough," she finished somberly when he paused to search for words. "Never mind. I'll find him. We will, somehow."

"Of course we will," Jennifer said. Robyn merely nodded. The cup slipped from her fingers and her head turned in on Aletto's shoulder. His fingers tightened briefly on her arm but it was doubtful she even noticed.

"Of course we will," he said softly. Now that Robyn couldn't see his face, though, he didn't look hopeful at all.

14

THREE days crawled by. Jennifer couldn't remember ever having been so anxious and bored at the same time, not even when she was awaiting her Bar results, or waiting to hear from Heydrich & Harrison that they'd hired her. At least then, there had been books to read—and no nagging, guilty feeling that someone's life hung on what she'd done, or might yet do.

They kept busy. Aletto managed his first ''real'' pushup, Jennifer ran and taught Lialla another throw. Edrith practiced new maneuvers with his bo. After the last puddles from the thunderstorm dried up, he took two of the horses and rode back to the roadside well, returning with enough extra water that Jennifer could bathe. It helped; there was sand in everything, the wind was nearly constant, her hair felt awful. She had to make do with a single rinse, which took away some of the sand and dirt and left her scalp feeling a little less rubbed. Not really clean. There was dirt ground into her knuckles, under her nails. The jeans that had been just a thought too snug when she drove to the Punchbowl were beginning to hang—partly lack of washing, but she could see where she'd lost weight. Robyn had definitely lost girth. Aletto, by contrast, seemed to be gaining, but that was no doubt muscle. He slept more hours than he was awake during the three-day stop, and worked out almost constantly when he wasn't sleeping.

He limped; visibly, he hurt. His temper wasn't good and he snapped at everyone but Robyn—though generally he apologized at once. No one took his temper seriously anyway; it was all too obviously the result of the pressure he put on himself and the resulting pain.

No one quite dared to suggest he take it a little easier. Robyn, who no doubt would have, was too preoccupied with finding her son.

She spent hours aloft each night, coming to ground only when she was glassy-eyed and staggering, or when it started getting light. She flew large circles at great height, flew low, taking in details of the darkened, distant landscape that would have been invisible to human eyes. There were no groups of Cholan nomads anywhere, no men who rode camels. No one who looked like Chris.

Fortunately, there were no more thunderstorms. One rolled over them the next afternoon, but the rain evaporated long before it reached ground. No lightning struck anywhere near them. Thereafter, it was simply hot: cloudless, airless until late afternoon. Hot.

Food was running low, to the point where even Robyn was finding it difficult to prepare anything filling and edible—besides the herb and rice soup. It was too hot for anyone to find soup remotely appealing, even after the sun set and it cooled off. Finally, Robyn and Lialla went into a huddle over their remaining supplies the third morning—breakfast had been oat cakes and tea. "Even I'm getting a little tired of oat cakes," Lialla said as she finished her tea. The tea wasn't much better; the water had a leathery taste once again and the herb an odd flavor of its own from improper storage. "We're going to have to do something about food, and Robyn and I both think the best thing is to send you for it, Edrith. There's a village down the road and just east of it, if this map is right." She held up a hand at once when Aletto set his cup down and shifted his weight. "Please. Don't have a better idea, please? I absolutely can't face any of this stuff one more night, and I can't take a fight right now."

"Just moving around," Aletto said mildly.

"Oh." Lialla eyed him suspiciously but he'd gone back to a study of his leather cup. "Edrith?"

He nodded. "We need water again anyway. Decide what you want; I'll go." He rode out a short while later with a handful of copper coin, the pack horse beside him and Aletto's under him. Robyn sat next to the nearly dead fire and watched him go, hand holding her chin.

"Thanks for not saying it, any of you," she mumbled. "I know it's my fault we're still here—"

"Oh, shut up," Jennifer said in good-natured irritation. "We don't need breast-beating right now either. Blame it on Chris for getting caught; at least he isn't here to argue with you about it."

"Three days," Robyn whispered.

"Three days isn't so very long," Aletto said. He patted her shoulder. "Come on, you were pretty stiff this morning, you come walk with me." He pulled Robyn to her feet.

"You and me," Lialla said mildly. She lowered her voice,

even though it was unlikely the now-distant Robyn would over-hear her. "She thinks he's dead, doesn't she?"

Jennifer sighed. "I'm afraid she does. She won't say, though. And I'm afraid I don't have the nerve to ask her right now."

"What about you, though?" Lialla persisted. "Do *you* think we'll get him back?"

"I don't think they've killed him. Why would they do that if he's a potential source of income?"

"Well, that little nomad said—"

"People say a lot of things, to persuade other people to act on emotion. Myself, I think they have him somewhere under wraps. Robyn could only see them in the open, after all. She says she hasn't seen tents or shelters except as part of villages or regular travelers along the road. Maybe these Cholan nomads don't use tents; maybe they've got underground shelters, or caves. I wouldn't mind either of those things just now; they stay cool no matter what it's like in the sun. There wouldn't necessarily be any evidence of either. Personally, I can see them waiting until we have to be good and worried; then they'll send the little jerk back to negotiate again."

"That presupposes they think we have reason to want him back, doesn't it?" Lialla asked. She settled down next to the fire, started to pour herself more tea, looked in the pot and wrinkled her nose. She set the pot back in the cooling ashes.

"I imagine members of a nomad tribe would simply assume we want him, that he's family or close friend to some of us. At least, where I'm from, desert tribes are composed of extended families."

"With Cholani, who knows?" Lialla said gloomily.

"I think we'll see something, soon—another note from Chris, or just another visit from our interpreter. I'll have to be careful, after my last performance. Let *you* or Aletto do the talking."

Lialla laughed briefly. "Keep your hands in your pockets. Especially if there are clouds. I nearly had a fit myself."

"Yeah." Jennifer sighed and braced her chin with her hand. "Nothing like calling down a royal curse, is there?" She stirred, got to her feet. "I'm going to run this morning, while it's still cool. You—?"

Lialla began to shake her head, stopped and considered. "I—it's something to do, isn't it?"

"Good for your legs and your wind," Jennifer assured her.

"I'll try."

They'd already discovered that Robyn's sneakers fit Lialla, if she undid her foot wraps and didn't try to wear either woman's socks. Lialla liked the lightweight, cushy shoes; since Robyn ordinarily went barefoot around camp and on the short, slow walks she and Aletto took, Lialla slipped into the faded sneakers, peeled out of all but the breeks and the lightweight, sleeveless overshirt. Jennifer tied her hair back, headband style, with one of the black haircloths; Lialla self-consciously copied that, shoved hair behind her ears the way Robyn did, matched Jennifer's stretch-out.

Jennifer kept the pace slow enough that she could talk, at least; after the first half-mile or so Lialla was limited to nods and shakes of her head, an occasional monosyllable. She paid close attention to the other woman's instructions: "Keep your breathing regular—see what I'm doing? Don't get your knees so high; keep them as close to the ground as possible." Lialla looked absolutely ragged when Jennifer slowed to a walk, but refused to turn back or wait.

"You're not just walking for *me*, are you?"

"I need this. The woman I used to run with told me to start slow and back off; I always liked that advice. At least, for the first few weeks; after that I get aggressive." She glanced at the red-faced sin-Duchess. "How are you doing? You sound better."

"I'm fine," Lialla panted untruthfully. She looked at Jennifer's bare legs with wistful eyes. "Except hot."

"It's getting warm out here. We'll take another run the same distance, then turn back. Before you ask, that's about the distance I started with. Maybe you need shorts."

"Perhaps. I'd never have the nerve to wear them, though, even out here."

Edrith returned several hours into the afternoon, while Jennifer and Lialla were napping under the high shelter; the noise he made on his return, the horses welcoming both their returning fellows and the water, woke the women. Just as well, Jennifer thought; it was windless and the sponging she'd taken when they got back from the ride had long since worn off. Besides, she was hungry.

Edrith had water, more flour, honey and tea, an enormous fresh loaf filled with some kind of meat stew, more rice and, tied to the back of the pack horse, a wooden cage containing two scrawny-looking young chickens. "I remembered what you said about a killed chicken turning deadly if I brought one back during the day. The woman I traded with was about to send these to market, and I swore to her by everything I hold dear to return her cage." He looked slightly bewildered at the face Robyn

179

made, and seemed to have an extremely difficult time understanding her reluctance to deal with live birds, though he listened patiently enough as she explained. "I see. You eat them, but you won't kill them?" He scratched his head and glanced at Jennifer, who laughed.

"At least I've never pretended anything different," she said. "Someone else wrings chicken necks and cleans them up, or I don't eat them. I don't even kill fish or clean them."

"Well, don't look at me," Robyn said huffily. "Being a modified veg doesn't mean you're automatically two-faced about these things, does it?"

"In most cases it does."

"Oh. Well." Edrith shrugged. "It's usually left to the cook, but since you're squeamish—"

"Got it right in one, kid," Robyn said firmly.

"Since you are, I'll deal with that. They'll be fine until tomorrow, if necessary, even the day after; there's a little bag of grain for them. The bread, however, will not keep. It was hot and fresh when she sold it to me but that was a while ago."

Robyn sniffed at it gingerly, shook her head. "It's red meat of some kind; oh, well. At least there's a lot of bread around it. Looks good. Thanks, kid."

Lialla held up another bag. "There's a small box with butter, probably very soft. You like that on bread, don't you?"

"Doesn't everybody?"

* * *

ROBYN slept most of the late afternoon, woke for a short while and slept again. After a cup of heavily honeyed tea, she walked into the dark, beyond the brush hedge; moments later, they heard her leave. Jennifer, who sat next to Edrith by the small fire, shook her head. "I wish she'd at least *say* when she's going. She'd be real sorry if someone grabbed her out there before she could shift." Aletto sighed, got up and walked over to his blankets, where he could be heard settling in for sleep. Lialla was out walking around the camp, keeping guard. Somewhere around midnight, Edrith would spell her, followed by Jennifer, who really wanted to follow Aletto at the moment and put some sleep between her and that two hours.

Edrith laughed dryly. "I'll wager the someone would be even sorrier. Even a goose can break a grown man's arm with a wing; did you know that?"

"No. I know a bird like *that* can snap a neck. But don't say so around Robyn, will you?"

"Of course not. It was market rumor all over Sikkre by the

time we left, though, you know: The wizard Snake dead, the three women missing from the Thukar's Ducal tower, the rather hysterical ravings of Snake's personal bodyguard, who saw a shapeshifted bird fly out the high window and only two human women behind before one attacked him. Was that you, or the sin-Duchess?"

"For my sins," Jennifer admitted.

"I wasn't really in doubt, you know," Edrith said. "You and Robyn are the first outlander women I've ever met, though there have supposedly been others about. It's odd to me you are so little alike, and Chris says you're sisters." He sighed. "I'm sorry I shall never see *your* world. Chris has made it real for me; so many things, so many very different kinds of people."

"I think you'd like it," Jennifer said. "I think you'd fit in quickly."

"I like the music he's told me about, some of the dancing. It's odd, you know? Very different from ours. But the music you sang for Dahven when we left Sikkre is close enough to some of ours. Very odd, don't you think?"

"There's a time problem," Jennifer said. "Apparently it moves faster where we were than it does here. You're not as technologically advanced as we are."

"That was Chris's word for it. He said, I mean—we have printing, but we don't use gunpowder; there are some things the same, but not others. He thinks we're at least two hundred years different from each other." He shook his head, laughed faintly. "So I don't think even when I'm an old man there will be any of these things Chris talks of. It's a pity." He leaned forward to stir the fire. "About Dahven. Jennifer, I don't believe he killed his father any more than Aletto does. The two of you seemed to me rather like one of the bard's tales, or those songs you two sang that night. Chris didn't see it, but I did. I wanted to say only that I'm sorry."

She swallowed. "You think he's dead?"

"No." He considered this. "By that, of course, I mean, I hope he isn't. If he played into a trap of his brothers', it doesn't seem likely he'll have survived it. We should not have let him go back."

Jennifer tugged the charm free and held it out where she could look at it. "We couldn't have stopped him. I tried; I think he'd have listened to me if anyone. I just wish he hadn't given us all his protections. I can't help but think it might have made a difference."

"Well." Edrith sighed gustily. "He's clever, you know. Even

more clever than Chris, and I truly expect to see Chris free himself and come back without nomads. Dahven—he's older, he's had more years to learn from Sikkre's markets, and from having such a father, such brothers.''

"Those twins," Jennifer agreed. "They were awful, simply dreadful. If he fell afoul of them—"

"They might have imprisoned him, you know. That's not good, certainly, but it's not dead, which is considerably more permanent. They might have killed Dahmec themselves and put their brother out of the way, in hopes that one of their father's sorcerers could make him confess to the death—"

"Please." She twisted around to lay a hand against his mouth. "Please don't. That's not better. Remember that I met one of those sorcerers. I'm not certain dead would be worse than what they might do to him.''

"I'm sorry," Edrith said simply. They were silent for a while. Jennifer finally stirred and rested her head against his shoulder.

"I'm glad you're with us, kid. I know Robyn is.''

"I'm glad I came. Sikkre—Vey is happy there; I know I was once. For a long time, actually. Being a thief is a boy's living, though; it's no guarantee of a long life for anyone nearing a man's years. If I'd stayed, I'd probably have been in prison within the year, or dead. Or sold to the Lasanachi.'' He was abruptly silent.

Jennifer waited for him to go on, finally asked: "Lasanachi?"

"Ship merchants. Also coastal raiders, depending on their mood at the time, or the phase of the moon, or politics back home, or—" He shrugged. "No one really knows. They trade now and again in Bezjeriad. I hear they put into Dro Pent harbor these days even though they warred against Dro Pent not that many years ago. They buy third and fourth sons, unwanted children, debtors or extra mouths from the various Dukes' prisons.'' He fell silent again.

"Nice guys," Jennifer said at last. Edrith nodded but wouldn't say anything else about them. She yawned, shook her head. "I hope Birdy isn't too long tonight; I don't feel right going to sleep while she's out like this.''

"I'd wake you," Edrith began.

She tilted her head to look up at him. "I appreciate that. But I try and keep touch with her via Thread. Hard to do that when you're sleeping.''

"I'd think so." He shifted, got to his feet. "I'd better check the horses.''

She watched him go, a line pushing her brows together. Hiding something. About Dahven? Her fingers sought the warm bit of silver and clung to it as though someone's life depended on that touch—hers or his.

* * *

THERE was no sign of Robyn anywhere near when she did search. Edrith came back, disrupting her efforts only slightly: She'd discovered that by keeping up a constant hum, it was nearly impossible for anything to break her concentration. The road was deserted at this near midnight hour. A large animal—dog-sized—moved across the dry lake bed at a goodly clip; another caravan camped around the water. One north of them. The herders had moved across the road the night before and now she could barely sense them at all.

* * *

IT was nearly dawn when Robyn returned. Jennifer was sleeping but she'd ordered herself to keep an ear and an open sense for any sign of her sister; she came awake at once as the bird crossed the camp slowly, banked and sailed down to the ground between the once again dry wash and the dry lake bed. By the time she was on her feet and moving, Robyn was already on her way past the horses, running despite obvious exhaustion. Edrith, alerted by Jennifer, had wakened and followed her, and was there to catch Robyn before she dropped. It was some moments before she could talk but she was nodding her head hard, pointing out toward the road.

"You found him!" Jennifer exclaimed. Lialla, who was on watch once again, came running, stopping only to catch up a water bottle; Aletto dropped down behind her to give Robyn a place to lean. She nodded sharply, tried to take the bottle, but her hand was shaking too much. Lialla brushed the hand aside impatiently and held a steadying hand under the older woman's chin, tilted the bottle against her lips. Robyn drank, tapped at the bottle then until Lialla took it away.

"Found him," Robyn gasped. "He's on the road—"

"Told you!" Edrith exploded joyously.

"Yeah, well, he's not with the camel guys; I don't know who they are. I knew if I went down, though, I'd never get back up and I was scared they might be the Thukars' men. We have to go get him!" Robyn finished in an urgent rush.

"We'll get him," Lialla said grimly. "Edrith, can you see enough to start saddling horses? Get moving."

"I'll help," Jennifer began, but Lialla shook her head and got to her feet.

"You'll scare them half silly. You pull down the shelters, pack things up. Robyn, can you ride?"

"Stop me," Robyn said flatly. She leaned forward, putting her weight on both hands. "Aletto, go help Edrith, I'll tell you the rest of it when we're moving; I'm just scared we'll lose him if we don't hurry. I'm all right," she added as the nera-Duke hesitated. "Just go!"

Lialla thrust the bottle into her hands. "Here, drink. You know you dehydrate when you do this, and you sound awful. I'll get the food packed and the fire out." Jennifer was already moving, heading for the sleep shelter where she'd left her high-tops. She thrust bare feet into them, strung loose socks through belt loops, left the laces trailing behind her as she crawled into the back of the blanket shelter to loosen ropes. Once they were looped together, the blanket and the one that had been under them folded flat, then rolled and tied for mounting behind saddles, she went for the tall daytime shelter. Lialla was stuffing things all anyhow into one of the larger bags; as Jennifer separated the two silk-cloths, the sin-Duchess stood and began kicking dirt over what was left of the fire. Jennifer undid ropes and separated ropes from silkcloth, spare blankets, three bos by feel. It seemed to take hours, but Robyn was still gasping for air when she knelt to roll the last of the blankets, roll the silkcloths around it and tie the bundle together with the last rope—a thick, unwieldy piece she had every intention of dumping in deep water as soon as they reached Bez Harbor. Some things absolutely begged to be replaced. Edrith came to take things away from her, passed Aletto, who let Jennifer load him up. She followed with the last of it. The laces tangled around her ankles; she swore under her breath and slowed to a more cautious pace.

Robyn stood, braced herself on wide legs, took one last drink of water and went over to the firepit to check for anything Lialla might have missed. "We're clear enough," she said shortly, still breathily. "Let's go, please!"

* * *

THEY made good time across the dry lake bed. It was dark, only a faint line of paler gray against black to show where dawn would eventually come, but Edrith had gone this way three times before now, and there were no burrows or unseen ravines to catch a person or horse unwary. The line of gray had extended to the entire sky by the time they reached the Sikkre–Bez Highway. This far south, it was wide open, only a few dry bushes to either side, a few flowering shrubs to show for the rain three days before. Robyn rode out onto the broad, flat, sandy surface of the road and turned her horse south. "That way."

Edrith came up beside her. "Rest just a moment; we pushed cold mounts pretty hard getting here."

"I want to know what you saw," Lialla said as she came up on the other side. Jennifer guided a cross, high-stepping animal with difficulty, finally drew it to a halt next to Lialla. Aletto was behind them both, attention divided between Robyn and the northward road, which he rather anxiously scanned.

"Don't know for certain," Robyn said. "Except Chris. He was sitting in the back of an open wagon. You couldn't miss him, that hair, those white sneakers. The people with him looked like men, mostly. Pale breeks like Lialla's, you know, all rucked up behind the saddlebow. Dark flapping capes. Two open wagons, a seat across the back of each. Three horses side by side pulling those."

Edrith considered this, and the others waited: Of them all, only he knew anything about this end of Rhadaz, little as it was. "Could be Bez merchants. The horse configuration isn't the Sikkreni style. They don't sound dangerous."

"There were ten, altogether," Robyn said. "They won't stand between me and my kid."

"They may not want to," Jennifer said and nudged her horse cautiously in the belly. It leaped forward, knocking into Lialla, who swore. "I need to get this damned monster moving before it eats my shoelaces, anybody mind? Maybe pick up the pace until we tire it out a little?" She was already well ahead of them, and had to raise her voice to be understood, but Robyn was at her side only a moment later, and the others right behind them.

"I don't mind," Robyn said. "I don't know how far, I don't think very. If anything, I was tireder tonight and it was harder to get anywhere."

"They might have pulled off to rest," Edrith warned. "Every one of you, keep an eye out, in case that's what they did."

Much too fast for her to read Thread. Jennifer gritted her teeth and concentrated on keeping what control she could of the horse, on not sliding off. On her right hip not cramping up, which at this point might be disastrous, and brought her visions of a fall right under the horse's hooves, or under Aletto's since he rode behind her.

They rode flat out for a few minutes, pulled back to a walk until the sun was just visible above the mountains. "Around here," Robyn said doubtfully. "The—everything looks different, you know?"

"I can believe it," Jennifer replied shortly. Her mount seemed well aware she was stiff, uncomfortable and—admit it, a little afraid because she couldn't find a good seat and the horse was full of itself after three days rest. The smell hadn't improved, or grown on her, during the days she'd had off, either.

The ground changed here, just a little: more sage again, a few dry, drought-stunted trees, and then the line of green that marked a stream. It didn't look as brightly green as the last one they'd stopped in, but the horses picked up the pace as they sensed water. Edrith, who had moved out ahead of them, stood in the saddle and waved, then pointed at an overgrown spot along the creek. "There's a cart or a wagon back in there," he called out. "I can't tell anything else. Could be them, though." Robyn bit the side of her hand and edged her horse forward, so she was right with him.

There was storm debris everywhere: large rocks, fallen slender trees with enormous, dirt-clogged root systems sticking up in the air. Thickets of dead brush piled behind that, twice as high as a tall man. Between two of these, the water ran, a fast stream gurgling over rock, falling in a three-foot spill to a deep pool, out and down an even higher falls. The crossing was above the first fall, marked by the footpath carved into a long-down tree spanning the water. Jennifer leaned forward in the saddle to peer into the trees. Level, early sun cast a hazy gold over everything and made it hard to see, but there might have been men there. By the time she reached dry ground once more— prudently afoot and leading the horse—she could hear them, though. The muscles in her neck had been tight with tension and worry; they relaxed now as she heard accented Rhadazi, two men discussing the cost of boot leather.

"Hallo the camp!" Edrith shouted. "We're from Sikkre, looking for a missing companion. May we join you?"

"Certainly," someone began, but a high, familiar voice interrupted him.

"Missing?" Chris shouted. "Hey, jeez, you guys, is it really you?" Aletto caught Robyn's horse as she threw herself to the ground, before the animal could run. Jennifer wrapped her reins around a heavy snag and followed. Chris, an unfamiliar yellow cape around his shoulders, met his mother partway, wrapped his arms around her and staggered back at the impact. He briefly buried his face against her shoulder. "Hey, Ma, it's all right," he said, loudly enough for the others to hear. "I'm fine." As Jennifer and Lialla came up, he smiled, but Jennifer's eyes were fixed on his hands. Chris made a face and hastily tugged at his

186

sleeves, pulling loose black cloth right down over his knuckles, but not before she had seen the deep, ugly, raw rope burns circling his wrists.

15

"HEY, ma, it's cool, don't sweat it, all right?" Chris held Robyn close and only Jennifer saw him tug surreptitiously at the sleeves of his black shirt, pulling them down well below his wrists, halfway across the backs of his hands. Or so she thought; when she glanced over her shoulder, Lialla met her eyes thoughtfully. Jennifer shook her head minutely. Lialla cast Robyn and Chris a swift glance, nodded as minutely. "Ma," Chris added in an intense, low voice, "you're getting my shirt wet and everyone's watching, you know?"

Robyn made a tremendous effort and got herself largely under control. She sniffed once, stepped back to look at him. "My God, kid, you look like hell," she mumbled. Chris gave a snort of laughter. The smile he offered her as reassurance only enhanced the gaunt lines running from his nose to the corners of his mouth, the unhealthy gray-under-tan of his entire face. There was dirt and dry grass or weed in his hair; his shirt was thick with dust; he'd washed his hands partway up, careful, Jennifer thought, of those dreadful wrists. Clean fingers only emphasized the grime of the rest of him.

He snorted again. "Yeah, about what you'd expect after being person-handled the way I was. I guess manhandled is okay, there weren't any chicks—women, sorry—in the party, as far as I could tell. Ultimate nonsexist costume, Ma, all you can see is eyes and hands. Before you ask," he added hastily, as his mother began feeling his arms and shoulders, "they didn't hurt me or anything. No torture, see, all fingernails right where they belong—"

"Stop that," Robyn protested weakly. "It's not any of it funny, Chris." But she took a step back and let go of him.

"Tell *me* it isn't. They coldcocked me, piled me on a camel, head down—avoid that if you can, it's no fun at all—made me

187

write rude notes to you guys and then stuffed me in an underground room that smelled so much worse than camels it must have held babies or sheep or something. Really gross, you know?''

"They didn't hurt your mouth any," Robyn retorted. She looked relieved, though, by the fact that he was kidding her the way he usually did.

"Yeah, well, none of them could understand me. I called them a lot of rude names in English, but that got totally boring after a while. I tried making faces at 'em—there was always just one guy at a time down in that place with me, they never did leave me alone. Anyway, I made faces and they just looked at me. Like real dimwits or something.''

"Probably figured you were trying to provoke them to jump you so you could get away," Jennifer said dryly.

"Yeah?" Chris demanded. "The way they had me trussed up, I doubt it. 'Course, I mean, we're talking about some serious Nervous Nellies here.''

"How did you get away?" Aletto wanted to know.

Chris shrugged. His ears were suddenly quite pink. "I wish. I didn't get away, I was rescued. Jeez, Ma, I feel like one of those damp Victorian girls in a Harlequin novel.''

"I wouldn't know," Robyn retorted dryly. "*I* don't read them.''

"Well, *I* sure don't. So I guess all those bodice rippers I found under the couch belonged to lovely Arnie—hey, easy!" Chris ducked as Robyn swung a practiced arm and clipped his ear. "You're supposed to be glad to have me back for at least a little while!''

"I guess you read them if you know what the women are like, huh?" Robyn asked dryly. "You got anything important to say, kid? I was up all night because of you. Literally," she added acerbically. Chris eyed her blankly for a moment, then went red right to his hairline once he realized what she meant.

"Oh." He glanced uneasily at Aletto, at Lialla and Edrith. Warily at Jennifer, who made a "go on" gesture. "Yeah. Well. Anyway, I intended to break out as soon as I could, I think that's rule one in the kidnappee's handbook. But the chances were absolutely zip. I hung out—God, I've lost track of time entirely! They gave me a little water now and again, apparently enough for them, but I felt like I was gonna dry up and blow away. The food was raunchier than junior high cafeteria food, it was so bad even *I* couldn't eat it. Well," he amended thoughtfully, "not much of it, anyway. So all of a sudden these guys start yelling and everyone splits. Next thing I know this guy"—he gestured with his head toward one of the men around him—"is sticking his head down through this trap door asking me in Rhadazi who I am and if I'm with the Cholani." He offered his mother a smile. "I said only by default and they hauled me out, dusted me off and offered me a ride." He feinted a punch at Edrith's arm when the Sikkreni came forward and grabbed him by the elbows. "Did I—tell me I saved you guys the money. I mean, did these guys?"

"A lightning storm apparently did it first," Jennifer said. "Which is just as well, since we didn't have as much as they wanted anyway. We'd have had to let them keep you." Chris groaned and made a face at her; he didn't look like he was taking the jibe very seriously, though. "You're all right, then, Chris, are you?"

He met her eyes warily. "Yeah, sure. Why?"

"We lost three days—"

"Three? Jeez!"

"—and it probably would be a good idea to make them up," she finished.

"Yeah, right." Chris nodded. "Right away, though? These guys were making breakfast when you rode up—"

"We have enough to share," one of them said, a young, red-haired man dressed in full tan breeches under a long, loose shirt and a swathing of red and gold headscarves similar to a nomad's turban. He spread his hands to take them all in; both index fingers bore large and costly-looking rings. "Particularly if you are a certain party traveling south, since my father has sent me on this journey to Sikkre in order to get what first-hand news I can for him. He's the Bez silver and brass merchant Oliendi, but he was Zelharri born. I'm his eldest and heir, Olar."

"I see," Aletto said. He considered only briefly, glanced at the others and apparently saw no serious opposition. He nodded then, and smiled what Jennifer had begun to think of as his politician's smile. It wasn't insincere, just—it changed him from the insecure and young-for-his-years nera-Duke. "Well. We are traveling south, certainly. And we'd certainly be grateful for food and tea; we've been on short rations the past few days." He held out both hands, clasped the other man's arms. Olar clasped his in turn.

"Good. We're not long from something hot; my cook can set another loaf in the ashes and start another pot of water. We always stop about here on a trading trip north and particularly until we've reached the highlands, we travel at night. Few do, but it's always struck me as far more sensible. We'll leave you before sunset tonight, but that gives us long hours for a meal, sleep and talk." He turned and raised his voice. "These people will eat with us, Mib, see to the food, will you? My companions are all employees of my father's silver trading company except Mib, who is responsible for the work on most of the wrought silver jewelry. He prefers to see to the purchase of his own raw materials. He's also an excellent cook." The men around the fire spoke or nodded as Olar indicated them with a wave of his hand and the resulting babble sounded friendly enough.

Robyn staggered and would have fallen if not for Jennifer's arm. "God," she whispered. "I don't know if it's reaction or just the dead tireds from being up all night. Literally."

"You said that before. I'm glad you can joke about it a little. It's probably some of both, Birdy. Let's get you over by that fire, shall we, maybe stuff a little food in you before you sleep."

"I should—" Robyn glanced at Chris doubtfully. He was introducing Edrith to the Bez merchant; in the early light, his face looked old and drawn, and Jennifer wondered whether it was all the pain in his wrists, exhaustion, or if there were some other injury he was hiding. Well, he wasn't going to hide it from *her*, not for long. Robyn would sleep long and hard once flat; Jennifer could tackle her nephew then.

She patted her sister's shoulder gently; it seemed less soft than it had only days before, and the underlying muscle was tight. Jennifer couldn't remember having ever felt muscle anywhere on her sister's arms before. "Robyn, you'd better sit down so you don't embarrass Aletto by passing out. Or Chris. I'll get our blankets and lay them out in the shade; personally I'm pretty tired myself and I'd like a good, long nap. This is probably about as safe as we're going to get on the road. I don't think anyone would dare jump us in the middle of a group like this."

Robyn nodded. "Yeah, right. Chris, why don't you come over here, talk to me? Let me poke you some more to convince myself you're real."

Chris had been talking with Edrith in a low, noncarrying voice. "Your little tax deduction is alive and well, Ma." He grinned impudently. "I need to go take a walk with this guy, though: I think I finally started taking in enough water."

"You're all right?" Robyn began worriedly. "Really?"

"Hey, I'm fine, I told you. I didn't pee for two days is all, they didn't give me enough water for that." Robyn turned bright red and he spluttered with laughter. "Anyway, you don't need to hold my hand, all right? I'm a little wobbly; I'd rather have

Eddie here than fall on my can and have to have someone come rescue me, thank you.''

"Wobbly?" Robyn's color was still high; she fastened on the one word anxiously.

"Mom, jeez." Chris sighed. "I got a little spooked, okay? Hanging out with guys who kept threatening to kill me. That doesn't do good things for your nerves, you know? And they didn't let me move around at all, so I also got stiff, and they didn't feed me much, so I'm a little sloppy in the knees for the moment. All the fingers are intact, as well as the fingernails, or didn't you notice? And just so you don't start yelling when I head for the bushes, I got a blister on the back of my heel so I'm limping a little, no big deal, okay?"

It was Robyn's turn to sigh. "No big deal," she echoed tiredly. "Anything starts to turn green and fall off, you talk to Jen or Lialla. I got your message loud and clear and I'm not messing with it."

"Good," Chris said flatly. "Not that there's any of *that* going on, nothing green, nothing falling off. I'll adjust the sock and the laces on my high-top so it's not rubbing, fix the funny walk right up. Don't sweat it, Mom. I'm back, nobody lost any money except the dufusses on camels, everything's fine." He paused, then quietly added, "I love you, too, Mom." He wrapped an arm over Edrith's shoulders and nodded. "Let's go, Eddie."

"Eddie?" Edrith asked; he didn't look certain whether he was being teased, insulted, or exactly what.

"You would be Eddie, in L.A., especially with a dweeb name like yours. So it's easier for me, all right?"

Edrith eyed him rather huffily. "Dweeb? That sounds like an insult, *Christopher Robin*."

"Gaaaa," Chris said in disgust. "I had to tell you about that, didn't I? Anyway, in L.A. you'd be Ed or Eddie, take your pick. And let's go before I start to float, all right?"

"Eddie." The Sikkreni considered this briefly, and suddenly smiled. "That's what they'd call me in El-ay?" He accented the first syllable, but the notion seemed to please him. "I like having an El-ay name, I mean, you know?" He guided Chris past the small fire, stopped to make a low inquiry for directions to the latrine large merchant parties invariably dug, and headed in the direction indicated.

"Yeah, well, it's easier for me to remember, you know? And you look more like an Eddie than an Ed—or an Edrith." Chris seemed to be having difficulty concentrating on the conversation, and he was definitely walking slowly and cautiously.

"Whatever they look like." Jennifer cast a swift, worried glance in Robyn's direction, but her sister gave the boys' retreating backs one sour look and followed Aletto over to the fire. Jennifer turned away to help Lialla pull bags from the horses and pile them away from the Bez merchants' things.

* * *

BY the time Chris returned, Edrith still supporting him, Robyn was curled up half-asleep, Aletto's thigh serving her as a pillow. His near hand lay on her hair, and he was drinking hot, heavily honeyed and spiced herb tea, listening to Olar. Jennifer sat close to the fire, sipping cautiously at the steaming liquid and wishing it were coffee—it reminded her of Robyn's favorite lemon-grass blend: It tasted odd and it made her nose run. She blotted it surreptitiously on the back of her hand. Of course Robyn had liked it; she'd drunk a cup of it down quickly, smiled shyly at the merchant party when Aletto introduced her as "My dear friend, Robyn Cray." It wasn't exactly what he'd said, though; the intonation had been warm enough for Olar and Mib to glance at each other in speculation.

Lialla had brought her blanket and now sat—not exactly behind Aletto but, Jennifer thought sourly, at least two paces behind the camel and offside. She understood by the location the sin-Duchess had chosen and by her downcast eyes and the arms folded across her chest that any input from the female members of the party would doubtless come from Jennifer. *I thought she said women are self-sufficient here,* Jennifer thought sourly, and then realized with a guilty little start that in Lialla's case it was surprising she had come so far at all. It wasn't in character; like Aletto, she was trying hard, but she wasn't up to her brother's manner with strangers yet.

She'll have to get there, Jennifer thought, *if she's to be of any use to him in getting aid from Bez merchants. Like this boy's father, who's lived in the south so long he has no intention of going home.* Curiosity about events up north was one thing; active support might very well be another, and Jennifer thought Aletto would need all the help he could get. She swallowed tea and forced herself to pay attention to the conversation between southern merchant and northern Duke's heir. It was still early days, and she had no idea whether Lialla would have done as much in her last days at Duke's Fort as she did now; even sitting behind Aletto might be an enormous step forward.

"We've had nothing but innuendo, rumor, gossip and the wildest tales in Bezjeriad," Olar was saying. "They say that Duke Amarni's son killed a man to keep that man from wedding his

192

sister, and—well, the rumors as to why are no fit conversation for mixed company. They say a sorceress of the old Duke's keeping brought outlanders to aid Aletto in his quest for his birthright, that the Emperor intends or does not intend all manner of punishment against any or all of the major parties involved in the matter." He glanced at Robyn and Jennifer curiously.

Aletto shrugged. He sipped tea and gently rubbed Robyn's shoulder; Robyn, eyes closed, smiled faintly. Jennifer thought she was probably nearly asleep already. "As to the Emperor's intentions, Olar, I certainly cannot say. The rest—well, as you have assumed, I am Aletto, and the lady there my sister. It was our uncle's intention to marry her to his cousin Carolan, and it is true that Carolan died when he tried to use force to detain my sister and myself in the household. I cannot regret his death; I did not like the man and know of no one who did save my uncle Jadek." He smiled rather deprecatingly. "I had no choice but to strike him down. My reasons included concern for my sister's well-being, but I doubt that was the tenor of the more hushed rumors." He looked down at Robyn; the smile softened. He moved his hand carefully from her and wrapped it around his cup. When he looked up, Olar was watching the two of them with comprehension.

One rumor set to rest, Jennifer thought dryly. *At least among these men. And subtly done, too.*

The man Mib pulled a round loaf from the fire and cut it into wedges, set out a bottle of oil and a pot of a runny fruit syrup. When it came around, Jennifer dipped her bread in the pot the way the others had. Apricot, she thought. A little odd-tasting; probably sweetened with honey when she was used to the taste of white sugar in her jam. Certainly not bad, particularly after what they'd had to eat this morning.

Olar chewed, tucked bread into his cheek. "Well. My father was concerned whether you still lived. He has no desire to return to Zelharri, of course; after so many years, he has many friends and good customers in Bezjeriad, and all my mother's family lives east of the harbor as they have for four generations or more. All the same, he's told me for as many years as I can recall how deeply he disliked and distrusted your uncle. A man he owed favors went to Regent Jadek and somehow came away with titles to the land where Father's shop and house stood. He had to give up all but the clothes he wore and whatever he could carry away in an hour or so; he's never forgiven that. He'd supplied your father with wrought silver ornaments and was loudly offended when Jadek sought the discounts your father never had.

"There's been little or no other rumor out of Zelharri, though a few men in the Regent's colors rode into Bezjeriad a day or two ago and began asking questions in the taverns around our quarter and down by the harbor.

"Sikkre, though: It's known an outland sorcerer was killed and that the old Thukar died, but not how. Mostly, it's said poison, though others will remind one of his rages and the weak heart his physicians warned him of, of the medicines he drank to deal with that."

"Digitalis," Jennifer said. "The man had an evil temper and I would have thought his color meant heart trouble. At one point during our discussions, his eldest son"—her mouth went dry and she took a quick, small sip of tea to cover—"asked his brothers and his sorcerer to bring the digitalis."

"They say," Olar went on doubtfully, "that Dahven has never wanted to take his father's place, though I know myself he bore responsibility for the market guard last year, for resolving disputes too small to bring to the Thukar's attention. It's a fact known to all that he did excellently well; he was honest and fair to all parties in a dispute, something most rare in Sikkre. They say, though, that after so many light encounters with women and after eluding his father's attempts to wed him and settle him down, he saw an outlander woman, an advocate and already a Wielder of Night-Thread. Gossip says he greatly desired her, but that the woman would not desert her companions unless he held the Thukar's seat—" His voice faded; his eyes, the eyes of his company, were fixed on Jennifer.

She shook her head; it was a moment or two before she could force any sound past a very tight throat. "I've no proof about the man's involvement with his father's death, of course; when we left Sikkre, Dahmec was still alive. And the rumor clearly implicates me, doesn't it, but there's no truth to it. I would never desert my sister and her son, to begin with, and I promised to help the nera-Duke gain what is rightfully his. Since I was brought to Rhadaz for that purpose, since I am not Rhadazi and know no one here but them, why would I leave them for a doubtful future in Sikkre?"

"You seem too sensible for such a course," Olar agreed. "Nor do the rumors link you by blood to the other outlanders. As a tale simply heard, however, it's telling, don't you think? A woman in a land not hers might well desert an even more uncertain future riding with the nera-Duke of Zelharri, since he has no armed guard to protect him and since Jadek might somehow win out—by force, magic, carefully placed bribes among

194

the Emperor's household.'' He met her eyes blandly. "A sensible woman might think all that out—"

Jennifer smiled and shook her head. "If she had the time to do so. But I only met the Thukar's eldest son over a luncheon table, and only for a few minutes.'' *Keep the rescue and the ride out of it,* she told herself firmly. *Unless someone calls you on it later, but how would they know?* Only Vey and members of the Red Hawk Clan knew, besides her own immediate companions; she doubted either would contribute to the gossip mill. *Gossip mill is right,* she thought grimly. *I feel like the cover story on a grocery store tabloid!* "I do not believe the man I met across his father's table would kill Dahmec to become Thukar,'' she went on easily. "It's not a sensible course of action—and whatever else he might be, he struck me as a sensible and intelligent man. And the only one of all three who showed any concern over the Thukar's health, or his temper.''

"Well," Olar's voice trailed off once again; he considered this, blank-faced, finally shrugged. "Who can say? It's one reason my father sent us north to Sikkre, to learn as much as possible, first-hand, and return to him with all the truth we can find. Setting aside rumor—or what of it a man can—it's true that Dahmec is dead, his younger sons rule in his place and wait the proving of Dahmec's new will. They say it was made only two nights before, and that it disowns Dahven and names the twins Thukars at his death."

"Well, then!" Jennifer exclaimed. "Why would Dahven murder his father, knowing he wouldn't inherit? And wouldn't that be an excellent motive for the new heirs to have done so, lest the old man change his mind once more?"

"Ah. But did Dahven know he would not inherit?" Olar shook his head, broke off more bread and stuffed it in his mouth. "One thing certain: We saw your group approaching from some distance off, and Dahven is surely not with you. If you are the outland woman rumor names, then other rumor can be safely dismissed: that he ran off with you."

"*I* haven't got him," Jennifer said evenly.

"We haven't seen him since we left Sikkre," Aletto said gravely; he glanced in Jennifer's direction briefly. He'd argued at one point to mention the caravan but apparently now thought better of that and decided to stick with Jennifer's simplified story. "And I'm concerned about him; Dahven is a good friend of mine, you know. We've known each other since we were very small boys. What else are they saying?"

"Little enough, that I immediately recall. Something about

the Lasanachi having been seen in Sikkre a few nights ago. But none of the back-market traders who deal with them report having seen them professionally.''

Jennifer turned as someone behind her made an odd little gulping noise. Lialla merely looked confused. Edrith had gone noticeably pale but when she shaped an ''Are you all right?'' at him he nodded and gestured faintly toward the merchants. She turned away. *Something wrong. Edrith knows something about this that I do not.* Her stomach tightened painfully; she set the cup of tea down and pushed it away from her.

''I do know,'' Olar went on, ''that there have been two Lasanachi ships come through the straights the past day or so: merchanters, of course, not raiders. One had already put into the harbor and its captain was dickering for supplies, but before the deal could be concluded or any coin exchanged, he simply left, in the middle of the night, too. And there was another ship beyond the harbor, I'm told—it's possible a message was brought concerning the rumors out of Sikkre. Many of the Lasanachi captains are sailing carefully these days, particularly since they were pushed out of Dro Pent with such heavy loss. Besides, they're nearly as superstitious as the Sink nomads; some believe the plague was put upon them by Dro Penti sorcerers. *That* kind of trading with the Lasanachi is strictly forbidden, you know.'' Olar turned to tell Jennifer rather ambiguously. ''But that doesn't mean it isn't done. And if rumor somehow reached their ears that Lasanachi were seen in Sikkre, particularly mixed with tales about the old Thukar's death, I think it very likely they would flee Rhadazi ports, fearing to be somehow named as responsible.'' He sighed. ''In a way, it's a pity they left. If you can persuade a Lasanachi to drink with you, there are always such interesting stories to be heard.'' He finished his bread, washed it down with the last of his tea. Behind him, the men were beginning to pack up the few bags they'd opened, and two of them had gone to rub down the horses.

Aletto stifled a yawn. ''If you don't mind, sir, we'll talk more later. We were awake the night and we've slept little worrying about our companion. But we've been sleeping during the hot hours, anyway. This is all so unlike Zelharri.''

Olar nodded. ''I once traveled to Zelharri when it was April and there'd just been snow. I could still see it in shadowed places along the road. Very unpleasant, nastily cold and damp. I would like to hear more about your journey, but I need sleep myself. It's a long stretch from Bezjeriad to here, particularly with the wagon, and especially when it's done all at once.''

Jennifer got up and went over to their horses. Chris and Edrith had crawled off moments before, Chris with a worried look in his mother's direction. She tugged her blanket free, and Robyn's—though it looked like Robyn wasn't going anywhere for the time being, and Aletto, at Olar's invitation, had shifted so he could lay down next to Robyn. Someone had put the fire out. Jennifer leaned rather wearily against her horse—it turned to look at her but didn't make its usual protest at being used for a prop—and looked around. It took her a couple of minutes to find Chris; Edrith was lying down, arms behind his head, but he was nearly invisible most times anyway. Chris sat cross-legged facing him, talking urgently and hurriedly—telling his friend what really happened, no doubt, because the expression on Edrith's face could only be described as appalled. Jennifer squared her shoulders, tossed the blankets back across the saddle and worked her way through fallen scrub and around a tight clump of willow to reach them. Edrith looked up; Chris stopped talking at once and slowly turned his head to follow the look warily. A little of the tension went out of his shoulders as he saw who was standing there.

"Aunt Jen. Jeez, you surprised me. Wonder if I'm gonna be this jumpy when people come up behind me?"

"Probably for a while. Most people would be," she replied mildly. He eyed her sidelong as she came over to kneel in front of him. "Hold them out, kid."

He gave her his best innocent look, which never fooled her in the first place; his ears and cheekbones were pink, an even better sign he was going to try and lie to her. "Hold what out?"

Jennifer snorted. "Yeah, right, great job, Chris. You've got the part, now cut the act. I saw the wrists right away."

"Oh, swell," Chris mumbled.

"Yeah, you'd think swell if your mother had been standing where I was. What did you do, rub them raw?"

Chris sighed dramatically; Jennifer folded her arms and waited. He sighed again, held them out, shrugging his shoulders a little to pull the sleeves up and bare his lower forearms. "It must be Mom's witch blood, Aunt Jen, you read me too well. Yeah, okay, I rubbed them, trying to get the rope to loosen up." He pulled his arms back and folded them possessively across his chest. "Touch either one of those and I'll murder you, I swear I will. They hurt like all hell."

"All right," Jennifer said. "Then tell me. Dragging it out of you won't be fun for either of us, but I will if I have to. Just tell me, get it over with."

197

"Yeah, sure. Easy for *you* to say." Chris closed his eyes, winced and shifted his hands so they weren't touching anything. "First time they tied me up, it wasn't as bad, but after I wrote that note I guess someone figured I might try to take off. Either that, or the guy lied and he could read English. Okay, I know, rotten logic, right? You know, I don't recommend having your arms pinned behind your back like that, either. In movies and on TV it doesn't look a tenth as tough as it really is. I thought my shoulders were gonna break off after a while."

Jennifer was inspecting her nephew's wrists, hands carefully kept away from them. "They're going to infect."

"Aren't *you* a comfort?" Chris asked dryly. Jennifer gave him a hard look, took hold of his fingers and turned his hands palm up. "Yeah, I know, Rommel's desert fighters had a bad time with infection, every little cut got green and gross. So why don't you just cure them, like you did for Aletto?"

"Oh, I'll try. It's just that this is—I don't know, Chris. It's not quite the same as a knife cut; they're rubbed. The stuff I used worked like stitches, I can't stitch a mess like that."

"*I* know that. While you're at it," he went on reluctantly, and suddenly with no trace of humor in his voice at all, "you might just take a look at the back of my head, okay? I think that's where the guy whacked me when they first showed up, I don't remember, but it really hurts."

"I'm not surprised," Edrith said. He'd come up onto his knees and was peering at his friend's scalp. "You've got a knot as big as I had that night and *I* didn't have to carry mine for three days." He leaned a little closer and sniffed gingerly. "It doesn't smell very good, Chris. Didn't they clean it?"

"You kidding?" Chris demanded. "They wouldn't get within a mile of me, if they could help it. They sure wouldn't let me loose to fix anything like that myself. Afraid I'd pound them all and get away, I guess."

"This we can deal with," Jennifer said. She'd come around to look at the back of his head, too.

"Yeah, well why don't you before Mom wakes up and realizes I'm about forty-five cents on the dollar?" Chris growled. He glanced at Edrith, who'd moved around to sniff at his wrists. "That means I'm a mess," he added.

"Seven coppers on a ceri, I think we decided? You told me about that expression before, don't you remember?" He took one last sniff, shook his head. "Your hands aren't pretty and they might scar but I don't think they're infected yet."

"Good. Aunt Jen, if you can't fix 'em, just wrap 'em in one

of those black scarves of yours; the sleeves will cover them. Main thing is to keep the dirt out and the flies off, if I recall correctly.''

"I'll try to fix them," Jennifer said firmly.

"Good. But if Mom finds out about any of this, you're in *big* trouble.''

"Says you, kid. But I have no intention of going through *that*; Robyn doesn't learn any of it from me, and we'll see what we can fix before she wakes up. That is, if you cooperate and finish the story. What about your feet?''

Chris squirmed and looked uncomfortable. "Um. Like I told you, I got this blister—''

"Crap," his aunt broke in acerbically. "Take them off." And when he glared at her, she shook her head. "Take them off, now, or I'll have Eddie here sit on you and I'll take them off.''

"God," Chris mumbled. "You would, too.''

"Not like it's your pants, kid," she said. Edrith laughed; Chris transferred the glare to him. "Come on. Robyn has spent the last three nights airborne, looking for you. Right now she's sleeping like a log but she might wake up. And I think all that devotion to a cause deserves a return on your part, don't you?''

"Yeah, right, make me feel bad, too," Chris growled, but he shoved his feet toward Edrith. "Here, since we all know what's going on, why don't you do the laces, 'cause frankly it hurts to use my fingers." Chris was silent while Edrith undid the knots he used to keep the bows from untying and tripping him. "Hey. If Mom's—tell me everyone doesn't know about Mom." Jennifer nodded. "God. How's *he* taking it?''

"Better than you'd think," Jennifer said. "He doesn't like it—''

"Tell *me*. You didn't see the look on his face in Sikkre.''

"I didn't have to; I saw the look on his face after you ran off with the camel boys and she got pissed and shifted." Chris grimaced, shook his head. He shoved one high-top off his heel with the toe of the other, pushed the second off with a grubbily stockinged foot. Jennifer's nose wrinkled involuntarily. "You'd better start washing those socks out, at least every couple of nights. You're going to lose them, and there's no K-Mart around the corner here.''

"Yeah." Chris sighed. "No decent music, no rap, no—I'd *kill* for a taco right now.''

"Bite your lip, kid. Last thing I need is to be reminded about things like *that*." She stripped the socks off gingerly and sat back to look at the soles of his feet. She could feel the blood leaving her face and she had to catch at the ground with both hands to keep from falling over. "Good Lord, Chris, what happened?"

"Shhh, not so loud!" he implored in an urgent whisper. "You think I want anyone else to see those?" He turned one foot over and forced the leg and his head around so he could look at it. "Great. They're uglier than they feel, and let me tell you, that's not good."

"No," Jennifer agreed. They were bruised black from heel to toes, swollen badly. Two welted cuts ran across the balls of both feet. "Tell me. And quit fooling around; I understand you feel like a damned fool, but just *tell* me. Get it all out."

"You're a lawyer, not a shrink," Chris pointed out peevishly, but he sat back and closed his eyes briefly, finally nodded. "All right. That makes sense, spill it, get rid of it. Right? It was mostly like I told you; except after I wrote the note, they ran a little rope around my hands and ankles; my hands weren't even behind my back. So, I flopped out in this really evil-smelling straw on my side, closed my eyes like I was going to sleep, right? And got my hands down where this little jerk couldn't see them, and fiddled the knot loose. It was a little harder getting to the ones around my feet, but the guy they had watching me was about half-looped on something, and trying hard not to fall asleep. Finally I got all the rope off and I guess he hadn't seen all of those movies where the guy plays deathly ill and when the guard comes over he gets jumped. Which is what I did. I checked all around through the holes in the frame of the building before I crawled out, needless to say. I mean, I wasn't totally stupid about it. But I knew it would be dumb to wait for night to sneak out; they could be sending another guy to relieve the first one at any time. So I finally just went for it, jumped out of the shed and ran like hell. Well," he shrugged casually, but his cheeks were even redder than they had been, "there were two of them on me like cats on a mouse, I don't think I got a hundred yards. They stuffed me back in the shed—it was like a half-underground thing, like a pioneer house, a lot cooler than the outside. Anyway, two of them held me down and the third went for this leather thing that looks like a carpet beater except they use it on the camels—" He swallowed and stopped speaking abruptly.

"Oh, Lord." Jennifer shielded her eyes briefly with one hand. "They beat the soles of your feet with—"

"Yeah, right," Chris said gruffly. "I mean, really, Aunt Jen. Would you go around telling anybody that—?"

"No. Guess not."

"So they did—that. Then tied my arms again, but behind me this time, and a lot tighter. I know, I tried for a little while to get loose because my hands were going numb. I got a little room so my fingers weren't going to fall off, but I could feel I'd been maybe a little too exuberant about it. They didn't do as good a job on my ankles, but they didn't put my shoes back on me, either. Those merchant guys found them on the sand, outside the shed."

"How'd they find you?" Edrith asked.

"Oh. That building? The Bez merchants sometimes keep extra feed for their animals in it, or if it's really hot and they're driving goats or sheep, they put them in there when they stop. It's not very far off the road—you know, I could *see* that damned road when I was running? God, I've never been so mad-frustrated in my life! Anyway, Olar said they'd traveled a little light as far as horse feed and thought maybe someone else had left some; it's like firewood when you're camping, I guess. Well, what they saw made them a little suspicious: these Cholani running like someone was going to murder them all—"

"They're cowards," Jennifer said. "At least, everyone tells me so, and the one I met certainly didn't do anything to dispel the rumor."

"I heard." Chris grinned fleetingly. "Right. *He* wanted to off me on the spot because you'd called lightning down on his head; the others apparently finally convinced him I might still be worth a little coin if they let you sweat for a while. But they *do* trade with merchants, and if they're close to the road it's expected they want to talk. These guys left everything behind, just jumped on the camels and split. So, fortunately the merchants got suspicious the Cholani might be earning money their favorite old way, and when they saw my high-tops in the dirt next to the shed door, they figured it at least bore checking out." He sighed. "I slept the rest of the afternoon. The one guy offered if I hurt anywhere they could give me a little stuff but they don't carry iodine and Band-aids. And I was too embarrassed to say anything. Fortunately for me, the guy who untied me did it in that shed; he couldn't really see much. I said stiff and sore and they pretty much bought it, and said they'd at least take me as far north as where you guys were. I just made sure I was pretty visible all the way, in case somebody on the good guys' side was looking."

"We all were," Jennifer told him. She was studying his feet. "We can at least do something about these and about your head,

I don't guarantee a full cure but it should be better. And Lialla has some salve we can put on your wrists.''

"Don't bring her into it," Chris said sharply. "You know she doesn't like me, and I'd really rather no one else knows, thank you.''

"She already does," Jennifer said. "She was back with me when we first came in, remember?'' Chris groaned; Edrith touched his knee and cleared his throat warningly. Jennifer turned as her nephew looked up. Lialla was coming toward them, moving with purpose. She held a small box in one hand; a wad of white cloth fluttered like ribbons from the other. She said nothing as she stepped onto the blanket and then knelt; she did look at Jennifer as if for reassurance.

"You're hurting," she said finally. "I saw your hands. I would have come sooner but Aletto wasn't yet asleep. If he'd come over, your mother might have woke up, and I thought you might not want that.'' Chris nodded, then set his lips in a hard line and wordlessly held out his arms. Lialla eyed them doubtfully, caught her lower lip between her teeth and opened the box of salve. She worked in silence, the only sound an occasional involuntary hiss from Chris. Lialla wrapped thin strips of white around her handiwork, sat back and blotted her forehead with her sleeve. "Jennifer, if you have a spare black scarf, it might be better to cover these, so Robyn doesn't know. I think he has a right to a secret like this; she'd think it was somehow her fault. She's gone though enough of that.''

"We all have. Sensible of you," Jennifer said. Chris glanced at her sharply; Jennifer shook her head minutely as Lialla bent down to look at his feet. She *had* already said most of what Lialla was now saying, but the sin-Duchess needed to build her confidence. And she and Chris needed to have a better working relationship, even if they couldn't wind up liking each other.

"I thought it might be something like this," Lialla said finally, and sat back up.

"You tell my Mom," Chris began threateningly. Lialla shook her head, silencing him.

"No. Didn't you listen?'' She drew and let out a deep breath in a clear effort to dispell anger. When she went on it was in a milder tone once more. "You think I don't understand about the shame that goes with a beating? I—this goes no farther," she added, and cautiously lowered her voice. "Jadek—my uncle—s-s-struck me, very hard, when I wouldn't accept Carolan.'' She was trembling and could suddenly barely force the words out. One hand went up to her face, touched the cheekbone. "Aletto tried to

202

stop him, to prevent the betrothal, and Jadek took his walking stick away. Just—broke it over his back. In—in front of horrid Carolan, Jadek's men and Carolan's, in front of our mother, Merrida—''

She broke off and swallowed hard. Chris, who had been staring at her in astonishment, touched the back of her near hand. Lialla started and looked up. "Don't worry, he won't hear about it from me, not ever. I'm glad you told me. God. At least all *I* had to put up with was a bunch of—of laughing nomads. That was—yeah. It wasn't good.'' He looked up at Jennifer. "So can you guys do something about the rest of this, or do we wait until tonight? Night-Thread, I remembered, see?''

"Maybe not,'' Jennifer said. "Meantime, though—'' She fumbled with the little belt bag, drew out the sapphire she'd offered the Cholani, two copper coins and four aspirins. "Here, two of these tablets are yours, kid.''

"Hey,'' Chris smiled crookedly. "You really do love me.''

"Don't do anything like this again, all right? I'm going to run out and then we're all sunk.''

"Right.'' Chris took Edrith's water bottle, swallowed the pills, and suffered Lialla to look at the back of his head.

"I really think *I'd* have to wait for dark,'' she said gloomily. "At least—'' she looked at Jennifer, who shrugged.

"I'm tired and *my* head aches, but I can see the stuff I'd need to use, at least for concusssion. I find that yellow hard to hear; you're better at finding the yellow than I am; you've done it one or two times more than I have. Why don't you at least try, and if you can't find it, we can wait.'' It was a lie—Jennifer could have laid both hands on the yellow Thread, and she could hear the Water Music sound of it just fine. The lie served its purpose, though: Lialla closed her eyes and concentrated hard, finally nodded.

"I—well, I see it, so I can try. If *you* don't mind, Chris,'' she added doubtfully.

"Hey, if it makes the lump go away and I can get my feet back in my high-tops before Mom wakes up, let's go for it.''

"You do the strangest things to Rhadazi,'' Lialla mumbled. "People don't talk like that.''

"Sure they do,'' Chris said. "*I* do.''

"Me, too,'' Edrith chimed in.

Lialla shook her head, but she was smiling faintly. Chris managed not to wince as she laid her left hand on his hair. A few minutes later he drew a relieved sigh. "Either you've got super aspirins or this lady does good work,'' he said. "Thanks, Li.''

The sin-Duchess looked a little startled, either at the compliment or at Chris's casual use of her brother's pet nickname for her. But she offered him that faint, abashed smile once more, glanced at Jennifer for reassurance, and went on to his feet.

Chris was gritting his teeth; he'd gone pale as soon as Lialla touched his toes and he looked as though he might throw up. "So, Aunt Jen, why are you humming? And—that's one of those things you used to play a lot on the stereo, um, Bach, right?" Jennifer nodded. She wasn't going to try and talk to Chris or anybody just now; she was tired enough that it was nearly impossible to stay so close to Lialla while she fingered Thread. *I could've done it faster and easier,* she thought, and, rather guiltily, *Poor Chris. Poor guinea pig.* But Lialla, though she was moving slowly, was actually Wielding in daylight, around other people, without argument every inch of the way. It was astonishing progress. *Wait until we find someone to talk to in Bez. This woman will have that silver sash yet.*

Chris was still stiff and uncomfortable when Lialla disengaged from Thread and sat back to wipe an extremely damp forehead. But his feet were no longer black and blue and the welted cuts had vanished entirely. He flexed them carefully, rolled onto one side and let Edrith help him up. "Yeah. This is great. Maybe I'll go down and soak 'em in the water; there's a little running and a pool where they watered the horses. I guess ours could use a drink, too, couldn't they?"

"Take the socks with you, kid," Jennifer said dryly. "Take them and wash them."

"Jeez, gimme a break," he protested. "I've been a hurting frog, you know?"

"Give us all a break," his aunt replied. "Your mother gets a whiff of those, she'll think your toes have all gone green and gross. You really want her poking at you?"

"You'd sic her on me. Blackmail, child abuse—"

Lialla looked from one to another in bewilderment. Edrith looked no less enlightened. Jennifer laughed. "Go. I'll bring down the bag of soap; *my* feet could use a bath before I try and sleep. So could my socks, but I'm not playing laundress for an able-bodied boy."

16

〜

HE merchants were gone an hour short of sunset, as soon
as the evening winds picked up to cool the air. Before they
went, Olar pressed a brooch into Aletto's hand and closed his
fingers around it. "Take this to my father; he'll know we met,
though he'd welcome you for yourself, and whatever news you
bring."

Aletto nodded, smiled, and pressed Olar's hand in turn. "My
thanks. Perhaps we'll meet again."

"Perhaps," the merchant said. He climbed onto the wagon
seat next to Mib, who held the reins. "If the political climate
were right, I am sure Father would *trade* in Sehfi once again,
and on a regular basis." He held up a hand to signal their de-
parture, used it to wave at the rest of the group as they edged
up onto the road. Aletto waved and smiled until Olar turned
around; his shoulders sagged then, his face sagged and he leaned
back against the nearest tree, closing his eyes.

"Gods of my fathers," he whispered. Robyn, who was sitting
cross-legged by the fire stirring a large pot of soup, didn't hear
him, but Jennifer, the only one of the party who'd remained to
watch the merchants ride away, did. She touched his shoulder.
He looked at her as though he didn't recognize her.

"If you're worrying about how well you did, don't," she said.
He smiled tiredly and shook his head.

"Not really. I—I remember my father quite well, you know;
I've merely copied his way of speaking to people outside the
family. I just—it's not me. I thought about it long before I left
Duke's Fort, of course. How I'd have to deal with people, if ever
my uncle allowed it. But that makes it so—I don't know. So
scheming, misleading people, playing them into thinking I'm a
nicer person than I truly am. But—" He shrugged. "I don't want
to bother you with this."

"Talk about it," Jennifer said. "In our world, people are voted
by all the people into office; I'm used to seeing the kind of outer
persona you're using. There's nothing wrong with it, if you're

not lying to people by pretending to be something very much other than what you are, you know. It may have been a persona for your father also; did you ever think of that? Besides, if you're only using it to cover a lack of experience and shyness—''

Aletto rubbed his chin and considered this. ''It's—I suppose that's a word for it. Shyness. Jadek never let me talk to outside people, really. Oh, servants, some of the armsmen. His relatives; and now and again I was allowed to walk through the market, though he maintained he worried about us and didn't like to have us out where anyone or anything could harm us. It was hard then, talking to people. I always felt as though they waited until I walked away to look at each other, to think that I wasn't—that I was faking the way I walk for sympathy, or that I made a huge fool of myself, laughing too much or saying too much, but of course since I'm a Duke's son they couldn't simply say so, could they?''

''No. But people who are shy feel that way. Not me, particularly. I've only felt that once or twice but I know people who experience it almost constantly. You aren't the only one; keep that in mind. When you traveled to Sikkre, though, why did Jadek permit that, if he didn't like letting you out of his sight?''

Aletto closed his eyes. ''That was—when Father still lived.''

''I'm sorry. Well.'' Jennifer patted his arm. ''I don't think what you're doing is wrong. I can see it bothers you, and telling you not to let it won't change that, I'm sure. All the same, you're doing a fine job, talking to people like Olar. He'll talk to others and word will begin to spread that the Duke's heir isn't as helpless *or* hopeless as his uncle would make him out to be. Your reasons are good ones; you know people *do* mistake shyness for arrogance. You don't want that, do you? And you *are* trying to raise support, so it certainly pays for you to make people like you.''

''It just seems like—I don't know, cheating?''

''Probably because you're an honest person. If you weren't, it wouldn't upset you.''

He groaned and closed his eyes again. ''Bezjeriad.''

''I know. We'll be there for a few days, won't we?''

''We'll have to, if I'm to raise support. Men like Gyrdan—he's given up everything to help me, but his family still needs to eat. There are always expenses. Palms to cover in Podhru, very likely.'' He shook his head. ''It nearly makes me ill, trying to remember all that's needed. Realizing how many people I'll have to persuade.''

Jennifer touched the back of his hand. He looked at her with dulled eyes. ''Remember that you may not have to do so much persuasion as all that. Most of the Zelharri refugees in Bezjeriad are there because of your uncle, aren't they?'' He considered this, nodded. The thought didn't seem to cheer him any. ''Also, don't forget you have all of us with you. We'll do what we can to cover for you, when you need a little respite. And I'm certainly willing to argue your cause. I've never tried political fund-raising before but I've been trained to be persuasive, you know.''

''Thanks.''

''You're welcome. You look exhausted, though. Is that all emotional strain from dealing with Olar and his friends, or are you as worn out as you appear?''

He managed a faint smile. ''I *am* tired. So much riding, all the rest I've been doing lately. Just walking—well, I suppose I've said it enough, it's all new to me. I don't think I realized how tired I'd become, just from walking. Though I *think* it's helping, a little. But I haven't slept well the past few days, since they took Chris. I was—well, keeping an eye on *her*.'' He gestured with his head toward Robyn.

''Why don't you go lie down?'' Jennifer asked. ''There isn't anything that needs doing right now; we aren't going on tonight, after all.'' They'd decided that an hour before, when it became clear that neither Chris nor his mother was strong enough to ride. In fact, Chris still slept in the shade, where Lialla and Jennifer had left him and Edrith hours before. ''Go on, you've earned it. And I think Birdy would like the company.''

''All right.'' Aletto turned to walk away, hesitated and came back to grip her fingers. ''Thank you. I still don't understand you; it's not your world, not your fight. You scarcely know us. And all you've done, thus far—''

''You forget, it *is* our world now,'' Jennifer said softly. ''And for the rest—if you offer most people a chance to do something decent and useful, they will. That's all.''

''It's not as simple as that; I know better.''

''No. Not quite so simple.'' She smiled. ''But I do think you've been around the wrong sort of folks for far too long. Pay close heed to those you deal with in Bez. I think you'll see there are all sorts. But an astonishing number of them are basically good.''

* * *

THEY wound up spending two full days resting. They had moved the first evening when Chris woke, farther back from the road along the ravine, and so away from any other merchants or others from Bez who might stop for the night. No one did. Once they heard a large party pass them by, several immense wagons

207

squeaking as they went along the road, and once a rider. They actually saw no one.

There was no argument this time when Aletto and Edrith both suggested following the road into Bezjeriad. Chris backed them. "There's a pass on my map. You know, people put passes in when they build roads because it's the easiest or only place to get through mountains. Do we really feel like crawling up over the slopes themselves? I've seen nature shows on TV where you lose half the livestock and most of the people, doing that. Besides, we haven't been exactly safe off the road, have we?"

"It's a matter of time now," Aletto said gloomily. "We've been so many days getting from Sikkre, I'd like to get this over and done with." He sighed heavily. "I do wish I'd known what this would be like, how long it would take. When I spoke with Gyrdan in Sikkre, when he offered to go on Andar Perigha and meet us in Podhru, I'd have suggested something different. It's so far from Bezjeriad to Andar Perigha, and Olar says the coastal roads are all up and down mountainsides and poorly maintained to boot, because there are very few people living along the coast."

"Why should anyone?" Edrith asked reasonably. "It's hot, windy, and nothing grows there except very thin goats."

"And everyone with any sense takes ship between Bez and the Emperor's city," Lialla said. "Perhaps one of the Zelharri refugees in Bez can arrange shipboard transport for us. We'll know when we get there, won't we?"

"I hope so." Edrith looked up from Chris's map—the new one Chris had drawn on yellow pad to replace the ransom-note copy he refused to have back at any price. "But another thing: I don't see that we'll be able to reach the city tomorrow, and I don't see why we have to. I have taken this road a time or two and I know of at least two places near the upper end of the bay where you can wait while I enter the town and at least find our merchants. Remember? I do: Fedthyr in the Street of Weavers, Kamahl at the wharves. Or, if both fail us, now this Olar's father. Under the circumstances, it might be better if the rest of you came in quietly after dark, don't you think?"

"City gates, the Duke's guards," Aletto began worriedly. But Edrith shook his head.

"The city gates are there only in case it's ever necessary to close them. That hasn't happened in over a hundred years. Duke Lehzin keeps the smallest personal force possible—partly because a large guard costs a lot to feed, clothe and house. And partly because he has a better understanding of trade than Dahmec ever did—leave your merchants and your ordinary citizens alone; the profits will stay higher than if you regulate everything."

Lialla nodded. "I read once that his father took the Emperor's idea of Dukedoms and applied it to his chief city: He's broken it into districts and made the people in each responsible for maintaining order—except in the harbor area, of course. There's a real, armed guard company there."

"Harbors everywhere are rough," Jennifer said. "I agree with Edrith; let's let him find our people, and the rest of us cause as little stir as possible. We don't want another mess like Sikkre, do we?"

"That won't happen," Edrith said firmly. "It's different in Bez. And you have me with you now, to keep you out of trouble. You know?" Chris snorted and gave him a shove, knocking him over.

* * *

THE second day spent in the camp was overcast and cool, a constant wind scattering fire ash everywhere. They were saddled and gone well before sunset, several miles down the road by full dark. The night was dark but clear and windier than ever, the road deserted except for two riders early in the evening, before full dark. They crossed the pass just after midnight by Jennifer's watch and reached oak forest two hours later. It was noticeably more humid here, and while the night air in the desert had been cool, here it was still warm. Jennifer shed her cloak and rolled up her sleeves, then edged forward to catch up to Edrith. "What kind of weather do they have in Bezjeriad?"

"Perfectly nasty," he said cheerfully. His forehead already shone with sweat. "In summer there can be such heat it feels like the air is full of water—impossible to breathe, particularly for the desert-bred like myself. Even at night—well, you can see how it is here, and we're not yet out of the high country. It stays hot. There are violent storms off the water quite often. Podhru avoids most of those, since it's at the very innermost point of the Sea of Rhadaz, but Bezjeriad Harbor faces right into open ocean. A number of years ago, they lost most of the piers to a grandmother of a storm. But even when it rained, it never got cooler."

"Got you," Jennifer said. She sighed. "New Orleans." She could see Edrith's puzzled look in the starlight, and laughed. "A city of our own, with a similar climate. I was born in mountain country but I lived most of my life in high desert. Hot at times, but dry. I've never traveled to the hot, humid parts of our country; I was careful not to even once I could afford the journey. It wasn't worth melting to me, whatever there was to see. Guess I don't have that choice this time, do I?''

''Well.'' Edrith shrugged. ''We won't be there very long, and it's early in the season. Not as hot, you know? And much too early for the storms.''

''So?'' Jennifer replied gloomily. ''We're bringing the storm with us.''

* * *

THEY stopped in one of the places Edrith knew, away from the road and down in a wooded ravine, but left the horses saddled and most of the packs in place. Robyn broke out leftover cooked rice to supplement the oat cakes, grumbled because Edrith and Chris vetoed a fire, and worried about snakes. Even she eventually slept, worn out from the long ride. They were on the way after only a few hours, well before sunrise. The air was thick, viscous; by midday, Jennifer could feel the jeans melting into her legs, the sweat running down her humidity-softened shirt from half a dozen sources. They fortunately hadn't much farther to go, though. Edrith reined in to point out a distant gleam of sun on water that he announced was the upper end of Bez Harbor; perhaps half an hour later, he led them into another ravine, this one wide and heavily shaded by brush and trees, a spill of waterfall just uphill of them and a narrow, deep ribbon of running water separating them from the southern side of the ravine.

Edrith stayed mounted, waited only long enough for the rest of them to dismount. ''I will be as quick as I can, though even I can't swear I'll return this evening. Be prepared, though, in case I locate either of Gyrdan's men and one is willing to shelter you.''

* * *

ROBYN turned away as soon as he was out of sight and pulled her braid up off her neck, twisting it and pulling it through itself to form a self-supporting chignon. ''Do we get a fire here? If I have to eat another one of those oat cakes, I swear I'll puke.''

''No problem, Mom,'' Chris said absently. He was still staring after Edrith. ''We're well off the road here. I'm sick of that horse fodder stuff, too. What else do you have, though?''

Robyn closed her eyes, rocked back and forth with her lips moving. She finally shrugged. ''I think biscuits again, maybe soup. Don't know, I'll have to look. You going to just stand there all night, kid, or can I get some help with the horses? Spare your poor aunt?''

''Yaaa.'' Chris turned and made a smirking, bratty face, pulling it back as his mother swung at him. ''Missed me. She needs to get used to horses, don't you think? Since the number of cars here is pretty low?''

"You *are* cruising for one," Jennifer said. She had been pulling at saddle straps but she let go now and walked away from the horse. "You do this, I go get wood. Do it," she added crisply, "or I tell your mother the truth about you." It was a line she'd used often over the past years, but at this particular moment it carried an additional message for Chris. He made the face in her direction, too, but he moved past her toward the horses, and Jennifer saw him tugging surreptitiously at his shirt cuffs.

There was a problem—how to get him away from Robyn long enough to check those wrists. They were healing, but not as quickly or neatly as she'd have liked. *Got to learn more about this damned thread.* Jennifer sighed. It was becoming the plaint of the hour, any more. She shook her head when Robyn moved to accompany her. "Better wait, lady. Snakes, remember?"

"God," Robyn said devoutly. "If I see one, I'll—" She found herself a patch of open ground next to the stream, eyed it doubtfully, and sat to pull off her sneakers so she could wade. Jennifer heard her yelp as her feet touched water. Colder than it looked, apparently.

She wasn't particularly enamored of snakes herself, though they didn't usually bother her. Here, with no emergency room to dispense antivenin, with no knowledge on her part or Lialla's of how to treat snake bites—she'd just as soon avoid the species entirely. She was extremely cautious about picking up sticks and branches if she could only see one end, and it took a while to get enough to do a proper fire. She went back for a second load and Chris, who had finished unloading packs and bags, came with her, leaving Aletto and his sister to rub down and water the animals.

She checked his wrists before they went back into camp. Chris was rather pale by the time she rewound the bandages. "They look a lot better. How do they feel?"

"Right now? Is this a trick question?" Chris tugged at his sleeves and scooped up a double armload of wood. "Actually, they have to be better; they sure couldn't hurt worse than they did when Lialla mangled them that first afternoon."

"I don't think that was all her fault," Jennifer said mildly as she gathered up her own stack of wood. "Something to do with a lot of scraped skin, maybe?"

"Yeah, I know," Chris said gloomily. He brightened a little. "Hey, you know, though? She's actually almost human, isn't she?''

"I think so. She's had a lot of problems, Chris."

"Yeah. At least Mom's boyfriends never pounded on me. And in front of old Merrida—God, wouldn't you want to *die*? Old bat didn't do anything to help her, though, did she? I'll just bet she didn't."

"Probably wasn't a lot one old woman could do against a roomful of armed men," Jennifer reminded him. "Besides, remember how Lialla feels about her own magic, about using it other than at night and in certain very proscribed ways. Where do you think she got that?"

"Oh. Yeah." Chris shifted his load, dropped a handful of long sticks and crouched down to pick them up. "Mom said that the night the Cholani grabbed me, Jadek found a way to talk to you. Boy," he said grimly as he stood up, "I wish that had been me. I'd have told him off, but good!"

"I did all right," Jennifer said mildly. Chris glanced at her, then laughed.

"Yeah, I'll bet you did. Let me guess; he figures we're being a lot too much help to those two, so he's offering half his kingdom and a free trip home if we pull their cards?"

"That means kill? Just the free trip home, and we only have to leave them stranded. Not bad, kid."

"Yeah, well, you know. I play—I *played* lot of the right kinds of games and read a lot. Keep telling you, reading all those law books wasn't the right way to go."

"Oh, I don't know, they're standing *me* in good stead just now. I seem to have a new job as local advocate," Jennifer said. She sighed. "Which means everybody shuts up and looks at me until I do the talking."

"Well, I always did think Aletto should let someone else do *that* for him. And I don't mean Lialla."

"He needs to learn how to take care of himself, Chris. I doubt he's going to want to hire me to do all his talking once he takes over."

"If," Chris said.

She shook her head. "When. Let's not give up on him; he's come pretty damned far for as short a time as we've known him. So has Lialla. Personally, I think it was there all along. They just needed to come out from under Jadek's thumb." She cast him a sharp, meaningful glance. "Rather like your mother and Arnold, maybe?"

"Ooooh. One below the belt, major low." Chris sniffed as they came into the open. "Soup." He sighed. "I really would kill for a taco right now."

Robyn heard him. She looked up from measuring peppers and herb mix into the kettle and gave him a smile. "Kid, I swear to you, if there's any way to fake it once we get into Bezjeriad, you'll get that damned taco."

Chris dropped his load of wood, checked to make certain his sleeves hadn't ridden up, and bent over to hug her. "Hey. They don't make mothers any better than you."

"Yeah, I'm a terrific mom." Robyn poured the last of the dried stuff into the pot, brushed her hands together and beckoned. Chris dropped down cross-legged. "I'm so terrific, I'm not going to do any of the things I threatened when I found these where you put them." She fished in her lap and brought up the battered partial pack of cigarettes. "You want to explain, maybe?"

"Jeez!" Chris sat back; sudden outrage showed in every line of his body and face. "You—jeez, I don't believe this! You went through my bag? Like, when? Right after I got grabbed? You snooped through *my* stuff?"

"I had a genuine purpose for getting into that bag," Robyn said flatly. She now looked as outraged as he. "You think I—what, you actually think the first thing I did after you disappeared—and I thought you were probably dead, God damnit!—was to pry into your personal stuff? Damnit, kid! When did I do that? When have I ever cared what you had, enough to snoop? I gave you certain rules, I gave you freedom to operate within those rules, I said I'd never double-check you, you think I'm *that* two faced? I want to know about the damned cigarettes, though! Taking something of mine is *not* anything that falls into the white-okay area."

Chris set his mouth in a hard line. Robyn waited. He finally shrugged. "Hey. You won't believe me anyway, but what the hell."

"Don't swear, damnit!" Robyn stopped short; Chris was suddenly fighting a grin and at the look on her face, he broke into laughter.

"Hell isn't swearing, damnit," he chuckled. He glanced around quickly to see Aletto and Lialla coming back from watering the horses a ways downstream, and lowered his voice. "You dropped the smelly, rotten, disgusting things in that busted-down building in Sikkre, when you and whosis were cuddling with the wine bottle in the corner. I figured you had more important things on your mind than a quick smoke—"

"God, where'd I get such a foul-minded kid?" Robyn demanded of the branches far overhead. "Here I actually went looking for you to get you back from those damned nomads—!"

"Yeah, well, what can I say? I'm worth it, right? Look, Mom. I swear I just picked the things up because they stood out, they were just down there in the dust. We were in a little bit of a hurry that night, if you remember, you and the Duke were out the front door ahead of me and already well down the street before I got to stick my head out. I stuffed them in the bottom of the Nike bag so nobody would find them later and know we were there, *and* to give back to you, and I just plain forgot." He spread his hands. "Look at it logically; why would I take your last six or whatever? It's not like if you said back home you'd quit and would I help or something. *Maybe* I'd have thought about it there, but there doesn't seem to be any point to it here."

"No." Robyn looked down at the crumpled pack and sighed. There was a long, uncomfortable silence. Robyn stirred her soup. Chris simply sat and watched her hand go round and round. She finally pulled the wooden spoon out of the pot, shook drops from it, and set it on a flat rock. She brushed nonexistent dust from her lap and sighed again. "Well. Look, kid, sorry I yelled at you."

"Sorry I yelled back." Chris considered this and chuckled. "Sorry I swore, too."

"Yeah, sure, smart kid." But Robyn managed a faint grin. "You know, I smoked one and the damned thing didn't even taste good?"

"Maybe Aunt Jen put a curse on them, go yell at her next time. Um—do I still get my taco?"

Robyn laughed. "You still get the taco. Right now, why don't you go get me a pan of water for this soup?"

"Pan—water—soup." Chris got to his feet, fished a blackened pot from Robyn's rather battered "kitchen." "So. How many biscuits you got going?" he added casually.

Robyn came up onto her knees to give him a shove toward the stream. "Bring me that water and maybe I'll think about telling you."

* * *

EDRITH was back before midday the next day. "I found Fedthyr, also Olar's father; they're in the same district. Didn't bother to go looking for Kamahl, but Fedthyr said he'd send a man of his own to let Kamahl know. He's expecting all of you and plans a gathering at his home tomorrow evening." He punched Chris's shoulder playfully. "He wanted to set it for tonight, but I persuaded him we'd be a while getting in and you'd doubtless want a few hours for sleep and to be made presentable. He's got daughters; Gyrdan didn't mention *them*." Chris rolled his eyes at the innuendo in his friend's voice and punched back—fairly hard, to judge by the look on Edrith's face.

"Gathering," Aletto said gloomily. "Well—I suppose I've asked for this all along, haven't I?"

"You'll do just fine," Lialla assured him. Her brother looked at her doubtfully, then briefly at Jennifer, who nodded. Robyn threaded her arm through his.

"We'll help, you know," she said.

"I know. It's just—I know." He looked over at Edrith, who was eating biscuits Chris had found for him as though he were starved. "When will you be ready to leave?"

Edrith tipped his head to one side and considered this while he chewed, nodded emphatically and swallowed. "Soon as you are. It'll be a warm ride, but we could be there just after sunset. Fedthyr said he would have water drawn for baths any time after the sun goes down tonight, and a cool dinner waiting."

Robyn sighed and leaned against Aletto. "A genuine bath. And food someone else fixes. It sounds just lovely."

He smiled down at her and touched her hair. "We'll do it, then." He looked up; Chris and Edrith were already gone, heading for the rough stack of baggage and saddles.

* * *

IT was at least as hot and awful as Jennifer had feared it would be: humid, airless. Not long after they started the sun went behind a thin haze of cloud; it didn't lower the temperature noticeably, nor did the mist of rain that fell once or twice during the afternoon. Damp jeans in a saddle, she thought gloomily. It made shifting her weight more difficult than usual because she stuck to the leather; her horse was in as difficult a mood as she was and probably as uncomfortable: Whenever she moved, it laid back its ears and turned to give her what she would have sworn was an evil look.

She stayed at the rear most of the afternoon, and at one point Robyn dropped back to join her. She pushed strands of hair from her forehead. "You gonna survive this, lady?"

"Yeah." Jennifer jabbed a finger in her horse's direction as it slowed and looked at her once more. "*You* might not, you keep that up."

Robyn chuckled faintly. "Chris said you two weren't getting along very well, I didn't know it had reached the death-threat stage." She sobered, and after a moment, asked, "You got a minute?"

"Got several. What you need, Birdy?"

"Well—yeah. Guess that's just it." Robyn stood in the stirrups, stretched, sank back. "This—bird thing. You don't mind if I talk about it?" Jennifer shook her head. "It does strange things to me, besides all the stuff you'd think. You know: It's just awful on my arms and legs, I thought I'd *die* from my lower back after that first time. It's tiring."

"I'd figured that, and Lialla said anyway; it's your muscle strength, whatever the shift turns you into."

"Chris's damned stories and the movies about werewolves don't go into that, either, do they? My damned luck it works the way it does here." Robyn shook her head. "Besides this other thing. It—when I was doing it so much, looking for Chris? But even before that: It—something gets into my mind. I—when I hit Snake, I didn't have any time to think, I don't think I was capable of thinking anyway, everything changed too fast, and the Robyn-part was way down on the bottom of the rest of it. Like one of the worst acid trips I ever took, way back when. A friend had to talk to me then for, oh, God, hours, until I could come out of it. That first shift—I don't know what I'd have done, if you hadn't been there to pull me out of it."

"You'd have shifted back," Jennifer assured her. She grinned. "Even without me singing Italian opera love songs to you."

"Well." A grin caught the corners of Robyn's mouth. "Yeah, that was funny. But when that guy tried to drag me into the barn? I was scared and then so pissed off, I deliberately used that to shift and he looked so stupid, so scared, I just wanted to—to—" Her voice trembled. She was quiet for a moment; her sister waited and tried to keep the alarm she felt out of her face. "I had to take off, get away from him, fast, or I'd have shredded him. That as much as worrying about Aletto kept me from shifting to protect Chris. I can *feel* the personality change as soon as the shift starts. I'm just scared it's going to stay with me, or that the shift is going to get so easy to do, maybe it'll just happen whether I want it to or not, maybe I'll start just—hurting people."

Jennifer considered this in silence for some moments. Robyn watched her sidelong. "Robyn. I wish I could just *say* right now. I don't know enough. I promise I'll find out for you anything I can learn in Bez."

"Without—" Robyn began anxiously, then stopped as Jennifer shook her head.

"Without implicating you. Of course. It's our secret. Since I don't know the answer, I wish I could just lie and tell you everything will be fine, you won't hurt anyone. Kill anyone." Robyn closed her eyes and shuddered. "Sorry. That's the bottom line, though, isn't it? Is it actually blunting your own beliefs about killing? Or just pushing them aside, or shuttling them off somewhere with your human shape?''

"God. I don't—''

"It can't be the former, really, can it? Because it wouldn't bother you so much right now, if the bird was changing your morals, would it?''

The older woman shoved blonde hair from her forehead again and considered this. "Well—no.''

"Are you still able to control the bird's—call it, more predatory feelings toward the subject?''

"So far,'' Robyn allowed cautiously. Jennifer patted her arm.

"That's what I'd have expected, considering it's you. Fortunately, it isn't *me* who shapechanges, I'm not in favor of killing people, but I'm a little more practical about it than you are. You know: Him or me, it's him every time, no question.'' She patted Robyn's arm again, withdrew the arm to catch herself on the saddle as the horse jerked forward. Chris or Edrith, now in the lead, had decided to put on a little speed. Jennifer groaned as her seat came into hard contact with saddle. "God, I'm going to murder those two, I don't think I can handle this.''

"Get your butt out of the saddle, then,'' Robyn said. "Am I sitting? I'm not. You have thigh muscles, you can handle it.'' She smiled to take the sting from the words. "Thanks, lady advocate. I'll get your bill, right?''

"In duplicate,'' Jennifer replied lightly.

"Seriously, kiddo, thanks for listening; I hate to bleed all over people like that, but I was getting a little worried. Drug personality shifts I've seen, I could maybe work that out alone. This, though—well. Anyway. I'd better go back to Aletto; the humidity is making him hurt all over. And he needs all the reassurance I can feed him right now, Bezjeriad and that gathering is eating holes in him. I'd like to strangle that uncle of his, what he's done to that poor boy. That's all two-footed and nonwinged me, by the way.''

"If he's hurting that badly, we can stop.''

"He doesn't want to—you know. Like he's holding us up because of his physical problems.''

"I know. He's probably making it worse, worrying.'' Jennifer thought a moment. "If he's really in misery, let me know. Scratch your ear, I'll come forward and insist on a halt because I'm about to die. That'll let him off the hook, and maybe you can rub him out a little.''

"I can try,'' Robyn said doubtfully. "I'll let you know. Personally, I think we need the stop anyway. So it keeps us a few extra minutes from reaching the gates, so what?'' She kneed her horse and cantered forward. Jennifer tightened her grip on the reins and swore in a low, angry voice when her own mount would have followed. The horse turned its head and glared at her, but slowed to stay in the rear.

17

THE road came down one last slope and doubled in width. It was noticeably smoother here, and now there were estates on both sides of them: enormous houses set well back from the road and often only visible as vast roofs above a sea of trees and flowering bushes, huge fenced pastures, sprawled outbuildings, cultivated fields and enormous herds. "Cows," Chris breathed reverently at one point. "Does this maybe mean real milk? And even possibly beef instead of all this other weird stuff we've been eating lately?''

"Just so long as you don't expect *meat* in that taco," Robyn said darkly.

Nearer the city, the holdings became smaller, until the road was lined by long, low houses surrounded by no more than an acre of land. Then half an acre. Finally, when they could see the lines of roofs inside the city walls and the walls themselves, the houses became one long building, two- and three-storied, each level edging out into the road past the lower level, inverted stair-steps that lay heavy shadow over everything.

The gates were enormous, solid metal of some kind, and held against the walls in open position by huge chains and locks; the walls were double, with a broad space of hard-packed dirt between, narrow doors all along both inside surfaces facing each other. They and the glassless window openings had a deserted, empty look, which Edrith confirmed: "The Emperor kept a large force here, a very long time ago. They lived between the walls, but the need for them has passed.''

The road broadened into a brick-paved avenue once it passed through the double walls. There were tall poles everywhere, lamps hanging by twos and threes from hooks. "Lamps?" Jennifer asked. "But I don't see any wicks; what kind are they?"

"Blue light, most likely," Lialla said. "It's a pretty common form; even I can do it, you know—given enough time and a little peace and quiet for concentration. I can light an already made one, anyone can—almost. Here, there's probably a contract for a lot of apprentice magicians to go around every night lighting them."

Silhouetted against a rapidly darkening pink and orange sky, towers, domes, roofs of all possible description. The walls curved out and away from them; the City seemed to go on forever in all directions. "Good Lord," Jennifer said reverently. "It's absolutely huge."

"Nearly a million people, according to Fedthyr," Edrith said over his shoulder. There was a pileup of wagons and carts, people trying to get out of the city with market goods, a few like Edrith and his group coming in. Beyond the gate, however, there was hardly any traffic at all, save a few people walking—and now, a young man moving slowly from lamp to lamp, pausing to mumble to himself. Lights glowed bluely, faintly in the dusk as he passed. "Sikkre has only half that many." Edrith led them down the avenue for some distance, turned right down a slightly narrower way, then left again. There were high walls marking the homes of the wealthy here, a broad expanse of grass and trees running down the middle of the street that looked to Jennifer to be at least a block from side to side.

She glanced over her shoulder nervously, realized what she was doing and forced herself to stop. She felt vulnerable, after so long in the desert, surrounded now by so much city and so many people. Apparently she wasn't alone, though: Lialla rode close to her brother, head down and hood falling over her face; her shoulders were hunched forward stiffly. Robyn's face was white and strained, even in the failing light; Aletto looked distant and cool, the way he did when he was worried. Edrith held as good a pace as he dared, without calling attention to them: There was even less traffic here than there had been at the gates, but all of it moved at a leisurely pace. Of them, only Chris took a genuine interest in the walls, some of which were painted or carved, in the park on their right, in the enclosed carriages or litters that went by at infrequent intervals.

After what seemed at least a mile to Jennifer, Edrith held up a hand and drew his horse to a stop, slid from the saddle and went to tap on a tall, broad door. It opened; Edrith spoke for a moment with the shadow figure inside, then turned to beckon his companions. Jennifer exchanged a dubious look with Robyn, dismounted and handed the reins to a slender boy nearly her height and clad all in deep burgundy. Robyn had stepped back so Aletto could bring his sister forward with him and held out a hand each to her son and her sister. She even managed a creditable smile, though her eyes were wide enough to show white all around. "Hey," she said, and glanced back at the dark opening where Aletto was just disappearing. He turned back and held out his hand; she let go of Jennifer's and took it. "Wow. Into the gates of, huh?"

"Shhh," Chris whispered. "Bite your lips, okay?"

The gate shut behind them and a bar slid into place with a terrible finality.

* * *

AN hour later, Jennifer was ready to laugh at her earlier thoughts—if formless fears brought on by heat, tiredness and strange surroundings could actually be termed thoughts. The inner yard of Fedthyr's home was a delightful mix of paving stone, grass, roses and other flowering bushes, a number of small pools and, just short of the entrance, an enormous rectangular fountain. Fedthyr himself was waiting beside the fountain to greet them. He was somewhere around fifty, perhaps, dark hair showing signs of gray. His beard was still dark, setting off a wide smile and making the very white teeth appear even whiter. There were four young people just behind him: the boy who had taken Jennifer's horse and was very much Fedthyr with thirty or more years erased; three girls who might have been between fifteen and eighteen. All three wore an extraordinary amount of jewelry over solid-colored loose dresses that were just short enough to expose one pair of bare feet and two pairs of very small shoes; one wore earrings that made Jennifer's lobes hurt just to look at them: long enough to brush her collar bones, ornately gold and silver, with three teardrop pearls dangling from the centers.

Fedthyr spread his arm wide in greeting, embraced Aletto—who managed not to look as astonished as he surely felt—and stood back to study him. "Ah. I am so glad to meet Amarni's son at long last. You have his look, but you must know that, yes? We will, I hope, talk later; for now, there are rooms, water, wine and a little food, fresh clothing. If you wish, sleep once you have had a chance to remove the Bez road from your back. Otherwise, send for me and we will take tea together. My son Enardi will go with you to show you and your men the way, and remain with you to give any assistance you need." Aletto performed introductions with cool, easy grace—rather as though, Jennifer thought with amusement, he'd been doing this all his life, with never a qualm. The amusement faded: Aletto's terror earlier had been absolutely painful to watch. She hoped she'd seen the last of it, as least while they were in Bez. Perhaps now his feet were wet. . . .

Fedthyr was polite to both Edrith and Chris and greeted them as equals. He was wildly charming to the women. The sin-Duchess allowed herself to be enveloped in an enormous hug; Fedthyr kissed Robyn's hand and both cheeks with enthusiasm. "The sister and the lady of Zelharri's nera-Duke! I am so pleased to have such lovely and important ladies in my house! And . . ." He turned to Jennifer and fixed her with a look that was a mixture of wariness and admiration. Jennifer bit back a grin; the man's daughters were giggling quietly behind him as though both used to and embarrassed alike by their father's exuberant ways. "You are the outland advocate who talked old Dahmec to a standstill, are you not? Now, that is a feat to brag of; you must tell me later how you accomplished it!"

Jennifer bit back a sigh, smiled pleasantly and let him take her outstretched hand in both of his, and nodded. The story was apparently beyond her ability to mend now. "I'm the outland advocate," she admitted. Fedthyr seemed to take this for modesty; he smiled widely, kissed the backs of both her hands resoundingly, and released them.

"My daughters will see to your needs, and those of the other ladies. Please, please do not feel shy about coming down for tea later, if you wish, I would so like to talk with all of you! But only if you feel able! Do not come down again solely on my account. We have several days, and I allowed it that no one comes to meet Duke Aletto until tomorrow, past midday. And even that"—he waved hands that shone with a number of gold and pearl rings—"we can discuss at another time."

* * *

AN hour later, Jennifer lay back in a large metal tub, toes playing with the ceramic rim, a pillow cushioning her head. Her hair was clean as it hadn't been since she arrived in Rhadaz, the last of the dirt gone from under her fingernails and the backs of her heels. The water was refreshingly cool, very lightly scented and right up to her chin—and a bucket holding more even cooler water sat on the floor where she could easily reach it. *How we could ever have thought disaster lay behind old Fedthyr's gates,* she thought lazily. It was an effort at the moment even to open her eyes.

Fedthyr's youngest had showed her into the room and then stayed with her, and she'd babbled continuously, on a wild variety of subjects. Ordinarily Jennifer would have gone mad from

221

five minutes of that kind of headlong, giggly, onesided conversation, but this time she had found it surprisingly pleasant. It had been after all a long time since she'd been able to listen to such carefree chatter and there was no real need for her to respond with anything but an occasional, "Uh, huh"—at least, once she'd persuaded the girl not to call her "Lady" or "Lady Advocate." They'd settled on "Jen," since Lasinay had the usual Rhadazi problem with her entire name. Lasinay was fifteen and enormously excited by Aletto's arrival.

"The Lady Lialla and Robyn have rooms next to yours; they're all joined by this common balcony, you see? I very much like the blue jins, I have heard of them from a friend of Enardi's— my brother, you know. They're an outland thing, aren't they, I never touched any before. The fabric is very heavy, isn't it? The fastener is heavy, too, how does that work?" She ran the zipper up and down for several moments, finally giggled and set them aside. "Are those also jins the—the light-haired boy wears?" Her cheeks were suddenly very pink. "And such shoes you both wear! How do you bear so much shoe around your feet and ankles? Will you wear those all the time you are here, or shall we lend you some? I have many pairs of shoes; my father is the greatest weaver in Bez but also he imports shoes and he also now owns a shop where others are made to order. Do you think our feet might be the same size? Do you mind if I test this shoe of yours, to see? Oh—it *is* large, but my feet are entirely too small, they embarrass me, but what can one do? The skirts are worn so short now one cannot hide tiny feet! Here in Bezjeriad we wash down in the little room, the privy, there is a separate compartment and Mindes stands on the shelf to pour water over you and after your hair is soaped, do you mind this, or would you rather do it yourself, and have her leave? I know some women are quite shy, my eldest sister, the one who makes and sells magic charms in the west market, she is one of those. The light-haired boy. He is called Chris?" Lasinay toyed with the pearl drops in one earring. "And he is the son of Robyn? I like the way his hair stands on end above his face; is this usual in your outland place? Is it as harsh to touch as it looks? Is Chris always so quiet around girls?"

Thinking back on the wild flow of speech now, up to her chin in cool, clean water, Jennifer chuckled softly. *Chris shy.* He'd have a fit over that one, when she told him: Chris was reputed by his mother (and himself) to have a very good line with girls— at least girls in his own world. He'd never lacked for dates for the movies or school dances, and Robyn had at one time complained—or bragged, more like—about the number of calls her son got from girls, though he'd never actually had a regular girlfriend. Here, though: She and Robyn had threatened him with half a dozen dire and painful miseries if he'd so much as *looked* at any of Fedthyr's daughters until he was certain what the ground rules were regarding merchants' female, unwed offspring. For all they knew, it was one of the Near Eastern Emirates all over; touching was death and even just looking a very poor idea. But judging by Fedthyr himself, Jennifer thought it likely the young women were protected within a household to an extent but not kept entirely from male company. Lasinay had confirmed this once she managed to insert the question into Lasinay's chatter.

"Father would never allow us to simply walk out with any man in Bez, though some of the Bez merchants put no such restraints on *their* daughters—well, past a certain age, of course. I myself have gone with the son of another merchant to two plays in the Duke's sector this spring, and not chaperoned. But Bez merchants encourage even more independence in their daughters than our fathers do; I think it is because for so long men like my father thought he would return at any time to Sehfi. Now—who knows? But we have more freedom than Lasanachi women, and the Holmaddi—well, my elder sister, not the charm merchant but the next one, she travels for Father, selling his outside goods in other parts of Rhadaz, *she* says being a Holmaddi woman means you did something dreadful in your last life, and that is how you pay for it! But Father has few rules for his children, trusting to our common sense, and to our honesty with him. And guests—well! Guests are another matter entirely, aren't they? Do these jins wash? And these soft foot covers? No, no, I will leave the shoes but the rest needs cleaning, we have a woman who does that, let me take them, and I will bring you something to wear for now—no, there, at the foot of the bed, Mindes already brought you a dress, it is mine, do you mind? Do you need your belongings from the horse? I will see they are brought up, but left outside the door until you are ready to come out of the bath. Are you hungry? There is fresh bread, our cook made it within the hour, and there is fruit and a very nice wine, also a cool soup, I will have Mindes bring the tray in for you."

It had been blessedly quiet in the room for a while after that.

Jennifer pried one eye open, idly watched her toes curl around the end of the tub. She pushed her shoulders out of the water and stretched her back, reached up to scrunch handfuls of hair while it was still wet. Of course, the humidity as well as the permanent were taking care of curl; her hair felt absolutely kinky at the moment. *Better than straight,* she thought and sighed happily.

Cool air on her arms and the back of her neck woke her up, a little. She leaned across the edge of the tub, let her fingers trail across a tiled floor and looked around. The room was larger than her bedroom at home, only a little smaller than the entire apartment. There was one heavy door, no windows, but the balcony Lasinay had mentioned took up most of the outside wall anyway. A length of pastel-colored gauzy stuff covered it, not quite blocking her view of trees and lights. A blue light partly illuminated the balcony, showing it to be wide, possibly covered—likely, she thought, in such a climate as this—with a solid, high outer wall. The room itself was pale cream—walls, floors, ceilings, furnishings—with a low, gauze-screened bed on a platform opposite the door, several piles of cushions in cream and rose, a round table and a low bench drawn up close to it for sitting. Uninhabitable in winter, Lasinay told her; since they'd never needed the rooms for themselves, they had never bothered to bring in glass or proper doors for them, merely closed them off during the heavy storm season.

If they'd cleaned and readied the rooms since Edrith's first trip into Bezjeriad, they'd done a quick and impressive job of it, Jennifer thought. Probably Mindes and the other servants. She hoped with a sudden qualm that the word meant just that, not slave.

A light blue silky thing lay over the bench for her to put on, a sheet-sized drying cloth next to it. Jennifer ducked her shoulders under the water a last time and climbed out. She *was* hungry, now that she was clean. And while she wasn't particularly shy, she certainly wasn't used to being walked in on. She'd better get dressed, fast.

She slid into the blue silk and tied the sash around her waist. *Wonder how Birdy's handling this?* She grinned. Better yet, wonder how Birdy was going to handle Chris and Fedthyr's youngest daughter. Fedthyr's *daughters*. The second girl had watched him right up until the time she'd escorted Robyn down a hall and around a corner, and lost sight of him.

Mindes tapped on the door, came in without asking and set a tray on the small table. She was back out the door again before Jennifer could more than thank her. Jennifer sighed and dropped onto the low bench. The bread was fresh enough to still be warm; the fruit was a sectioned orange and a handful of just-washed grapes. A smaller plate held a soft scoop of butter and a larger scoop of soft cheese, lightly dusted with some herb she couldn't readily identify. The wine was a pale peach color and too sweet for her tastes, but there was also a pitcher of water. She drank nearly half of it before even breaking into the bread.

She stopped, bread in both hands: a familiar-looking bit of yellow had been hidden under the small loaf. Somehow she wasn't surprised to see Chris's writing on it. "Hey, Aunt Jen, I went out with the boys, okay? Mostly 'cause Enardi got a look at my arms when I cleaned up and his family uses this guy when someone gets sick or hurt—like a doctor, I guess, with a pointy hat and a wand instead of a black bag. After that, he wants to show us around, take us to meet some friends. There's a note here for Mom, see she gets it, okay? You tell her the truth and you're dead meat. I won't get in trouble, before you worry, do I ever? Forgetting the nerds on camels?" The usual little heart followed by a C, and a p.s. "Can I get another handful of paper from you, if I don't find any in the market? I think this was my last and it's hard to write this small."

Jennifer crumpled her note and stuffed it into the toe of her shoe, where it would at least be out of sight for a while, then glanced at Robyn's. It was notably shorter. "Ma, I'm out with the guys, I won't break anything I need for riding, but Eddie and Enardi are with me, what trouble can I get into? I won't go after the girls and I'll stay out of bars. What can I say? Bright lights, big city. . . ."

Jennifer smiled, picked up her tray and carried it onto the balcony, then down to the next room, yellow note fluttering between her fingers. "Hey, you," she called from just outside Robyn's curtain. "You decent?"

"Never in my life," Robyn replied promptly. "Why should that stop you? C'mon in, kiddo." Robyn was still soaking, long blonde hair hanging wet and dripping over the edge of the tub, knees protruding. She applauded silently as Jennifer edged past the blowing curtain. "Oooh, class act, you look good in that thing. Let me get out of this tub and see what one does for an old broad."

Jennifer set her tray on the table—the room was very much set up like her own—and went to the door to check the hall. As she'd half suspected, Robyn's dinner sat on the low bench right next to it; Lialla's was already gone. Jennifer freed a hand to wave as Mindes came hurrying up from an alcove somewhere near the turn in the hallway that led to the stairs. "It's all right, I've got it. We're used to serving ourselves." The woman looked very confused, perhaps a trifle put out. Robyn was blotting water from her legs. She wrapped the large cloth around her hair, turban style, pulled the lightweight fabric over her head and belted it. "Purple," she said doubtfully.

"Mauve, Birdy. Good on blondes, really good on you."

"Yeah. Like those poly-silk dresses of yours, built to show every bulge, every lump—"

"Take a good look at yourself, woman," Jennifer said mildly as she set Robyn's tray next to hers. "Think you'll find you sweated most of those off these last few weeks."

Robyn made a face but obediently turned and twisted to look down her body. "Yah. New form of exercise; I'll take it home and give Jane Fonda a run for her money. Hey, though, you know? I think you're right. If I'd tried this on before our trip to the Punchbowl, I'd probably have killed myself. Um—d'you think this is a wear-it-in-public thing?"

"Possibly a little lightweight for that, but I'll wager it's acceptable for guest wear in Fedthyr's house."

Robyn grinned. "Yeah. I'll just bet he'd love that! I was thinking, poor Aletto, all he's ever seen me in is a pair of scroggy jeans and that wad of black thing I couldn't ride in—I bet he'd like it."

"Lasinay—the youngest—didn't say anything to indicate it wasn't a mixed-company garment." Jennifer picked up the silver jug of wine and put it on Robyn's tray. "Here. I tried it and I can't drink it."

"Oh." Robyn looked at it for several silent moments, finally shook her head. "I'd better not. You know, if I'm being introduced as—well, the way they're introducing me, I won't dare drink anything the whole time we're here."

"You could probably go right ahead this evening, sleep it off, might be good for you."

Robyn considered it and shook her head again. The drying sheet came loose and damp hair fell around her shoulders. "I—thanks anyway. I haven't had any since Sikkre, that night we got out of the tower. Sometimes I even forget about it. I guess I'll have to learn how to just take a sip and tell myself I don't want more, at least in places like this where it's not just *me* people are going to see if I get smashed. Aletto said he wants to not, anyway; he's afraid his reputation is everywhere by now, thanks to Jadek. You know: sulking in his room and drinking all the time. If I can help him quit—" She shoved hair away from her face and wound the long, still wet stuff into a knot at the base of her neck. "You know, I wish people wouldn't introduce me as his lady."

"You don't like the sound of it?" Jennifer swallowed bread

and smeared butter on more. It was almost too salty for her taste and had an odd, white color.

"You know I do. Except it scares me. I have a track record like—well, it's more losers than *I* ever want to count. I don't want to—I feel like I'm taking advantage of him; he's only twenty-eight, Jen! And how many women has he ever *talked* to before?"

"You're all right," Jennifer told her. "I'd think about the last part of what you just said, though. You think he'll find someone prettier, younger—"

"More politically suitable," Robyn broke in gloomily.

"I think you're underestimating him. Are you in love with him?"

"I don't know. I don't know if he feels like that about me, or if he just thinks he does because no one else has been nice to him, besides his mother and his sister." She sighed, picked up a soft lump of cheese, sniffed it and popped it in her mouth. "Mm. Good stuff. Well, anyway, I said I'd help him and I will. Just by being with him, though, people don't hassle him any more about being hot for Lialla; did you notice Olar?"

"I noticed. I'd wager Aletto did, too."

"He did." Robyn dabbed the torn end of her bread in cheese, bit it off and began pulling grapes from their stems. "Oooh, grapes with seeds, you can't hardly find them like this any more."

"Nifty," Jennifer said dryly. "Here, this is for you."

Robyn read Chris's note, and sighed. "Why am I not surprised? Oh, well, poor kid, I've been feeling rotten all along about all the stuff he's missed. I really will get out tomorrow or the next day and find a way to get the stuff and make him something Mexican. I mean, I can handle doing without, I did without for too many years."

"I know. So did I, in college. I can think of fifty things I'd have right now, if I could, but—" She shrugged. "You manage. I can feel poor Chris mourning his music sometimes and it really hurts me. How do you fake rock music in a place like this?"

"Yeah, I know." Robyn finished her grapes in record time, took a sniff of the wine and set it aside. "Ech, reminds me of one of those early seventies pop wines, you know, fruit juice to hide that it's bad stuff to start with, and about six pounds of white sugar? Even I can't drink that." She nodded emphatically. "Good. If that's the kind of stuff they serve here, I may be safe."

Jennifer stood up. "I'd better let the woman collect these; she was a little miffed that I took over her job, I think. I hope the word is 'job,' anyway."

"Biyallan's phrase for it, when I asked her, was 'We have seven servants, low for the area; we only support six poor families.' I still had to ask, because it sure made *me* nervous, the way she said that, but I guess she meant it literally: They pay them, and apparently it really is enough to keep one of the poorer families from the south end of Bez city in food and shoes. Even I can't argue with that. Leave the trays. It puts my hackles up, too, but what are you going to do? I'd rather upset me than offend someone who's only trying to do her job." She looked up. "By the way, is my kid really all right?"

Jennifer paused on her way to the balcony. "Sure. Why do you ask?"

Robyn snorted. "Don't try to fool me; he was a big ball of pain when we found him. You think after all these years I can't tell when he's hurting and trying not to worry me?"

"Yeah, I guess so. Don't worry about him; he had a crack on the head that wasn't looking very good, but Lialla fixed it for him, and the headache that went with it." Robyn seemed to be satisfied by this, and Jennifer made her escape before it occurred to the older woman she might not have received the entire truth.

* * *

WHEN Jennifer came out her door, Mindes was carrying both trays away, both jugs of wine on them. She looked at the outlander woman, brow wrinkled. "There was something wrong with the wine?"

"No, everything was fine, thank you." Jennifer wondered if she was being overly effusive from embarrassment, but decided she had more important things to worry about. Probably the servant did, too. "The water was wonderful; we both missed clean water in the desert. The wine just wasn't as interesting."

"Oh." The woman didn't look as though she understood yet, but she wasn't going to worry about it, either. She went off with the trays, slowing only long enough to call over her shoulder, "To the foot of the stairs and through the first door to your right. The Merchant is in the chamber there, with the young Duke."

The Merchant, Jennifer thought with amusement, both capitals very audible. Oh, well. Better than what she'd expected; she didn't know if she could have held a straight face for "The Master." Particularly not when applied to a sweet, chubby little charmer like Fedthyr.

Young Duke was funny enough.

* * *

JENNIFER stayed only long enough with the two men for Robyn to appear—and take her place. Robyn looked almost awake,

228

ready to charm Fedthyr right back; she, by contrast, felt suddenly very nearly asleep. She was glad she'd been there, though, when Robyn entered the room. The look of sheer delight on Aletto's face should have been enough to satisfy even a doubter like Birdy, Jennifer thought as she dragged herself back upstairs. She tapped on Lialla's door, looked in; the sin-Duchess was sound asleep, curled in her little wad and covered by a thin sheet, all except for one strand of reddish-brown hair.

She met Lasinay and the eldest of the still-at-home sisters, Eveleah, coming from their own apartments, farther along the hall. "You look tired," Eveleah said sympathetically, "so we won't keep you. But the sin-Duchess said you were looking for a Wielder, just any advanced Wielder, is that so?"

Jennifer nodded. "To talk with. I badly need information she can't give me, some help with certain things."

"I sent a note to our eldest sister, who creates charms and sells them in the market. She's no Night-Thread Wielder, but she has a good relationship with old Neri. He's a Pale Gray Sash; there can't be much he doesn't know. He's old, of course, and probably rather set in his ways. But I gather from the sin-Duchess that is not just an attribute of *his*."

"No," Jennifer said dryly. She bit back a yawn.

Eveleah shook her head and took her youngest sister's elbow. "Well, I can see how very tired you are. Of course, Neri won't see you until after dark tomorrow at the earliest—if he does at all. Sleep as long as you like; perhaps we can talk tomorrow, before Father's old Sehfi friends begin to arrive."

"Sleep well," Lasinay added brightly. Jennifer let her eyes close briefly as she moved away from them and into her room. There ought to be a law, she thought, against anyone that alert when *she* was so tired.

* * *

The bed was not as soft as she had feared it might be; the sheets were soft, no additional covering needed. Jennifer slept for well over eight hours and woke to sun touching the trees in the park that divided the wide residential avenue, to Robyn's voice next door, and then Chris's. Wonderful to wake clean once again, with fresh food and clear, cool water to drink. She got up and pulled the blue thing around her, walked onto the balcony. The air was almost cool at this hour. *Perfect time for a run,* she thought, and looked wistfully down at the park. She doubted seriously anyone here would understand if she expressed a desire to run through the park, given Aletto's and Lialla's initial reactions. Even Edrith, who'd seen and done more than they, seemed

229

to think she was half-mad. "Oh, well," she sighed, and turned away. There would be time later, once they were on their way again—provided of course, they didn't go by ship. "There will be time, once we get back to Sehfi and Aletto runs Duke's Fort," she told herself firmly.

It wasn't impossible, just odd, after all. Most Rhadazi women weren't treated like third-class citizens, and they *were* expected to learn how to fight—if only defensively. To ride. Certainly a clever woman—a noted advocate—could convince the women of Zelharri that running was an important part of being in condition to either fight—or avoid—an attacker. "Hmmm." Well, it was a thought, anyway. Even if it wouldn't make up for turning her back on that lovely, cool and shaded lawn, forgetting about the white shorts and running shoes, for going downstairs for breakfast instead, so she could impress Fedthyr with her advocacy and help Aletto persuade The Merchant to at least persuade others to back him, or to provide money if not physical assistance.

Chris came out onto the balcony as she was turning to go in. "Hey!" He flashed her a smile, held up his arms—bare to the elbow and not even visibly scarred.

"Smooth," Jennifer said. "You out all night, or did you get some sleep?"

"Jeez," he said, but the disgust was mock. "You and Mom. She wanted to smell my breath; can you believe it?" He turned both arms palm up, then palm down before stuffing his hands in his jeans pockets. "That girl, Lasinay? She's kind of cute, but does she talk? I mean, is something wrong with her voice? I said hi to her last night when we went out, I said good morning just now when I came up the stairs—nothing." He frowned as Jennifer broke out laughing. "What? What's so funny; what'd I say?"

"Never mind, kid. Take too long to explain, and I'd like something to eat."

"You'd better hurry up, then; Mom took too long getting dressed, and that Mindes was at the door with a tray for her. Says she feels like an invalid. You should have seen *her* last night, when we got in—giggling at the old guy's remarks like they were really funny."

"Shhh," Jennifer said in a low voice. "Keep in mind the old guy lives here, will you? And he's daddy to the three cute chicks?"

"Well, hey—yeah. I don't look totally dumb, do I?" Robyn yelled something Jennifer couldn't quite make out from her room, and Chris turned to yell back, "See you down there, Ma!" He turned back to his aunt. "She just went down to find Aletto, why am I surprised? Yeah, so, Enardi took me and Eddie—"

"Eddie and me," Jennifer said automatically. Chris cast his eyes up.

"Took *us* to this old guy, awfullest bad breath you ever smelled, like forty-five years of garlic or something? God! Anyway, he took all the bandages off, made 'tch, tch' noises over them—so that was cool, I knew he was a doctor then, right? Anyway, put my arms in this stuff, felt like pickle juice on a paper cut, thought I'd *die*."

"Sounds like a doctor to me," Jennifer agreed. Chris laughed.

"Yeah, funny, I wasn't laughing then, I was using all the words Mom likes best under my breath; Eddie kept making faces trying to crack me up. So after a couple minutes, they quit hurting, and the old guy with the Van Helsing breath—"

"With the *what*?"

"You know, Peter Cushing played him, the guy who drove the stake through Christopher Lee's heart when he was Dracula?"

"It was also a book, you know."

"Sure, years ago. Well, anyway, they quit hurting and he pulled them out of the brine and wow, all gone! Cost me half the money I had on me, which wasn't that much but I was going to get a bow maybe, to replace the one that got crunched up in that village, the first time we got in the fight? But I'll have to do that later today."

"You might get stuck here, Chris. Just so you know. All these people coming over to meet Aletto."

He shook his head. "Don't think so. Besides, I got it figured. Couple things: the way old Fedthyr looked at me—the hair, mostly, I guess. The old doctor did the same thing; so did a lot of older guys when we were cruising around last night. Old people don't take to that much change; you know guys Mom's age used to come down on me for the haircut back home. But guys like Ernie—Enardi, *you* know—and like Eddie, and a bunch of Ernie's friends, I can talk to them. And you trust me, Aunt Jen: Some of these old guys like Fedthyr and Olar's dad—they have it so good here, big houses, servants, nice clothes. Ernie says his dad talks about going home, then two minutes later he's on about how grim winters were, snow and all that. Those guys won't go along to back Aletto, even if they do send money. But someone like Ernie, or Olar's little brother—he's nineteen and he wants to work leather for belts and carry bags, that kind of stuff. Does really swell designs and all, but there's all these guys

231

in the market here already doing that. He thought about importing semiprecious stones from the south somewhere but there are a couple of guys and a woman doing *that*. So anyway, if he goes to Sehfi with Aletto, then he's backup for Aletto: 'We move here only if the nera-Duke does, and if he does, we really set up a market.' You think that won't help?''

''Don't know, though I have to agree it sounds good. Some people in Sehfi are bound to look on them as competition, of course, but others might see them as a boost to the economy,'' Jennifer admitted. ''But if you're networking with useful people, who am I to slow you down? It's more your speed than Aletto's, too. Just keep in mind—''

''No girls you have to pay for,'' Chris intoned flatly and drearily, but his eyes were wicked. ''Stay out of the taverns, no fights on the docks, and don't break or lose anything you need to stay on the horse and hold the bo. That cover it?''

''More or less. Make nice with Fedthyr's daughters but don't play too close.''

Chris's ears were suddenly noticeably pink. ''Well—right. The middle daughter, Biyallan? She's old enough to decide on her career—they make a thing of it on the kid's seventeenth birthday, did you know? I think I'm a little behind, huh? Biyallan was thinking about some kind of trading company between maybe Cornekka and Bez, but according to Ernie, since she found out Aletto was coming through, she thought maybe something with branches in both places but centered in Zelharri. Ground-floor thing again, you know.''

''Mention it to Aletto, when you get the chance; Biyallan may be too shy.''

''Ernie says she knows her own mind—sounds like maybe a little too strong for *me*. At least she talks, though: not like Lasinay. I wish,'' Chris added irritably as Jennifer began laughing once more, ''that you'd tell me what's so damned funny.'' Still laughing, she finally managed to explain. Chris ran his hand through his hair, swore and separated it into spikes again. He managed a faint grin. ''Yeah. Think she likes me? She's kinda cute.''

''Also two years younger than you are,'' Jennifer pointed out.

''Well—so? You see that Nike bag of yours? I think I put your hair spray in it, and I can't find it.'' He started for the door, stopped with it half-open. ''Um. Listen, I don't know how far to trust Mom. I know you have scissors in that trunk of yours. How do you feel about trimming the extra stuff off my hair? *Very* carefully?''

"Is it my life if I screw up? Sure, kid. By the way, is that hair all over your jaw?"

"Hey, she noticed." Chris rubbed his chin and looked both embarrassed and pleased at the same time.

"You going for the Miami Vice look?"

"Hey. I *was* thinking about a mustache, just to see—anyway, the Miami Vice look appeals to me a *lot* more than the alternative; have you *seen* the thing Aletto takes to his face? God, it must be a foot long and sharp enough to—"

"Up to you, kid. About the spray, I don't have the Nike bag, don't you—wait. Is that it under my so-called trunk and the spare food bag?" Chris dove on it, unearthed the gym bag, fished out the can of spray. "Take it all, kiddo. We'll do something about your hair later, when I'm sure I'm awake."

"Yeah." Chris leaned back in the door for a parting shot. "I'd like your eyes open when you lay into my scalp." He was gone before Jennifer could formulate a suitable retort.

18

ת

IT was late morning and already too warm when Biyallan and Lasinay came to take Jennifer to their eldest sister's shop. Lialla, after a quick, worried argument with her brother, was persuaded to go along. "He says it's all right," she said doubtfully as they left the house and walked across the shaded grounds. "I felt like I let him down last night, sleeping."

"Conserve your strength," Biyallan said with a dry laugh. "Father will have simply *everyone* here, all hours of the afternoon and most of the night. Here, are we buying this afternoon, or simply visiting? Because if there's much to carry, we should take the kitcheners' cart."

"A few of your sister's charms?" Jennifer said doubtfully. She exchanged a look with Lialla, who shrugged.

"We can use certain supplies, but not until we're ready to go on. And what we get depends on a lot of factors." She shrugged again. "A few charms. At the most."

"Good." Lasinay clapped her hands together. "Mindes and

Fyoran like to keep the cart handy, in case—particularly on a day like this, when so many visitors are coming. But I prefer to ride the open cart, anyway.''

Biyallan made a face at her and gave her a shove toward the main outer gate. ''Because Oliendi's younger sons so often take the open cart into the market, that's why.'' She turned to Jennifer and Lialla. ''It's something only Bez has, I think, though one of the Emperor's men thought it sensible enough to want to import to Podhru: small wagons travel around the districts and the market. For a small copper, they'll take you almost anywhere within the walls, but there's little room for more than a single shopping bag.'' She held up a limp cloth and string bag by its wide leather shoulder strap.

Jennifer nodded. ''Chris mentioned them this morning, after he went out with your brother. Shared taxis.''

Lialla gave an exasperated snort, but her eyes were amused. ''You have to ignore this woman sometimes, she uses these outrageous *words*—''

''Outlander,'' Lasinay nodded. ''You know?''

Jennifer groaned. ''Oh, God. You've been talking to Chris, haven't you?''

''No—my brother.''

''Gods of the Warm Silences,'' Lialla said reverently, with a helpless little smile. ''It's spreading.''

* * *

THE wagon, when one finally came by, was only large enough for the four women and the other three girls already in it. There were cushions on the wooden seats, something Biyallan assured them was unusual. ''Most of them have canopies for the rainy season, though it's little help if a wind is blowing.'' The wagon dropped the three girls on the broad avenue that led from the north gates; it picked up two older, bearded men who sat close together discussing money in low, intense voices. Jennifer watched the city go by, fascinated, and let Lialla carry the conversation with Fedthyr's daughters.

It was going to drive Chris absolutely crazy, she thought: not medieval or Renaissance, particularly—though some of the clothing had the tied-on Renaissance look of the Franco Zeffirelli-produced opera she'd seen the previous year. There was a flavor of the Near East here, too, but the women seemed to wear what they chose, face veils were conspicuously absent, and there was a freedom to the way they walked that would not have fit in most of the eastern Mediterranean countries she knew about. Byzantine? Not that, either, though she knew less about the historic eastern countries.

One thing certain: The climate might be similar, but there was no resemblance between the people here and those of early New Orleans. Whatever else they might be, they weren't Americans.

Where the devil are we? Jennifer wondered as Biyallan paid the wagon driver and led them across a nearly deserted, sunny square. Chris had thought they'd arrived where they'd left. Then again: Chris knew only what he read. Who was to say this place was their own world with certain changes? In any event, the land masses didn't particularly track. She shrugged it aside. Where they were, was Bezjeriad. In the company of a young man and his sister in need of funds to allow him to regain what should have been rightfully his three years before. *Keep that in mind, Cray,* she told herself firmly. *You have enough trouble staying in the "real world" here, without fiddling with it.*

Fedthyr's eldest daughter Marseli was a tall, angular woman of perhaps Robyn's age; like Robyn, she was pale-skinned and blonde, her eyes a very deep blue—like their father's first wife, Lasinay had explained. There was an air of brisk competence to the woman as she came around the small table that was the room's only furniture and held out both hands to Biyallan, then hugged Lasinay. Biyallan introduced the other two. "Sin-Duchess. Jeni—? Jen. I'm very glad you've come to my shop. I'd hoped to be at Father's last night to greet you, but one of his friends has a ship going out, and that always means extra work for me." She made a very faint grimace. "Even though the Lasanachi do not fight us or bring us their outsider fevers these days, so many men aboard ship are superstitious. Of course, it is profitable for me—another ship or two this month, and I could move the shop into better quarters. Biyallan, have you broached your notion to Father yet? She," she told Lialla, "has hopes of serving as my northern branch, if your brother is successful in his bid against your uncle. I would certainly be willing to invest what I can in your cause, to see the girl properly started."

"I—well," Lialla squared her shoulders under the novice blacks and tried to look as though she'd done this before. "I can't speak for Aletto, of course, though I know there is only one maker of charms in all Sehfi's market, and she is both old and unwell; she only makes healing charms—and love potions, of course."

"Well, of course," Lasinay said. Her two sisters quelled her with a mild glance.

"If she had an heir who sought to carry on her practice—but

she hasn't. I know, I spoke to her not long before we left Duke's Fort. Come tonight, if you can; talk with my brother.''

"I intend to,'' Marseli said. "My husband can package what I've made for the sailors and make the delivery before the *Bay Cutter* sails. Better he does anyway; have they warned you to avoid the docks?'' She glanced out the open doorway, measured shadow with a practiced eye, and added, "Let's go down to Adlaki's, I'd like a glass of orange and one of his fresh buns; we can talk there and watch the people and the water.''

* * *

THERE had been a very sweet orange drink at the cafe; to Jennifer's great pleasure, there was also coffee—tiny, very hot cups of it, already slightly sweet, with another cup of cool milk to pour into it. The buns were sweet, too; crusty outside, warm and soft inside, filled with bits of dried apricot and covered in raisins. She ate two and washed down most of the last with a second coffee. Lialla and the sisters watched in astonishment as she drank the second cup black. "Wonderful,'' she said with a happy little sigh. "Never mind the climate, I may come back *here* to live, if the coffee's all like this.''

"It's better here than some places,'' Marseli replied. "Don't you care for milk?''Jennifer pushed it across the table; Lasinay snagged the cup and drained it.

"Sometimes—but not in coffee. Why don't you import coffee to Zelharri, too?''

"Because you'd be the only one to drink it?'' Lialla asked pointedly.

Biyallan laughed. "Perhaps so—but things are changing, you know. Here in Bezjeriad, it was once only Bezanti. Now, of course, there is an entire district mostly Zelharri, but there are a few outlanders, outsiders chased from their land by the Lasanachi, southerners from just across the sea in Fahlia and Derra Vos. Even Sikkre, they say, has an influx of Dro Penti, other Zelharri, even Holmaddi and certain nomads who have decided to sell their carts and camels and live within solid walls. As for Podhru—one cannot tell one sort from another there, any more. There are more of us Rhadazi everywhere. The Emperor's councils speak of the need for new roads between the Dukedoms. There are actually new towns along the road from Sikkre, and our eldest brother says Whindsey is becoming nearly a city itself. But now, let's talk a little more. What kinds of charms would you like from me? And what arguments do you think I should bring with me tonight on Biyallan's behalf, for your brother?''

* * *

THEY returned to Marseli's shop an hour later. Lialla chose several of the woman's charms: blurring stones, two pendants similar to the one she'd used in Duke's Fort to "hear" up and down the hall, when Thread failed her. At Jennifer's suggestion, she also took two similar to the one Dahven had worn, to let him know when others were using magic to search for him in particular. Lialla either did a reasonably good job of covering her displeasure at requiring charms, or was thinking of them as backup for the others in their party. Or perhaps she'd begun to rethink that attitude also. She showed embarrassment only when Marseli refused to take payment for the items, and would have argued it, but the woman had already wrapped them in a black cloth and stuffed them in Lialla's hands, closing the fingers around it. "No, absolutely. After all, you are here to seek assistance, aren't you? How silly then for me to charge you. Think of it as *my* assistance."

Lialla considered this briefly, finally nodded. Her face was still flushed. "Thank you." She turned to look out the doorway at shadow that now covered most of the square. "They—my brother will be expecting me; I suspect we should go, and let you finish what you were doing when we came in." She glanced at Jennifer. "There was also the matter of medicines; we've used almost everything of what we had—"

"I know a good place for you to go," Marseli said.

"Perhaps we won't need most of the things on that list after tonight," Jennifer reminded her. "After we talk to this Neri."

Lialla sighed. "Who knows?" she asked gloomily. "But we should probably get back. This is a new thing for me, you know; simply going out where and when I choose. Aletto isn't any more used to it than I; he's bound to worry."

* * *

IT was a very long afternoon; Jennifer took enough time to wash her face and hands in cool water and to pick her hair out so it fluffed around her face. The blue dress was gone, replaced by a mint-green one embroidered at the cuffs with gold leaves and swirls. There was a pair of thin-soled sandals with matching gold patterns on the band of leather across the instep. They weren't going to be wonderful for standing in, she thought, but bare feet wouldn't be any better. "And they're much better with the dress than the high-tops," she told herself. There was no mirror in the room; she checked her hair and face in the reflection in the water bowl. Dahven's pendant lay against her throat. She touched it, turned the cord so it hung straight, and went downstairs.

Marseli apparently hadn't been joking: The room where she'd

talked so briefly the night before with Fedthyr and Aletto was packed with people; they spilled into the hallway, out onto the patio, sat on the edge of the fountain and were spreading across the grass. Fedthyr had clearly been watching for her, though: He caught hold of her elbow as soon as she reached the foot of the stairs, and escorted her around, introducing her to what seemed hundreds of people—she lost track of names almost at once—and repeating with pride every time: "You know the story about the outlander advocate and the late Thukar that came down recently from Sikkre? Well, *this* lovely woman—" After the first few introductions, she managed to take it in good stride. It was, as she reminded herself, all for a very good cause.

Robyn and Lialla stayed near Aletto at first, but Robyn finally moved out on her own, talking to the women. She wore mauve again, richly embroidered on the sleeves and back. Someone had braided her hair and worked a thin purple ribbon into the plait. She looked ten years younger, Jennifer thought. *Chris should have stuck around to see this; he'd be proud.* But Chris, with Aletto's approval, had taken Edrith and gone off with Fedthyr's youngest son. According to the note he left in Jennifer's room, they intended to come back in the early evening, before the party ended, so those they'd talked to could meet the nera-Duke.

She and Lialla would probably just cross paths with them: They had an appointment to meet Neri an hour after sunset, in Marseli's shop. "I'd arrive a little early, if anything," Marseli warned. "He's perhaps a trifle set in his ways, and he won't tolerate lateness in anyone."

Someone pressed a glass of wine into Jennifer's hand; she carried it until she could find a place to set it down and managed to snare a tall pottery mug of an orange drink. It didn't taste particularly good, but the mug in her hand kept people from forcing more of that sweet wine on her. Robyn, she noticed when she got near her sister late in the afternoon, had done the same thing.

She lost count of the number of times she had to tell the story of her confrontation with Dahmec; lost track of faces after a while. At one point, she found herself alone, edging sideways through a crowd, catching phrases here and there: "I hadn't expected so much of Amarni in him." "—well, yes, but if he doesn't find a way to trick Jadek, the man is utterly without scruple, you know." "I myself would *never* go back to Zelharri; do you remember that last spring in Sehfi, before the old Duke died? Snow up to a man's belly and a wind that took out all my fruit trees!" "Well, my daughter really had no interest in Sehfi, either, but the boy she's marrying has an interest in family land there, do you know Ibric? His family, their forests adjoin the late Carolan's on the north—'' ''Yes, but if he can't take Duke's Fort, I'd not only be out the money but Jadek isn't a man to take that kind of opposition lightly. I know, the Emperor has laws against vendetta, but when has that stopped anyone like Jadek?'' ''You can't think the boy will lose, can you? It's not just the two of them with our money, it's old Gyrdan and half Amarni's ex-iled guard. That would make even Shesseran think a second time, wouldn't it?'' ''If the boy wants to go, who am I to stop him? It's a wonderful opportunity, Aletto's bound to be generous to those who help him now, when he's Duke.''

And on and on. It was running about fifty-fifty, she thought: people worried about their money and their families, others see-ing it as the perfect chance to get in on the ground floor with a new regime. She wondered how Chris and his friends were man-aging but dismissed that; she'd know soon enough. Right now she wanted a few minutes in her room, flat on her back; the shoes were just as impossible for standing in as she'd thought they would be. And she wanted a drink of water; the orange stuff was bearable cool, but warmed by the room, the outside air and her hand around the mug all afternoon, it was perfectly dreadful.

And she wanted a few minutes—just a few—to organize her thoughts. It wouldn't be long now before Marseli came to take her and Lialla to meet Neri, and she wanted to have her list of questions and needs ready.

* * *

CHRIS, Edrith and Enardi had taken over a corner of one of the larger coffee shops on the southern edge of the market, not far from Marseli's shop. Here, over bread, cold sliced beef and cheese, they were talking with a number of Enardi's friends. At least, Chris talked when anyone asked him directly about Aletto, or about Lialla—otherwise, he pretty much kept his mouth closed and listened to Enardi talk about financial matters, business, various trades. Things he'd never really thought much about be-fore. After all, he'd figured on an after-school job at one of the minimum-wage burger chains this year, community college if he couldn't somehow swing anything better. History degree and God knew what he'd do with it, unless he decided to teach. All this merchant talk was as much another language, almost, as what the Cholani nomads had babbled at him. At least the food was good. He ate, listened, tried to pick up what he could, to see if he could figure who was pro-Aletto, who just in it for the money, who was too chicken to stick behind them if the going got ugly, so he could fill Aletto in later. It was some time before he noticed Edrith had gone.

* * *

EDRITH had understood more of the merchant-talk than Chris, but it interested him less. Besides, he thought as he eased quietly out the door and into the market proper, that was Chris's job, to evaluate people, to impress those who wanted to meet a genuine outlander, to pick up support for the nera-Duke. Edrith doubted any of them were greatly impressed by the presence of an impoverished Sikkreni, even if they didn't know how he'd kept himself fed for so long.

He wondered very briefly if Aletto and the others worried about turning him loose in Bez, fearing he'd steal and get caught, embarrass them all, but he decided probably it hadn't occurred to them. Chris at least understood, under all the pulling of chains, as Chris called it, that a kid living on the edge of starvation did what he had to to stay alive. That anyone did. Robyn understood. Jennifer—she never seemed to pay attention to things like that; to her he was simply Edrith, one of them. He respected her for that as much as he liked her for her quick wit and her dry humor. Aletto—well, he and Lialla were noble, after all; considering that, he got on very well with them.

And because of what he was, who he'd been, Edrith thought there was something *he* could do that none of the others could. While Chris was reading the sons and daughters of merchants, he, Edrith, could read the market, and see what rumors moved among its stalls. Whether word had spread of the nera-Duke's arrival—doubtless it had, even to the poorest huts south of the docks—and more importantly, whether any of Jadek's men or the Thukars' were here, looking for them. Edrith moved into shade and stood, gazing about until he had a feel for what was around him. He moved with an easy stride into the midst of late afternoon shoppers and no one paid him any heed at all.

He paid a small copper for a heavy cloth pocket to hang from his belt and spent several moments talking to the man who ran the stall—one of several bunched together in the front of an old, shabby wooden building. There were a few rumors about Aletto, the ones he'd already heard abut Dahven and the new Thukars, about Dahmec's death. He drifted past more buildings, a few new individual buildings—one of these, if he'd understood Enardi right, was the one Marseli wanted to purchase. He must be nearer the harbor, then—though not too close, since this area still had a feel of prosperity, and even the packed-dirt walks were clean. He glanced up at the sky, picked out shadow—no easy trick here, where everything was canopied over and buildings and stalls ran so close together—and turned to head west.

The change was gradual, but after he'd been walking awhile the stands became smaller, less well maintained; the overhead canopies were smaller and patched, or put together of several older ones. There were holes in fabric, letting sunlight through to fall on piles of used clothing, shoes and boots with perhaps a little more wear to them before they fell apart. The smell of fish everywhere. A seller of already worn magic charms; what she had to offer looked like the sandals on the blanket across from him: a few more wearings but not too many. Edrith slowed, put his hands behind his back and looked at the bits of wrought copper, carved wood, and tried to start a conversation. The old woman cast a practiced eye over him and refused to be drawn; she clearly knew the look of a browser and had no intention of letting one come between her and any possible sale. He sighed and turned away. And stopped as though someone had hit him.

The old man sitting cross-legged behind the rotting gray blanket with its few pairs of sandals and two old mismatched boots was arguing with another man—younger, perhaps, skinny and with a desperate, hungry look in his eyes Edrith knew all too well. It wasn't the look of the man, though—or the smell of him, he reeked of fish—but the boots hanging from his hand. *I know those boots,* Edrith thought dazedly. *I know them.* He forced himself to move on before the old woman at the charm table could begin to wonder what he was up to, slid into shade once more where he was less obvious, but could hear the old man and his customer.

No, not customer, he realized. The fisherman—he couldn't be anything else, not smelling like that—was turning one of the boots over. He knelt, held it out cautiously, as though fearing the old man would snatch it from him. "There's thick sole leather, Poli, and look at the color on the fold."

"The size is a small one," Poli objected sharply. He touched the boot with one finger, drew it back and put it in his mouth. "And they're thick with dried salt. I'd need to clean them, to make back what you ask for them, Dighra."

"Six ceris," Dighra said flatly. "It's small for a man's foot, but what difficulty is that? A man's small foot or a boy's large one—"

"What boy has so much money as to purchase these?"

"The salt could be washed from them by the purchaser. You could simply brush them while you sit here, instead of glaring
241

at those who might otherwise buy your things," the fisherman added persuasively.

"Hah." The old man spat. "I couldn't pay six, not for Duke Lehzin's own boots. Three perhaps." He touched the leather once again; Dighra snatched them back.

"Six or nothing." He turned away. "I'll bring them by to-morrow, Poli. If I don't find another buyer between now and then. Think it over."

"It'll still be three!" the old man shouted after him. Edrith slid around the next table where a pair of children sat watching a tray of sticky sweets and waving a branch to keep the flies away from it. The man Dighra was moving at a fast walk down the muddy track toward the docks, boots tucked under one arm, fingers firmly fixed in the cuffs. Edrith stayed right behind him.

His mind was a whirl. *Dahven's boots. Gods of my mother, is he dead then? But how did he come here?* There was one way to find out—at least, he'd find out where the skinny little man got the boots.

Dighra turned up a narrow alley just short of the open docks and glanced behind him. Edrith hovered at the entrance to the alley, waiting until he turned away, then sprinted as fast as he could. The smell of fish assaulted his nostrils; the man's sleeve was greasy under his fingers and he nearly let it go in disgust. The man whirled around but couldn't make himself let go of his precious bundle to strike out. Edrith backed him against the wall. The knife he wore at the small of his back was in his hand. "The boots. Where did they come from?"

"F-f-f-found them?"

Edrith shook his head and smiled grimly. "Didn't find them. Where did you get them?"

"There was—they were on the beach, two nights ago, I just—"

"No. I can tell when a man's lying to me, it's in the eyes. And you're not good at it. Let's make a bargain, shall we? Let's say I want the boots, and I'll pay you six ceris for them."

The man eyed him warily, swallowed. Looked at the knife, back up into Edrith's eyes. "Eight," he managed finally.

Edrith laughed, and Dighra shuddered. "You'd better learn to pretend courage, if you want to play games like this, my friend. But, a bargain. Let's say, ten ceris, for the boots and the man who wore them."

"Why?"

"Say he's someone I know. The reason doesn't concern you. Ten ceris do, don't they? Ten ceris—and I put the knife away without using it?"

242

"I didn't hurt him! I swear I didn't—!"

"Then take me to him, let me see that for myself." His heart rose and he felt slightly dizzy; surely it wasn't possible Dahven was still alive? *Don't hope, this poor creature might be saying anything to save his skin.* Gods knew he'd done that himself, once or twice. He didn't dare let that thought soften him, though. "Take me to him," he repeated, and gently detached the boots from the other's suddenly nerveless fingers. Dighra looked momentarily as though he wanted to protest; he spared another brief, frightened glance for the knife, turned and started back down the alley; Edrith stayed right on his heels, the knife now out of sight but tucked in his hand against his leg. Where he could use it, if necessary.

It wasn't far: They followed the little alley to its end, came out onto hot sand under high, thin clouds. The haze, as usual, did little to break the heat. Dighra pointed to a small shack, one of perhaps twenty huddled together near the south end of the docks where two large trading ships and several transfer boats were moored. "There. You have the boots, give me the money."

"We'll see inside first. Not that I don't trust you, of course." He didn't. And he was frightened, suddenly. Afraid of what he'd find there—afraid of how he'd tell Aletto. And Jennifer.

But when the fisherman pushed the patched door curtain aside, sunlight fell into the single tiny room, illuminating the pile of filthy covers that filled at least half of it. The man lying on them was nearly as filthy: He was ragged, bearded and gaunt, but there was no mistaking Dahven. And as light fell on his face, he groaned and flung an arm over his eyes.

19

S OMEHOW, he found the ten ceris—nearly the last of his money—and gave it to Dighra, who turned and immediately fled. Edrith worried only briefly that the man might be in search of the dock guard or of his own kind for support, but he dismissed that: The dock guard would be the last people a man like Dighra would want. If anything, Dighra would wait somewhere until Edrith left, then come back. *That* wasn't likely, though; he'd be too afraid.

It didn't matter; Dighra wasn't important any more. Edrith knotted the ragged curtain up and crawled into the little room and moved so his body shaded Dahven's face. "Dahven? It's me, Edrith. Can you move, can we get you out of here?"

"Edrith?" The voice didn't sound much like Dahven's and he had to bend close to hear it. "How can it be you?"

"You beat us to Bezjeriad, apparently," Edrith managed lightly. Inside, he was more frightened than ever: The man's forehead was hot and wet. Sweating sickness, or something very like it. No wonder the fisherman had run.

"Yeah. Came by ship. They didn't want me any more after—Bez Harbor—something. Can't complain—about that." He was trying to speak lightly, too. He sounded dreadful. "I'm glad it's you. Didn't want anyone—to see me like this."

"I know." Like Chris. Edrith had never felt or really understood that kind of shame, especially for something that wasn't your fault in the first place. Hardly the place to argue that, though. "I'm—thirsty. There was water—" He brought up a trembling hand to point, let it fall across his chest and closed his eyes. Edrith turned away to feel around the little room. The sun was in his eyes, making them water; he couldn't see anything but sparks of light and black shadow. "That man. Found me on the sand. Lasanachi left me. Brought me here. I said I'd pay him, don't think he believed me, though. Got sick. I feel awful," he finished in a whisper.

"I don't doubt it—wait. Found something—" Edrith sniffed at the jug cautiously, tipped it and put a finger to the liquid, touched it to his tongue. "This thing had wine in it, bad stuff. Water in it now." He shifted around, got an arm under Dahven's shoulders and eased him up a little; Dahven was a dead weight, but he managed to get a little water down. "Can we move you?"

Dahven shook his head. "You and me? I tried earlier, just for the water. I—just can't. Couldn't even reach the water, stupid, isn't it? I could only think, if the Lasanachi came back, and I couldn't do anything at all, even then I just—just couldn't." He tried to smile. "Funny. I could only think of the time I had that wine at The Four Bells—"

"The stuff Mirso was supposed to get?"

"Gods but I was sick that night! You half-dragged me all the way back to the old walls." He fetched a little sigh, a second. "I haven't even that much strength, Edrith. I'm—sorry." Fingers pulled at his shirt restlessly, then caught hold of Edrith's

244

wrist. "You'd better go; when they come back they'll take you, too. They're—I would—don't let them, Edrith. The market stories don't tell you half—"

"Shhh. Dahven, don't; it's all right." Edrith blotted his friend's forehead with the hem of his own shirt, poured a little of the water on that and blotted the rest of his face and his throat. "There are no Lasanachi anywhere in all the Sea of Rhadaz just now; they ran several nights ago. The merchant housing Aletto told us."

"They'll come back—"

"No. I won't let them take you away, even if they do." This seemed to have been the right thing to say. Dahven sagged back against the blankets, eyes closed; his fingers relaxed and fell back onto his chest, where they now lay still. Edrith sat motionless until he saw the other's chest move, sighed faintly and began to think furiously. Dahven needed medical care; he was dangerously ill and in pain. The hand Edrith had used to hold him upright while he drank felt sticky and was smeared with blood. It was worse than what Chris had gone through, much worse, and with only one young and inexperienced Sikkreni to help him. . . .

But that kind of thinking wasn't useful. He touched Dahven's shoulder, then removed his hand. He seemed to be asleep; better not to turn him over. Find a physician like the one who'd treated Chris's wrists, and bring him here? But to find one he dared trust! And then, bringing one out here; what dweller in such a hovel could afford the services of a physician? Suspicious, it would look. And there were most certainly men in the market looking for just that sort of suspicious activity.

Dahven didn't seem to know what had happened in Sikkre— his father's death, his brothers' taking the Ducal seat. Well, this was scarcely the time to tell him. All the same, with Sikkreni guards looking for all of them— Jadek might have no personal use for Dahven, but would certainly sell him to his brothers. Jadek wouldn't care if Dahven were alive or dead, but probably the new Thukars would find it less embarrassing if there were nothing to do but mourn a foolish brother and burn his body, Edrith thought grimly.

That wasn't important just now, either, but it was hard for him to focus on what was. Most importantly, he wouldn't dare move the man in full daylight. Someone would see them, the wrong someone. Even if no one did, though, where could they go? *If this were Sikkre,* Edrith thought in some despair, *I'd know the answer, I'd have a dozen places Deehar's men would never locate, and physicians or healers who owe me favors.* Here, though: He couldn't go to Fedthyr; the merchant might be willing to aid Aletto but how would he feel about a sick man accused of killing his father, however noble? Would anyone here believe he hadn't killed Dahmec? Just as likely they'd send for Sikkreni armsmen to return him to his younger brothers—less fuss all around. What Edrith had seen so far of the Zelharri merchants, their first thought was money, their second caution. Not the best of allies, not for Dahven.

But even if Fedthyr were eminently trustworthy, there were dozens of people filling his house just now.

There seemed to be only one answer; not a good one, just the best he could devise. He roused Dahven to drink a little more water, got him flat again and mopped off his face; it was already slick with sweat. "Listen. I have to leave you, to get help. We'll come back after dark, find a place to move you where it's safe. Get medicine for your fever. Do you understand? I'll come back after dark, that isn't so many hours now. Can you manage?"

Dahven smiled weakly and gripped his fingers. "Hours. Edrith. Don't worry about me, I'll sleep." And indeed, Edrith thought the sick man was asleep before he edged outside and got back to his feet. *Little warm sand gods, I hope he believed me. I think he is certain the Lasanachi will find him first.* But there was nothing to do about that, just go, find help. Get back here.

He wasted a moment debating about the boots, decided finally to take them with him; if he left them, Dighra might simply return and steal them again. Someone else might. And Dahven was going to need them, Edrith promised himself grimly. He moved quickly across the sand, edged cautiously into the alley and hurried through it, around the narrow way where the used shoe merchant still sat, thinking hard the whole way. By the time he reached the cleaner and more prosperous portion of the market, he had a plan—not much of one, but probably the only one he could put into effect himself, in the time he had. He finally came back to the cafe where he'd left Chris, but the corner where they'd been sitting was filled with older men, all arguing some obscure religion or other. Edrith backed out, looked up and down the street, up at the sky. It really was nearly sunset, later than he'd thought; likely they'd gone back to Fedthyr's house. He knelt to fumble through his pocket. One copper—two. He'd thought the last coins had gone to bribe that fisherman. Fortunately not: It wouldn't be that difficult to walk from here into Fedthyr's district, certainly not for him, but there was the matter of time. Chris had told him Jennifer was going out tonight to meet with some old Night-Thread Wielder. He absolutely had to find her first.

* * *

IT seemed to take forever to find one of the carts that was willing to go near the gates, without going ten other places first. He sat in the rear, one leg jiggling wildly, finally jumped down when the cart would have taken him away from the long park and back to the main north-gate avenue, ran along the edge of the grass. The servant guarding the gate fortunately recognized him, tousled and sweaty as he was, and not only let him in but helped him avoid most of the partygoers. He ran up the back stairs, down the hall to where the women were quartered and tapped on Jennifer's door—no answer. His heart dropped, but a moment later, Lialla's door opened and both women came out, Lialla in proper Wielder novice blacks, but Jennifer in her familiar jeans and sneakers, the blue shirt unbuttoned partway and sleeves rolled neatly to her elbows. She looked businesslike, competent—ready for anything. *Thank all my mother's gods for a capable woman,* Edrith thought devoutly. He drew a deep breath and then a second to ease his laboring chest, then beckoned as Jennifer looked up and saw him. Lialla glanced in his direction, but had knelt to deal with one of her sandals. "Jen, this Wielder—you're going there now?"

"Yes." She studied him curiously. "You're sweating and absolutely white. Are you all right?"

"Fine. Well—winded. Where is he?"

"Marseli's shop. He didn't want strangers in his home, I suspect. Why?"

"Just—need to know. Will you be long?"

She shrugged. "Don't know. I doubt it. Lialla says we'll be lucky to get much time out of him if we're not apprenticed to him, and Marseli says he's impatient and old both." She was still gazing at him in concern. "Something *is* wrong. What?"

"Nothing. Honestly. How are you going?"

"Marseli's husband Dowbri is coming; he has a small cart. He said he'd bring us back later, so he can meet Aletto."

"If—" Edrith drew another deep breath. "If I come with another wagon, and ask you to trust me, and to come with me—will you?"

"Of course." She turned to look at Lialla, who was adjusting black scarves nervously. "I'd better go; she's getting worried about the time. So am I, for that matter. Is it safe for you to wait outside that shop?"

"I'll be somewhere about; I'll see you." He gripped her hands as she would have turned away. "Thank you. You were the only—well, never mind. Just—thanks."

* * *

JENNIFER went down the back stairs with Lialla just in front of her. Moments before, she'd been nearly as jumpy as the sin-Duchess, worrying about how this old man would accept them, whether he could answer any of the questions she'd written down, what he could—or would—show them. She was suddenly glad she'd written down what she wanted to know; her mind had gone completely blank. She followed Lialla across the kitchen court-yard in that same bemusement; managed to shake herself enough to respond politely to Marseli's husband—a broad-shouldered, hefty man with a long red beard and very blue eyes that fixed for one startled moment on Jennifer's blue-clad legs. Lialla held a desultory conversation with him—what she'd seen of Bez thus far, what she thought about it, how she liked Fedthyr and his house—leaving Jennifer free to get herself together.

What was Edrith up to? she wondered. She pulled her sheet of yellow pad from her back jeans pocket and studied it in the rapidly failing light. *One thing at a time,* she ordered herself firmly.

* * *

NERI was waiting for them, pacing the little shop, though they were if anything early. Jennifer took an instant dislike to him: His face was very pale, set in lines—like Merrida's—of deep disapproval and sour disappointment; his eyes and mouth held a knowing, self-important expression like Merrida's that was just as irritating. Jennifer bit back disappointment of her own and hoped the similarities didn't mean he was as arbitrary; that he knew more. *At least he's here,* she told herself. *And he's two levels above Merrida; that has to mean something, doesn't it?*

He wore black except for the very prominent, broad swath of silvery gray that ran across a thick middle. The rest of his garb was a welter of scarves and short robes that left her feeling smothered; his neck was wrapped right up to the chin in thick cloth. The thighs of his breeks shone, where he'd rubbed greasy hands on them; Jennifer had seen too many of Chris's jeans like that when he was younger to mistake the look. He smelled strongly of sweat, almost overpowering in the small back room of Marseli's shop until the shop owner pulled the thick door open and had her husband pop the shutters from the chamber's single window. Sea-flavored air, only slightly cooler, puffed into the room. *Wonderful,* Jennifer thought. *Salt air, old fish and male sweat.* She was suddenly glad she'd eaten nothing since midday. Neri walked back and forth across the room once again, stopped at the far wall and fixed both women with a look, transferred it to Marseli, who set a single thick candle in a glass shroud on the table, shrugged, smiled at Lialla and left them. Dowbri had already gone out the back door; Jennifer could see his shadow in a blue light where he was squatting over some task in the little packed-dirt yard.

The old man adjusted scarves, settled the gray sash and nodded at them. He didn't come across to greet them, and Jennifer was relieved. He was bad enough from where he was, and his glare intimidated her. Maybe she could keep that to herself, though, from a distance. She hoped so: Better to bargain from a position of power than to feel like a truant kid and know the other person senses it.

He crossed to the opposite wall, leaned against it. *God.* He had a limp even more noticeable than Aletto's at its worst: one leg was shorter than the other but he had obviously adjusted to this years since and showed none of Aletto's emotional discomfort as he took long strides that jerked his upper body back and forth. To Jennifer's distress, when he leaned against the wall he swung his short leg back and forth. With an effort, she pulled her eyes from that, looked up to meet his sardonic, black gaze. "You are the outlander advocate," he said finally. "And you, old Merrida's second apprentice. Who backed her to name *you* fit to Wield?"

Lialla swallowed and when she spoke, her voice was thin and a little high. "Um. Erryn, her old teacher." She swallowed again. Jennifer stepped on her foot and frowned at her; they'd had it out for over an hour in Lialla's room before coming here, and the woman was losing the little confidence she'd built up already. Lialla glanced at her, comprehension in her eyes, and shut her mouth. *Don't babble,* Jennifer had told her. *Draw a deep breath, force as much air out with your words as you can, to keep it from wobbling, if you're still scared when we get there. Don't let him spook you, damnit; he puts his breeks on one leg at a time, just like you do.*

"I'm Jennifer Cray. Merrida had little time or energy to talk with me when she brought us through to help Lialla and her brother, and Lialla has taught me a great deal, but of course not as much as a person at Meridda's level could. I need to know more than I do." She stopped then. The old man was shaking his head and giggling.

"Heh." He wiped his eyes, then his nose on a black sleeve. "Merrida couldn't teach water to flow downhill. She cheated and bribed for that Green Sash. Did things to *me* once that—

249

well, that's not your business and I haven't all night. I'm an old man, need my sleep. You." He pointed a long, trembly finger at Lialla suddenly. She jumped. "Show me the Thread for listening." Lialla closed her eyes, reached, and Jennifer set her jaw. "Like that? That's how she taught you?" He giggled again; Lialla glanced at him sidelong, like a shying horse, closed her eyes again when Jennifer increased the pressure on her foot. She herself was able to deflect the worst of the vibration Lialla was setting up by a very faint hum, a Bach flute piece not quite loud enough to be heard by anyone else. But Neri turned his head to fix her with a hard eye. *What is this?*

"Music," she said flatly. "If there's a better way to keep myself out of what she's doing, tell me; I find it very uncomfortable."

"Of course you do, unguarded. There *is* no better shield than music against intrusion by another's Wielding," he added, almost mildly compared to his earlier snapped remarks. "But I wonder how *you* found that out, since old Merrida has less music sense than that lamp, and I can see already she taught this girl all wrong." Lialla opened her eyes and looked at him; her face had sagged into lines of misery and he glared at her. "It isn't the end of everything! You can relearn, can't you? If you want it as much as you think, you can!"

"All those years," Lialla whispered. For a moment, Jennifer thought she might burst into tears, and probably the old man would desert them. But the sin-Duchess swallowed hard and sounded almost calm as she asked, "Will *you* teach me?"

"I? No! Too old! Too busy! Find another Wielder, a younger one." He laughed rather nastily. "There are plenty of pretty young men scrambling for position in Podhru, young Wielders. A few I taught, some of Ibarneffy's classes—classes, huh! But a number of those are good; find one with muscles and a lean face, the things you young women like, persuade *him*." Lialla was blushing and he laughed again. "Enough," he said abruptly. "I said I'd show you things, talk to you both tonight. I will, if you ask sensible questions and pay heed to the answers, if you show you're worth my time. Besides, it will be *such* a pleasure to undo that woman's—well, call it craft if you will. Wretched creature, deserves everything she gets, maybe worse. You," he snapped at Jennifer as he leveled a finger at her nose, "will find music as you just used it to be a shield that will keep others from touching you by means of their own magic—not simply other Wielders. It will blur even more effectively than the Thread itself. Keep that in mind, particularly if you are the objects of such search as the market rumor says. You"—he shifted the finger Lialla's direction—"will relax and consider Thread, so that when I demand a task of you, you can do it; you are entirely too overwrought to do any good at all. Wait—did Merrida not show you *this*? Grasp it so—no, listen, it sounds—that is right. That Thread. Run it through your fingers, in and out, concentrate upon it. Fool old woman, not to show an excitable novice *that*!" He mumbled under his breath for a few moments. "Go ahead, use that, ready yourself. And you—you have questions, do you? Well, then, ask!"

To his credit, Jennifer realized much later, he answered most of her questions without further comment—probably figuring he'd be out of Marseli's back room all the sooner—and only now and again flatly refused to talk about something. He didn't much like her assertion that she could use Thread during the day, but wasn't as upset about it as Lialla had been. "Mmm. Well. Nothing I've ever done, why bother? Day's for sleeping, or other things, never needed it then. If you do, and you can—why not? Wager Merrida'd say otherwise, heh." He was silent for several moments after her next question, finally shrugged. "Can't say why anything would work differently because it's sun up there instead of moon or stars. Test it, why don't you?"

But she got nothing from him on the subject of Hell-Light save a harsh diatribe worthy of one of Lialla's early ones: Hell-Light was evil, dreadful, a created magic, separate from Thread entirely. Jennifer decided, prudently, not to ask about the compacted knot of Threadlike stuff that had been in the deserted hut, fearing they'd lose him entirely.

He put Lialla through everything she knew, and each time stopped her, showed her different ways to work Thread than those Merrida had taught her—he laughed at her red string and cat's cradles, sang or hummed at her in a reedy but well-pitched voice to illustrate how certain Thread sounded, scoffed at Merrida's insistence on certain ways to hold the stuff. "Bah. Nothing of the sort. Get a good grip on it, rest is just foolery. Old Merrida making herself important, making things difficult for you." He stopped her when she started looking glassy-eyed and frustrated, sent her into the little yard, just outside the open door, to work at it. "Remember the first thing I showed you, young woman, work that Thread first, calm yourself. A frantic Wielder is worth less, almost, than a certain nasty old woman." Lialla simply nodded and left; she'd tried defending Merrida at first—more out of loyalty and reflex than any remaining belief in her old instructor, Jennifer thought. But Neri had merely laughed raucously, covering her stammered remarks with loud chuckles, and she'd finally given up.

Neri then eyed Jennifer, folded his arms and swung his short leg. "It's a pity. You have more talent than the old Duke's child: you could very possibly obtain a White Sash if you wanted it. You don't, do you?"

"No—at least, to be honest, not just yet. I don't think I ever will." Jennifer spread her hands. "But I have only been in your world—not even thirty days yet, unless I've lost count. I was an advocate in my world; there's no magic like this there and I wouldn't have wanted anything to do with it if there had been. I had plenty without it. Here, though . . ." She sighed. "It seems I do nothing but explain that I said I'd help Aletto. I can't do that if I don't understand what I'm doing. It's important to me that I do not fail for lack of knowledge, or someone else's lack—or the stupidity and arrogance of anyone's teacher."

Neri laughed briefly. "Which could be Merrida—or myself, if I fail you tonight? You have a sharp wit, woman, to go with that sharp tongue. It's a rarer commodity than the ability to Wield. However. Pay close attention to what I do now, and how I do it. You need a better way to heal injuries or ill health, you need a way to communicate which works better than the one you worked up by yourself—that was clever, tugging at the girl's rope to warn her. But you don't need me to tell you how clever you are. You need to know how to make a protective circle. I'll show you as much as you can absorb."

"That's quite a lot," Jennifer said crisply. "Begin."

* * *

It was very near midnight when Neri left them. To his credit, he'd given them considerably more time than he'd originally agreed to, and when Lialla offered him coin, he refused it. "Remember everything I taught you and learn more. Rise above the Black Sash that disgusting old woman bound you down to; that will be payment enough." He turned away from them, then, and simply faded away—like a sour-tempered Cheshire cat, Jennifer thought irreverently. She could feel Thread shimmering where he'd been, a vibration that moved rapidly away from them: He was utilizing the near-black Thread that reminded her of a Rimsky-Korsakov processional, all horns and snare. By now he'd already be back in his own small house. He'd shown her how to use that—Lialla had been past taking another single idea by that time—but Jennifer had found herself too nervous to try such a form of transport, and watching him fade out like that, even sensing him whole a distance off, didn't encourage her to try it.

After all, she'd be essentially dissolving herself; what if all of her didn't make it? It reminded her of all Chris's science fiction stories about that kind of transport, old *Star Treks* where the machinery malfunctioned and people became a collection of really disgusting bits and pieces. *Ugh.* And this wasn't even science, it was something she found far less safe. When she'd asked Neri, he hadn't prevaricated: Things did go wrong, now and again. It didn't seem to worry him. *It won't happen to me, no sir,* Jennifer thought flatly. She wasn't certain she could have used it anyway; it took a *lot* of concentration and energy, more than anything else she'd tried thus far.

Right now, she very likely couldn't have lifted a pencil with Thread. Her mind felt sieved and utterly limp. Poor Lialla looked half-asleep.

She'd nearly forgotten Edrith, and her promise to him, but he was waiting when Marseli and her husband came out to drive the sin-Duchess back to Fedthyr's house—and no doubt a still very much ongoing party. It must be costing Fedthyr a fortune to put up so much food and drink.

Lialla showed little interest when Edrith tried to explain. "I'll bring Jen, but we may be a while. There's something I think we need."

Marseli nodded and settled Lialla next to her. "I'll remember that. And if anyone asks, I'll tell them so." Her husband turned the wagon to head out across the blue-light lit square. Edrith waited until they were a distance away, then lifted a handful of reins and turned the long, flat wagon the other way. The animal—a small, dark mule—picked up its ears and started at a slow walk down a narrow, cobbled street, heading toward the harbor. Jennifer settled herself cross-legged on a thick pile of blanket and clutched the high sidewall. There was no seat, just carrying space, about seven or eight feet of it, she thought.

They rode in silence for some moments. Edrith glanced in her direction. "You look awful, Jen. Are you all right?"

"Fine, physically anyway. Mentally, I'm worn out." Her fingers quested by her side and behind her to ease the lump on which she was sitting: a fighting staff shoved under them—no, two of them. It brought her a little more awake, and set off an alarm in the back of her mind. "Edrith. Where are we going?"

He smiled, and she thought that it took him an effort to manage that. That his eyes were strained. Difficult to tell in the uneven and infrequent light. But he had looked pretty dreadful when he'd caught her outside Lialla's door; how could she have forgotten that? *I didn't realize how spooked I was about going to see that old man.* The back of her neck was prickling suddenly; anticipation, fear—perhaps both. Edrith's smile slipped and was gone for good. "Down by the docks—below them, actually. Some huts out on the sand." The mule slowed even more as the blue lights became fewer and the poles holding them more widely separated. "It's not a good place, day or night, but—" His voice faded away.

"Why?" she asked finally. The voice was high, thin, and couldn't possibly have been hers.

Edrith glanced at her again. "I found Dahven. He's alive, but very ill, I think he's hurt, too. The—Lasanachi—" He shook his head. "Never mind that, it's not important for you to know. I hated to leave him there, but I couldn't carry him, it was still daylight; that part of the market even busier than the main districts. And he couldn't walk." He shrugged. "I am truly sorry about the harbor—"

"Never *mind* that. I don't care. If he's alive—" She swallowed, and Edrith touched her hand. When she stayed quiet, he went on.

"I didn't know who else I could get. Aletto wouldn't dare leave Fedthyr's party, Robyn wouldn't be any use down here, Lialla— Chris is meeting with Enardi and some of the other sons and daughters of the merchants for Aletto."

"I know. He told me." It hurt to talk.

"If he can persuade any of those people to back Aletto, they'd—well, you know." She heard him swallow, and remembered with a pang that he'd known Dahven for years. "I don't know any of those people, I didn't know if I could trust anyone. But I knew I could depend on you in a fight," Edrith went on after a few moments. "Because of—well, who and what you are. And because it's Dahven." He lapsed into silence. She was staring straight ahead, scarcely seeing the narrowing streets or smelling the noxious mud the mule was splashing up. She became aware of him finally, watching her worriedly.

She sat very still. Her skin felt like someone had just rubbed it with block ice: chilled and aching, scraped. *Breathe*, she ordered herself. *Like you told Lialla. Air behind the words, so they don't tremble.* "How bad is it?"

"Fever—the man who'd found him thought sweating sickness. I did too, at first, but it's different. This is exhaustion and—well, he's been hurt, I don't know how badly, I didn't want to move him around."

She nodded numbly. "Do you think he's still alive?"

"I—yes." She couldn't tell if he believed that or not. It

254

sounded good; she'd take it because just now anything else was unacceptable. "But he's being sought—"

"I know that."

"I mean, here. Today. When I was back in the market this evening to find a blurring-stone, before I borrowed this wagon from a friend of Enardi's, I heard. There are Sikkreni in Bez, men openly wearing the badges of the Thukars' in-house guard. They've been all over the market and down on the docks, asking questions—about the Lasanachi ship that left Bez so suddenly, about a man of Dahven's height and size. The man who lives in that hut tried to sell Dahven's boots; that's how I found Dahven. And I scared the poor man half to death, but he may outgrow that, given enough time—and he may try to sell something else."

"Oh, God," Jennifer said. She wrapped her hands around each other and squeezed until her fingers hurt.

"We're close now; it'll be all right."

"Is there anything else?" she asked.

"No. Just a question: Will you be able to use that bo, if we're attacked?"

"Try me," she replied grimly.

"Good. Perhaps we won't need it. I brought two and those blankets so we might carry him to the wagon; it's all soft sand and the wagon would never make it."

"We'll make it," she assured him. "I couldn't Wield right now to save any of us; there's simply nothing left. I haven't been so good with that under fire anyway."

"You've been fine. A last thing: something Chris told me you did for him, before he and Aletto went into Sikkre's market that first night. The knife you gave him and what you said." He bent down and drew something long and dark from his boot. Jennifer eyed it sidelong as he held it out. It was a dagger rather than a knife, she thought; the blade was dark steel, nearly a foot long, very slender but it felt strong enough. The handle was wrapped in soft suede. "Could *you* use one of these if you had to?"

She hesitated only a moment, took it from his hand and ran the blade through a belt loop, jamming it in place so it wouldn't fall out and cut her foot off. One edge and the tip were hellishly sharp. "Trust me. I can do anything I have to tonight." *Except Wield*, she thought unhappily. *As Birdy would say, my lousy luck*. But luck was something you made for yourself. Right now, she was her own luck, and Dahven's.

She fingered the little silver charm around her throat, as the mule turned down a very narrow, muddy alley.

* * *

"You ready?" It was the first thing Edrith had said in several very long moments. Jennifer nodded, realized it was too dark for him to see her and whispered: "Ready." Edrith pressed her hand. Something hard in his fingers—he leaned over to breathe against her ear: "Blurring-stone. Hides the cart as well as anything could. Have to hurry, though; anyone could trip over it."

"Got you," she breathed back, slid from the wagon and gathered in one of the blankets before catching hold of her bo. The single thickness of black fabric she'd wrapped around one end where her hand gripped it for walking felt reassuringly familiar in a world where suddenly nothing was. Even Edrith—she'd known him for weeks now, and suddenly he was as alien as everything else: the smell of his skin and of his breath, the mule, the stuff they'd used to grease the wagon wheels, the wood itself. The blanket was unmistakably wool but scratchier than any wool she'd ever owned and there was an underlying smell beneath the lanolin. The narrow alley reeked of long-dead fish, other things much less savory; it squelched unpleasantly under her high-tops.

Her mind reeled; she took one involuntary step back. A slightly damp but reassuringly hard wall caught her across the shoulders and held her up; a moment later, Edrith was beside her, leaning over so he could whisper against her ear once more. "That's good, stay against the wall, no one can come up on your left side that way. Set your feet down easily, so they don't splash if there's more puddles." He took her agreement for granted, she thought; simply tugged on her sleeve to give her the direction, and set out.

He was hard to see at first, even though her eyes had had several moments to adjust to the almost complete lack of light. But suddenly there was an opening ahead, a flare of yellow light beyond it that might have been a lamp or torch. Something that was pale under starlight and had to be sand. Edrith jerked his head urgently in that direction and increased his speed a little.

They came into the open two shallow breaths later, and he stopped, abruptly. Jennifer, just behind him, had little warning as someone shoved hard against her right shoulder, forcing her into the open. She spun about on one heel, dropping the blanket somewhere behind her. Two men blocked the alley.

"Look at that," one said. "A stick of a boy and a woman in those outlander breeks!"

"We need money," the second said. "*Your* money."

"Do I look stupid enough to carry money in a place like this?" Jennifer snapped at him. "Or to give it to you if I did?" She heard Edrith draw in a sharp breath. He was swearing softly as he moved up next to her, blankets somewhere off to one side and the bo dangling loosely from his hand.

"You can't be too smart," the first man retorted. "Coming to a place like this at any hour, with only a boy to protect you, clad like that. Why, I wonder?" Jennifer bared her teeth at him. She was aware of the Sikkreni at her side darting nervous little glances her direction. Maybe she'd be horrified later, too; right now the Cray temper was heating her blood. The man took a step forward, held out a large hand. "Not that I much care. Give me what you've got, maybe you'll come out of it alive."

"I intend to," she replied flatly. "You may not have that option." He glanced at Edrith, at his companion, and she laughed. "Come on! Don't let fear hold you back!"

It hadn't really been a plan, just what her self-defense instructor had once said about getting them mad and off-balance enough to attack first. She retreated a step and pivoted her back to Edrith's, bent both knees. Her attacker must have taken it for fear, he was already coming, both hands outstretched to snatch her. The bo slid through her hands, just like Chris had taught her; she tightened the two-handed grip, straightened her legs and caught the man right between the eyes. He dropped as though poleaxed. Edrith brought his through in an underarm swing and slammed it up under the second man's chin, lifting him off his feet and throwing him backwards.

Jennifer had already shifted her grip on the staff so she could pick up the blanket; she turned her back on the two men and peered toward the nearest huts. She could hear Edrith dragging first one out of the way, then the other. He came panting back to gather up his own things. "They're under the shadow of the wall, where no one will see them right away. But you—that was *crazy*!" he hissed against her ear. She bit back a laugh, knowing it would echo all over the docks.

"No—mad, as in angry. Where is he?" Edrith cast up his eyes, gestured with his head and started forward.

The fighting high left her as abruptly as it had come on, and for one horrible moment she thought she might fall, her legs had gone so weak. *Later,* she thought grimly. *Don't you dare worry about anything else right now, woman!* Anything—else— Her feet slowed again as Edrith knelt before one of the little shoulder-high huts—a collection of wooden crates, bits of board and canvas washed in from the harbor; it looked as though one puff of wind would utterly destroy it. Edrith pulled aside a bit of cloth that blocked the hole that must serve as a door; his head and shoulders vanished inside. Jennifer came up to where she could touch it, bo clutched in nerveless fingers. After what seemed an eternity, he sat back on his heels, nodded to her. "Alive. Hurry," he mouthed. She nodded, dropped blanket and staff, fell to her knees and edged forward, past the salt-stiff rag he held onto.

A little light came into the room; the torch up by where alley ran into sand, two lamps a little farther along the clutch of hovels, a distant blue-lamp in a second- or third-story room. It was enough, just, to see the man who lay half in and half out of utterly disgusting rags. Her heart dropped; this could not be Dahven! There was nothing here of the man she'd known, however briefly, in Sikkre, and on the road—!

But as she shifted to come near him and lay a hand against his forehead, his eyes opened. A faint smile moved his mouth, half hidden in ragged beard as it was. "Gods of my ancestors," he whispered, and his fingers stole up to catch hold of hers. "Is it truly you, or have I died and found the paradise the Emperor's priests promise?"

"You talk so much, and you might," Jennifer whispered back; as humor it was pretty poor, but he seemed to understand the intent. Suddenly it was easy; like when Robyn had broken her arm, when her friend had panicked in deep water. She could be calm and strong for Dahven, too. "It's all right, Dahven. We're here. But there's very little time; we have to get you out of here, to someplace safe."

"You, and Edrith?" He shook his head; droplets of sweat from his forehead fell across the backs of her fingers. "You can't. I'm too weak for any walking—"

"Shh, don't worry about that, that's our problem."

"You can't—"

"I can and will," she hissed furiously. "You're ill and this is a dreadful place, there are horrid men everywhere and your brothers have sent guards to look for you!"

"You go," he began faintly. His fingers had already slipped from hers.

She bent down and touched her lips to his. They were cracked and salty, unresponsive. "Not *ever* without you," she replied against his ear. "Not ever again in this lifetime, do you understand me?" He opened one eye, then the second. Gazed at her in silence. For a long, frightening moment, she feared he hadn't understood anything; then his hand recaptured hers, and he brought it to his face, held it briefly against his lips, and he nodded.

"You're trying to shame me into moving, I know that trick too well," he managed. They both looked as Edrith bent down

258

and whispered, "Hurry up!" Dahven drew a breath, blew it out in a gusty sigh, successfully fought a cough, and said, "What must I do?"

"Wait. Don't do anything, save your strength," she ordered. She moved around to get her arms under his shoulder, shifted her weight so she was nearly sitting behind his head, and scooted backwards, dragging him, rags and all, out the doorway. A deep furrow of sand marked their passage. "Watch him." Jennifer glanced up at Edrith, crawled back inside and brushed furiously, filling in the rut. Let anyone who came here later think the man had left on his own feet; don't make it so obvious they'd had to drag him. She backed out once more, held the curtain aside with one shoulder and threw the regular occupant's bedding back inside. "Anything of yours in there?"

Dahven sat on the sand, supported from behind by Edrith, both hands out to help him keep his balance. "Nothing I want to keep," he whispered. "Let's—get this over and done."

"There's a cart," Edrith said softly. He turned his friend a little and pointed. "Through there. We can carry you, a stretcher."

"No. Let me try—" Edrith gave Jennifer blankets and his staff, wrapped an arm around Dahven under his shoulders and forced himself upright, bringing the other with him. Dahven set his teeth, let his eyes close and somehow managed to set one foot in front of the other. It took them three stops to cross the narrow strip of soft sand, and Edrith was sweating nearly as freely as Dahven by the time they came onto a narrow row of flat rock that marked the end of beach. Jennifer moved from side to side, keeping an eye out for anyone who might have been behind them, lurking among the dark little huts.

"Careful," Edrith whispered. "Sand on this, bad footing."

"So's mine," Dahven replied; it would have been a better joke if he hadn't so obviously been hurting. *Don't think about Dahven,* she ordered herself fiercely. His pain, pity for him—both threatened to overwhelm her, if she gave them the least chance. *Get him somewhere safe; that's what you're good for right now!* She set her jaw and edged around them to check the alley. The two men who'd accosted them earlier lay where Edrith had left them: One was breathing very loudly, the other making a little whimpering noise under his breath. *I hope your damned head aches for a week, you rotten bastard,* she thought viciously, and then forgot about them. A scraping, slithering noise brought her around; Dahven had fallen, taking Edrith down with him. She dumped everything to help, but Edrith was shaking his head at her, gesturing furiously the way they were heading. She came back around in a low crouch, scooping up the bo from the welter of things at her feet. She couldn't see anyone; it was too dark in the alley for that. She could hear them, though. Men, up close to where they'd left the cart, making no real effort to be quiet.

A deep voice, the Sikkreni accent very noticeable in the echoing little space. "How much farther, you?"

The second voice was high with fear and trembled. "Only out there, sirs, the sand, he's still there, I saw him an hour ago, sleeping! I didn't dare go in, he's fevered—"

"We'll worry about that. You come, show us."

"Pay me here—"

"No. Come with us or—I thought you'd see it my way." And then the sound of feet splashing through puddles, squelching through mud. The clink of something metal against a stone wall. Jennifer bent down to throw the blankets as far ahead of herself as she quietly could, gestured without turning for Edrith to pull Dahven aside, away from the two fallen men and out of direct line with the alley. She went down onto one knee, fighting staff balanced across her thigh.

Edrith came up on her left almost at once, on hands and knees, pulled his bo toward him and stayed low. She glanced at him, eyes asking the question it wasn't safe to voice. Edrith made a very small gesture: behind them, still. He leaned close, tugged at her hair and put his mouth almost on her ear. "Couldn't move him quietly. Safer where he is. Sorry."

She shook her head minutely, then reached cautiously to free the dagger from her belt loop. Dahven was safer behind her, all right: Anyone who wanted her man was going to have to go through *her* to get him. Edrith touched her near hand, laid a finger to his lips as someone stumbled just short of the alley entrance. She gave one very short nod; she wasn't issuing challenges this time, not with stacked odds, a helpless man at her heels—and men coming toward them who fought for a living. Who might even have fought her people out in the desert, which would take away her last element of surprise. She stayed low until one of the Thukars' men came into the open and turned back to say something to the man directly behind him, then rose silently to her feet, bringing the bo up with her. The tip slammed into the base of his skull; she brought it back across the forehead of the man following him. Edrith leaped up and to the left; someone waded into the wad of blankets Jennifer had thrown and staggered, swearing furiously before the air went out of him and he doubled over, arms clutching a staff-bruised belly. Edrith

260

dealt him a second crack on the temple to make certain he stayed down. Someone dove forward then and caught Edrith at knee level; suddenly the two men were rolling back and forth, making footing dangerous. Jennifer went back to one knee but remained where she was, as much a shield as possible for Dahven. She was peripherally aware of the two men fighting next to her, rolling bodies, flailing arms. Of the ragged, skinny man who edged past the Thukars' well-clad ones to hare off down the sand, heading toward the lit docks. The man who'd given Dahven shelter, and then tried to take the last thing he owned, even before he was dead. She could have murdered him, given him the slowest, most painful death ever devised by one human for another. *Coward. He'd have sold the boots from the feet of a sick man!* She dismissed him from her thoughts with an effort that left her knuckles white.

Two, no, three men still stood. She heard someone swear in a deep voice down near her feet, heard the hollow *thwack* of wood striking bone and a long string of words Merrida's enforced Rhadazi lesson hadn't encompassed.

One of those standing—a large, bulky-shouldered man who wore a brimmed hat with some kind of metal emblem on a wide band— came forward only a pace before he was caught in the blankets. He swore briefly, stopped at once, eyes fixed on her. "I see you, woman. Get up." Jennifer came slowly upright, moving easily. *Charles the First would be proud of me, not a tremor anywhere,* she thought wildly. She let the bo trail by her side, out of his line of vision. One more step, just one, and she'd take him; the wad of fabric around his ankles would do what surprise didn't. He stood where he was, though, and gestured. The man standing just behind him bent to drag off the fellow who'd tripped in her soft trap, came back to gather up blankets and toss them aside, then glanced at her, over to where Edrith was still wallowing in the sand with his opponent, hesitated as though uncertain where he would be the most use. The hatted man ignored him and leveled a finger. "Woman. Who is that?" She shook her head. "Answer me!" he thundered. *One of Birdy's old boyfriends,* Jennifer thought sourly. Well, he wouldn't frighten *her* into saying anything she didn't want to tell him, not at any time. Tonight—

She held her silence long enough for him to realize he hadn't jolted words out of her, then laughed coldly. "Come and find out," she replied, and shifted slightly so the second man couldn't move out and blindside her. She knew this fellow now; he'd been one of Snake's guards in the Thukar's palace. The one she'd slammed into the wall with one of the few judo throws she knew. *Damn.* No wonder he'd stayed where he was; he wasn't going to let her close enough to possibly humiliate him like that a second time. All the same, he didn't look particularly wary. *Half again my size. Probably still thinks that's all that counts.*

"You're the outland advocate," he said. "I should have known."

"I doubt it. You don't look that smart."

"I only have to call, others will come."

"Go ahead. I'm not afraid."

"No?" He took a step forward and snatched roundhouse at the bo, pulled back and ducked as she snapped it at him. She pulled it back and inwardly swore. He was faster on his feet than she liked. With room to maneuver—but she didn't have that right now, not with Dahven behind her. And Edrith—she didn't dare look to see how he was doing, but she suddenly realized she hadn't heard anything out of him in several moments. *Half my kingdom for a bloody three-strand Thread rope, right now,* she thought sourly. Her opponent came back upright and feinted with his left hand, snatching at the bo once more with his right. Fast hands, too, and a damned long reach. "You should be afraid, woman."

The third man dropped out of her line of vision as though someone had possibly crawled across the sand and swept the legs from under him. Edrith yelled out, "Got him, Jen, you know?" She laughed aloud; the Sikkreni guardsman stared at her. "Me afraid? I'm not the one trying to stay out of reach. Is the big, nasty man with the big, nasty sword scared of a little stick?" She saw Edrith leap up from the sand and throw himself on the hesitant man who'd been trying to look like he was backup for the head guard. "One to one, pretty boy," she added, and laughed again. "Come on! You want Dahven? You'll never lay a hand on him!"

He snarled something that must have been an obscenity and knelt swiftly; she came down in a crouch, bo angling down, but he wasn't trying to tackle her as she'd feared—or hoped. The back of his head would have made a fine target if he had. Instead, he caught up the end of something fabric, long and lightweight—perhaps a cloak—and snapped it at her. It slapped hard across her jeans, nearly tangled her legs. She leaped like a rope-jumper, throwing herself free of it, evaded a second throw. She swore, twisted and snapped it hard; the tip cracked across her elbow and she yelled at the pain. He laughed, twisted it up and drew it back for another swing. "Get away from him, he's our business, not yours, woman. Do you know I can break your arm this way?''

''Crap!'' she spat, and threw herself sideways as he snapped at either the end of the bo or her head. The crack was too damned close and it made her ears ring. She wasn't sure he was lying; didn't matter, it *hurt*. ''You couldn't hit one of those hut walls from the inside, you pile of camel droppings!'' She came back upright, too soon; the tip of the blanket struck her cheekbone, just below her right eye. Light exploded through her head, momentarily blinding her; a hand ripped the bo from her fingers and she found herself falling, wind driven from her as he fell on top of her. Dahven's motionless fingers were under her shoulder, a large man in dark looseweave wool straddling her, her bo between his hands resting on her throat. He was panting; his teeth were bared in a humorless grin.

''I warned you to move away from him. It didn't need to come to this. Now: A little pressure, and no more outland advocate.''

''You won't dare,'' Jennifer said flatly. She could feel the bo pressing, making it difficult to bring air into her throat; a little more and she'd black out. *Fast,* she ordered herself. *Think fast, stop him, you're no good to Dahven unconscious or dead.* ''Too many people will be unhappy if I'm found dead.'' He pulled the bo back a little to consider this.

She had maybe one final chance. *I told Birdy, if it came to this. A fatalist would say I'd asked for it by saying as much, him or me.* But she hadn't heard any sound out of Edrith since she fell; it might all be up to her now. Dahven—this man wouldn't so much as lay a finger on him; she'd cut it off his hand first.

Her right hand was pinned under his left forearm but her left was still free. Practically touching the suede-clad dagger handle. *Fate, you could call it, all right. He's made his own luck.*

He was still thinking. Finally he nodded and lifted the bo from her throat, setting it aside. ''No. I suppose I don't dare kill you, whatever I'd like. For making us look foolish back in Sikkre— I'd murder you for that alone; I'll likely never hear the end of it. A sorcerer dead, nothing but three women in the chamber with him—and then, his guards wrapped like sides of mutton! I saw three of everything for the next four days; I owe you for all of it. But their Honors Dayher and Deehar surely will want to question you. After—well, the Regent Jadek has openly offered them a good deal of money for you.''

''I'm glad to hear I'm so popular,'' Jennifer said sweetly and struck: She brought her right knee up sharply, aiming for nothing in particular, only to cause him as much pain as possible while she

263

freed the dagger. It took him high in the thigh, bulging his eyes. He folded nearly double and tried to roll away from her, but Jennifer caught a handful of his hair, rolled with him and drove the dagger up in a short arc with all her frustration and anger behind it. The blade slid into his belly and angled up with astonishing ease and a disgusting, wet noise. He gagged, shivered and loosed his hold on her. She threw herself backwards and off him as blood ran across his chest and down his fingers. As she stared at him, the bleeding slowed, stopped. There hadn't been much to begin with. Less than she'd ever have thought.

Edrith had her by the shoulders. "That's the last of them; by all the gods of your world and mine, don't think about it now, just move!"

"I'm not." She gazed expressionlessly at the dead man. *Someone should probably say whatever is said here. I should feel something.* She did: relief that it wasn't her sprawled there with a dagger in her. She bent to retrieve the blade. It came out as easily as it had gone in, something that might haunt her later. She drove it deep in the sand a few times to clean it, shoved it back through the belt loop and slewed around to catch hold of Dahven's arm. He was still unconscious. "Don't worry about me, Edrith, I'm fine! Let's not make that"—she nodded toward the dead man—"a stupid gesture. Let's get Dahven *out* of here, get him somewhere safe!"

20

S HE lost several minutes; haste, rising fear there might be more men, hiding in the alley where she couldn't see them, now that Thread-sense wasn't working, fear for Dahven, who was rag-limp and mumbling to himself. Suddenly she found herself seated cross-legged next to Edrith but facing the rear of the cart, a blanket-wrapped Dahven sprawled out with his head in her lap. "Damn," Edrith mumbled. Jennifer jumped as though shot.

"What? What's wrong?"

"Not much. Just lost the blurring-stone, though."

"Don't stop to look for it!"

"No, wouldn't. Just in case, though, can you—?"

She drew a deep breath and tried to let rising panic out with it. "I can try." *Thread?* she thought desperately. *What Thread?* "I can't blur, sorry. There's another thing, but it only works against magic. Just go."

"Where?" He already had the cart turned, though, the mule heading at an easy clop out of the dockside market.

"I don't—Marseli's house." In her own world, she couldn't think of a situation where she'd impose on such a brief acquaintance. Here—she smoothed wet, stiff hair away from Dahven's hot forehead and began to softly sing. Edrith cast her a startled glance, but she couldn't have been heard above the noise the wagon made. And maybe it would keep the sick man quiet. He turned back to put his full attention on the mule and the wagon.

The little shop in the square was dark and had a deserted, empty air when he pulled up. Jennifer looked around, shook her head. "They might not be back from Fedthyr's yet. I don't know any of the people Chris is with, do you?"

"Not really. Olmic, this is his cart and mule. His mother's blankets. But which of them we could trust—I wouldn't chance it, not with *his* life in the balance."

"No."

"We can't take him to Fedthyr's—"

"No."

Edrith clenched his jaw and thought hard. He sighed finally. "I told myself when I was asked to come south with you I'd never steal again, and I meant it. I didn't think I'd ever be glad I knew certain things. Wait here; I can open the lock on that door." She turned a white, set face in his direction, merely nodded.

"Whatever you have to do," she said flatly. But as he slid down from the wagon bed, they both heard an approaching cart. It was Dowbri. He pulled up next to them, looked at Edrith, at Jennifer. In silence at Dahven. Jennifer glanced at Edrith but he seemed as uncertain as she. She forced herself to sit very still then, waiting for the merchant to speak first. He finally shook his head and when he spoke, he sounded calm, unhurried— utterly, almost frighteningly normal. As though, Jennifer thought, he hadn't taken in what he saw before him. "It's been a long day, hasn't it? I need to put my mule and wagon away, if one of you would hold the gate for me?" Edrith went where he pointed and fumbled in the dark with an unfamiliar catch. Dowbri jumped down and crossed the short distance between wagons. He leaned across the side board, then got a grip on Dahven's shoulders, slid an arm under his knees and simply lifted him bodily from the borrowed cart, edged through the just-opened gate with Jennifer right on his heels, the bo in her hand. Edrith pushed the gate the rest of the way open, caught Jennifer's sleeve and held her back long enough to murmur against her ear, "I'll return the cart, come back myself later for you." She merely nodded and ran past Dowbri to open the door into the back room of the house. Edrith brought the merchant's mule and cart into the yard and latched the gate behind himself, climbed back into the borrowed one and turned the mule toward Olmic's mother's house.

He was going to have to fight not to simply fall over backwards and sleep; he was desperately tired, bruised in a dozen or more places and he ached everywhere else. There was a cut on the back of his left hand where one of the Thukars' men had come a little too close with a knife, and sweat stung it. "I gave up thievery for this?" he asked aloud. The mule slowed a little and flicked an ear his direction. He flipped the reins across its back. "Gave up a comfortable life of hand-to-mouth, cadging bad wine in taverns, sleeping in rubble for all this? My mother always said I wasn't too bright; I begin to suspect she was right." He laughed quietly; somehow, that restored him a little. Enough. He'd be all right. He could only hope that Dahven would.

* * *

DOWBRI had bundled Dahven through the door and laid him along the wall shared by the shop, and was now in the shop itself, searching for something. Jennifer leaned back against the wall and fought exhaustion and sudden despair. In the combined blue light and candlelight, the blanket-wrapped man looked truly dreadful. Now that she'd gotten away from the fight, she was beginning to stiffen alarmingly; everything ached and there was a puffy bruise on her cheek, her right wrist felt sprained and fat, the fingers limp. Blood on both her hands. Some part of her mind was still functioning, though: She was still singing, humming really. Dowbri came back from the shop, several small boxes filling large, capable hands.

He smiled. "You're safe here, you know. Marseli had Neri put a full protective spell around the shop, to keep her trade secrets her own."

"Oh." Jennifer considered this blankly and slowly eased herself down the wall. "Just as well, I was getting hoarse. I—I'm sorry," she added awkwardly as the merchant sorted through containers. He looked down at her. "For subjecting you to this. You don't know me well, you don't know him—"

"I can put a name to him, though I won't," Dowbri said quietly. He opened a flat wooden box, took a large pinch of something from it and dropped the stuff in a cup, added water to it and held it out to her. "This is for you, you need it. If the name I have were to match the one you could give me, then I want no apology. I met him, once or twice, when I was running the caravan for Marseli myself—before her elder brother took it over and let me stay here with her. This one is a good man, he never killed anyone, let alone the one they say he murdered."

"I know," Jennifer said. She stroked wet hair back from Dahven's neck; he mumbled something, his head rolled back and forth fretfully.

"He's a good administrator, also; he realizes there are things beyond a straight profit margin—better than our Lehzin, who has a mind for trade and money, and for peace, but is too conservative. This one—he'd be good for Sikkre, though he'd be the first man to deny that, unless he's changed greatly. But—" Jennifer swirled the cup, sniffed doubtfully at the contents and drank. He was mixing another now. He shrugged, gave her an abashed smile and went back to his pile of boxes. "They say we're civilized, we Rhadazi. They point to the nomads, to the Lasanachi, or to folk two days' sail south of the Sea of Rhadaz who still live in small tribes and war constantly against each other. And they say we're not like any of those; we're more prosperous and so clearly much better. We're not so civilized as the Emperor's councils brag, when a thing like this can happen, when nothing is done to stop men from riding into Bez to steal people away."

"Your own Duke," Jennifer said tentatively. She let Dowbri lift Dahven, took the cup and held it to his lips, her other hand on his cheek. He opened a glazed eye, let it close, obediently drank when she urged him to it, but she doubted he'd known her. *Oh, God, he'll die,* she thought suddenly.

Dowbri got back to his feet and shook his head. "Don't look so frightened; he'll be all right, I promise you. He'll sleep now. And Marseli can help him after she returns. There's a man we can send for once the sun's above the walls; he's good with fever." He carried the boxes back into the shop, came back at once and closed the door behind him. "Duke Lehzin spends this time of year aboard his barges, outside Bez Harbor and east, where there are lagoons deep and private enough to hold the network of ships they tie together to make him a spring palace. Don't mistake me, he's a good man. Most of our people are, but what does a man like me, an ordinary merchant, know about dealing with determined armed men who bribe with coin and

267

threaten with knives? The Duke is like most; he's not entirely aware of the uglier aspects of Bez. There aren't as many as in Sikkre, and parts of Podhru are truly dangerous. But Bez isn't all clean streets and happy, well-to-do citizenry.''

"I saw that, tonight," Jennifer said. She laid a hand on Dahven's cheek again. Stubble prickled her palm; he didn't move. "He's—"

"He's all right. *You* swallowed a stimulant; you looked as though you needed one. He got a sleeping draught." He squatted down and studied her face. "You've been hurt. I have salve for that, if you like. And your hands—"

She shook her head cautiously; it was beginning to ache in earnest now. "That's not my blood," she began. The air around her vibrated, richly; all it once it was simply there: Thread. A little faint but she could hear it, touch it. Disorienting, as tired as she still was. Dowbri went through a small door that must lead to their private apartments, came back with a deep, footed pottery bowl and thick, dark cloths. Water sloshed to the floor as he knelt, dipped fabric in the water and held one out to her. He sponged the sleeping man's face with the other. Jennifer managed a faint smile. "Thank you." There was blood on her face, too; the tip of the cloak had broken the skin. She blotted it cautiously, scrubbed the rough material down her hands. The nails were still dark, underneath and around the cuticle. Unimportant. Thread—if it left her again—

She closed her eyes, shut Dowbri away—shut them both away—and concentrated on Thread. *That,* Neri had told her, a yellow but different, thicker stuff that she almost would have sworn had a good, danceable beat. It healed, more quickly than the variety of things she and Lialla had used on their wandering journey south. The knot of bruising on her cheekbone unraveled on touch, the ruddy glow of headache had no snarl of Thread but she took hold of the thick yellow and spread it, thinning it like pie crust or Robyn's biscuit dough. The dull red, and the pain, were smothered in short order. The ache in her bones was nothing in comparison, and she'd worry about that later. Now she was able to concentrate, now she could think about how much inner strength she might have.

Perhaps it was like a battery; charged all the way it would work for some time, but partly charged it would fade almost at once. She wouldn't waste what might be finite strength on herself. She knew damned little about fever; Neri hadn't shown her, she hadn't asked. She'd simply have to trust Dowbri's judgment on that. But she'd seen the way Dahven moved, getting to his feet; how he'd shuddered whenever someone touched his back; and now she remembered the things Edrith had said. Lasanachi. Hurt. All the dreadful pirate movies, the Roman galley movies came back to her and for an awful moment she thought she'd be sick. *There isn't time for that, don't!* she ordered herself furiously, and opened her eyes to find Dowbri sitting back on his heels, the damp cloth in his hands.

She liked him; she wouldn't have suspected so much quiet strength from meeting him earlier, from half-listening to his conversation with Lialla. Now he put the cloth back in the bowl and studied her. "There is always gossip in a market, you know," he said. "The past night or so, there's been even more, and some of it contradictory. Some says Lord Dahven murdered his father in order to have Sikkre's throne and the love of an outlander woman, while other holds that his father in a peevish fit sold him to the Lasanachi for servitude in the rowing ships, and altered his will knowing no man would return alive from that."

"The Lasanachi," Jennifer echoed blankly.

"They buy men, though not openly in Rhadaz. But it takes fifty or more to row one of their merchant ships and even though they have only a few such ships they constantly search for rowers. Those who take the oars don't survive long." He bent forward to shove the unconscious man's left sleeve up; the arm was much darker than Jennifer remembered it, as though he'd spent long days under a hot sun. But there was a pale mark about three inches wide just above his wrist. "That's the manacle mark, where a man's bound to his seat," Dowbri said.

"Oh, God," Jennifer whispered. She could feel the color draining out of her face and without the wall she'd probably have fallen. She wrapped both arms around herself, clutching at her upper arms. "I—there's more. His back."

"Don't—" Dowbri began; he caught her hand as she reached for Dahven's shoulders. She looked up at him through blurred, wet eyes and shook her head.

"You said he's out—unconscious. Maybe he'd hate it if he thought I knew; I'd never want him to know if it were reversed. If I can make it better before he wakes up—" She shook her head, brought a hand up to rub across her eyes. "I'm not making the best sense in the world. Part of me doesn't want to know, believe that. I can't just leave him. Not if he'll hurt."

Dowbri let go of her hand, set it gently aside and rolled Dahven over. She blotted her eyes a last time and set her jaw, tried to smile. It must have looked awful. "Do you know, I'd barely

269

seen blood in my life, before Merrida sent me to fix Aletto's arm? I'd never seen injury by human violence. I can't bear knowing he hurts. And if I can—'' She laid a hand on the ruins of a linen shirt that might have been white or cream once. Likely, she realized with a pang, the one he'd worn the night they left Sikkre in the trader caravan. Dowbri lifted her hand and the shirt both, so she was holding fabric away from skin; he produced a small nail knife and cut through the remains of embroidery worked around the throat. The material practically dissolved as the metal yanked at it. The dark ruin of skin swam under her eyes. *Don't look. Don't think. Just do it, quickly.* She closed her eyes and shifted into full awareness of Thread.

Neri had shown her a way to block outside pain when she was healing; it was only partly successful. She kept her eyes fixed on Thread-vision, her concentration focused only on that. *Don't look. Don't think about it,* she reminded herself now and again. The thick yellow healing Thread was suddenly heavy; it dragged at arm muscles already worn almost beyond bearing. Somewhere along the line, though, the pain in her wrist vanished; indirect healing, possibly. She finally drew back into reality, leaned against the wall. She lost track of time for a long moment; of everything. When she looked up, Dowbri had gone but she could hear him walking around overhead somewhere, and when he came back he had a pair of the square lightweight linen sleeping cloths in his hand. One went across Dahven's too-dark back, covering him right up to shoulders still faintly scored with pale, long lines; the other, folded into fourths, went under the man's cheek. ''I'm going out to unharness the mule and feed him. Marseli's brother should be bringing her shortly; your young friend is probably on his way. Will you be all right?'' Jennifer nodded; her head ached again and there wasn't anything left in her to fix it.

She didn't care, she thought dully as the merchant went out into the yard and through to the separate area where the mule and his wagon were kept. So much had happened since Fedthyr's party began this afternoon; doubtless she'd never recall a tenth of it later. But that could only be good. Already the fight in loose sand—the *two* fights—were something that might have happened to someone else, that grim woman herself someone else. She bent forward and turned her head so she could listen to Dahven's breathing, so she could feel his face with her own. His skin was hot still, but he was no longer as restless.

She'd have to leave him. They'd expect her to be in her room tomorrow morning—*this* morning—in that vast merchant's estate up by the north gates; there might be questions otherwise, and

270

she couldn't chance that. She was terrified to leave him, not afraid of trusting Marseli or her wonderfully calm and competent husband—just afraid. She wasn't leaving Bez without him, though. As she sat back, his eyelids fluttered and he mumbled something. "Dahven?" she whispered.

Silence. Then: "It really is you, isn't it?" His fingers moved, touched his face. "I feel a little cleaner. Where are we?"

"Friend's house, in Bez," she assured him.

"Oh. Good." Incurious, she thought—but fever did that to you. "*You* didn't wash me, did you?"

"No."

He managed a very faint smile; it faded at once and his eyes were more closed than open. "Not—I wouldn't mind, ordinarily." He fetched a thin sigh; the fingers found hers and tightened. "I'm sorry. Truly. You weren't supposed to know, not ever."

"It's all right."

For a moment, she thought he might argue with her. He sighed again instead. "Jennifer. Don't leave me."

"Never," she assured him, and brought his fingers to her lips. He smiled; she shifted her weight so her hip was on the thickness of blanket and eased down onto her elbow, next to him. Edrith could figure out something to tell Fedthyr, or maybe Marseli and Dowbri could; she wasn't going anywhere tonight. When Dowbri came in moments later, she told him so.

"We'll manage a tale for my father-in-law," he said softly.

"Good," she said, and edged the elbow under her. The cloth under Dahven's head was thick and wide enough for them both, the blanket under her not thick enough to protect her from hard wooden planks, but she was suddenly much too tired to care. Dahven's breath was warm against her shoulder; his fingers still gripped hers tightly. It was the last thing she was aware of for a very long time.

* * *

WHEN she woke, the room was warm and stuffy, full of sunlight, and Dahven gone. She staggered up, disoriented from the hard, dreamless sleep and not enough of it. Marseli, apparently alerted by the noise, came from her shop. "You've wakened, good. Your nameless friend is there"—she gestured toward the family rooms—"getting a decent wash. The man who saw to my fever last spring is with him. Sit," she ordered as she moved on toward the door she'd just indicated, "and wait. I'll bring food." She was back in moments with a deep dish containing small fragrant loaves; in her other hand, a round metal pot and two thick-sided, nonhandled mugs. "Coffee. I remembered, you see?

It's from the shop where we drank together, you recall that? I sent Dowbri for it and we kept it in the ashes next to the warming pot.''

"Oh, God," Jennifer said devoutly and ran a hand through tangled dark curls. "There never was such a true friend, Marseli. Anything short of my life—"

"Well," the woman replied comfortably as she drew up a stool and pointed Jennifer toward the other, "I need very little, you know. Though I admit I hope you'll press my cause for my sister with the nera-Duke, it wasn't in my mind when I thought of the coffee.'' She filled a mug, pushed it and the plate of bread across the little table before picking up her own mug. "Tea,'' she explained as she sipped gingerly. "Your friend is a little better this morning than when Dowbri found you last night; he said I'd better assure you of that first off.''

"Thank you." Jennifer concentrated on filling the mug with black, hot, sweet liquid, with tearing a loaf and biting into nearly white, soft bread flavored with nuts and spices.

"Better, but not particularly good," Marseli said. Her usually cheerful face was somber. "He should have had treatment for that fever some time since, you know. Dowbri says he'd been— well, never mind, there's no mark on him that *I* saw."

"Good." Jennifer drank half the cup at one long swallow, chewed and swallowed a bit of the bread. "I'm sorry to have done this to you. Truly.''

"Don't be. Oh, I understand how you feel; I'd feel the same if Dowbri were—like that, and I had to find him shelter in a strange place. He's safe here, and I'm honored you thought of me, and felt trust when you did.''

"I do." Jennifer nodded. "I—" She shrugged. "Frankly, I don't know what comes next, Marseli. He can't stay here; those men knew he was in Bez.''

"One doesn't know anything, any more," Marseli replied darkly. "Or so Dowbri heard when he went to fetch coffee and bread." Jennifer closed her eyes and shuddered. "Never mind. He's safe here a day or two. You won't stay much longer, I don't think. I thought the nera-Duke sounded anxious to be on his way when I met him last night; after this attack and renewed market gossip and rumor, he'll be all the more glad to go.'' Marseli drank tea, set her cup aside and leaned forward on her elbows. "Also, my uncle tells me that Casimaffi—he once sold carved logs to be made into door frames and window frames for the houses of noble and wealthy in Zelharri, but came south with my father—Casimaffi has offered Lord Aletto passage on the

Windsong. It is to leave for Podhru in two nights, on the tide. If Enardi understood them both right, it is the nera-Duke's intention not to come to the wharves but to meet the ship at Long Point, when it puts in for the night.''

''Ship,'' Jennifer echoed. ''Lialla said that might be a more sensible way to reach Podhru, because of the roads—''

''Perhaps so. But Casimaffi—'' Marseli shook her head. ''He is a dear friend of my father's, I've known him and called him Uncle all my days. But I'd be no friend at all if I did not tell you that Casimaffi has been a frightened man for many days now. It's Enardi's belief that Jadek somehow reached him and terrified him into silent compliance against Lord Aletto, or perhaps bribed him. Not everyone is the nera-Duke's friend, of course.''

''No one of us expected that,'' Jennifer replied. ''Casimaffi— did I meet him?''

''Doubtful. He spends most of his time dealing with his accounts or supervising the loading of his three ships in person. I know very little, mostly my brother's notions; understand that.''

''I understand. Better to trust that and feel foolish later than trust wrongly.''

''I knew you had wit,'' Marseli replied. ''Now. Your friend. I sent Father a message last night that you were still here when I arrived home, and that after Neri left we talked until we lost all sense of time. He won't find it odd that you spend your nights here. So you know.'' Jennifer nodded. She didn't think she could have spoken, just then.

* * *

DAHVEN was a little less feverish, perhaps, but he was barely aware of her helping him onto the blankets, helping him drink the liquid left by Marseli's physician. He slept almost at once. She touched his face—even thinner and grayer now that Dowbri had shaved it, and the line of pale skin where beard had been did awful things to the normally attractive lines of his cheekbones—bent down to touch his limp fingers against her lips, and tangled the leather thong with its charm around his wrist, where he'd be aware of it when he woke.

Dowbri offered to take her back to Fedthyr's place; she finally gave in and let him. Easier than dealing with foreign coins, with the odd transport system. And, as Dowbri pointed out, there was a splash of blood on her jeans. No good calling attention to herself, and to that, just now.

* * *

FEDTHYR was not yet up when she arrived, and the boy at the gate who let her in said The Merchant would not be about for several more hours. ''The party ran until nearly sunrise, Miss,'' he added.

Chris was waiting in her room, curled up asleep next to her bed, a pillow pulled under his ear. She nudged him with her foot. ''Whatever you're guarding, I think it's gone,'' she said.

''Jeez.'' He sat up, rubbed his eyes and staggered to his feet. ''I should smell *your* breath, lady. Edrith looked like all hell last night, and when you stayed out, I got worried.'' He gave her a quick hug and started for the door, eyes still only half open. ''I'll start the cross-examination later, okay? Right now, I need a little real sleep in my own bed, thank you.'' He was gone before she could think of anything to say. She tossed the pillow back onto the bed and turned away from it. She needed a bath; there was still blood under and around her nails, her high-tops were disgustingly brown, and Dowbri was right about the blood: It was on her jeans; a few splatters dotted her chambray shirt, too. *Do it now,* she urged herself, *before anyone sees.*

She got a little sleep after that, before Robyn came looking for her. ''Missed some party, kiddo. Almost too much for me, though: I'm starting to feel like a Republican's wife or something, never smiled so damned much at old men in my life.''

''All for a good cause, Birdy,'' Jennifer managed through an enormous yawn.

''Yeah, right, I'll bet the Inquisition said that, too. There's an informal luncheon today, not nearly as many people, thank God. Mostly Aletto and the money boys locked up in Fedthyr's back room, talking about what, when and how much. So we can get what we need and get *out* of here.''

''I'm all for it,'' Jennifer said. She'd slept in the slightly damp but now stainless jeans; she sat up now and pulled on the scrubbed high-tops. ''Marseli says there's a lot of rumor around.''

Robyn snorted in exasperation. ''Well, just figure: A bunch of ordinarily very straight businessmen all of a sudden start throwing parties and bouncing off the walls? Sure there's rumors! Aletto's ready to go as soon as he has enough money to get supplies and to get him inside Podhru. Chris says half a dozen or so of the people Enardi's age—I can't help but think of them as kids, honestly!— will be leaving for Podhru tonight, some overland but most on one of the ships; they're lodging some petitions, about setting up business in Sehfi, *you* know. Something about a new road between Bez and Zelharri, too; I guess they need permission and money to start something like that.'' She shook her head and sighed. ''Politics.

God. I can't believe I'm *doing* this to myself! I don't think I can live with it.''

"Don't decide anything too fast, either way," Jennifer warned as she dug through her handbag for a pick and began separating curls, working out snarls.

"Don't intend to," Robyn retorted from the doorway. "By the way, if you're interested, I put Chris a burrito of sorts together late last night."

"Really?''

"Yeah." Robyn grinned. "Should have seen us trying to fake ingredients. Actually, the only thing missing is jalapeños, and there are *plenty* of hot peppers around here to fake that. But the kitchen staff *really* liked them and so did Fedthyr. You could probably get one for breakfast, if you wanted it.''

Jennifer shuddered. "God forbid. A little later, though— Pretty clever, lady.''

"No worse than trying to make food out of government surplus and food stamps," Robyn replied. "I think Chris and Enardi did something about beef, though; I have a nasty hunch he's going to be showing that poor cook how to make hamburgers next.''

"Hey, why not?''

"Well—okay," Robyn allowed. "Why not? I have to get down there; Aletto needs all the support he can get right now, I think he lost ten pounds yesterday, just from sheer spooked.''

"I'll be down in a few," Jennifer assured her.

* * *

ALETTO did look as though he'd gone through a war since she'd last seen him, but he was holding up better than she ever would have hoped those first few days. And Fedthyr, who didn't know him well, seemed unaware of the nera-Duke's tensions. The afternoon party stretched on for hours, but at its end, Aletto had the promise of financial aid—enough at present to fill a large purse, to fill a supply wagon if they chose to travel overland. There would also be funds for Aletto to draw upon in Podhru, through various friends of the local merchants. And the offer of ship travel, which Aletto, after a short consultation with the others, accepted. Jennifer kept her mouth prudently shut; Casimaffi was sitting on Robyn's other side, talking nearly nonstop, positively radiating common sense and good will, while Fedthyr beamed at his friend as though he'd been responsible for the ship himself. The ship was supposedly large and stable enough to carry half a dozen or more horses in a special holding stall on deck, particularly on the run from Bez to Podhru, with the wind always at the ship's back and the seas running with the boat.

Aletto, they decided, would prepare for the journey and would take his party out to Long Point, and wait there, two nights from this. Casimaffi spread his hands wide and smiled, exposing very even and small white teeth. "I do not guarantee that the *Windsong* sails that very same night, understand; often there is a night's delay because of the things coming in to be unloaded from one ship to another, because of the tides or the wind. Please understand this and have patience. The ship will be visible for several leagues before she comes near the point; the land is open all around. You simply camp and wait for us." Aletto accepted this, Jennifer thought, without much concern over details and what she saw as holes in the man's logic. How did he intend to get horses out to the ship, for one thing? Surely if it depended on tides to get it from Bez Harbor it was too deep-drafted to come right into shore. Casimaffi jokingly offered to send for his scribe and make a written contract; Aletto waved this aside as unnecessary—as he clearly was meant to do; Jennifer had seen entirely too much of that kind of dealing, and double-dealing—and of the results. She could only hope this time they wouldn't be fatal, and hope to get a chance to speak with Aletto before they set out, to talk some sense into him.

The chance never came; Aletto spent most of his waking hours with Fedthyr and other Zelharri merchants, or with Robyn. She herself spent hours talking to Marseli, getting medicines and charms, serving as go-between for Aletto and Marseli and arranging the early stages of Marseli's new Zelharri trade. Her nights were all for Dahven. His fever broke the second night, but he was weak, fretful—and, she thought, ashamed that she had been one of those who found him. He spoke little and ate less, slept a lot. She tried to remember how Chris had reacted to his comparatively mild beating, how she would feel if Dahven had found her instead, black and blue, shivering with fever and, just possibly, with terror of being recaptured. *Give it time*, she told herself. *You don't really know him, after all; you can't possibly know how or why he's reacting the way he is.*

Edrith spent most of his time down in the marketplace, walking around, looking for the best prices on the kinds of food Robyn wanted to take, even though Aletto now held this was unnecessary, since they would be taking ship and Casimaffi assured him his captain would feed them. Edrith also was scouting rumor, though he seldom passed on any, except to Jennifer. Chris moved back and forth between Enardi and his friends, his mother, Edrith. He had more energy than the rest of them combined, and Jennifer wondered if he slept at all.

SUDDENLY, there was no time left. Jennifer gathered up a small bundle and shoved it into her handbag, let Dowbri put the rest of the things she'd obtained from Marseli in a large pack. She hugged the merchant woman hard. "Everything you've done for us—I can't thank you enough."

"Thanks aren't necessary between friends," Marseli replied and hugged back, thin arms pressed hard against Jennifer's back. "Take care, and visit if you return here, that's all."

"I will." She walked through the shop, into the back room. Dahven sat with his shoulders against the wall, a cup of water held carefully in both hands. He set it down, looked up at her. "Your promise," she began. He managed a smile.

"I swore I'd come. It's wrong, though. I belong in Sikkre."

"I agree," Jennifer replied calmly, though the very thought made the back of her neck crawl. "But not now. Get strong first. Get a few allies. Get Edrith, as soon as Aletto can spare him, if nothing else." He took hold of her hands. She gripped his in turn. "Besides. You promised. If you break that, I'll come after you, I swear I will."

"I don't doubt you." He bent forward and turned her hand so he could kiss the thumb. "I can't think why you would."

She smiled. "I can't, either. I'm a grown woman, too old for fairy-tale nonsense—"

"Why you'd want a man like the one I've become," he interrupted flatly, "No, don't talk, listen. *Please.* Then go, swear you will. And then I'll be there tonight. Please." She looked at him, looked away from a chill, urgent, stranger's face, and nodded. His voice was the faintest of whispers now; it couldn't have reached Marseli in her shop, Dowbri out by the wagon. It went through her like a knife. "My father sold me to the Lasanachi, the night I left you. For a bag of coin. They put irons on me, beat me senseless when I tried to fight them. I rode in a cart under full sun, no food or water, and that night they brought me aboard a ship and fastened me to a rower's board." He held up his left arm, her fingers still caught in his. The wide white mark was still very clear; it would be for weeks yet. "That's—like a scar that runs right through me, can you see that? They—I was fool enough, even then, to think a man might defy them and keep his heart or his soul, or even a little of both." He turned his head away, stared at the wall. "I was wrong. What they did—but you know some of it, don't you? It was you with your Wielder's magic that healed what skin they left on my back, wasn't it?" She nodded, blinked furiously to keep the tears from showing. "It's a pity your Night-Thread can't go beyond skin and bone,'' he whispered, and suddenly released her fingers. ''But perhaps there's nothing left inside to mend.'' He bent forward, let his forehead fall into his hands. ''Now you know. Please. Just—go.''

Somehow, she found her way to her feet and, blindly, to the door. She caught hold of the frame, swallowed hard and turned back. He hadn't moved. ''Now I know,'' she said huskily. ''It doesn't change anything, not for me.''

''Aletto,'' he said finally. ''I never wanted to do this to him.''

''No,'' she said. ''He's not quite the boy you saw last in Sikkre. Dahven, you're not thinking normally. You can't expect to, not just yet. Give yourself time, please.'' He shook his head. ''There'll *be* time. Trust me. And you remember your promise to me.'' He brought his head up, looked at her blankly. ''You'll come. You swore.'' He nodded. She turned away and walked into the muggy, misty late afternoon sunshine.

21

🜚

THE sun had set only moments before; five riders moved through the crowded gate area and onto the broad roadway. A loaded wagon followed, a mule pulling it, two saddled horses behind that. Another man on a small but extremely nervous gray; people moved to give it a wide berth. They rode slowly up the broad road, slowed only briefly where the road to Podhru joined into the Sikkre-Bez highway. This wound away into trees and brush, already narrowing. Aletto, in the lead with Edrith at his one side and Robyn at the other, gazed as far down the road as he could and shook his head. ''I'm glad we don't take this far. Enardi's wagon would break a wheel the first night.''

Don't count on any of that, Jennifer thought from just behind him, but kept the thought prudently to herself. She'd tried, just once, earlier in the day, to persuade Aletto at least to keep his options open, and he'd practically taken her head off. Enardi, who drove the wagon, exchanged a glance with her; he shared her concerns, she knew, but wasn't going to voice them, either.

And, of course, it was possible the *Windsong* would meet

them—tonight or tomorrow. She had no hard proof that its owner intended otherwise.

Dahven: He'd come. He'd promised her. *By all the gods in my world and his, though,* she thought in despair, *how can I possibly help him put himself back together, after what those men did to him?* Would he even let her try?

They moved on down the east road, moving slowly over a washout, over ruts and holes and loose rock that made footing treacherous for the animals. The wagon creaked ominously as it rode over obstacles, twisting in ways the maker had surely never intended.

An hour or so later, just short of complete dark, the land began to rise, to dry out and the trees now grew farther and farther apart. It was still humid but not as unbearable as it had been down in Bez, and Jennifer wondered suddenly how she'd stood it. She must have been half-asleep the entire time. Aletto called a very short halt and came back to consult with Fedthyr's son, who stood on the wagon seat and finally pointed.

"The headland is just there—another half-league along the road and then at right angles to it. We can set up the tent and build a fire; there's a ledge that hides most of the headland from the road, but the fire can be seen by *Windsong*'s captain."

"Good." It was the first thing Robyn had said in hours; she knew nothing about the controversy between her sister and the nera-Duke but she sensed the tension and was reacting to it. "Let's go."

There was a very light wind when they finally led the horses out across open ground, stopping a dozen or so feet back from what had to be a very sharp, long drop. Jennifer could hear water crashing against rock down there; she had no desire to go see what it looked like, or how far away it actually was. She unhooked bags with fingers that moved a little slowly—they'd lost their familiarity with the knots, in so short a period. The saddle came next. The horse—well, it smelled as unpleasant as the last one, but it seemed to have a better personality. She gave it a pat, brushed the hand on the gray riding breeks she'd worn in public since rumor filtered from the dock markets about two men who claimed to have been attacked by an outlander in the heavy blue trous such outlanders so often wore. Even Chris had been prevailed upon to change from his jeans until they were on the road once more.

Enardi unhooked the mule and the two riding horses and went off somewhere with Chris. Robyn piled rock where a fire would be partly shielded by the rocky slope behind them, open to the sea, and with Lialla's help got one going. Chris and the merchant's son came back with dry branches and a thick piece of tree root that had to be shoved in at one side and fed into the fire a bit at a time. "Can't believe you folks don't have saws," Chris said. Edrith smiled, shook his head; Chris lapsed into silence.

Enardi roused himself a while later and offered to unpack the tent. Robyn vetoed that vigorously. "The weather's good, it's almost cool enough out here for sleep, and I'm not hanging around while a bunch of guys try to put up a tent for the first time in the dark."

"I did one like it—well, once," Enardi amended honestly. Robyn merely snorted and shook her head. She used both feet to give the tree root a shove, stood up to fold her blanket double and curled up on it. Chris and his two friends moved away; Jennifer could hear them talking a short distance off, but couldn't hear what they were talking about. Not her business, she thought sleepily. Lialla wandered away as far as the wagon, came back with a blanket and spread it out back away from the cliff. Jennifer bent forward to stretch out her back, eased herself down. After a moment or two, she sat back up. The boys were momentarily quiet, Robyn asleep or nearly so. Aletto was sipping water from his bottle, watching the water. He glanced at her, went back to his study of the ocean.

"Lialla told me last night," he began abruptly. "About the things our uncle said to you, that night in the desert. You hadn't told me—"

"No. I'm sorry, I quite honestly forgot."

Aletto shrugged. "It's not surprising. Lialla did, too: At least, she never remembered when we were together. Just as well. If I'd known then—" He looked at her again. "It's all out of my hands, isn't it?"

"How do you mean?"

"You know," he said gloomily. "In Sikkre, it was so simple. Gyrdan swearing to me, all that. I knew my uncle was wrong to keep Zelharri—oh, don't look at me like that, he *was* wrong. He still is. I haven't given up. I wouldn't dare, would I?"

"And that's the real problem, isn't it? That—oh, before it was a soldier backing you, a man used to taking risks and weighing them. Gyrdan knows what he's getting into."

"Partly," Aletto admitted. He shifted, cautiously so as not to waken Robyn. "I ache so from trying not to limp, just from *standing*, you can't think!"

"You should have told one of us. Here, I have aspirin." She reached for her shirt pocket; Aletto touched the back of her hand and shook his head.

"Chris told me about your aspirin. Save them."

"They're for need, they won't save forever. There's Thread, too, if you'll trust that."

"I—well." He shrugged. "Never mind. Later. What you said about Gyr, it's partly true, but it's more complex than that. In Sikkre, it was my desire to become Duke, and Gyrdan's to back me. Now so many people want so many different things! How can I possibly sort through them all? Or know which of them I can depend upon, which merely smile at me because I can make them wealthy, or guarantee they become a power back in Bezjeriad, or their family does—?" He spread his hands helplessly. "Sehfi's market is depressed, it has been for years. Even I, ignorant as I was, knew as much. There are other towns that need markets, or new trades, but how does a man as untried as I am deal with this? Without offending every man and woman who already sells in Zelharri, or has a trade there?"

"I don't envy you," Jennifer said. "There aren't any easy answers, *life* is a damned complex thing."

"I'm discovering that," he replied ruefully.

They sat side by side in silence for some time. Finally, Jennifer stirred, fished a single aspirin from her pocket and held it out. "Take it, please. *I'll* feel better if you do." He did; she waited until he'd swallowed it. "Do you still intend to go on?"

"Do I have a choice?"

"Oh, I think so. Is that the worst of it for you? Being afraid you don't?" He considered this. Shook his head, then shrugged. "There's always a choice. It wouldn't make you popular among certain merchant families in Bezjeriad, but your head is the one on the block, not theirs. They'll only be out a little money if you quit, or if you fail."

He laughed quietly. "Succinct. If anyone had told me I'd get more use out of an advocate on this journey than a fighting guard—what did Chris call them?"

"Brutes with broadswords," Jennifer said after a moment's thought. Aletto laughed again.

"If anyone had told me that, I'd have thought them mad." He sobered again. "There's the other thing, though: Jadek said my mother—?"

"He *said* she's pregnant," Jennifer said bluntly.

Aletto closed his eyes, counted on his fingers. Shook his head. "She cannot be very near her time, do you think? I'm—I noticed very little those last days in Duke's Fort, but I think I would have seen that."

"He didn't say. She might not really be."

"He has no reason to lie. I'm still heir, at least, by law. Jadek can't change *that*. Unless something happens—"

"Unless you die," Jennifer said evenly.

"Unless my uncle finds a way to kill me," Aletto replied; his voice carried no expression but his eyes brooded darkly on the distance. "If he manages that, in such a way it appears to be an accident—well, he's good at those, isn't he?"

"Your father?" He nodded. "You think Shesseran would accept two such accidents? Surely not!"

"You don't understand our Emperor. It need only *appear* accident. However much rumor followed, however unlikely the circumstance. As things are now, Jadek would probably prefer to have me at home, locked in my rooms, and hold to the pretense of playing regent for a mentally deficient sot. If he had his own heir, though—gods. He could simply kill me, assume mourning, petition the Emperor for Father's duchy—and quite likely get it. It's known Shesseran would ignore any rumor to maintain an outward appearance of peace, as things now are."

Jennifer stirred indignantly. "As they now are! Is he mad?"

"Who knows?" Aletto shrugged gloomily. "Who ever sees him, personally, save his family and his inner circle? It doesn't matter; he rules. That matters. If he was faced with either of those situations, I know he'd give Jadek what he wanted and forget about it at once. Either way, I'm as good as dead, if Jadek gets hold of me."

"Well, then, he won't. But you were as good as dead anyway, and no one's killed you yet, have they?" Aletto gave her a sheepish smile and shook his head. "Don't give up now, not just because of what Jadek said. He surely knows how you'd take it; perhaps he's lying."

"Possible, I suppose. All right. I won't give up anyway; I *do* have Father's stubbornness in full measure." He leaned forward to shove fresh sticks into the fire, winced as he sat back. "All the same, Jadek is better at this game than I am—"

"Only because he's played it for so long. He hasn't won yet." She got to her feet and stretched hard. "I'll be back in a moment, I think it's my time to watch, isn't it?" He nodded. "Get some sleep, then. I'd be willing to wager you haven't had much at all these past few days."

"You'd win," he said somberly, but she thought the set of his shoulders wasn't as tight as he turned back to watch the sea.

* * *

WHEN she came back to the fire, Aletto was curled up next to Robyn, one hand protectively across her shoulder. Lialla sat on the edge of Jennifer's blanket. "I'm not very tired," she said. "I thought perhaps I'd watch."

"If you want to." For a moment, she thought Lialla might be in a confiding mood, too; but the sin-Duchess merely nodded and went back to her place away from the fire. Jennifer could sense her fingering Thread, testing some of the things Neri had shown them. She drew her blanket away from the fire in the other direction, past the wagon, worked herself down flat and began to quietly hum: Donizetti this time. *Una Furtiva Lagrima* was a tenor's aria, but no one else *here* knew that.

* * *

THERE was no ship by the gray hour before dawn. Enardi shook his head when Aletto roused him for his share of the watch and told him. "I'll have an eye for intruders of any kind, but it's the wrong hour for a ship; the tide would be out now, *Windsong* has to be still at the docks." Aletto merely nodded and went over to his blanket. Jennifer pried open an eye, sat partway up.

"Anything wrong?" she whispered as Enardi walked over to the wagon.

"No ship. Maybe tomorrow night," he whispered in reply. But he didn't look any more confident of that than she felt.

* * *

THE tent was set up when she woke again. It was dark cloth, deep gray with a darker awning all along the front, wide enough to sleep all of them in reasonable comfort, while there was plenty of space under the awning for twice their number to sit. Fedthyr had provided that, together with a number of serviceable but thick rugs to serve as a floor, and three blue-light lanterns on poles for the interior.

The wagon had shaded her but in a very short while the sun would clear it. It was warm anyway, where she lay. Jennifer blotted a damp forehead, pulled the hair away from her neck and sat up. Aletto was walking in the direction of the road— limping, rather. At least he was carrying his shoulders right, but he had the look of a man leaving an argument. Lialla came out from under the awning, opened her mouth to shout something after him, shrugged and turned away with whatever it was un-said. *God. Already?* Jennifer thought gloomily. Lialla turned and walked off along the edge of the cliff and vanished into a clump of dry-looking, wind-bent trees. Robyn now stood where Lialla had been, gazing anxiously in the direction Aletto had gone. She saw Jennifer and came across to her. "Hey, you have any ruby slippers? I'd like to clonk my heels together and get out of this place."

"Left them in my other purse," Jennifer replied. Robyn laughed. "What was all that, or do I want to know?"

"I didn't think it was anything. She said something about Podhru and he said it didn't matter and then he said something about Thread and she said she didn't care, she wasn't going to Wield any more and he jumped all over her." Robyn cast her eyes heavenward. "I don't know."

"If I'd been there, I'd probably have strangled her," Jennifer said. "After all I've gone through with that woman, trying to build her confidence!"

"Yeah, well. I think she was just pulling his chain. She's been in a bad mood about magic ever since you two went to see that Neri, though."

"Makes sense. He basically told her she'd been doing everything wrong right from day one."

"Strangle Merrida instead," Robyn said crisply.

"I may, if Lialla doesn't beat me to it. Don't pay attention to her, she'll come out of this and she'll be fine."

"Yeah, well, she's damned hard to live with in the meantime. You coming over with the rest of us, get some of that sweet bread before the boys eat it all?"

"God," Jennifer said. "Don't tell me—"

"Ernie fortunately eats no more than a real human," Robyn said. "I'll never adjust to that name, darn Chris, though, Enardi's just as hooked on the idea of an outlander name as Edrith—damnit, Eddie—is."

"Swell. Chris tried Anglicizing Aletto yet?"

"What do *you* think? I told him if he even suggested 'Les' to him, I'd throw his high-tops over the cliff."

"Les. God."

Robyn giggled suddenly. "Yeah. Could be worse, though. Could be something that Anglicized as maybe Oscar—"

"Allawishes, spelled A-l-o-y-s-i-u-s?"

"Clyde—"

"Herman—"

"I knew a Herman once, he was all right. Maurice?"

"Stop," Jennifer begged. "Just—enough." From somewhere inside the tent, Chris yelled Robyn's name. She turned and called back, "Coming!" and started for shade. Jennifer followed.

Aletto came in as she was finishing her second, slightly stale roll and washing it down with cool coffee from a heavy pottery jug. Marseli's parting gift; she'd have to drink the last of it today, it would be awful by morning. The nera-Duke glanced quickly around, eased himself down next to Robyn and mumbled, "Sorry."

"Why?" she asked. "You weren't shouting at *me*."

"I know you don't like it."

"Maybe I'm getting better at putting up with it. Here," she added. "I saw how you were walking out there. Was that bothering you last night when we stopped? You promised me—" She shoved at his arm. "Down," she said flatly. Aletto sighed faintly but obediently went flat and rolled onto his stomach. Robyn began kneading his thigh. "God, that's tight. You spent too long on your feet that last afternoon."

"I know." He sighed again. "It's hard—"

"I know it is. You just have to ease them over to someplace you can sit and *do* it. You're the Duke, you know. They do, too. You don't want the problem to show like it is right now, you'll have to keep that in mind."

"I'm sorry."

"Don't be. Just remember. We'll work on it."

"Gods," he muttered. "That ship. It'll be worse than Fedthyr's house, no time or place to even talk in private—"

"There's always someplace and always time. We'll all manage." Aletto raised his head slightly so he could look at her. She nodded firmly, reached up to press his face back to the rug.

* * *

JENNIFER finished her coffee and went out. It was shady here, but the air was still and she needed to walk. If Dahven came—*when* he came—but that wouldn't be for hours. Dowbri planned to wait until the crowded hour at the gates, to bring the wagon with a number of parcels bearing Marseli's seals, and his "cousin" to help him deliver it. Likely he wouldn't even need the story; lower market rumor had given an alarming number of details about the fight by the little huts on the sand below the docks, but according to Edrith, who'd spent most of his last two days down by the fish merchants' stalls and on the docks themselves, no names had been spoken, not even in whispers. And the city guard showed no sign of searching out any truth that might be hidden in the gossip.

The Sikkreni had vanished; it was said there'd been blood on the stones, some spilled in the sand. The stories centered around that were wildly varied and none of those Edrith heard bore any resemblance to truth. Nothing was said about the Thukars or Sikkre, no body was found. The two men who claimed to have been assaulted and robbed were trading their story for wine to anyone who'd buy, and listen. No one seemed to take them very seriously, though: Edrith thought they were too well known for anyone to doubt who'd done the attacking.

"You're as jumpy as a cat, I swear." Chris's voice; she gasped and came around sharply, a hand clutching at her shirt front.

"Jesus, don't *do* that!" she managed.

"Yeah, well, this isn't the place to not pay attention to what's behind you, remember?" he retorted. "Anyway, sorry. But what's chewing on you? You've been really strange since you went to play Night-Thread with that guy Ernie's sister knows. The stuff does *that* to you?" She shook her head. Chris folded his arms and tipped his head to one side thoughtfully. "Maybe land in a fight with the big boys?"

"Who, me?"

"Yeah, right, you lie about as good as I do, Aunt Jen."

"Jen. This 'Aunt' stuff sounds funny, don't you think?"

"I always thought so. You're trying to distract me, I must be on the money, huh? You and Eddie out half the night—he won't say anything, why don't you tell me what the hell you were up to?"

"Don't swear, damnit."

"Yeah, funny." He shook his head. "Come on, let's take a walk, you haven't run in about a week, you'll get fat and soft."

"Thanks, kid, I needed that."

Chris grinned very briefly. "What I'm here for, you know. Come on, I'm not up for a run, you can walk in long britches and spare poor Ernie's virgin eyes the shorts this time. Ground's too rough for running, anyway. You know, he might just come with us, if the ship doesn't show. He sure does want to." He took her elbow, turned her away from the camp and started up toward the road. Jennifer sighed but went with him. A walk could only help; if all else failed, it would eat up some of the time between now and nightfall. On the other hand, Chris saw a damned sight too much and he was entirely too sharp.

They reached the road in silence, turned to walk east. There was a little shade here, tall trees and here and there bushes. The road ran around a bend, downhill; the shade deepened, trees arced overhead, forming a canopy. Breeze soughed through the upper branches, and enough came through where they were to make it bearable.

"Is it the ship?" Chris asked abruptly. "Ernie says it won't come, he says old Chuffles—the guys call Casimaffi that—is so scared of Jadek he practically pukes every time he thinks about him. Ernie thinks Jadek maybe got to Chuffles, it just wasn't like him to offer us a free ride on his boat."

"That's what Marseli said. Just not to trust the man. He didn't ring true to me, I tried to pin him down but Aletto was getting visibly worried I'd drive off an ally so I had to back away."

"Yeah. *That* guy needs a keeper," Chris growled. "But he can play Duke when he has to, can't he? I mean, I talked to enough of the guys my age and he like, *really* impressed Fedthyr and his friends, you know?"

Jennifer laughed and increased the pace slightly as they came into a more open area. "You're certainly getting a feel for how to mangle Rhadazi, aren't you?"

"Hey, lighten up. Chill out, you know? Am I actually hurting anything? You think about the kind of trouble I could have got into in Bezjeriad—did I even drink? Or do any stuff, or anything?"

"How would I know what you did?"

"You could probably figure it out. Hey, slow down some, will you? You think I'm Flo Jo?"

"Let me see your fingernails," she demanded. He laughed; Jennifer slowed just a little as they started uphill and came out into the open. "Wonder why that place *we* are is so dry and rocky and everything else around here looks like they could film jungle movies?"

"Who knows? You're distracting me again, Jen. *You* could figure out what I did in Bez—pretty easy, I'd think. Even if no one else said anything. Kind of like I did."

"You did?"

"Wow, great acting, lady," he said dryly. "You got the part. Yeah, coming in hours after Lialla. Maybe you were talking to Marseli part of the time, but that doesn't figure in things like Eddie borrowing Olmic's wagon, or that he had his bo and another with him when he got the wagon—Olmic got curious about that; young, healthy-looking guy like Eddie walking around with two staffs, you know? All that sand outside your door and next to your bed, where you kicked off your shoes?" Jennifer groaned faintly. Chris glanced at her, turned his attention back to the road. "Why don't we turn around and head back? All this fresh air and exercise isn't good for my growing young body. Why don't you just tell me what you and Eddie were doing out there on the sand?" Silence. "And whose blood that was?"

"I—"

"To paraphrase someone recently, spit it out, you'll feel better. Come on, Jen," he said flatly. "You look awful. *You* fall apart on us and we're in deep you-know-what. Or would you rather have me keep working it out and maybe get some wrong answers?"

She slowed a little, finally nodded. "You would, wouldn't you? All right. I was out there, with Edrith—"

287

"Eddie. He actually took you into *that* part of Bez? After dark?" Silence. "Instead of me?"

"You were busy, remember?"

"Yeah, well, I could have—"

"Dumped everything and made people wonder? Lost Aletto support?" She shook her head. "Don't look so offended; he thought of you first. He took me because I was available. And because he found Davhen." She glanced at Chris; he merely stared at her, stunned into silence. "We got him out just before the Sikkreni would have."

"Jeez. Look, just tell me, okay?"

It got easier; she kept back only the last things Dahven had told her. Those were his. Chris had apparently heard all the rumors about Lasanachi ships, though; he'd gone a ghastly white, and she stopped, grabbing his arm to stop him. "Are you going to pass out? Put your head down; I can't carry you."

"Yeah—well." He bent over, bracing his hands on his knees. "It's just—you know, those goofs with the camels, the Cholani. It brought it back. You're sure he's okay—"

"He's fine, I should know. Trust me." He cast a disbelieving glance up at her but said nothing. "He's coming with us. Dowbri said they'd be here by dark tonight. He couldn't very well come with us if he couldn't ride."

Chris laughed grimly. "Right. Me, too. I never did believe in that damned ship. Look, though, that guard, the dead one—"

"The one I killed, don't tiptoe around it, kid. And don't worry about it. This is the first time I've talked about it since it happened. It's like a story, something that happened to someone else. Too much, too fast, all of it strange."

"Terrific. Guess I shouldn't have brought it up then, huh?"

"Doesn't matter. I might feel something later; it can't touch me right now. You better?" He nodded and straightened up. "Then let's get back, shall we?"

* * *

ALETTO was restless most of the afternoon; he slept off and on during the heat of the day, rose to prowl the ledge. During one of his pacing sessions, he stopped to talk to Lialla, who was leaning back against the wagon wheel, setting tiny stitches in the hem of one of her scarves. Apologizing, by the look of them both. He came away from her slightly less tense; Lialla let the sewing fall to her lap and watched him walk off, shook her head and picked up the needle once more.

Jennifer slept, but unpleasant dreams kept her from a proper rest: In one of the few she recalled, Dahven had been walking away from her, ignoring her when she called to him. She'd begun running but somehow, however fast she ran he was always just as far ahead of her. He never looked back, the only sound was her calling out his name in increasing desperation. She woke with tears running down her face. Late in the afternoon, she crawled back inside the tent to wet a cloth in the washing-bowl and blot her face and neck, then went back out to lie in shade on her stomach, chin propped on her arms. She stared out across the edge of the cliff, out to open sea. The water was a very deep blue this afternoon, white-capped. Surf crashed echoingly far below. There was no sign of any ship, no sail of any kind, though they'd been assured they would be able to see it by late afternoon. That it would be visible not long after it swung around the tip of Harbor's End.

If it came—she'd be afraid to take it. Aletto wouldn't think twice about it. But a ship would make a much better trap than Long Point, though she'd considered that possibility more than once this afternoon. People waiting for a ship might not keep an eye on the road, might not watch their backs. Her people had proven fairly resourceful in a fight so far; they'd evaded traps. The ship—once on that, once on the sea, there'd be no way out save to jump overboard and chance sharks.

And Dahven. If he were taken prisoner aboard another ship— Dear God. She swallowed, shook her head fiercely. No! She forced herself onto her feet, went in search of her handbag, dragged out paper, the six-inch ruler a temporary agency had passed around the law firm some time ago, a pencil. "You're going to make sheet music," she told herself firmly. "You're going to sit in the shade, and make the paper, and then you're going to start filling some of it in." He'd asked her about notation, in that Red Hawk caravan. Just now, she'd have given a lot for one paperback novel; this would simply have to do.

* * *

THE ship was still nowhere in sight, though now the sun was slipping behind the horizon. Aletto was increasingly snappish, inclined to read "I told you so" into almost anything said to him. Robyn went for a short walk to get away from him; Lialla was napping— or pretending to—in a far corner of the tent, scarcely visible against the dark canvas. Chris and Edrith had built up a fire and Chris was sketching out one of his maps for Enardi on the pad of paper he'd borrowed from Jennifer. Jennifer had turned half of another yellow pad into manuscript paper, and nearly half of that was now covered with notes: melody line notes only. She couldn't concentrate enough to manage anything else, even if she could remember without an instrument in her hands.

The yellow pad was back in her handbag now. She was ready to begin sorting through her other bags—anything!—when she saw Robyn look down the road toward Bez. A moment later, she could hear it, too: a wagon, not a company of armed men. A familiar set of long brown ears came into sight first; moments later, she could see Dowbri waving. And next to him— She started forward as the big man swung his wagon off the road. Aletto caught up to her a moment later, then passed her at a near run.

"Dahven! Is it—it really *is* you?" The wagon stopped, Dahven climbed down and turned to grip his friend's arms.

"Who else? I told you I wanted to come with you, you know."

"Well—but that was just a joke, wasn't it?" Aletto looked him up and down; his hands fell away and the smile slipped. "I forgot. Dahven, I'm sorry—"

Dahven shrugged. "What? Father? Let's not talk about that, shall we?" Aletto looked relieved. Jennifer came up and Dahven smiled, leaned over just enough to bestow a light kiss on her hair and wrapped a possessive-looking arm around her shoulders. She braced her knees; a considerable amount of his weight was in the arm and he still looked too pale. The worry must have been in her eyes as she looked at him; he continued to smile but sent his eyes warningly in Aletto's direction. "I myself have heard the most outrageous stories, very few of them true, I assure you. Don't worry about them, Aletto. That's all behind us for now." For one brief moment, he became serious. "Let us put Zelharri in your hands first, then you can help me turn out my brothers." He shrugged broadly and added in a much lighter voice, "That's how they do it in tales, after all. Isn't it?"

"In the best ones. Well—all right." Aletto gripped his arm again; the concern was still in his eyes, belying the wide smile. "You look thin, my friend."

"A little fever recently, that's all. *You* look as though you've grown muscle in those shoulders, and that's a respectable grip you have. Someone has been forcing you to work, haven't they?" Aletto shrugged. He looked both shy and pleased. "I am glad to see it, you needed muscle. As for me—it's simple, really." Dahven's arm tightened around Jennifer's shoulders. "By the time I returned to Sikkre after seeing you off, I realized I couldn't live without this delightful lady. But since even this lady isn't worth wading through the Great Sink for, I took ship to Bez. Well, my luck held. I think Jennifer was the first person I saw, once I reached land."

Aletto blinked at this outrageous and clearly at least partly untrue tale. He opened his mouth once, closed it again, finally shook his head. "Amazing luck," he said finally.

"And," Dahven finished with a flourish, "here I am. If you don't mind company. It's a long ride back to Sikkre and my brothers seem to have turned my apartments into counting-rooms while I was gone."

"I think we can find a place for you," Aletto said, deadpan, but he'd finally entered into the spirit of the thing, and his eyes were dancing. "Provided the lady doesn't mind."

"Oh," Jennifer said mildly. "I don't mind."

"Not even if I can't offer you half of Sikkre, the way rumor says I did?" Dahven demanded lightly. "Dowbri, didn't you bring messages for Aletto? Jennifer, if you find me water, I'll promise you half of Sikkre."

"What, I have to earn it?" They walked off together, rather slowly; Aletto remained by the wagon as Dowbri dug through one of the small packs. "That was neatly done," she added in an undertone. "Didn't want him to see you walk yet, did you?"

"I don't want his sympathy," he said, his voice as low as hers. But there was an edge to it.

"I know that. Why do you think I went along with all that nonsense back there?"

Silence. She got him around the front of the tent, under the awning, got him down and seated before Aletto and Dowbri started after them. He was rather short of breath, much too pale and sweat beaded his forehead. After a moment, he shook his head, touched her hand. "I'm sorry. I swore to myself I wouldn't do that—I've hurt you again."

"Don't. I'll worry later about whether you yell at all your women when you're mad at the world—"

"That isn't fair," he protested faintly. "I've never yelled at any woman; I didn't yell at you, Jennifer."

"No—you snarled. Don't look so shocked, my friend. I've got a mind and a mouth of my own, you must know that by now."

"I watched you talk Father to a stop, remember? Even I could never do that."

"Anyway, I know you don't feel well. I'd probably have snarled worse than you did, if I felt like you look. I'm just wondering how you think you'll keep Aletto from getting to the truth."

Dahven shook his head. "You think he doesn't know it? He's heard rumors, *he* knows what the Lasanachi are like. He'll never ask, that's all I care about."

291

"It's your decision," she said mildly and poured water into her leather cup. "Here, if you're keeping up the pretense, Aletto's on his way over, take this and drink."

He drank, handed the cup back to her. "I feel awful. Does it show so much? Because maybe it's better if I don't—"

Jennifer was shaking her head and he fell silent. "Don't you dare say it! Or think it. I told you, if you go, so do I. Don't try to convince me you're not worth it, either, I won't listen to you." She glanced up as Aletto and Dowbri passed them, heading down toward the edge of the cliff. She refilled the cup and held it out. "Shut up, in fact, and drink."

He did. When he set the cup aside, he was laughing. "Nasty tempered little sand gods, what have I done to myself?" He gripped her fingers and pulled her down next to him. "Are you always this way?"

"Only when someone I love is acting like an idiot."

"I'm not—well, perhaps I am. Let's forget it for now. I won't try and leave. I'll pretend I'm worthy. Does that satisfy you? And are *you* responsible for the change in my good friend Aletto?"

"Maybe a little. Robyn has done more for him, so has Chris."

"I'm very impressed. You told me, I wouldn't have believed it. Jennifer. This isn't going to be easy."

"I know it."

"I have nothing to offer you. My brother's men are looking for me, it won't take them long to know which way I've gone."

"They've harried us all the way from Sikkre, even without you."

"It's so odd, knowing my father's dead. I can't believe it, somehow; I can just see him hiding behind the fountain in the family dining hall, waiting to catch the twins out— I don't know. I should hate him; I did. He was insufferable, he was arrogant. All I can feel is sorry, now he's dead. Even after what he did to me."

"I know. Mine—never mind. I'll tell you, someday. When there's time."

"The ship won't come," Dahven said flatly. "Casimaffi was paid off; his son says he's gone into hiding and the *Windsong* on its way down to the south sea; it left last night. Dowbri wouldn't tell me so, but I think he's afraid this place is a trap, that we'll have to leave here tonight. I don't know how well I'll be able to stay on a horse."

"We have Enardi's wagon. Aletto knows you had fever, you told him. Sleep in the wagon, if you have to. In a day or so, you'll be keeping up again."

"I intend to. The rest of me—"

She turned, laid a hand across his lips. "Don't. Don't try to tell me you're worthless; if you say things like that you might begin believing them, but I never will."

"If they're true—"

"They're not!" Silence. He took her fingers in his, held them against a slightly scratchy cheek. "You can do anything you have to, anything you want."

He managed a faint smile. "You're trying to shame me again, it won't work."

"I'm not trying to shame you. I love you. Don't try to change that, Dahven. If you don't love me anymore, if that's true—"

"That's not true!" he protested.

"Good. Don't try to push me away for a shock to your system. Not because you've lost faith in yourself. Besides, I won't let you." She shifted so she could look out to sea. "No ship. I knew there wouldn't be. But right now, I feel like I've been kicked."

"Lot of that going around." Chris's voice came from somewhere above them. He knelt to grip Dahven's shoulder and momentarily seemed at a loss for words. He finally grinned, nodded and said, "Glad to see you again, Dahven, I hear you're coming with us. That's great. Listen, you two, are you up for a nice long ride tonight? Because I think Aletto's finally given up on the free ride, and I *really* don't like this place, and I'm gonna be really pissed off if we have to start out with a fight, you know?"

"Got you," Jennifer said. "How soon?"

Chris glanced at Aletto, who was gesturing sharply out to sea. Dowbri stood with folded arms, listening. "How about, like, now? As in, we drop the tent, fold up and go while we can still see where the road is?"

* * *

ALETTO came back from the edge moments later, his face pale and set. "We can't stay here," he said. Chris nodded.

"Already heard; tent's coming down right now." He glanced at Dowbri. "Hadn't you better go, before your name gets on the wrong list?"

"I'm not worried," the merchant replied lightly. "Here, you get those bags out and onto the cart, you start folding rugs, I'll take care of the tent." He looked over his shoulder, assessing the rapidly darkening sky.

Enardi came up beside him. "Tell my father I'll take good care of his wagon, will you?" Dowbri smiled, shook his head and pulled a fat leather wallet from his belt. It clinked heavily, as though full of coin.

"Fedthyr sent his own message. This—and a warning not to lose that mule." Enardi looked abashed, but he took the wallet and threw it under the driver's seat.

* * *

SOMEHOW it was all done; the horses saddled and packed, the goods packed into the wagon and tied down. Enardi drove the wagon out onto the road to wait and to listen and watch—though it was by now nearly too dark to see anything save the comparatively light road. Edrith went with him. Jennifer fastened her handbag in place, checked around the ground where the wagon had been, to make certain nothing had fallen off. Lialla was gone now; Aletto helped Robyn into the saddle. Dahven sat one of the two spare horses a little stiffly. He managed a smile for Aletto as the nera-Duke and Robyn started toward the road, turned to gaze off down the hill westward.

Jennifer mounted and he rode over to join her. "All right?" She held out a hand, gripped his. "All right. Let's go."

The wagon was already a faint shadow in the gloom; behind them, she could just hear Dowbri's cart on its way back to Bezjeriad. Dahven a worrying but warm presence beside her, at least for as long as he could hold to the saddle. Before them, a narrow, rutted road led on through rough country. They couldn't see very far; fortunately, she thought. It was daunting enough, without that.

But the road itself was very probably going to be the least of their worries. And just now, the prosperous civility of merchant Bezjeriad seemed as far away as the Emperor's city.